Ramsay

A Sign of Love Novel

Mia Sheridan

ISBN-10: 153463648X
ISBN-13: 978-1534636484

COVER ARTIST: MIA SHERIDAN
FORMATTED BY MIDNIGHT ENGEL PRESS

To Angie, Addie, Lucie, and Callie. I'm glad to call you sisters, but even happier to call you friends.

The Aries Legend

The myth of Aries tells of two children, a brother and sister, who are sacrificed to the Gods. At the last minute, they are saved by a mighty, winged ram. For his strength and heroism, Zeus places the ram among the stars and his golden fleece, sought by many, becomes a symbol for that which is most precious

PROLOGUE

Brogan

She was waiting for me.

My feet moved softly but swiftly over the grass I'd mowed that afternoon, driving the mower so the result was a wide expanse of grass striped in alternating light and dark green. Sometimes I did a checkerboard pattern, and other times I chose diamonds. My dad always shook his head in disbelief when I told him I created the patterns without mapping them out on paper first, or without using string, even on the first line of my design. *When he was sober enough to notice anyway.* It was true, though. I just saw it in my head and computed where the turns needed to be, instinctively knew where I needed to move to ensure each line was straight. I couldn't say how, I just did.

The spice of the cut grass mingled with the tanginess of the potted key lime trees lining the garden and the sweet headiness of the honeysuckle growing nearby. My mind blanked to everything else as it attempted to separate the myriad of scents. My skin prickled, and I walked more quickly. The smells weren't unpleasant to me, but I couldn't think clearly when I was around something overly fragrant, and I *wanted* to think. I wanted to think about *her*.

"Lydia," I whispered, loving the way her name rolled off my tongue, the way the hard *d* smoothed into the soft sound of the *a* at the end, leaving off like a sigh. I wanted to picture the delicate lines of her face, I wanted to imagine her hair—a cascade of summer sunshine falling down her back—and her eyes, a shade of blue and green so perfectly mixed I never could quite figure out their actual color. And I wanted my mind's eye to see the sweet curves of her body, the way the fullness of her breasts pressed against her tank tops and spilled out of her swimsuits, the way her waist flared in slightly and then curved out again to the feminine roundness of her hips and arse. I felt myself swell in my jeans and frowned. Just the image of her made me hard. But even so, I *made* myself imagine my eyes moving down Lydia's slim legs all the way to her perfectly formed feet. Even her toes were sweet.

I wanted to take a few minutes to picture all of her so when I saw her in person, it wouldn't be obvious how arrested I was by her beauty. Picturing her always helped soften the impact—ever so slightly—of the reality of her right in front of me. Still, she knew how she affected me. I could see it in the way she held her shoulders when I was around, as if she knew very well she was being watched and liked it. I could see in the self-conscious tilt of her head and the way she glanced at me to make sure my eyes hadn't left her, the way she gave her hips an extra sway for my benefit.

Lydia was a princess, the only daughter of Edward De Havilland and his new wife—Lydia's stepmother—Ginny, multi-millionaires and owners of one of the largest privately held construction and real estate firms in the industry. Plus, she had a protective older brother. She was spoiled, pampered, self-indulgent, an incorrigible flirt, and I very well knew it. And yet I couldn't manage to stay away from her.

"Bloody eejit," I muttered to myself.

I was the son of Lydia's family's gardener. *The gardener*, who had taken my sister and me from a small county in the mid-east region of Ireland to America three years ago for a supposed "better life" after our mam died. The gardener, who had promised things would look up for us here, and instead was grappling with the bottle as much or more so than he'd been doing back home. *My dad.* Sean Ramsay, a piss artist and useless prick. And so I picked up the slack for him so *he* wouldn't get fired, because we were desperate for the salary, desperate for the healthcare the job provided. The doctors' visits my little sister, Eileen, needed were endless. Endless and expensive.

He kept promising he would quit, and I kept hoping. Some days he did better than others, but today wasn't one of them.

I was seventeen, but some days I felt seventy.

When my dad still managed a good handle on his drinking, he had Mr. De Havilland hire me to work part-time after school as one of his assistants. So now, if anyone saw me, they believed I worked in that capacity. Or at least that's what I hoped. What they *didn't* know was I often worked late into the night on the De Havilland grounds, ensuring no one realized my dad had already abandoned most of his duties.

Lydia's father had also noticed the patterns I mowed into the grass, and when he asked me what my math grades were like, I'd told him I had been taking advanced college level courses since ninth grade. He'd looked impressed and asked me if I might be interested in working for his company during the summer. Excitement and pride had filled me, and I'd readily agreed. It might mean we could finally afford some of the treatments the doctors recommended for Eileen. And maybe, just maybe, someday I'd earn enough to date Lydia.

Yes, Lydia was a princess, but when she smiled at me, my heart did somersaults in my chest. When she laughed, it sounded like the sweetest music, soft and pitched in a way that was nothing except pleasing to my ears, not in the garish way some people had of laughing—laughter that made me grimace and want to stick my fingers in my ears. She was everything soft and beautiful and feminine, and she made me want in a way I both loved and hated. And despite her princess status, she never looked at me in the way her friends did—a mixture of disdain and lust—when they came over to swim or attend parties at her house, as if they were interested but ashamed they were. No, Lydia was a practiced flirt, but there was something more about her that drew me in—not just her stunning beauty, but a depth the other girls her age didn't have.

I loved it when she'd seek me out and chat with me while I worked. I lived for those moments. I loved the way she teased me, but never in a way that felt mean or condescending. And no one else made me laugh the way Lydia did—often surprising me with her wit.

I spotted Lydia standing under a sycamore tree next to the stables before she'd turned around, but by the way her shoulders straightened, I knew she had sensed me. She took her time turning, flipping her hair over her shoulder and inclining her head and smiling her dazzling smile.

"Mo Chroí," I said, approaching her slowly.

"I told you not to call me that, Brogan. I'm *not* a princess," she said, cocking her head and letting her eyes run down my body. I fisted my hands to remain still, to keep my blood cool enough that I didn't harden under her slow perusal, giving her immediate proof of her power over me. "Thanks for meeting me." She licked her lips once, her eyes holding nervousness I hadn't seen before. *What was she up to?*

I narrowed my eyes slightly, putting my hands in my pockets and leaning one shoulder against the trunk of the tree. The sun had begun to set, the sky behind Lydia painted in bright shades of pink and orange.

"I—" She licked her lips again, crossing her arms over her chest, plumping her breasts. "Well, here's the thing, Brogan. I've never . . . well, I've never been kissed before."

Shock momentarily rendered me mute, and my mouth went dry. I wasn't sure where this was going, but the subject matter was shooting off warning sirens. I willed my expression to go blank and took my time answering. "I find that hard to believe. You've got every fella within ten miles interested in ya." She was only a grade behind me, and although we didn't attend the same school, I'd heard plenty of guys talking about her, even though they only knew her by sight. Greenwich, Connecticut was a small enough town.

"Ya could put out a casting call," I joked cautiously. "I'm sure there'd be a line of lads around the block." *And I'd line up, too, because I wouldn't be able to bloody help myself.* "I imagine Myles Landry would be the first one to arrive." Myles was a neighbor and he was always over sniffing around Lydia. I'd watched her flirt and dazzle him more than I'd cared to. But that's what Lydia did. She flirted and dazzled and played her little games. And all the while my stupid heart yearned for her, wishing I was enough.

"Ha ha," she said. "The thing is, Brogan, I want *you* to be the one to kiss me." She took a step closer, and I took a step back.

"Why?" I demanded. Why was she doing this to me? Making me hope for things I could never have? Didn't she know she was driving me crazy?

"Why?" she repeated, tilting her head, her expression perplexed, her blue-green eyes blinking. As if she should have to give me a reason.

"Yes, why would ya want *me* to kiss ya? I'm the gardener's son, not exactly in your social circle. It's not like anythin' could come of it." I didn't have the money to date someone like Lydia right now. She'd want to be taken to the movies, out to eat, expect flowers and gifts, and who knew what else. We could barely afford to put food on the table at home, and I had a voracious appetite that never, ever seemed to be satisfied. I was wearing shoes too small because my feet had grown four sizes in the last year and our budget couldn't keep up.

She laughed softly and shook her head. "You always *say* something like that, Brogan. I don't care about any of that."

I let my eyes roam her face, trying to detect deception in her expression. I didn't think I saw any. But of course, she hardly knew what she was talking about. She had no idea the extent of our financial straits. *Oh you would, Lydia. If you really knew my situation, you would.* "Anyway, ya didn't answer me question."

Lydia looked up at me through her lashes, causing my heart to race. "I want you to kiss me because you're one of the most handsome boys in Greenwich, and you don't even know it. Because I like the way you look at me, the way you watch me. But even more, I like to watch you, too." She stepped closer, and I held my breath. "I like how your accent gets a little thicker when you talk to me. I like how serious you are, so different from the other boys. I like the look you get on your face when you dig your hands into the soil, as if . . . as if you're feeling it with your whole body. I want to know if you get that same look on your face when you touch *me*. I want to know what you're always thinking so hard about. And I want you to kiss me because I want to know what your lips feel like on mine." The last word came out breathlessly, and my heart started pounding harshly in my chest. She'd thought all those things about me? I hadn't even known she thought anything about me at all when I wasn't right in front of her.

She leaned closer and I caught her fragrance, feminine and delicate like her—warm and clean with just the barest hint of . . . vanilla maybe? I wanted to put my nose against the perfume of her bare skin and close my eyes. I wanted to see what else I could detect in her subtle scent. She tilted her head up higher, looking at me, asking me with her eyes to kiss her.

"Aye, Lydia, I'll kiss ya, but I'll not do more," I said. She was right, my accent was thicker when I talked to her, and my voice sounded hoarse, shaky. I couldn't help it. I didn't seem to have any control around her—not with anything, not my body, not my voice, not my thoughts. She must know how desperately I wanted to kiss her—how I'd been dreaming of kissing her since the first day I'd seen her.

Lydia smiled and then held her hand out to me. "But not here. Let's go inside where we can be alone." *Oh Jaysus.*

I removed my hands from my pockets and took her hand in mine, following behind her. Her hand was so soft, so warm, and before I even realized what I was doing, my thumb began making slow circles on her skin, attempting to learn the texture. With difficulty, I forced my thumb to still.

She led me to the back door of the stable and shut the door behind us once we were inside. The smell of hay and horses overwhelmed me and for a moment, my mind went fuzzy. But when Lydia led me to a decently sized room, where there was a cot that the men who worked in the stable could use if there was any cause, like one of the mare's birthing a foal, and closed the door, the smells lost their pungent quality and I was able to focus again.

Feeling some apprehension about being totally alone with Lydia in such a private location, I pulled her hand, halting her. She turned, staring up at me again. "What's wrong?" she asked.

"Nothin'. This is good, right here," I said. She'd been leading me toward the cot and I knew *that* was a bad idea. I'd kiss her once and then I'd leave. Some small alarm still rang inside me, but I ignored it, knowing I was helpless to resist her. In the end, I'd do as she wanted me to do whether it seemed like a good idea or not. I knew it, and she bloody well knew it, too.

Lydia stepped closer to me until our bodies were barely touching, and she leaned up on her tiptoes and gently pressed her mouth to mine. I felt the soft press of her lips as if every nerve ending was focused right there where we were joined. Hot desire raced through my veins, and I made a small choking sound. Her eyes opened and something soft and understanding appeared in her gaze. She moved slowly and sensually as one hand came up to the back of my head, her fingers weaving through my hair, the soft scratch of her nails over my scalp causing my skin to prickle. Lydia's other hand went around my waist, resting there like a warm weight. I put my trembling hands on her hips, bracing myself, and closed my eyes, focusing on the feather-light brush of her lips.

Tentatively, I reached my tongue out to taste her, my nerves stretched as tight as a bow, my senses on overload in a way I'd never experienced before and wasn't sure how to manage. The mingling of pleasure and pain wrapped around me, holding me tightly in a strange embrace, an exquisite torture. I couldn't figure out which sensations to focus on. *And somehow Lydia seemed to know.* She dropped her hands from my hair and my waist so the only parts of us touching were our mouths. I sighed against her lips, learning the taste of her, a subtle sweetness mixed with a hint of richness, like milk and honey. *God, it was good. Better than good.* Completely fascinated, I delved my tongue into her mouth to get more of it, and she let out a little whimper, causing me to harden painfully. Her tongue met mine, wet and warm, and so very,

very soft, drugging me, and yet causing my senses to sing. Our tongues danced and thrust, and I pressed my groin against hers, seeking some relief, and finding only more sensation that was both maddeningly pleasurable and searingly painful.

I used all my willpower to pull away, my lips coming off Lydia's with a wet pop. She gazed at me, confusion and need warring in her expression. It took me off guard. I'd only ever seen Lydia look fully in control. "Was that your first kiss, too, Brogan?" she asked uncertainly.

I looked away, trying desperately to control my breathing. "Was I that bad at it?" I asked, shooting her a small smirk I didn't feel.

She shook her head. The expression on her face was almost one of . . . *wonder.* "No, it wasn't that. It was incredible, and I love that it was a first for both of us. I just . . . you're trembling." She took my hand and pulled. "Come sit with me on the cot." When I hesitated, she added, "Please." And so I followed. *Again.* When we sat down, she scooted closer and ran a finger down my chest.

"Lydia," I groaned.

"Can I see you?" she whispered. "Please, Brogan? I want to see you." She began tugging on my T-shirt and I let her, lifting my arms as she brought it over my head. I sat before her, hardly breathing as her eyes raked over my bare chest. I knew I was fit. How could I not be? I did physical labor eight hours a day most days. But I'd never been naked before anyone. And this wasn't just anyone. This was Lydia, the girl who made my guts clench with nothing more than a glance. I felt vulnerable and afraid. I watched as Lydia's delicate throat moved in a swallow. "God, you're beautiful," she said. "Is it okay if I touch you?"

I nodded. I was incapable of anything else. She reached her hand out slowly and ran her palm down my chest, using her index finger to move over the ridges of my stomach, stopping at the sparse, dark line of hair under my naval that disappeared into my jeans. I sucked in a breath as her gaze moved down to the erection straining through my pants. Her eyes met mine in question, and she must have seen something in my face that gave her permission, because she reached down and ran her hand over my shaft. "Oh God," I groaned, helplessly pressing myself into her hand. I couldn't believe this was happening. This was . . . I couldn't think. I could only want. And I wanted Lydia. I'd wanted Lydia for what seemed like forever.

We lay back on the cot, and she unbuttoned my jeans and slipped her hand inside. When she wrapped her warm fingers around me, I jerked in her hand and groaned, lying perfectly still, just focused on the sensations. *Pleasure and pain.* She brought her lips to mine again as she stroked me, and I turned my mouth away from her. It was too much. Too much all at once. She continued to stroke me and after a minute, she sat up and took her tank top off, followed by her bra. Her gaze stayed on me as she undressed and when her breasts popped free, I barely resisted the urge to moan at the sight alone. She was so beautiful it hurt me a little. Her breasts were full and high, creamy white where her swimsuit had covered her skin from the sun. Her nipples were a pale pink and already hardened. *Jaysus, so pretty.* Barely hanging on to control, I sat up and tasted them, rolling one around my tongue. Lydia gasped, but only pressed toward me. "You're making me ache, Brogan. I want you. I never knew . . . Oh," she gasped. I sucked a nipple into my mouth, learning the texture of that intimate skin, like velvet with barely discernible, soft ridges at the very peak. And her skin, yes, it was clean with a light hint of vanilla—maybe a body wash that still barely lingered. She rolled out from under me, my mouth coming off her breast, but before I could question what she was doing, she stood and shimmied off her skirt and underwear and then removed my shoes and socks and jeans. I watched, dazed. *I should stop this. I should.* It had gone too far and I couldn't figure out how it had happened.

But then she was lying next to me, warm and soft, and I forgot why this wasn't a good idea. In that moment, I barely knew my own name. My senses were focused only on her, naked in my arms, and it felt so blessedly good, so right.

Lydia . . . Lydia.

She kissed me again, and I reached between her legs and felt the slippery evidence of her arousal, rubbing it between my fingers and then bringing my hand back to the place that made her buck and yelp. She was so slick, so lush. "Oh God, Brogan, yes, please. Don't stop."

We touched, and explored, and stroked until we were both moaning and panting. My blood was swirling through my veins in a fiery frenzy. And yet all the while, Lydia seemed to understand that I couldn't take too much at once. She seemed to know when to withdraw her hand from one spot so I could focus on what she was doing to another. She seemed to understand that for me, there was a fine line between pleasure and pain, that my senses were overly acute. She couldn't know, of course, because I'd never attempted to explain how it was always this way, but she reacted to my body as if she *did* know, as if she understood this about me better than I did. And I was lost. When I moved over her, there wasn't an ounce of hesitation in her eyes. She opened her legs, and she welcomed me.

I pressed inside her, inch by inch, gazing into her face. Her beauty. *Mesmerizing.* I was awed that I was inside her . . . or nearly. When I came to the barrier of her virginity, I met her eyes, full of trust and wonder, and whispered, "I'm sorry, I'm so sorry, sweet Lydia. Mo Chroí." And then I pressed inside, tearing her. She cried out in pain. I wanted to comfort her, but it felt so blessedly good that I could only bring my forehead to hers, holding myself still by sheer force of will, gritting my teeth to stop myself from thrusting, while she became used to my invasion. Why did it have to be that something that felt so wonderful to me hurt her? I had never imagined anything feeling so good as her hot muscles clenched around me, pulling at me, stroking me from deep within. "Are ya okay?" I finally managed. She nodded, and I began to move, groaning with pleasure at the tight friction surrounding my throbbing erection. Sweat broke out on my back. I knew I wouldn't last long.

"Tá tú gach rud atá go hálainn dom," I breathed.

You are everything that is beautiful to me.

Lydia sighed, tipping her head back and wrapping one leg around my hips. After just a handful of thrusts, I felt an orgasm tightening my abdomen and swelling my cock even further. It was the first time I'd ever been inside a girl. With one final thrust I came, the pleasure washing through me and causing goosebumps to form on the surface of my skin. Groaning, I collapsed beside her and attempted to catch my breath, finally looking at her. Her eyes were slightly stunned, but her expression was introspective, as if she was deep in thought. My heart froze. Did she regret this already? I doubted she'd had an orgasm—she had to be disappointed. I didn't know what to feel. There was joy tightening my chest, but there was also insecurity and confusion, and I tried to remember how this had come to be. "Are ya okay?" I asked her again, repeating the words I'd said the moment I'd taken her virginity. *I'd taken Lydia De Havilland's virginity.*

"Yes, are you?" she asked.

I couldn't help chuckling. "Yeah. I just . . . I'm not sure exactly how this happened."

Lydia gave me a small smile, leaning up on her arm, her breasts drawing my attention and amazingly making my cock throb again. "I know," she said. I nodded curtly, feeling suddenly awkward. I reached for my jeans and handed Lydia's clothes to her, looking away as she used her underwear to wipe the smear of blood off her left thigh. We both dressed quickly. I wiped my sweaty palms on my hips as I turned to her.

"Lydia, I—" I started, reaching for her hands. The door flew open behind me, hitting the wall with a sudden bang. *What?* Adrenaline burst through my veins. Myles Landry was standing in the doorway. *What the feck?* As he took us in, a look of perplexed anger took over his face.

"Lydia?" he asked, his brow furrowing, eyes darting between us and then down to the rumpled blanket on the cot.

I looked at Lydia and her face was white, her expression arrested.

"Why'd you ask me to meet you here, Lydia?" Myles asked, an edge of hostility in his tone. My body went ice cold. Lydia had asked Myles to meet her here after she'd asked *me* to meet her here? *Why?* I looked back to Lydia and my heart thudded dully in my chest when I saw the expression on her face: knowing guilt. She'd set me up. She'd wanted Myles to find us here. A game? I had been the unknowing player in some game of hers. Myles's jealousy maybe? Getting him back for some misdeed? Stupid that grief instead of anger should grip me in that moment. All the worse that I didn't remember it hurting this badly when I'd found out my mam had died.

Lydia was shaking her head, her expression still stunned. "I'm sorry," she whispered, turning her eyes my way, big and bright blue in that moment, no green at all. "I really didn't mean for it to go that far. I only meant for him to find us . . . kissing." The last piece of my heart cracked.

"What's going on in here?" My head swiveled back to the door as Stuart De Havilland stepped into the room. Lydia's older brother. *Shite.* I knew things had just gone from bad to worse, and yet, I couldn't manage to feel anything. I was numb.

Just as Myles's had done, Stuart's gaze went from Lydia to me to the cot and back to me. For the first time, I noticed a smear of blood on the light blue blanket. I watched as rage filled Stuart's expression. He stepped toward me. "What the fuck did you do to my sister?"

"Stuart!" Lydia screamed, stepping forward.

"Don't, Lydia," I managed, stepping forward, as well. "What happened here is a private matter. Excuse me." I went to step around Stuart but he pushed me, his hands braced on my chest so I flew backward, slamming into the wall. Lydia gasped. I clenched my jaw against the sensation of hard wood jarring my body and stood up straight, meeting Stuart's eyes. At seventeen, I was already bigger than him at twenty-one. I could kill him right here if I wanted to.

"Did you rape my sister, you lowlife piece of trash?"

Rage raced through my system and in a flash I stepped forward and swung on him, nailing him straight in the jaw. Lydia shrieked again as her brother went flying backward, stumbling and catching himself. "You motherfucker!" he yelled, his hand coming up to his jaw, blood dripping from his lip.

"Of course he didn't *rape* me, Stuart," Lydia yelled, her voice high-pitched and panicky. She hurried to Stuart and stood in front of him so he wouldn't attack me . . . I assumed.

She had done this. My Lydia. She had done this. No, not my *Lydia. Never mine.* Grief clogged my throat, and I almost choked on it.

Stuart narrowed his eyes at me. We stood there for several tense moments, the only sound in the room my own harsh breath. "Add this up, math genius," he finally said, a nasty edge of mocking in his tone. "You taking advantage of my sister plus you being a disgusting piece of garbage equals me throwing your family off my property. Be gone by morning." I froze, my heart hammering.

We lived in the small house at the edge of their property, reserved for the gardener. Right this minute my dad was passed out in bed, and Eileen was watching cartoons on the couch in her leg braces. Edward De Havilland was ill, and he was a fair man—although he might not be if he found out what I'd just done with his daughter—but his son was *not* a fair man, and for the time being, Stuart De Havilland was in charge. He was going to make me beg, here, in front of Lydia and Myles. I let out a long, slow breath, my face growing hot.

"That's not necessary, Stuart, please," Lydia said weakly.

"Shut up, Lydia," Stuart said, pushing her aside. I clenched my fists more tightly. Even though she'd just used me cruelly, my instinct to protect her was strong. Grief and anger now competed in my heart. I bloody hated myself.

"This is not me father's fault, Stuart," I said. "Be fair about this."

Stuart's eyes narrowed further. Several heartbeats went by before he drawled slowly, "Get down on your knees and beg me, scum."

My heart faltered, but I wouldn't flinch. I wouldn't give him the satisfaction.

"Stuart—"

"Shut up, Lydia!" Stuart yelled again. I didn't even look at her.

"Get down on your knees and beg me for your father's job, and I'll let your family stay," Stuart said, his eyes filled with something that looked like barely contained excitement. He'd never liked me, had resented me for some reason I didn't understand. He was finding some sick glee in this. Silence reverberated around the room. I would not do this for my own father. I would not do this thing for him. But for Eileen . . . for her, I would beg.

I went slowly to my knees, not breaking eye contact with Stuart. "Please don't fire me father. I will not touch your sister again. Not as long as I live." I heard Lydia's quiet cries but vowed not to meet her eyes. *Refused to.*

"Kiss my feet and the answer is yes."

I gritted my jaw so hard I bit my tongue. The metallic flavor of blood filled my mouth. *Eileen . . . Eileen* . . . I chanted in my head, picturing her sweet, innocent face, the freckles that dusted her nose and cheeks. I leaned forward, my body vibrating with rage and shattered pride. Before I'd even made it halfway to Stuart's feet, his leg jerked out and his boot caught me square in the jaw. I flew back, letting out a startled moan as I landed on my arse on the floor, hot pain radiating up my face.

"Changed my mind. Get your flea-bitten family out of here . . . by morning."

I jumped to my feet, dizzy with the conflicting emotions pommeling my heart. I could barely see through the fog of humiliation. I went to step toward Stuart, but Myles, who I'd all but forgotten about, took a step toward me, putting his hand on my chest. I swiped it away. "I think it's best if you just leave, Brogan," he said quietly, pity emanating off him. I hesitated, still breathing harshly.

"Good boy," Stuart said, reaching in his pocket and throwing something on the ground at my feet. I looked down. It was a one-hundred-dollar bill. "You got paid yesterday. That should cover today." Shame and self-hatred was a raw ache in my gut. I could feel heat burning under the skin of my neck, but I bent slowly anyway and picked up the bill. We needed it. Now more than ever. I stepped around Myles, exiting the room and not looking back.

As I strode across the lawn, the sky a dusky blue, the sprinklers came on. The cool water felt good against my overheated skin and I didn't change my course, simply walked through them. Out of the corner of my eye I saw who I thought might be Lydia racing toward her house. I refused to turn my head. Stuart De Havilland had told us to be gone by morning. We wouldn't wait that long. We'd be gone tonight. We'd leave right that very moment. And as God as my witness, I would *never* beg anyone for anythin' again. Not *ever* again.

CHAPTER ONE

Lydia – *Seven Years Later*

"Earth to Lydia, hello," Daisy said, waving a hand in front of my face.

I laughed softly, grabbing her hand and squeezing it before letting it go. "Sorry, was I drifting off again? I've got way too much on my mind. Start over and I swear you'll have my full attention." I took a sip of champagne and focused on my friend.

Daisy waved her hand in the air, taking a sip of her own champagne. "No, I don't blame you for ignoring me. I was only complaining about my new eyebrow lady and how the arches she creates are completely sub-par."

I laughed, training my gaze on her perfectly—as always—sculpted brows. "I do see what you mean. You've been ruined. I can't believe you'd subject the public to the disturbing vision that is your eyebrows." I pretended to shudder.

"Oh shut up! Seriously though . . ." *Shut up, Lydia . . . That phrase . . . why does it always cause a cold chill to move down my spine?* I knew why of course—my brother had yelled it repeatedly *that* day—but I wondered if those particular words would *ever* cease to unnerve me. *Shut up, Lydia.* ". . . so I'm counting down the days until Mariposa's maternity leave is over. The nerve of her."

I laughed, Daisy's banal chatter lightening my mood. "The nerve of her to reproduce?"

"Exactly. So tell me what has you so distracted today."

"Oh the usual. The business, Stuart, *finances* . . . all very boring."

Daisy gave me a sympathetic look. "I thought things were looking better with the business."

I sighed. "I thought so, too. It seems like every time we get a break, something else happens to set us back again. And of course, Stuart doesn't help." My spendthrift brother who still lived as if we could afford to be extravagant. Ever since my father died and Stuart had taken over the company, things had gone from bad to worse. Upon my father's death we'd discovered the company was in more debt than my father ever let on. Possibly because it was still a situation that could have been managed had the person taking over had a semblance of fiscal restraint or management skills—neither of which my brother possessed. I sighed to myself. I did love him, but I also frequently wanted to kill him. I also missed my father terribly. His kindness, his intelligence, his love. Despite the irony, I wished he were alive to have as a sounding board about how to get us back into the black.

Daisy patted my hand. "It'll be fine. You know what you need? Some good sex. When was the last time you had some? There's nothing like a good thorough fucking to lift the spirits."

I choked on a sip of champagne and Daisy grinned. "If only I had a candidate," I said, laughing. I did love Daisy—she came across all polish and style, but she was liable to say the most outrageous things just when you needed it. But Daisy was a trust fund baby who had never had to worry about money a day in her life. She didn't really know what it felt like. Up until recently, I hadn't either. Life had happened, and now I'd learned lessons I'd never expected to learn. And not just about money. I took another sip of champagne. "Things will be fine. Of course."

She nodded. "Did you know the family that bought your estate put it up for sale a couple months ago?"

I stared at her for a moment. "Why?"

She shrugged. "I heard rumors about a big job offer overseas, but I didn't know them. They've already moved. I think it's still on the market."

My heart clenched. God, if only I had a way to purchase it back. I sighed, letting that thought float away. I didn't, and there was no use wishing for something that was an impossible dream.

"How's Gregory?" I finally asked to change the subject.

Daisy's eyes shifted away. "Oh, busy as always. But I guess I knew what I was signing up for when I married him. If he didn't look so hot in a suit, I'd have given up on him long ago."

I gave her a small smirk. "Is he working today?"

"Yup—closing a big deal." I thought something like doubt moved through her eyes, but before I could question it, she smiled brightly, pointing out some girls we knew who'd just arrived and launching into a story about one of them.

I nodded, drifting off again, as my eyes moved over the people at the garden party, laughing, talking, and enjoying appetizers and cocktails. *All so carefree.* Why did I feel so . . . *trapped?* Trapped, standing here in the middle of the wide-open lawn, the summer sun shining down on me. Trapped and restless. It didn't feel like it was only the financial issues my family was facing. But I couldn't put my finger on it exactly. There had to be more though, didn't there? More to look forward to once we were able to get the business back on solid ground? More than the world I'd been raised in, the world of endless social events, shopping, and surface chitchat that, these days, went in one ear and out the other. I couldn't help it. I'd thought working as the vice president at our family company would fill something in me that felt empty, but it hadn't. It was challenging—Stuart ensured that—and it was interesting and fulfilling in its way, and rather than simply being the figurehead I could have been, I chose to be very involved with the business, getting my hands dirty, so to speak, along with the rest of the staff. But it still didn't offer that . . . *something* I'd been hoping it would provide. *Oh, shut up, Lydia, you don't even know what you want. How can anything fulfill you when you're so clueless as to what you're missing? Shut up, Lydia . . .*

Shut up, Lydia . . .

"Lydia," my stepmother said, seemingly coming out of nowhere, air kissing my cheek, the heady fragrance of her perfume—the Chanel N°5 she'd worn ever since I'd known her—lingering in the air around me even after she'd leaned away to air kiss Daisy. I barely held back the sneeze that threatened. "Daisy darling," she said, and Daisy greeted her with a small smile.

"Ginny," I muttered, taking a long drink of champagne. "You look perfect as always."

My stepmother ran a hand over her sleek, blonde updo, not a single hair out of place. "Why, thank you. And you look," her eyes ran over me, assessing my outfit, a nude maxi dress with a floral design, "lovely." I resisted scowling and instead took another sip of my champagne. No one had the ability to make the word "lovely" sound critical quite like my stepmother. *Ex*-stepmother actually. She had recently remarried. "Is that from last season?" she couldn't resist adding on.

Of course it was from last season. Ginny was well aware of Stuart's and my financial situation. Did she think I was still splurging on expensive designer clothes? *Naturally.* Because it's what she herself would have been doing in my situation.

"Oh hello, Jane!" Ginny called, looking behind me. Always looking behind me to see if someone *better*, more interesting, more popular, more able to serve her needs, might be around. But I was happy her focus had moved away from me, even momentarily. "I'll be right over," she called, a large smile on her face. "We need to discuss the Bough Center charity banquet."

Looking back to me, her smile wilted. "I hate that bitch." Her eyes narrowed in on me again. "You really should try to mingle, Lydia. There are quite a few eligible men here. You're not getting any younger. Strike while the iron's hot and all that. When was the last time you went on a date?" Her eyes homed in on my face, making a disapproving clicking sound and then bringing her own hand to her eyes as if smoothing wrinkles away she'd seen on *me.* As if they might be contagious. Classic move to make me feel self-conscious without saying a word. Although I couldn't deny Ginny's skin was perfect, even though she was ten years older than me. In the past, I would have beelined for a mirror to find out what fault she had evidently spied in my complexion, in my outfit, in my overall being. But now, it only made me want to shake my head in exasperation of her shallow put-downs. Perhaps it came from having bigger fish to fry than the size of my pores.

"Carter Hanes is right over there by the bar," she went on, pointing out a tall, thin man with light hair. I already knew Carter Hanes. In fact, I'd gone out on a date with him the year before, and he'd licked my face when he kissed me. I shuddered at the memory. My stepmother was prattling on. "He's not the most handsome man, but you and he would make a good pair. His father is worth billions *and* he's unwell. Near death I've heard." There was a note of glee in her voice, as if she'd just shared a piece of good news. *Had she thought about my father in such terms once upon a time? Near death?* Her face screwed into a frown. "Well, Mindy Buchanan is swooping in on him, and now you've missed your chance."

She clicked again, looking around to see who might be listening in—apparently Daisy didn't count—before she leaned toward me. "When your father died, and we found out about all his debt, you didn't see me sitting around waiting to be rescued, did you? No, I went out there and found Harold, married him, and solved my *own* problems. You need to stop being a martyr and take the initiative like I did. I'll be back after I've chatted with Jane. Don't move." With that she dismissed me, sashaying off toward Jane, leaving me to ponder how exactly marrying a man for his money was solving your own problems. I shook my head. There was no point in trying to analyze Ginny's flawed, selfish logic.

Daisy put her hand over her mouth, stifling a laugh. "Wow. She's . . . something, isn't she?"

I rolled my eyes. "I can't even believe I came to this," I muttered, draining my glass. As a staff member walked by with a tray of champagne, I switched out my empty flute for a full one, smiling a thank you.

"Of course you did," Daisy said. "It's *the* social event of the season." She winked at me. I smiled half-heartedly, barely able to remember a time when any of this was important to me, when I'd tried to please my stepmother—a never-ending impossible task. Since I was having financial issues, she thought she would *help* me find a rich husband—in her mind the perfect solution. *God.* To her credit, she wasn't gossiping about Stuart and me. These people would all turn their backs on us in a heartbeat if they found out the extent of our money problems.

"I feel like I might die of boredom," I said. "But even worse, Ginny will be back. I have to hide." God, I was a twenty-three-year-old woman with a job and my own home and I was still hiding from my stepmother at parties. *Ex-stepmother. Even worse.* "And get drunk while I'm at it."

Daisy laughed. "I'll come with you." We grabbed a couple more drinks and started making our way across the lawn to an outdoor balcony overlooking the party below. As we began to climb the steps there was a group of women descending. I resisted the urge to groan, instead taking a large sip of the champagne I was double fisting.

"Why, Lydia De Havilland, I haven't seen you in *forever!*" Lindsey Sanders stopped in front of me, looking me up and down in that bitchy, assessing way she'd always had. "Hello, Daisy," she said, shooting her a thin-lipped smile before focusing her attention back on me. I sighed internally. I wasn't in the mood for Ginny, and I was even less in the mood for these women. My old high school friends. It could be argued that Daisy was shallow sometimes, but these women took it to a whole new level. It might have been somewhat acceptable when we were fifteen, but not now. I'd grown sick and tired of the constant competition, the utter phoniness, and we'd had a big falling out at the senior prom when Lindsey had accused me of trying to steal her date. I'd had zero interest in her date. As a matter of fact, I'd had zero interest in *my* date. I'd been struggling with more complex issues than they'd been capable of understanding, and they had nothing at all to do with stealing the muscled college guy Lindsey had brought to a stupid dance. I'd stopped hanging around all of them after that and they still hated me for it—assumed I thought I was too good for them, I supposed. The truth was, I simply didn't have the stomach for it anymore. I'd grown out of all the trivial nonsense, but they never had.

"You look nice," Lindsey went on. "Not every bottom-heavy girl would have the confidence to wear a floral print. You always did take fashion risks though. We all admired you so much for it." The phoniness dripped from her voice. I held back the laugh that wanted to escape my throat. I knew I wasn't bottom heavy and so did she. Once upon a time, that comment would have had me on an immediate starvation diet. How sad that I had cared *so much* what these petty girls thought of me. "So what have you been up to?" she asked, taking a sip of her drink and looking around as if she couldn't care less.

I plastered on my own phony smile. "Oh, you know, not too much—"

"Lydia's too modest to say that she's insanely busy running a multi-million-dollar company, Lindsey." Lindsey raised one perfectly sculpted eyebrow before Daisy went on. "What have *you* been up to? I'm sure it's thrilling, and we *must* hear about it sometime. But not now. Right now we're needed upstairs. Nice to see you!" And with that, Daisy grabbed my arm, and I was forced to stumble behind her, letting out a small laugh before stifling it in a cough. I grinned back at Lindsey and her group of followers who were all glaring after us. I'd been the leader of that group once upon a time . . .

While I was still looking back, before we were far enough away not to overhear, Lindsey turned to Daphne Hanover and said, "She still acts like she's lady of the manor even though, if the rumors are true, she barely has a pot to piss in." And then the sound of their laughter rang out, piercing me in the gut. Maybe Ginny wasn't being as discreet as I'd hoped.

"Ignore them," Daisy said, grabbing my arm and pulling me into her as we walked. "You were better than them then, and you're better than them now. They very well know it and it *kills* them."

Daisy and I climbed to the balcony and sat down at a stone table with an umbrella over it. Looking over the rail, I watched as Lindsey's group joined a small crowd gathered around a tall, dark-haired man. A brunette in a pale pink dress was standing at his side. Something about the man caught my attention, the way he held himself slightly away from those around him, even as people tried to lean in to talk to him. There was something . . . familiar. The only person I'd ever known with those mannerisms was Brogan Ramsay. I took a quick inhale of air, my heart lurching at the thought. But . . . *no.* This man was too tall, too broad, and the way he held himself was too self-assured to be Brogan. And there was no way he could be here. It was just . . . just because I'd been thinking of him earlier. *Shut up, Lydia.* Yes, that was it.

But I squinted my eyes, trying to look closer. I couldn't make out the man's exact features from this distance, but from what I could see, he looked gorgeous. If my own vision hadn't told me, the gaggle of women—now including Lindsey—vying for his attention, preening and prancing around him despite the woman at his side, would have clued me in. And the woman at his side, although she wasn't touching him, she was clearly possessive, turning her shoulder toward women who got too close, flipping her hair in what looked like annoyance.

"Daisy," I asked distractedly, "do you know who that man is?" I inclined my head toward him and Daisy followed my nod, watching him for a moment.

"No, but he's something to look at, isn't he?" We were both quiet as we stared. "I don't think I've ever seen him before. Should we head on down and introduce ourselves?" She winked at me.

I shook my head, biting my lip, the same strange feeling swirling in my belly. "No," I said, looking back to where he stood. "He has a date. Anyway, I think he's leaving." The brunette at his side had just leaned in and whispered something in his ear, and he'd nodded and started shaking hands with those around him. Daisy and I watched as he strode off, the woman at his side. There was something in the man's walk, too. A familiar movement. I frowned, confused again. Shaking my head slightly, I took a big drink of champagne, dismissing the strange feeling. *It just couldn't be.*

Just as the couple were about to exit through the gate that led to the steps at the edge of the garden, the man looked back and up, and I swore our eyes met. I jolted slightly, frowning again, a shiver moving down my spine.

Later, after having both successfully drunk too much champagne and avoided my stepmother and any more run-ins with old high school friends, I said a quick goodbye to the hosts and made my getaway with Daisy in her chauffeured car. We hung out at her house, laughing and talking for a few hours until her husband arrived home and I'd sobered up. Daisy's driver took me to my car, and I made the trip back to my apartment in New York.

As I approached the door to my building, I got the strangest feeling I was being watched. Shivering in the warm early-summer air, I paused and turned around, looking up and down the tree-lined street but not noticing anything unusual. After a moment, I dismissed it as nothing more than the sun and champagne-drenched mind of someone who'd had a long day. Shaking my head and laughing softly at myself, I opened the door and went inside.

CHAPTER TWO

Brogan

The underground, high-stakes poker room was the height of lavish opulence, decorated in shades of black, gold, and red, the materials rich and sumptuous, ornate crystal chandeliers causing light to bounce off the mirrors surrounding the upper portions of the walls. Quiet, classical music drifted through speakers mounted somewhere in the ceiling.

This moment had been a long time coming. I was going to savor it.

The man across from me pulled at his collar as he turned over the card he'd just been dealt. I could smell the tang of his sweat even from the other side of the table. Even if I hadn't been counting the cards, I'd know he believed he had a good hand by the slight widening of his eyes, the way he glanced around quickly to see if anyone else had noticed his reaction. His knee bounced. He had a good hand, but he wasn't entirely sure it was enough. And it wasn't. The king of diamonds I needed to make four of a kind was at the top of the pile. I placed two cards on the table and signaled the dealer, who dealt me two more. Ten of hearts, king of diamonds. I kept my face expressionless, bringing my glass to my lips. I tipped the bartender here exorbitantly well to make sure every other drink I ordered was free of alcohol. This particular round was the real deal. I took a sip, letting the brandy slide over my tongue. At first fiery and sharp, smoothing into soft toasted marshmallow, vanilla custard, a dash of pepper, and then transforming into a nutty oak flavor as it slid down my throat.

Savor, enjoy.

The man across from me had long ago passed *savor* and had moved on to *slurp*. He signaled the waiter for another. Of course, he was too foolish to know that drinking and gambling didn't mix. Or too weak to resist any and all vices offered to him and then to mix them haphazardly, just as he was doing now. And he was about to go down. *Hard.* A boot to the face. Metaphorically, of course. I resisted the wolfish grin that wanted to spread across my face.

He suddenly looked up at me, meeting my eyes through my glasses, narrowing his. "Have we met before?" he asked. I casually signaled the dealer for a cigarette and leaned forward as he lit it, letting the smoke waft in front of my face, tamping down my senses violently, working not to become overwhelmed, not to grimace. I hated the smell of cigarette smoke, detested it. The man across from me watched the smoke rise, as if in a trance, immediately distracted by the swirling vapors.

"I don't believe so," I said, slurring my words slightly, making sure there was no hint of an accent. I'd worked long and hard to do away with it. He looked back at his cards, pulling at the collar of his tux again.

The other player at the table—a tall, blond man—folded. I caught his eye so briefly; it was only a bare flicker of the lids. An acknowledgment only he would see, much less understand. A sign only two people who had spent years on the streets together, surviving, cheating, looking out for each other, becoming brothers in the truest sense of the word, would recognize. *Fionn.* He turned and walked out of the room. He had done his job—he'd driven up the stakes.

The security detail wandered by, his hands clasped behind his back, eyeing our table. This establishment knew enough to watch me, knew enough to suspect me of something they'd never prove. I wouldn't let them. Counting cards was no effort on my part anyway. I did it without even thinking, without even concentrating. So it was unlikely I'd ever be suspected if I handled myself appropriately and discreetly. And I rarely played now anyway—I certainly didn't need the funds, and my vices were few, gambling not being one of them. I hadn't played in years. That is, until *he* started playing here. And now it was only the two of us sitting at this table in this high stakes room.

Savor, enjoy.

The man was intently focused on his cards, considering doing something very, very stupid. *Do it. Do something stupid.* I knew very well he needed to win—he needed to win desperately. His company was suffering, and badly. I knew because I'd made it my business to know. But I didn't think anyone else knew what dire straits he was in. Not even his family. But I moved that thought aside quickly—I needed to concentrate.

"Let's make this interesting," I said, adding a slight slur and a hiccup to the end of my statement. "What do you say we up the stakes here?"

The man's eyes flashed to mine. I could see the desperation in them as clear as day. God, he was a bloody *shite* poker player. I'd almost feel sorry for him if I wasn't savoring his impending downfall so much.

"What are you thinking exactly?" he asked, trying and failing to keep the note of anxious excitement out of his voice.

"I'm in for five million," I said, downing my drink.

The pulse jumped in his throat and he stared at his cards for a beat. *Do it, do it.* "I'm sorry to say I don't have that kind of capital available," he said.

I lowered my lids and shrugged. "Well, it's been fun." I signaled to the man at the door for my tux jacket.

"Wait, wait." Sweat had broken out on his forehead. "I own a company and I'll sign it over to you if you win." He glanced at his hand again, obviously trying to provide himself confidence in his own ridiculous offer.

I laughed. "What would I want with some unknown company?" I signaled the man by the door again.

"It's worth ten times what you're putting in." He was lying. It was barely worth five million at this point. But I didn't care *how* much it was worth. I wasn't trying to make a profit—not a financial profit anyway. A personal profit? Well, that was a different story. I narrowed my eyes, holding my hand up to the man walking my way with my jacket. He nodded his head and turned.

I looked down at my hand, allowing a miniscule frown to crease my brow. I swayed to the left slightly, caught myself, and shrugged. "Oh, what the hell! Right, André?" I forced out a loud, obnoxious laugh. The beefy security detail with the earpiece walking slowly past nodded at me, his expression cold and removed.

Looking at the dealer, I asked, "Is there someone here who will record this bet?"

"Absolutely, sir." The dealer signaled to a man by the door who came over with a book and wrote down the terms while the man across the table downed the rest of his drink, his knee bouncing uncontrollably. I assumed a bored expression as we both signed our names.

He laid down his hand, three jacks. Just as I'd thought.

"Let's see what you've got," the man said shakily. Nerves seemed to have sobered him a bit. But his face was flushed, the subtle glee in his eyes telling me this was the thing that kept him coming back: this moment right before it was revealed whether he would win or lose. That addictive, excited hopefulness that had taken down so many men before him.

I paused.

Savor, enjoy.

And then I turned my hand over, revealing my four kings. For a moment he simply stared, as if the math wasn't adding up. His face flushed bright red, and he looked like he was going to throw up.

"I believe I just became your boss," I said nonchalantly, allowing my accent to slip through. I tilted my head, removing my glasses. "Actually, now that I consider it, I believe we have met before. Stuart De Havilland, am I right?" I stuck my hand out, a wild satisfaction moving through my blood. "Brogan Ramsay." Stuart's face blanked and then slow comprehension dawned in his slightly inebriated eyes as he stared at me, his face finally blanching of all color. He gaped. "So very nice seein' ya again." I smiled. It felt wolfish. And this time I allowed it.

CHAPTER THREE

Lydia

"Morning, Carl," I said, breezing through the doors of De Havilland Enterprises, removing the coffee, two sugars, no cream, from the drink holder and placing it on the front security desk.

"Morning, Lydia. Have I told you lately that I love you?"

I laughed, kissing him quickly on his grizzled cheek and heading toward the elevator bank. "Every morning, Carl. And I'll still never get tired of hearing it." I grinned at him and stepped into an elevator as it dinged open in front of me. Balancing the other three coffees in the drink holder, I switched my briefcase to my other hand and pushed the button to the upper floor.

I'd woken up this morning with a hopefulness I hadn't felt in months, a certainty that everything was going to be okay. I had a meeting with my brother at nine, and we were going to go over the quarterly reports. We'd recently won several large construction bids, and there was every reason to believe we'd win several more. Based on the numbers that came in this morning, we'd come up with a plan and even if I had to cut my own salary in half—again—we were going to get back into the black, so help me God.

Going with the *when you look good you feel good* philosophy, I'd put on one of my prettiest work outfits, an elegant, fitted sapphire wrap dress and nude heels and spent extra time on my hair and makeup.

Stepping out of the elevator, I greeted Charlene, Stuart's secretary, and placed a coffee in front of her. She was on the phone but mouthed thank you to me. I winked and used my shoulder to open the door of the conference room, walking inside and setting all my things down on the edge of the large mahogany table.

Once I'd gotten all my things situated, I peeked my head out the door. "Hey Charlene, has Dave in financials dropped the reports off yet?"

"There wasn't anything on my desk this morning. Do you want me to call down?"

"No, that's okay. I'll wait until Stuart gets in." I called his cell, but it went straight to voicemail, and so I drank my coffee in the conference room, going over a few emails on my laptop. When Stuart still hadn't arrived forty-five minutes later, I put my things away and headed down to my office, asking Charlene to let me know when he got in. Why did I have the sinking feeling my brother was at home in bed, nursing a hangover as he so often was on Monday mornings these days? I sighed, the hopeful attitude I'd arrived with quickly dwindling.

I walked back up to Stuart's office about noon, but Charlene just furrowed her brows and shook her head. I sighed, turning to leave, when the door opened and my brother walked in. I startled at the look of him, bedraggled and pale. "Stuart?" I asked, walking toward him. "Good Lord, are you sick? Why'd you come in—?"

"Go into the conference room, Lydia." I frowned, and started to ask him what was going on when he cut me off. "Please." That startled me more than anything. I couldn't recall the last time my brother had said please.

"Lydia, do you—?"

I shook my head at the start of Charlene's question. "No, Charlene. I'll call you from the conference room if we need anything." A pit was beginning to form in my stomach. Something bad was going on. Something I was pretty sure I didn't want to know about.

The door clicked quietly behind us. Stuart went and stood at the head of the table, his hands on the chair in front of him. I could see that a fine sheen of sweat had broken out on his brow.

"What is it?" I asked quietly. I felt myself bracing, drawing inward against whatever he was about to share with me.

"I . . ." He ran his hand through his dark blond hair. It already looked like he'd done that far too many times this morning. "Jesus, Lydia, I'm sorry. I'm so damn sorry. I . . ." he let out a long, shuddery breath and then met my eyes, "I lost the company."

I stared at him, my mind grappling to understand what he was telling me. I shook my head. "Lost the company? That's impossible." I laughed, a brittle sound. "You can't *lose* a company, Stuart. What are you saying?"

"I lost it in a card game. I gambled it. I gambled the company."

I blinked at him: once, twice, three times. "I don't understand," I said, speaking very slowly. "I think you better help me grasp what you're trying to say here."

Stuart raised his arms and dropped them, anger coming over his expression. "I fucked up! I bet the company in a high-stakes poker game, and I fucking lost, okay? I was with our lawyers all morning. I signed it over. It doesn't belong to us anymore. Is that clear enough for you? Are you comprehending?" he spit out.

My blood pressure was skyrocketing, and I felt nauseated. "Don't," I said, my voice a hiss. I pulled a chair back and sagged down into it. "That can't even be legal. Surely there's a way to undo this—"

"There's not. Not unless I want a hit put out on my life. Or maybe yours. Fuck, Lydia, there's no way out of this. I was so close. It was right within my grasp. All our problems . . . solved! *Right* there and then," he snapped his fingers, "gone." He pulled the chair back that he'd been standing behind and sagged down just as I had. "We're fucked."

I shook my head back and forth, reeling. This couldn't be happening. He'd gambled the company? No way out? *A hit . . . on his life?* On mine? *What the hell?* "No, no, I can't believe this. No, Stuart. Maybe I can talk to the person who bet against . . . what? What is that look on your face?"

Stuart put his head in his hands and raked his fingers through his hair again. After several tense moments he brought his face up, his expression even paler if that were possible. "I haven't told you everything. I . . . Jesus—"

"Just spit it out, Stuart. It can't possibly get any worse." Only it probably could. And knowing Stuart, it would.

"The man who owns the company now," he swallowed, his eyes pools of despair, "is Brogan Ramsay."

My heart stuttered, my breath faltering. I clutched the edge of the table. "Bro . . . Brogan Ramsay?" I breathed.

"Yes, his father used to work—"

"Yes, I know who Brogan Ramsay is! How, though? I don't understand." My heart was pumping out a staccato beat in my chest. I felt like I might faint if I didn't remain sitting.

"You think I do?" he yelled, throwing his hands up again. "He's a *psycho.* He's been plotting this. We fired his father, do you remember?"

"*We*?" I hissed. "*We* did not fire anyone, you did." Images were assaulting my brain, unbidden. *A summer twilight . . . his lips tasting me, his body pushing into mine . . . the look of . . . reverence in his young eyes . . .*

"Because I was protecting you!"

I groaned, leaning my head back on my chair. I remembered it *very* differently, and I was damn sure Brogan did, too. But I wasn't going to argue with Stuart about this now. I needed to try to fix this. "Where can I find him?"

"No, Lydia. You're not going there."

I licked my lips. "We were friends . . . of a sort, once upon a time. Maybe he'd listen to me, Stuart. I have to try." Plus, I owed him an apology. It had been a long time coming. I'd wanted to apologize to him for so many years. I still carried it like a sliver deeply embedded in my skin. *Stuart* owed him an apology, too, but I couldn't be responsible for Stuart. *Clearly.* "Give me the address. I don't have the energy to argue with you." I felt drained, zapped completely of the hopefulness from this morning.

"I'll go with you then."

"No, I think you've done enough damage. I'll go alone."

"He's not the same as you might remember him. He's . . . different . . . dangerous. He tricked me." The last part came out sounding like a whine and a wave of disgust washed through me.

I rubbed at my eye. Dangerous? Brogan? I remembered him as sensitive and intense. "I'm just going to talk to him, Stuart. Do you have a better idea? Another solution that you haven't put on the table?" I asked angrily.

"No," he said, his shoulders slumping. "I'm sorry, Lydia. I'm so sorry." He put his head in his hands again.

I couldn't muster any compassion for him, not in that moment. "Then give me the address."

"It's a business address."

"That's fine—even better. There'll be plenty of people around."

"I don't think it's that kind of business." He raised his head, his expression a mixture of fear and dejection. But he reached into his jacket pocket and brought out a business card and pushed it across the table. I reached out and grabbed it.

****

I followed the instructions from my GPS to the address on the business card, pulling up in front of a nondescript red-brick home in Woodlawn, a neighborhood in the Bronx known as Little Ireland. All this time he was so close? After he'd left—*don't sugarcoat it, Lydia, after he'd been kicked off*—our property, we'd looked for him and hadn't had any luck. It was as if his family had simply disappeared. I'd even wondered several times if his father took Brogan and his sister back to Ireland after that day. *That day*. I cringed, as I always did when I thought about it. I sat in my car for a few minutes, staring at the building, working up my nerve to go inside. Stuart had said it was a business address, but it looked like someone's home. Taking a deep breath, I stepped out of my car into the muggy air, straightening my dress as I crossed the street. One glance at the clouds above told me we were about to experience a summer shower.

The brass knocker had the head of a ram on it. My heart rate had sped up, and I worked to calm my breathing as I lifted the knocker and used it to rap twice.

I was about to come face to face with Brogan, after all this time, all these years.

After a minute, I heard footsteps coming toward the door and stood completely still as it was pulled open. My breath came out in a whoosh when I saw a boy, no more than fourteen standing in front of me. "H-Hi," I stuttered, clearing my throat and pulling my spine straight. "My name is Lydia De Havilland. I'm here to see Brogan, that is, Mr. Ramsay."

The boy raised one brow, letting his gaze roam down my body in a suggestive way. I stiffened and gritted my teeth. *Insolent little brat.* "Is he in?" I demanded.

"Aye," he stood back and waved his arm, indicating I should come inside. I hesitated only briefly before stepping over the threshold. The foyer was nondescript, lots of dark wood and a faded oriental carpet on the floor. It was devoid of furniture or wall hangings.

I jolted slightly when the door slammed behind me, fidgeting with my purse strap and waiting for instructions from the boy. He appeared to text something on his phone, then put it in his pocket, and gave me another gesture to follow him. I did, walking down a hallway and turning into what appeared to be a waiting room. There was a large leather couch, several bookshelves lining the wall, and a coffee table with a few financial magazines on it.

I sat down on the leather couch and the boy sat down next to me. I scooted over slightly and smiled at him politely. His eyes swept my body again, a cocky smirk on his face. My God, the boy didn't even have facial hair yet. "How's the form?"

"Excuse me?"

"What's the craic?"

"I'm sorry, I don't—"

A door on the other side of the room suddenly opened and a tall, dark outline stood in the doorway. "Rory."

The boy—Rory—stood abruptly and moved around the table. I stood, too. "Sorry, Mr. Ramsay. This fine thing is here to see ya." I did understand that. I pulled myself straighter. My heart was now a frantic drumbeat in my chest as I stared at the man I'd only known as a boy so many years ago. My nerves stretched tight, tension coiling in my stomach. I was suddenly having difficulty pulling air into my lungs. He took a step closer, into the light, and it felt as if time stood still. Brogan Ramsay stood in front of me. He was *all* man now, tall and broad, his black hair cut shorter than it'd been the last time I'd seen him. He removed a pair of black-rimmed glasses, and I stared at his face. It was the same and yet different. I recognized the ice-blue beauty of his eyes, framed by thick, inky lashes and black, slashing brows, and the sensual shape of his mouth. But the difference showed in his strong jaw and sculpted cheekbones—the bone structure of a full-grown man. He was even more beautiful than I remembered. The girl in me swooned and melted just a little. But I wasn't a girl, I was a woman, and I stiffened my spine. I wasn't here to swoon.

His gaze finally moved from Rory to me and lingered on my face for one startling moment as my breath caught, his eyes hard chips of blue ice. I froze under his cool assessment. He looked away as if in disinterest, and I released a breath.

"I told you I require a visitor's name, Rory."

"I sent it, sir."

"You didn't."

Rory swallowed. "Phone's acting the maggot, sir. Strangest thing. Lydia De Havilland." He swept his hand toward me as if I were royalty, but Brogan's eyes didn't follow it. A small muscle twitched in his cheek.

"Get it fixed. Go now."

"Shur look it. I'm gona head on." Rory rushed from the room, not looking back. My gaze returned to Brogan, taking him in. He wore black suit pants and a gray shirt, open at the collar and the sleeves rolled up to show strong, tanned forearms, those same forearms I used to stare at as he worked in my yard.

"Hi, Brogan," I said softly, unmoving. Emotions were assaulting me, so fast and furious I hardly had time to analyze them. They overlapped, swirling together to form a ball of nerves in my stomach, a tightening in my chest. Something seemed to flutter through my veins.

"Lydia, it's been a long time. How can I help you?" His voice was deep, smooth, completely unaffected. Bored even.

I stiffened. "You don't know why I'm here?"

He paused and then turned, heading back into the room from which he'd emerged. "Would you care to sit down?"

I followed him into what I saw was his office. He tossed his glasses onto the top of a large, black desk in the center of the room and sat down in the chair behind it. I hesitated momentarily before taking a seat in the chair across from him.

"It *has* been a long time," I said, replying to the comment he'd made a few moments before. "I'm glad to see you're well, Brogan." I cleared my throat. "What exactly is this business?" I asked, sweeping my hand around, indicating the building as a whole.

"I'm in life insurance." There was some kind of amused gleam in his eye I had no idea how to interpret. I noted he no longer had any trace of an accent. I wondered if that had come naturally, or if he'd worked to rid himself of it. Either way, it seemed a shame. I'd always loved the lilting sound of his speech, the way he sometimes threw in Irish slang that I had no idea how to interpret. The way the boy, Rory, had just done. I remembered laughing and asking him what certain sayings meant. I'd known a few . . . long ago. Sometimes they still came back to me, unexpectedly. *He'd called dandelions piss-in-the-bed. What are you doing down there? I'm clearing out the piss-in-the-bed.*

I cleared my throat again. "Insurance. Oh. Okay. Well, good. Obviously you're very successful."

Brogan tapped his fingers on his desk as if impatient. "As to your previous question," he went on, apparently ignoring what I'd just said, "yes, I do know why you're here. I imagine it's because your brother is still a coward and a moron. Sending his sister to do his bidding? To clean up his mess?"

I swallowed, heat flooding my face. Outside thunder rumbled. "He didn't send me. I insisted on coming. But yes, I am here to clean up his mess." I licked my lips nervously.

"And how exactly are you going to do that? Are you offering to purchase the company back? There'll be a surcharge now, of course."

Surcharge? "I . . . I can't. We don't have the capital to do that. I'm hoping we can come up with some other arrangement."

He lifted one dark brow. "And what did you have in mind?"

I looked to the side and then back to him. Truthfully, I hadn't arrived at a plan before rushing over here to beg Brogan for mercy. And now I saw the folly in that. "We were friends once, Brogan. I'm hoping you'll—"

He suddenly slammed his fist down on his desk, his face contorting into a mask of fury. "We were never friends. You tricked me and lied to me. You cost my father his job. You have no idea what you cost my family."

I swallowed heavily, shaking my head. "I . . . I know. I did trick you. It was an awful, selfish thing to do. I've wanted to apologize for so long, I even—"

"I have no need of your apology, Lydia."

"All the same, Brogan—"

"No," he gritted out harshly. Rain began pelting against the windows. "You don't get to throw a sorry at me in order to assuage your own guilt. I don't want it. Keep it for yourself, *princess*." He added the old nickname mockingly.

My God. He hated me vehemently. After all this time.

I studied his face, hard and set in his anger. "Stuart was right. You did this on purpose. You *planned* it. You tricked him into losing the company to you."

"Tricked him? Hardly. Your brother's problems are of his own making."

"I know that, Brogan. Believe me, I do. I'm under no illusion as to my brother's weaknesses, his vices. But please, we employ so many people. They all depend on us for their livelihoods."

"Ah, now you care about peoples' livelihoods? How refreshing."

I opened my mouth to respond, but he interrupted me, plowing ahead. "Anyway, what makes you think I'd put anyone out of work? Except, of course, you and your brother. As the new owner, I've taken it upon myself to look into De Havilland Enterprises. At first glance, it appears things could be turned around if it was being run by someone who wasn't a gambler, a drug user, and a fucking self-serving waste of oxygen."

My heart dropped. He might not take the company apart, but the business my father had worked his fingers to the bone for would no longer be in our family. It would have broken his heart to know . . . *oh God.* And all because of something *I* foolishly did seven years ago.

I pulled in a lungful of air, a lump forming in my throat. Whether Brogan agreed or not, I *had* thought we'd been friends . . . once, long ago. *Before.* I searched his face for the kind, sensitive boy he'd once been, but saw nothing of him in the hard lines of this man's face. I didn't know him anymore. This man was a callous stranger.

"There's nothing I can do, is there?" I asked. I licked my lips, pulling the bottom one between my teeth.

Brogan studied me, his gaze skittering to my mouth and back to my eyes. Tapping on his desk again, he appeared to be weighing something, some decision. "How much do you want ownership of De Havilland Enterprises back, Lydia?"

My throat went dry. "I . . . I'll do anything, Brogan. Anything." My face flooded with hot shame. But it was true. In that moment, I would go to any lengths to fix this mess. For my father, for his dream, I'd do anything. It was his legacy, the only part of him I could still care for in this physical world.

Brogan chuckled, a sound filled with disdain. He rubbed the edge of the leather inset on his desk with his index finger, my eyes following the movement for a moment. He'd always been such a sensual person, always touching something, his hands lingering, caressing, seemingly entranced by textures . . . He had covered his accent, but not that. I grasped onto it—finally recognizing something in this man that had also been in the boy. "Anything? Would you beg for it? Would you get down on your knees and beg?"

I froze, my heart seeming to stop before it picked up an erratic beat, my gaze meeting his. "Is that what you want me to do? Is that what this comes down to? A payback of some sort?"

"Actually, Lydia, some interest has accrued since *I* was asked to beg. If we're considering a payback, your begging would have to be on a much larger scale. Grand even."

"What does that even mean?"

Brogan looked off to the side, seeming to be considering something. Moments ticked by before he finally looked back to me, his light blue eyes a soft and startlingly beautiful contrast to the harsh expression he wore. "Here's my offer: Come work at my home as I used to work at yours. Do as I ask you to do and every day, you will beg me for your company back. If you do it well enough, I'll consider your request."

I gaped. "Are you out of your mind?" I hissed.

He shrugged nonchalantly, his face impassive now. "It's been said."

"Said? Said by whom? Because I'd be inclined to agree. It's a disgusting offer. You're a pig."

"That's been said as well." Brogan chuckled, leaning back in his chair again, flashing me an arrogant smirk. I blinked. I'd never seen Brogan smile that way before. I remembered a different smile—sweet and slightly shy. *That* smile used to make my heart flutter. *That* smile used to make me giddy with desire. One of his front teeth overlapped the other just a tiny bit and I'd noticed the way he'd run his tongue over it when he seemed to feel unsure. When I had kissed him, I'd run my tongue over it, too, and it had thrilled me in some way I hadn't been able to explain—even to myself. I swallowed at the memory, not allowing myself to think any more about it. Because while it was true that his smile had filled me with want once upon a time, when he'd smiled at me all those years ago, his eyes had been warm and full of affection, full of yearning. Not now. Not anymore. He shrugged. "The operative word is *offer*. You're free to accept or decline. But it's the only offer I'll give you—the only chance you'll get."

"And what type of *work* would I be doing at your home exactly, *Brogan*?" I asked tightly.

He steepled his fingers. "I'm not sure yet, *Lydia*. All kinds of things probably. I guess ya could consider it a jack-of-all-trades position of sorts. Or would the expression be *jill*-of-all-trades?" He smiled again as I simply stared.

His phone buzzed, and he pulled it toward him, glancing at it quickly. "I'll have to wrap this up. I have more important things to attend to. Consider my offer," he shrugged, "or not. Either way. I'm assumin' ya have my card since ya found me."

I was still staring at him, my teeth clenched together, disbelievingly. It didn't escape my notice that his accent had emerged during those final sentences. I stood up and, without another word, left Brogan Ramsay's office, slamming his door behind me. *Oh God.*

CHAPTER FOUR

Brogan

I attempted to control my breathing. Lydia De Havilland had just slammed out of my office, and I still couldn't catch my breath. The fact made me want to hit something.

I'd seen her from afar several times, even followed her home a couple of days before for some reason I still couldn't explain. Gathering information on the De Havilland family, I'd told myself. All the better to know how to proceed with the acquisition I'd planned of their company. But that was flimsy at best, and I bloody well knew it. And even though I'd seen her from across a party, and across a street, I hadn't been prepared for the impact of her right in front of me. I hadn't needed Rory to tell me her name so I'd *recognize* her. I'd just wanted to be *ready*. But I hadn't gotten that, and the entire time she'd been in my office, it had felt as if the ground was rolling beneath me.

Lydia had matured into a stunning woman—even more beautiful than I'd remembered. And *back then*, she'd had the power to steal my breath right from my lungs.

Her golden hair was shorter than it'd been, shoulder length now, but it still looked as soft and lustrous as I remembered it. I rubbed my fingertips together as if the gesture itself would conjure up the feel of the blonde strands on my skin. I longed to touch her hair again, and that small longing alone filled me with impotent rage. Her face had lost the roundness of youth, highlighting her delicate bone structure, and those beautiful, almond-shaped blue-green eyes. I put my head in my hands and massaged my temples and then raked my hands through my hair. Just sitting in the same room as her made me *hungry* in that same desperate way I'd felt when I could never get enough food, never feel the satisfaction of a full belly. Only it was worse because this hunger would never be satisfied, nor would I let it.

When she'd walked into my office, I'd had the urge to lean toward her to catch her fragrance. That had shocked me. I was used to unconsciously leaning *away* from people when they got too near, or holding my breath as they passed. I didn't enjoy the smell of others for the most part—and I could detect too much. It felt like an intimacy, and most often, it was an intimacy I didn't care to partake in. But it'd always been different with Lydia. She had *always* appealed to me in a way no one else had. Chemical makeup didn't change, I supposed. Pity for me.

My mind went back to a summer evening seven years ago, the night my mind wouldn't let go of for some insane reason. I could still feel Lydia in my arms, could still recall her delicate scent, the flavor of her mouth, the sound of her sigh as I'd pushed into her tight body. *Why?* Why was I still so damned affected by her? I'd been a boy the last time I'd seen her. I was a man now. A man who'd been with women who had much more sexual prowess. Beautiful women who knew tricks in bed that would make an innocent princess like Lydia De Havilland go scarlet. I'd had experience far beyond the teenage fumbling I'd known with her. My time with Lydia had been but a moment. *And yet . . .* I shook my head of the memories and forced myself to move past the brief moments in her arms to the one that had come next.

The humiliation. The rage. The hopelessness. The grief.

The memory of what she'd done still pulled tight like an internal scar every time I thought about it. Not just what she'd done, but what she *hadn't* done. She hadn't defended me. She'd basically stood by while her brother shamed me and made me beg. I hated her for manipulating me, for making me *hope,* and for the weakness I'd felt. And I couldn't forgive her for it. I wouldn't *ever* forgive her for it.

And that was it. If I exacted the revenge I'd been imagining for so long, I'd be free of her. Exorcised of her ghost, the one that had been haunting me for seven years. Of *Lydia*, of the memories, of the shame that still burned deep in my gut. I'd finally be able to let her go. Because I'd succeeded in turning everything around—now she was the one who needed *me.*

Now she was the one begging.

"Well, what's the craic?"

I raised my head as the door swung open. Sitting up, I attempted to smooth my ravaged hair. Fionn eyed me as he dropped into the chair Lydia had occupied only a few minutes before, his big body sprawling. His shirt was wet from the rain. "Not much." I answered.

Fionn whistled, leaning forward. "That Irish accent says otherwise, mo chara." He laughed softly, and I gave him a glare that only made him laugh harder and pretend to shiver. How in the hell had he detected my accent? I'd only uttered two words. "What a fiendish glare. Is that supposed to work on me?"

I sat back, leaning my head on my chair and staring up at the ceiling for a minute. "Lydia De Havilland came here."

"Ah."

"Yeah, ah." I raised my head and looked at him. His expression held sympathy and the vague hint of worry.

He raised his eyebrows. "Well, now I understand the state of ya. Did she offer to buy her company back?"

"She can't. She doesn't have the funds." *Which I'd already known.*

Fionn shrugged. "Well, that's that, then. She'll have to find a new job. Good luck to her."

I felt a tick start up in my jaw. Fionn narrowed his eyes and inclined his head. "What's that look?" he asked.

"I told her she could come work at my home and serve me and beg for her company back every day, and I might show mercy."

Fionn gaped at me for a moment, then reclined back in the chair, his arm hung leisurely over the back, studying me. "That's a fret."

"You could say that."

"What were ya thinkin'?"

I gritted my teeth. "I was thinking," I said slowly, enunciating each word, "that it's her turn to get down on her knees and beg *me*, that's what I was thinking."

"Her *turn* to beg ya? Ya haven't left her much choice, have ya? Is that what ya really want?"

I shrugged nonchalantly. "We'll see."

"And do ya have any intention at all of returnin' her company?"

"No."

Fionn was quiet for a moment. "This is all gona go arseways, ya do know that, yeah?"

Probably. "No. I have it under control."

"What's the plan, then? And what's the time limit on this bloody madness?"

I shrugged. "I'll make it up as I go along. I'll see what pleases me."

Fionn chuckled. "What *pleases* ya. Aye. Because ya already look so *pleased*." He sighed. "Completely arseways. It doesn't even make any sense. Why do this to yourself, mo chara?" he asked softly.

"Satisfaction." *Peace. Payback. Revenge. A cleansing.* A hundred reasons and I didn't even need one. I was the one who held all the power now.

"Aye, if ya say so. But I helped ya because I thought takin' the company from Lydia's brother was what was gona bring ya satisfaction. I gotta say, ya look many things, but satisfied ain't one of them."

I shrugged. "Another opportunity presented itself. I decided to take advantage of it. Why are you here?"

He sat up and sighed. "I work here, remember?" He raised a brow. "And now that ya have your archenemy by what I can only assume is a very pretty throat, we have some actual business to attend to." I narrowed my eyes at his mocking archenemy comment, but he only grinned in that disarming Fionn way—the way that had gotten us out of some scrape or another more than once. "And *then* we're gona go get ourselves good and ossified and find us some women of questionable moral attributes."

I stared at him for a minute, but then chuckled. I could never stay annoyed with Fionn for long. And truthfully, getting good and drunk could be a good thing. I sat back as he went over the jobs we had going on that week.

Fionn had been by my side practically since the day we'd left Greenwich and moved to a small rat-hole in the Bronx. I'd had less than a month left of high school, but had never graduated, instead scrounging for every side job I could get to support my family. My father had looked for work but sunk into a deep depression when he didn't find any. Then his drinking had only increased, until he was drunk more often than he was sober. Which left me in charge of Eileen's care. And so I'd done what I had to do, some of which would sadly follow me for the rest of my days. All because of what had happened that evening in the back room of Lydia's stable. All because of *her* betrayal.

But I'd had a trusted friend in Fionn—at least I'd had that. A scrappy kid a year younger than me who'd moved with his parents to New York City from a town very near where I was from in Ireland. His parents died in a horrific car accident, and as they didn't have any close family left in Ireland, he'd had nowhere to go other than the streets. But one thing you could say for the Irish, we took care of our own. People did what they could for us, sharing their food no matter how little they had, hiring us to do odd jobs. But for me, it hadn't been enough. Because Eileen had needed more, and I'd vowed never to let her down. I was all she had.

And I dreamed that one day I wouldn't have to scrape and do without, I wouldn't have to check my pride at the door, make sacrifices I didn't want to make, do things I cringed while participating in. I dreamed that one day I'd make my own rules. I dreamed that one day I'd feel *safe*. One day I'd be at peace. And I'd finally achieved my goals. I'd finally arrived at a place where I could turn my attention away from merely surviving to making the people who'd torn my world apart pay.

I didn't know exactly what I wanted from Lydia. But I wasn't overly worried. If her presence became bothersome to me in some way or another, I'd simply tell her to leave, *and* I'd keep her damn company. No matter *how* much she begged. I'd add it to my empire. I didn't need the money, but I'd make it successful; I'd make it my own, and I'd find satisfaction in that alone.

A small feeling of guilt niggled at me, but I squashed it down. Taking the De Havilland company meant I'd be taking it out of the family. And Lydia's father, Edward, had been a decent man who had been proud of what he'd built from the ground up. In actuality, I'd respected him more than I'd respected my own father. And he'd always been fair to me, more than fair—he'd been kind. I'd heard that he'd passed four years before and I'd gone to his funeral, standing at the back of the cemetery so I wouldn't be seen. But I'd seen *her.* My eyes hadn't seemed to be able to look away as she'd mourned in her black suit, a pair of sunglasses on, and her hair held back in a black headband. And then her brother had come up and put his arm around her, pulling her close and comforting her. And she'd let him. And why shouldn't she? He was her brother. And I still couldn't figure out exactly why watching them together had felt like another betrayal. Was she supposed to have banished him from her life after what he'd done to me? *She* hadn't even cared enough to come after me. To expect anything at all from her was ridiculous. And yet it had *ached.* I hated them—hated the whole lot of them. And now they'd pay. And I'd enjoy every minute of it. I wouldn't allow anything less.

CHAPTER FIVE

Lydia

I sat at my computer in my pajamas, tapping a pen against the edge of my desk before dropping it in frustration. I'd started to write a draft of the email I intended to send Brogan, but decided typing it out might be easier. And then I could just go ahead and press send. I picked up his business card—a thick, white cardstock with black print. Elegant and strong, just like the man. Or at least just like the *look* of the man. Setting the card aside, I placed my fingers on the keyboard, typing in his email address. Stuart's voice rang in my head, the words he'd yelled when I'd told him what Brogan had offered. *He said WHAT?* he'd raged. *He wants my sister to whore for him as payment for my loss? Who the fuck does he think he is? I'll kill him!* Empty words when he was completely at Brogan's mercy, when he had absolutely nothing to bargain with. Still, the look on his face had told me he meant what he'd said. If he could get away with murder, he would.

Brogan,

I find your vague, arrogant offer disgusting and vile. Nonetheless, I have no choice but to accept it if—

I deleted what I'd written, frowning. Did I really think Brogan wanted me as his whore? I had the feeling he didn't. In fact, the way he'd looked at me—with disgust—told me all he wanted was to humiliate me. And I had to believe he had plenty of *willing* candidates, if he was looking for sex. He was a gorgeous man. I sat up straighter. I could do it. I could take some humiliation if it meant saving the company my father had loved. If it meant saving the jobs of those we employed. I didn't have to be happy about it, but perhaps playing the game would be the best plan. *More game playing.* I'd grown up and washed my hands of playing games with people years ago. But apparently Brogan had not.

My only other option was to wipe my hands of this mess, go out and get a new job and move on. My heart sank. Could I really move on like that without even trying to convince Brogan to let us have our company back? To *buy* our company back on some sort of payment plan? If it was even the most remote of possibilities, I had to try. I had to find out what Brogan required of me and what he was willing to give—if anything. I had to. For myself . . . *for my father*.

Brogan,

I appreciate the offer you have so generously presented—

Delete. I brought my foot up on my chair, hugging one knee for a moment, closing my eyes and picturing Brogan as he'd been as a teenager, picturing those light blue eyes, all the more stunning because of his dark coloring. They seemed like a trick of nature—something that made his male beauty impossibly stunning. Thinking of them now brought a strange ache, as did the memory of the way he'd always looked at me with those piercing eyes of his. It had been . . . *adoring.* It had appealed to my teenage vanity, of course, but it had also appealed to something else—something deeper, something I'd wanted to explore. Why had he adored *me* of all people? The boy who seemed to never, ever make a decision lightly, to never do anything without *intensity* and forethought. That day in the stable I'd begun to understand that whatever it was between us was far more than superficial. The strength of it had startled me. And as much as I hated to admit it, I still felt pulled to him, at least physically. Of course, I had to figure most women were. "Gah," I said, putting my knee down and sitting up straight.

The thing was, despite everything . . . despite this terrible situation, despite that Brogan hated me, that he wouldn't allow me to apologize much less accept it, despite that he'd decided to use his money to take ownership of our company, I couldn't help the feeling that had swirled in my gut when I'd seen Brogan earlier—not just shock and confusion, and distress, but . . . *pride.* I was *proud* of his obvious success even though he apparently intended to use it to destroy me. I hardly knew how to organize my own emotions. I was *still* reeling.

Brogan,

I accept your offer. Please let me know where I should be and when.

Lydia

I paused only momentarily before hitting send. Taking a deep breath, I stood, walking to the bathroom off my bedroom to brush my teeth. As I was finishing, I heard a ding from my computer and returned to see I'd received an email. I walked slowly to the screen and inhaled a sharp breath when I saw who it was from. I'd assumed he'd make me wait. With shaking hands, I opened the email.

Lydia,

I'm pleased. You may start tomorrow at four p.m. Below is my address.

Brogan Ramsay

Oh holy hell. I frowned, chewing on my lip as I noted the address of his home in Greenwich. *He lived in Greenwich?* How long had he lived there? It had to be only recently that he'd bought the house. Greenwich was a small town—surely I'd have heard? And suddenly it hit me—the man I'd seen at the garden party recently. That man had been Brogan.

"Oh my God," I whispered. I *had* recognized him. I had just been too discombobulated and shocked since everything had happened this morning to revisit that moment at the garden party. God, I'd *known* it was him, and I'd talked myself out of it. The smooth way he walked, the controlled way he held his body. The way in which he had always stood just a little farther away from other people. *But not me*, he had never held himself away from me. Things had apparently changed though. In the most dramatic way possible.

Anxiety assaulted my nerves, and I took several calming breaths. Okay, this was fine. I could do this. And even *better* that I'd be in a town I was familiar with—where I had friends. Well, sort of. I supposed classifying the girls I'd gone to high school with as friends might be stretching the definition. *Quite a bit.* I had Daisy. At least I had her. But would I tell her about this? God, the humiliation. How could I? I'd cross that bridge when I came to it because as of now, I really had little idea what I was getting myself into.

Brogan and I would have to discuss terms once I got there. Certainly he didn't intend for me to "work" for him for some interminable timeframe. Surely he'd grow weary of this game, too? Or would he? He couldn't possibly expect me to be some sort of slave labor forever.

All right, I wasn't going to worry about this tonight. I was going to get a good night's sleep and not imagine scenarios that may or may not come to pass. I climbed into bed and shut off the light, laying my head back on the pillow, the vision of pale blue eyes drifting through my mind.

****

Sleep never came. I crawled out of bed the next morning at seven a.m. after I'd tossed and turned through the night. After a long, hot shower, I blew my hair dry and dressed in a pair of white pants with thin pin stripes and a green blouse. I was going to go into the office for a couple hours to get things settled. I paused as I slipped on my pumps. Was Brogan going to *allow* me to work at my office during the day—even remotely? I groaned—I supposed, *technically*, it wasn't even my office anymore. But that was the purpose of this. The *purpose* of this was that I was going to play by his rules, allow him to exact his revenge, take back his power, whatever he considered it, and then we'd part ways, me in possession of my family company. I would do as he asked me to do, and I'd persuade him to do the right thing. Okay, admittedly, it was a long shot. Perhaps an *impossibly* long shot. But somewhere deep inside, I had to believe there existed the sensitive boy I'd once known, even if only a shred of him was left. I *had* to believe as much, and I had to believe having access to Brogan was going to allow me to convince him to give back what was rightfully mine. If I didn't have hope, I basically had nothing.

Another thought made me pause. What if whatever "work" Brogan Ramsay asked me to do was of an illegal nature? I frowned, recalling his place of business. He'd said he was in life insurance and yet, I'd seen nothing that would indicate that was true. There hadn't been as much as a sign on the door or a computer on his desk. And his only employee had been a frisky adolescent. I'd had the impression that whatever his "business" was, it was sketchy at best. Insurance salesman, my ass.

Attempting to turn off my mind, I drove to De Havilland Enterprises and made my way quickly to Stuart's office. Surprisingly, I found him standing in front of the window, looking out at the city beyond. I was surprised to see him there—unless we had a meeting, I usually didn't expect to see him until after ten. I wondered how long it would be until one or both of us were escorted off the premises.

Stuart turned when he heard me enter, and I caught sight of the flask in his hand, and his bloodshot eyes. *Ah.* Now I understood why he was here so early. He'd never gone to bed. Well at least if I was losing sleep, he was, too.

"Would you like some coffee with that?" I asked sarcastically. "To at least *pretend* it's morning."

He turned, his expression tight. "No." He took another swig.

I dropped my purse onto a chair. "How is this helping anything? I'm the one who has to go live with a virtual stranger who is looking to make our whole family pay for something that happened seven years ago. The least you could do is present a semblance of strength for me today." I loathed that my voice sounded overly high-pitched. I took a deep breath and removed some files from my briefcase. "I need you to take care of something for me later this afternoon. I'm leaving early and this needs to get done. You're the only one who can do it besides me. Do you think you can manage it?"

"Stop the condescending bullshit, Lydia. Just tell me what you need done and it'll get done." Stuart was back to staring out the window and didn't turn around. I gritted my teeth. As usual, Stuart had gone from livid anger to sulky self-pity. I wasn't surprised, but I also didn't need to contend with it. Not today.

"Okay, thanks," I said, feigning nonchalance. "I'll text you when I know more."

I picked up my briefcase and my purse and went to leave his office when Stuart said, "Did you know our father planned to give him a job here? Said he was some kind of math genius, and we'd be lucky to have his talent at De Havilland Enterprises." I turned, one hand on the doorknob. Stuart laughed softly, no humor in the sound. "Ironic, no?" He took another long draw on his flask.

I regarded my brother, a small frown tipping my lips down. He continued to stare out the window, his shoulders bent, looking broken. I hadn't realized—he'd been *jealous* of Brogan Ramsay. All those years ago, he'd been green with envy because our father had recognized something in Brogan that had impressed him. My father with the incredibly strong work ethic and business savvy had never been impressed with his lackadaisical son. My father was a good man, but when it came to my brother, he'd noticed every weakness, every *difference,* and more often than not, looked at him with disapproval.

"Take care of your brother, Lydie," my mother had said right before she'd died. "I know he's older, but he's not strong like you." Stuart had only been fifteen at the time and she'd known. I couldn't help the small spark of sympathy that ignited in my chest. There were many things I didn't appreciate about Stuart, but he was still my brother. In actuality, he was the only family I had. And my mother had asked me to look out for him.

He turned toward me. "Take care of yourself. Be . . . safe."

I nodded, offering him a small smile. "I will. I promise. Things will be fine." I walked out and closed his office door softly behind me.

I spent the rest of the day wrapping up loose ends, telling my secretary I was taking at least a few vacation days. In actuality, I had no idea what was going to happen, or whether Brogan was going to allow Stuart and me to have jobs here in any capacity. If I was here next week, all the better. I could continue on, trying my best to pull the company out of the mess it was currently in, just as my plan had been the day before.

By two p.m. I was leaving the office. I refused to say goodbye to anyone as if I wouldn't be returning. To do so would be to abandon hope. Plus, as far as I could tell, none of the staff had any idea anything was different than it'd been yesterday, so I'd have to wait for Brogan to clue me in on exactly how that was going to be handled. Of course, I could only hope he could be taken at his word as far as ensuring the rest of the staff stayed on, whether that was true of Stuart and me or not.

A large part of my job was managing the department heads, and they were all competent in their roles. They would do just fine without me there. Reminding myself of this as I left De Havilland Enterprises put my mind at ease.

I returned home quickly and pinned my hair up and took another quick shower. I then packed a bag with a week's worth of clothes. Surely it wouldn't take me longer than that to convince Brogan to come up with some terms we could work with. I hesitated over what exactly to take. Hmm . . . what did a girl pack before submitting herself to her slave master? *Good grief.* How had my life ended up here?

I got in my car and pulled the address up on my GPS that Brogan had emailed. I turned on an audio book for the forty-five minute drive and attempted to focus on the story as I drove. Worrying was useless, and I had no idea what I was walking into. Imagining the possibilities would only serve to work me into a nervous wreck. All the same, by the time I pulled off my exit, I knew I hadn't absorbed a single word of the novel.

I navigated my way to Brogan's address in Old Greenwich and drove down the long driveway to pull up in front of a gorgeous pale-gray Nantucket-style shore colonial right on the waterfront. *Wow.* The boy who had once been a gardener's son sure had done mighty well for himself. Clearly there was money to be made in the *probably shady* insurance business. This home had to be upward of six million dollars, if not more.

There were no other cars in the driveway, but Brogan could very well have parked in the three-car garage in front of me. I got out of my car and grabbed my bag from the backseat, surveying the house in its entirety. Was this part of the reason Brogan had chosen to have me come here? So I would see just how affluent he was now? To highlight how far *we'd* fallen, and how far *he'd* risen? Well, if so, he'd already been successful. That fact was clear. As clear as I could imagine the view was to the Long Island Sound from every room in this elegant home.

I walked around to the front of the house and used my hand to shield my eyes as I looked out over the water just beyond a wide expanse of grass, mowed in diamond shapes. Interesting. Brogan did his own yard work? Either that, or he'd found a gardener to adopt his style. I doubted it, though. I thought back to seven years ago. I hadn't only noticed Brogan physically back then. I used to watch with fascination how detailed he was in everything he did. Intent. Focused. The precision of the work in front of me spoke of Brogan Ramsay and Brogan Ramsay alone.

There was a spacious wrap-around porch flanked by endless summer hydrangeas already in full bloom, the decadent, round, blue flowers a favorite of mine.

Taking a deep breath, I knocked once on the door and then waited. It was several moments before I heard footsteps approaching. The door swung open, and Brogan was standing there in jeans and a navy blue T-shirt. I pulled myself up as straight as possible. "Hello," I managed. Brogan nodded and stepped back, allowing me room to enter. I did, looking up and around at the two-story foyer. "You have a lovely home."

Brogan thinned his lips and nodded, pushing the door so it swung shut with a small click. "Follow me, I'll show you to your room." *Well, this was uncomfortable.*

"Room or *cage*?"

Brogan shot me a scowl. "I left you a choice in this matter, Lydia. Feel free to leave now if you've reconsidered."

I followed him up a flight of stairs, my eyes caught by the stunning view out the window of the upper floor. I was right—all the way to the Long Island Sound. "No, I haven't reconsidered. But I'd like to discuss terms. We didn't—"

Brogan turned into a room and I followed him, the words I'd been saying dying on my lips as I took in the luxurious accommodations. I was pulled immediately to the French doors that led to a widow's walk providing a beautiful, clear view of the water. I could imagine standing here with a cup of coffee in the mornings, watching the sun rise. *Temporarily, of course.*

I turned and looked at the bed, a large canopy with plush, white bedding. The far wall featured a fireplace flanked by two tufted, velvet chairs, and a door that must lead to the bathroom. The only other furniture was a chest of drawers and a nightstand.

I turned suddenly back to Brogan and he startled slightly at my abrupt movement. I thought I caught a fleeting expression of nervous anticipation, but when I blinked, his face held only neutral boredom. "This is . . . this is beautiful," I said anyway, biting my lip. "Can we talk now?"

Brogan cleared his throat. "Actually, no, I have a business call I need to make. I'll see you later at dinner."

"Oh, okay. Um, dinner? Do you cook, or should I . . . I mean, will that be part of my . . . duties?"

Brogan seemed to consider that. "Actually, yes, that will be part of your duties. You'll probably want to go shopping for some food, though. I haven't had the chance to get to the grocery store for a while."

The sudden picture in my mind of this aloof, powerful man strolling through the frozen food section glaring at the potpies and sending searing glances at the English muffins made me want to giggle. I stifled it. "All right then." I'd plan to discuss the terms of this arrangement over dinner. I eyed him. "And on what schedule does my begging begin?"

Brogan had turned toward the door but now halted and pivoted toward me. I shrunk back as he took two long strides before he was right in front of me. "When would you like to start?"

I raised my chin. "Does it matter what I want? I thought I was at your command. Isn't that the whole point of this?"

Brogan stared at me for several heartbeats but didn't say a word before turning and leaving my room, closing the door behind him.

I released a breath, walking to my bed and sinking down on it, lying back, and staring up at the canopy above me. Okay, well, here I was. And at least going to the grocery store would give me something to do with my nervous energy.

****

An hour later I was back at Brogan's house with an armload of groceries. I wasn't the greatest cook, but I could manage. I'd been living on my own since I returned from college, and I'd learned to make do for myself, especially since I was on a budget and went out to eat as little as possible. Of course, if this whole business with Brogan didn't work out in my favor, I'd be on an even tighter budget. Jobless. Or maybe I'd be better off. As it was, I was putting practically every dime of my own paycheck back into the company. I had to hope it would be worth it, but in the meantime, I was shopping the bargain racks and clipping coupons. Not that I would ever let Brogan know that—it would probably *please* him, and I wouldn't give him the satisfaction. He knew we were bad off—he didn't need to know the particulars of my personal finances. Or, that when I'd first thought to shop for this year's swimsuit at Target—which surprisingly enough, had really *cute* swimsuits—I *didn't* get to shop at all. There was no extra money for this year's anything really. *My new reality.* At least I was prepared for what might be to come. And at least I now knew Target was great for swimsuits. And clothes. And purses. And home décor. Target was awesome. *Anyway.*

I unpacked the groceries, opening cabinets to determine where the dry goods went. The kitchen was a large open area with custom white cabinets and white subway tile. There was a large island in the center and a breakfast nook off to the side with a pretty garden view. Brogan's home was luxurious, but it also managed to be very homey and comfortable, too. Despite growing up very close to here, in a luxurious home as well, it had never had the relaxed feel of this home. I looked around. Perhaps it was the décor—Ginny had always decorated using showpieces rather than anything you could actually use with any practicality. And even my mother, though she'd been warm and kind, had leaned toward formal furnishings. Brogan's home was decorated in just the opposite way—it seemed as if all the pieces, though beautiful, had been chosen specifically for comfort. But there was also a decidedly female influence—I wondered if he'd hired a decorator. *Or perhaps he'd been married . . .* I didn't really want to ponder on why that thought sat heavy in my belly.

I headed toward the stairs to drop my purse in my room and noticed that the door to what I'd seen was Brogan's office was open and Brogan was gone. I called out his name softly and then waited, but there was no response. He must have gone out.

After leaving my purse in my room, I returned to the kitchen and moved the kettle off the stove—a kettle! What man owned a kettle these days? I prepared a baked chicken, roasted Parmesan potatoes and green beans for our dinner, and then poured myself a glass of wine as I waited for Brogan to return.

An hour later, I'd drunk two glasses of wine, my stomach was growling and there was no sign of him. Should I call him? I went and retrieved his business card from my purse and dialed his number. It went straight to voicemail. Sighing, I dished up my own plate and ate alone, sitting in the breakfast nook, staring out at the garden, colorful with summer flowers.

I cleaned the kitchen and wrapped the plate I'd made for Brogan and left it on the counter.

What in the world was going on here? Anger assaulted me as I climbed the stairs and put my pajamas on and climbed into bed. Didn't I even deserve some common courtesy? Apparently not. Despite my anger and although it was early, my lids began to close as soon as my head hit the pillow. I'd barely slept at all the night before and the two glasses of wine had done me in. I was asleep in mere moments.

CHAPTER SIX

Lydia

I woke early and showered and dressed before heading downstairs. Although I had slept hard and hadn't heard Brogan come in the night before, it was obvious that he'd been home. The food I'd left out was gone, there was some junk mail on the counter that hadn't been there yesterday, and a chair had been left pulled out from the table. I saw a note on the island and picked it up.

Lydia,

I'll be home at six with a guest. Please have dinner prepared for two.

What. The. *Hell?* No explanation about why he hadn't bothered to turn up for dinner last night, no information about what I was supposed to do today, no plan for when we'd have a conversation about the terms of this ludicrous agreement, just . . . *this?* I crumpled the note up and threw it across the room. Picking up my phone, I dialed his number for the second time. Straight to voicemail again. I let out an angry growl and dropped my phone on the counter with a loud clack.

Was his plan to bore me to death? Or maybe I should look at this as a nice little vacation? Perhaps I'd lie out on his deck and soak up some

. . . a loud crack of thunder sounded out the window and rain began beating on the glass. I slumped down onto one of the bar stools and put my chin in my hands.

No, I was not going to sit here and do nothing. He'd "hired" me to work off our debt, and that's what I'd do. I got started in his kitchen cabinets, organizing everything by item and then alphabetizing it all. After a quick lunch, I moved on to his room, knocking first and then opening the door slowly, peeking inside as if he might be there, hiding in the shadows. I stepped inside, looking around at the large master. It looked somewhat similar to the room he'd given me only the bed wasn't a canopy and was made up in dark gray linens, and there were no chairs in front of the fireplace, only a large, soft-looking area rug. There were no personal items I could see, and I decided not to open his dresser drawers—for the moment anyway. Instead, I went to his bathroom and organized his medicine cabinet in the same way I'd organized the kitchen. He only had a few items—toothpaste, a toothbrush, floss, deodorant, shaving cream, a comb, a bottle of Tylenol, and nail clippers—so it didn't take long. It felt extremely personal to be going through his bathroom cabinet, but that's what he got for leaving me with no direction. If I had to make it up as I went along because he'd left me to my own devices, then he couldn't complain. Still, there was a tight feeling in my gut as I went through his personal spaces that I couldn't exactly explain to myself. All this time, all the days I'd wondered about the boy, and then the man . . . and now here I was in his bedroom.

I looked over at the bed again, wondering what he looked like when he slept. Did that intense expression he wore smooth out as he traveled to the land of dreams, or did he hold on to that tight control of his even in sleep? And how many women had slept here with him? How many women knew him intimately, *as I had . . . once and only once?* Shaking off the thought, I went into his closet and began organizing his clothes by type and color. His clothes mostly consisted of dress shirts and pants, a few ties, and several racks of shoes.

When I was done, I left his room, that same strange feeling of sadness lodged in my chest. That had been a bad idea. I would be better off with no reminders that Brogan Ramsay was a flesh and blood man. Though I had thought of him often over the years, with a mixture of sorrow and regret, I'd be better off remembering he hated me and was out to punish me in whatever way brought him satisfaction. Going through his clothes and personal items had not helped my own cause. Still, it might annoy him so at least I had that.

As I stood staring out the window, I caught movement just beyond some trees to the side of the house and leaned closer, straining my eyes. It had stopped raining, but water droplets were still dripping down the glass, which made it difficult to see. I walked quickly to the front door and made my way across the soggy lawn and through the trees, emerging in another driveway in front of what looked like a nice guesthouse, smaller than the main house, but in a similar style. There was a car driving up the driveway and I watched as it turned out of sight. Someone was staying here? I turned and walked back to the house.

I dialed Stuart's number, and he picked up on the second ring.

"Lydia. You okay?"

I gritted my teeth. It sounded like Stuart had been drinking, his voice slurred. What I was doing out here at Brogan's house wasn't going to make a damn bit of difference if Stuart was drinking himself stupid rather than maintaining our business until I could get back. I'd likely return with some kind of plan worked out between Brogan and me, and the company would be completely worthless. "Yeah, I'm fine."

"He hasn't hurt you?"

"No. It seems like he's planning on using me as his housekeeper. I'm supposed to cook him and a guest dinner tonight." I opened the refrigerator and started looking at what I'd bought yesterday that I could make for dinner.

Stuart let out a breath. "Did he tell you how long you'd have to be there?"

"No. I haven't talked to him yet. I'll let you know when I do, okay? Are you all right?"

"Yeah." He sounded sullen like he was having a pity party. "I've been fired. My replacement showed up today and the new management watched as I cleaned out my office. Not surprising . . . but . . ." His voice drifted away.

I froze for a second, hearing how upset Stuart sounded. *And so it begins. Would he fire me, too?* "Oh," I breathed, leaning against the counter. "Stuart, I'm sorry. I was worried that would happen, but I hoped . . . Well, this will turn out all right. Will you be okay?"

"Once Brogan Ramsay is dead in the ground," he murmured.

"I don't think we need to get that drastic. Hold tight. This will work out. I'll call you as soon as I can, okay?"

"Okay, whatever you say. Let me know if you need anything." I heard liquid sloshing as if he'd just taken a drink out of a bottle. *Yeah, I need for you to grow up and start being a responsible man, Stuart. Start thinking of someone other than yourself.* I held my tongue. He'd just been escorted out of our family company. Maybe it wasn't the right time for a verbal lashing. And maybe he wasn't the only one who needed a drink.

"I will. Stuart, I . . . I love you, okay?"

"Yeah, I love you, too. Bye."

"Bye."

I stood in Brogan's kitchen for several minutes, trying to get hold of my emotions. I was resentful of Brogan for the situation we were currently in, but I was angry with Stuart, too. Here I was serving at my master's mercy and he was . . . *drunk?* I could barely afford groceries and he was still drinking? Where exactly was he getting the money for that expensive vice? And after he'd gambled away our company? I let out a shaky breath. God, my life was in tatters. And now I might have to figure out a way to make my car payment. Or maybe it was time to get rid of it entirely—I had prepaid the garage fee in the city for the year, but it was coming up for renewal in the next few months and I probably wouldn't have the funds to pay it. Truthfully, I no longer lived a lifestyle where maintaining a car in New York City was reasonable. Maybe I should start preparing my résumé, *but what employable skills did I actually possess?*

I headed to my bedroom where I took out my laptop and logged in to my email account, my muscles tense as I waited to see whether I was locked out or not. I wasn't. So Brogan had had his new management team fire Stuart, but not me? My heart rate decreased slightly. I had to believe that was a good sign, that at least Brogan was considering working with me on this. The next department head team meeting wasn't for another couple weeks, so hopefully all would be resolved by then.

I spent the next few hours catching up on emails and a few work items I could do from my computer, thankful that although I wasn't in the office, I could keep my finger on the pulse of the company so to speak. Then I went to a recipe website and looked up a few ideas, emailing the one to myself that I finally chose.

Returning to the kitchen, I pulled the recipe up on my phone and got the ingredients out of the refrigerator. Again, I poured myself a glass of wine while I cooked. So far, I had to say, this portion of the revenge plot Brogan had going on was pretty weak.

At five forty-five, I heard a car pull up in the driveway and checked the fish I had just put in the oven. It still needed about fifteen minutes, so I hoped Brogan wasn't expecting dinner early. I heard the front door being opened and left the kitchen to stand in the foyer. Brogan came in first, a smile on his face and I almost startled at the unexpectedness of it. But then I saw why he was smiling. He was talking to a woman who was entering the house behind him as he gestured her into the foyer. He caught sight of me and his smile wilted. "Lydia," he said, nodding his head. The woman stepped fully into the foyer, a smile on her face. She was gorgeous with long, red hair and legs that went on for days. She looked at me questioningly, but Brogan didn't introduce us.

"Um, dinner's not quite ready," I said to Brogan. He took the woman's light wrap, and I couldn't help but to notice that her figure was perfect in every way as the entirety of her dark purple dress was revealed, deeply cut at the chest, showing an ample amount of cleavage.

Brogan moved his eyes from her to me, as if with difficulty.

Something tightened in my chest. "That's okay. We'll have cocktails in the living room. What would you like, Anna?"

"I'd love a glass of white wine," she said. "Do you have a chardonnay?"

I looked at Brogan and he looked at me, raising his brows when I didn't answer. "Oh, uh, yes," I finally said. So I'd be, what, serving them tonight? I pressed my lips together. "Let me get that for you." I plastered a fake smile on my face. "What would you like to drink, Brogan?"

Brogan put his hand possessively on Anna's lower back and led her toward the living room, turning his head slightly and saying, "Just water."

I gritted my teeth and turned back to the kitchen. This was fine. I was going to serve Brogan and his date. He could have assigned me worse tasks than this, I supposed.

I checked on the fish and then the items on the stove. I'd made pecan-crusted halibut with couscous and roasted asparagus.

When I walked into the living room with their drinks, they were both sitting on the sofa with their knees touching as Brogan laughed at something Anna had just said. Laughed! I'd rarely even seen him laugh when he was a teenager. He'd just gotten this warm look in his eyes and they'd crinkle slightly at the corners in this endearing way . . .

Without making eye contact, I put the drinks down on two coasters on the coffee table. When I looked up, I saw that Brogan was watching me, his tongue running over his front teeth. His eyes moved away and I glanced at Anna whose eyes were moving between Brogan and me. I cleared my throat. "Dinner should be ready in ten minutes."

I turned to leave when Anna put her hand on Brogan's thigh, giving me a cool smile, and said, "I don't think I caught your name. I'm Anna."

I turned fully toward her, shooting a quick glance at Brogan. His eyes were shuttered as he took a drink from his water. "I'm Lydia. It's nice to meet you." I gave her a small smile and then turned and left the room as quickly as possible. I could hear her asking Brogan in a whispered voice who I was, but I didn't try to listen for his answer.

As I set two places at the table in the formal dining room right off the kitchen, I wondered if Brogan was having me serve him and his date to inspire some kind of jealousy? Why would he do *that*? Or was he simply trying to cause me embarrassment with the fact that I was now so lowly I was reduced to serving him and his girlfriend? Or one of his girlfriends at least. I did note that she was a different woman than the one I'd first seen him with at the garden party. Apparently he wasn't lacking for dates. What *was* the actual point of this? Because the truth was, I *did* feel a smidge of jealousy and I didn't like it at all. I didn't want to watch Brogan with the beautiful woman in the other room. I could certainly accept that he was with another woman—all these years, I'd figured he was. When I'd thought of him, I'd assumed he was probably with plenty of women, perhaps even married, perhaps even with children . . . A lump formed in my throat and I swallowed it down. But assuming something and having to be a party to it were two very different things. And the truth was, I could admit to myself that I had never fully let go of my feelings for Brogan Ramsay. I wasn't even sure exactly how I felt about him—especially now in my current predicament—but what I *did* know was that I'd rather be lots of other places than where I was now. *Suck it up, Lydia. You agreed to this.*

I squared my shoulders and returned to the living room where Anna was leaned in to Brogan whispering something in his ear. Her hand was between his thighs, resting just above his knee. His gaze met mine above her turned head, and my eyes widened at the direct eye contact. "Dinner's ready," I muttered, pivoting back toward the kitchen. God, I *hated* this. And I hated him. I hated that this was bothering me. I hated that he was doing this to me just because he could. He was doing this to prove that he held all the control. Like a spoiled toddler, he was going to show me who was in possession of all the toys. And yet, he knew nothing about me now. He knew nothing of the things I'd experienced since that day seven years ago. He didn't know that I'd suffered, too. He didn't know because he hadn't attempted to find out. *He probably hadn't cared and really, I guess I couldn't blame him, and yet it hurt all the same.* And so this was who Brogan Ramsay had become: a man who took pleasure from exacting any petty revenge he could on a person he knew nothing of anymore.

I took another sip of wine, feeling anger move through me. I held on to the emotion tightly—it felt so much better than the jealousy, the hurt. Perhaps I deserved all three, but it didn't mean I had to like it.

The fact remained, though: I did have to endure it. I'd agreed to as much.

Brogan and Anna came into the dining room. Anna shot me an annoyed look. Clearly, she'd rather be alone with Brogan. Who could blame her, really? I'd be uncomfortable if I were her, too. I'd serve dinner and make myself scarce.

I brought the dished-up plates to the table and refilled their drinks. "If you don't need anything else—"

"We might. Stay nearby," Brogan instructed. I felt my nostrils flare, but I simply nodded and left the room. In the kitchen I poured myself a second glass of wine and sat at the island flipping, unseeing, through a magazine of neighborhood coupons that was sitting with the other junk mail.

Anna's feminine laughter drifted from the dining room. I heard Brogan call my name and froze, getting up slowly and walking back into the dining room where I saw Anna had pulled her chair closer to Brogan.

"What can I get for you?" I asked, clasping my hands in front of me and smiling placidly.

Without turning to me, Brogan said, "I dropped my napkin. Will you bring me a new one please?"

Or you could simply bend down and pick it back up, you arrogant asshole. "Of course." I retrieved another napkin from his linen drawer and took it into him.

"Thanks," he said, not looking at me. I held the napkin out to him, but when it became clear he wasn't going to take it, I set it down on the table, my knuckles rapping against the wood. The noise caused him to glance up at me, those blue, blue eyes meeting mine. My heart squeezed.

"God," Anna moaned, putting a forkful of halibut into her mouth, "this is so good." She licked her bottom lip slowly and giggled, putting her fork down and sliding her hand across the table where she used her index finger to run along the top of Brogan's hand. "My compliments, Lydia. This food is almost better than sex." She looked pointedly at Brogan. "Almost." She turned her eyes toward me, clear hostility there now. *And why?* I'd done nothing to her.

"Well," I said, shooting her what I hoped was a fake looking smile, "I really wouldn't know. I've only been with one man, and it was an extremely *unfulfilling* experience."

Brogan's body went rigid and Anna's eyes narrowed. "That's a shame, Lydia. Maybe you should get out more." *Like right now,* was written on her face.

"That's a good idea, Anna. If there'll be nothing more, I'll leave you two to enjoy your date." I didn't give Brogan the chance to reply before rushing from the room. I grabbed my phone off the counter and headed up the stairs. I'd come down later—after they were gone wherever it was they'd end up going—and clean the kitchen then. Was she going to spend the night here? I ran my fingers over my forehead. So this was his plan. How stupid I was to even consider that he'd brought me to his home to use me as some modern-day sex slave. He was going to keep me here to show me how very *wanted* he was by other women. How very little he wanted me. Why? Because he'd thought all those years ago my tricking him meant that I hadn't cared for him at all. And yet, if he cared enough to go to such extreme lengths to prove something to me, didn't it also prove that *he'd* cared and cared deeply? *Had* cared? *Did* care? I sighed. *Oh, Brogan.* What is this you're doing?

And now he knew he was the only man I'd ever been with because I'd blurted it out in a moment of anger. I cringed. I hadn't thought that out. I hardly wanted *him* to know that.

I undressed and took a long, hot shower and then put on a pair of cotton shorts and a tank top I slept in. I hoped Brogan wouldn't try to call me downstairs to serve dessert. Oops, I hadn't made dessert. Well, Anna would appreciate that—she wouldn't have to wait to get Brogan upstairs and into bed. I put in a pair of ear buds and turned on Spotify on my phone, lying back on the bed.

Something woke me. I blinked, trying to grasp where I was for a moment, moaning aloud when I finally did. I felt like I'd been sleeping for hours. My eyes adjusted to the low light and I turned over, bringing my knees up and wrapping my arms around them, loneliness assaulting me in the darkness of this strange bedroom.

"Were you lying?"

I startled, letting out a small yelp and jerking upright. Brogan had turned one of the chairs flanking the fireplace and was sitting on it, leaned forward, his elbows on his thighs as he watched me.

I allowed my heart rate to slow for a few moments, removing the now-silent ear buds. My playlist had ended. "It's not okay to come into my room without permission."

"You went into mine."

Ah, so he'd noticed. "Not while you were in there," I defended.

"That makes it better?"

"I . . . what do you want? I didn't think midnight visits to my bedroom were part of our deal, not that we've defined the terms of our deal since you stood me up last night." I scooted to the side of the bed, running my hand through my hair, trying to work out some of the tangles.

"Were you lying about having only been with me?"

I stared at him in the dim light, his features softened, the color of his eyes subdued. "No, I wasn't lying."

"Why?" he hissed.

I jerked back slightly. "Why what?"

"Why haven't you been with another man in all this time?" He stood suddenly and stuffed his hands in his pockets, turning toward the window.

"Maybe I didn't find the experience particularly pleasant. Maybe I haven't been eager to repeat it."

He didn't turn, didn't react to what I'd said. I wasn't sure if he really wanted the truth here, or whether it was to satisfy some morbid curiosity. I released a slow breath, biting my lip. "I don't know. I guess I just haven't met anyone it went that far with. Between my dad passing, and the problems with the company . . . I just . . . my focus hasn't really been on dating."

"But before that?" he asked, still not turning. There was a note of something I wasn't sure how to define in his voice. Almost a sad weariness.

I swallowed. *Before that* . . . I waved my hand around. "Before that, I realized it was much more fun playing games with a whole handful of boys than just one," I lied. "More fun being a tease than actually giving in." It seemed to be what he wanted to believe and he wouldn't get the truth from me. Not under these circumstances. He already had enough leverage against me, plenty to hurt me with. I would not give him more.

He turned after several tense moments, his jaw ticking. "I see."

No, you don't. I nodded, standing and walking to the door where I opened it and then crossed my arms, waiting for him to leave my room. "You shouldn't keep Anna waiting. I'm sure she's wondering where you snuck off to in the middle of the night."

"Anna's gone."

"Well that was . . . fast."

He studied me from where he stood by the window for several tense seconds before tilting his head minutely, his eyes narrowing as he walked toward me. I willed myself to stand still, not to look away as he approached me. When he got within a foot, I dropped my arms and backed up slightly, my back hitting the wall next to the door. I wished he wasn't so tall. Standing this close to me, I was forced to tip my head back and look up at him giving him an unfair advantage. I stiffened my spine. "We took such alternate paths after that day, princess." He stepped right up to me, leaning toward my ear. I felt his warm breath fan my neck and shivered slightly. Unconsciously, I inhaled to catch his scent before I realized what I'd done. I remembered him smelling salty with sweat when I'd known him before. *I'd loved it.* It had spoken to my body in some primitive way my mind didn't understand completely but thrilled at all the same. He didn't smell like sweat anymore, though. Now, he was a man who looked as if he'd smell like some expensive cologne. But even this close, I could only detect clean skin and soap. But of course, Brogan Ramsay wouldn't wear cologne, would he . . .?

"My family was completely destitute, see. We couldn't even put food on the table after your brother kicked us out." I closed my eyes. *Oh God. Oh, Brogan, no.*

He leaned back slightly and ran one finger down my cheek as he shrugged. "You ever feel hunger, princess? Real gut-wrenching hunger? The kind that makes you want to pick a fistful of grass and eat it just to stop the incessant painful gnawing in your stomach?" I let out a gasp of anguish and Brogan's lips tipped up. "Oh, I don't want your pity, princess. See, I had a few things going for me. As it turns out, there was a whole slew of rich, married women in New York City willing to pay good money for a vigorous fuck with a young, strong boy." My eyes widened, shock cutting through me like a blade as I stared into the angry, ice-blue depths of his eyes. "I was able to support my family fucking in hot tubs, limos, once on the bar of an exclusive dinner club after hours." He smiled but it didn't come anywhere near his eyes. "In so many delicious positions. You have no idea, princess. Would it shock you to know I loved every minute of it?"

I stared at him, the expression on his face challenging and cold and yet . . . his eyes were filled with . . . stark pain, something I imagined he didn't even realize was there. It prompted me to recall things I'd once noticed about him. I'd been fascinated by the way his senses seemed so . . . acute. I had never asked him about it, but then the one time we were together, when I'd touched him, I'd known I was right. He was lying to me now. I wasn't certain if I should trust my gut on that or not—it'd been so long since I'd spent any time with Brogan. But I didn't think that sort of thing changed. "It must have been very difficult for you," I murmured.

Confusion washed over his features as he took one step back. "Difficult?" He attempted a smirk. "Hardly."

"All those women . . ." I tilted my head sucking on my bottom lip for a moment as I watched him closely. His eyes leapt to my mouth and then quickly back to my eyes. "All the smells, the textures, the way they must have clawed at you . . . It must have been very difficult for you."

He froze, his expression arrested as he took another step backward like I was a venomous snake who had struck out at him. I felt no satisfaction in the wound I knew I'd just inflicted, only sorrow.

"Ya know nothin' about me," he said, but his voice was raspy, his accent suddenly appearing and betraying some emotion I wasn't sure I could put my finger on.

"Don't I, Brogan? I did once. Once, we were friends," I said softly. *And for me, more. Much more.*

He laughed. "Ya were a spoiled little princess who thought slummin' it with the gardener's son a time or two made us friends? Is that what ya thought? We were never friends. We fucked once and that's it. And as ya said, it wasn't even very satisfyin'."

"Don't make it dirty, Brogan. Please don't do that," I said, a hitch in my voice that I couldn't hide.

"Why not? Isn't that what ya did by settin' me up? It was dirty before it ever began, Lydia, wasn't it? A dirty trick."

I shook my head. "I know but I—"

Brogan stepped forward, swearing softly. "I promised myself I wasn't gona discuss this with ya." He stepped closer, staring me down. "You're an employee of mine now, nothin' more."

I lifted my chin. I would not cry. I had survived worse than this. Brogan thought I was still a self-serving princess. And yes, perhaps I had been. Once. Perhaps I had been petty and maybe even unknowingly cruel, an insatiable flirt who didn't always consider the feelings of others. A princess who played games instead of being honest about my feelings. But I had been a teenager. He was a full-grown man now, and if treating me this way was going to give him something he needed, then let him have it, whatever it was. Suddenly I was too drained and weary to care.

Our gazes held for long moments and I swore I saw something intense—*yearning*—in his eyes, and it made my heart clench.

I opened my mouth to say something, to try to make some sort of peace between us. But then Brogan's expression went carefully blank, and he stepped back once more. "I'm having a cocktail party this weekend," he said evenly, enunciating every word. I blinked as my mind struggled to catch up to the change in topic. "A housewarming of sorts. I'll need you to work it. The caterers will be here Saturday morning to begin setting up, along with the band and the florist. I won't be back until then."

"O-okay. And what should I do until Saturday?"

"I'm sure you'll come up with something." With that he turned and walked out the door.

I fell back against the wall, tilting my head up as tears filled my eyes and blurred the high ceilings above me. I'd known what happened that day must have hurt his pride deeply, had understood the overwhelming anger it must have caused. But I hadn't known he'd suffered the way he'd just described. All these years, when I thought of him, I hadn't imagined he still carried such raw pain. *God, Brogan, I didn't know. I didn't know it still hurt so much.*

CHAPTER SEVEN

Lydia – Sixteen Years Old

The rain beat against the library window. I tilted my head, leaning my cheek against the cool glass as I snuggled into the plush cushions of the window seat. I ran my finger down the pane, following the trail of a lone raindrop. I loved rainstorms, loved being inside while it beat down on the roof and wind whipped at the trees outside the window.

A small sound caught my attention, and I turned my head to see Brogan standing in the doorway. He looked surprised to have been caught and took a step back. "Sorry," he mumbled.

I stood quickly, running my hand over my hair and giving him a big smile as I tilted my head in the way Ginny did when she talked to men she found attractive. "It's okay," I said, my heart rate increasing slightly the way it always did when Brogan was near. I walked toward him, trying to put a little extra sway in my hips. Brogan's eyes moved quickly down my body, and I felt a little thrill of delight run up and down my spine. "What are you doing here?"

"I was just pickin' up me dad's paycheck," he mumbled, holding out the envelope in his hand as proof. "I should get back. It's really lashing." He nodded his head toward the window indicating the rain and I grinned, and I could feel that it was the dumb, wonky grin that showed too much of my eye teeth.

I straightened my mouth before he looked back at me. "I like it when you talk like that," I said, smiling and tilting my head.

He looked confused for a moment and then ran his hand along the back of his neck as he bent his head forward on a smile. My heart flipped. He was so heart-stoppingly handsome, and he had little to no idea. That was the part I liked best about Brogan. He didn't even seem to understand his appeal.

"Stay a minute," I said. "At least wait until the rain lets up a little bit. It's not like you can work outside tonight."

He hesitated, but when I turned and walked back into the library, shooting him a look over my shoulder, he followed. *Yes.*

I went back to the window seat and sat down, and Brogan took a seat next to me. My gaze moved to his fingers running absentmindedly along the silky tassels of the cushion we were sitting on. He was always touching something in that way, as if memorizing its texture. A gentle heat moved through my veins. I wondered what his fingers would feel like doing that to my skin. I wondered if he'd like the texture of . . . me. I bit my lip, and his eyes moved to my mouth, causing a wave of satisfaction to wash over me. But then his eyes shifted away, out the window, and a fleeting expression of sorrow moved across his face.

"My mam used to say God gave us rainy days to let us know it was okay to take a day off now and then." And even though his eyes remained sad, his lips tipped up in one of his rare, sweet smiles. Butterflies fluttered in my belly.

His mam. I considered him for a moment thinking that perhaps he and I were more similar than different. Maybe that was another reason I was so drawn to him. I missed my mother, too. So much that sometimes it was still hard to believe she was gone. Sometimes in my secret heart of hearts, I pretended she wasn't. I pictured her right upstairs, sitting in her bedroom brushing her long blonde hair and humming softly to herself. I left her there in my mind and it didn't hurt quite as badly as picturing her in the cold, hard ground.

"You miss her very much," I said softly. He had never spoken of his mother before, even during the times I stood and chatted with him as he worked. He leaned back against the wall behind him and I let out a breath, happy he was relaxing in his seat and that he might stay and visit with me for a little while.

"Every day."

I nodded sadly and waited for him to say something more, but he seemed to gather himself. "Did ya know the Irish have hundreds of different ways to talk about the rain?" he asked, obviously changing the subject. I tilted my head, looking at him quizzically.

"Like what?"

"If ya say it's only spittin', it means it's just drizzlin' a bit. Pissin' is a heavier rain that might keep ya inside. Rainin' stair rods is a soakin' rain that will ruin your shoes. Hoorin' will have your windshield wipers set at top speed. Lashin' will wash ya right down the storm drain and hammerin', well, entire towns have been known to disappear in rain like that."

I was laughing as he spoke, and he looked at me with a warm gleam in his light blue eyes, our gazes meeting, lingering, and then parting. *I love you,* I wanted to say, blinking at my own thought, feeling suddenly insecure and off balance. When I looked back at him, Brogan was watching me, a small, confused frown on his face.

I cleared my throat. "Why so many?" I asked, but my voice sounded breathy.

He shrugged, his smile contemplative. "It rains a lot in Ireland. I guess ya know what's frequent or important in certain places based on the number of words for any specific thing." He paused. "There are also about a hundred ways to describe gettin' drunk." He looked away, his lips thinning and a grim look taking over his expression.

"Do you miss it?" I rushed in to fill the silence, wanting to sway his mood back to playful again. But I also genuinely wanted to know. I wanted to ask him so much about himself. Did he have a lot of friends in Ireland? Did he want to go back someday? How did his mother die? Did she have cancer like mine? I felt a sudden urge to touch him, to let him know I wanted to be his friend. I wanted him to ask about me, to ask me what I felt like inside, and I wanted to tell him, not just because I had no one else to tell—my friends and I didn't discuss things like that—but because I liked him so very much.

My hand lifted to reach toward his when there was suddenly the clicking of heels on the marble floor growing louder in the hallway.

Brogan jerked to a standing position just as Ginny turned the corner. She stopped in the doorway, cocking one slim hip, looking back and forth between Brogan and me. "Why hello, Brogan. How nice of you to come visit us up at the house."

I resisted the urge to roll my eyes. Sometimes the things Ginny said came out sounding so bitchy.

Brogan gave me one last glance and turned toward the door. He nodded at Ginny as he passed her. "Nice to see ya, Mrs. De Havilland."

She turned her head and looked back at him moving down the hall toward our front door before looking back to me. She clicked her tongue. "You've really got to stop *cavorting* with the help. I see you bothering him relentlessly while he's working. Honestly, Lydia, you may as well just pick up a rake and help him out if you're going to be hanging off him so much."

I stood up and crossed my arms. "Cavorting?" I asked. "We were only talking. And I don't bother him." I pouted. "He likes talking to me, too."

"It really can't come to any good." She walked across the library to the liquor cabinet and poured herself a glass of wine. She held the bottle up in my direction, and I shook my head no. I'd shared several glasses with her before and had to drag myself out of bed for school the next morning feeling like death warmed over. Despite our somewhat close age, I'd wanted Ginny to be a mother figure, but Ginny wanted to be my . . . friend. I was beginning to wonder if she'd be of any real use in either role. But she was all I had.

I made a scoffing sound in my throat. "Myles says I'm the prettiest girl in Greenwich," I bragged, frowning immediately at my attempt to impress her. *Should I even bother?*

Ginny gave me a smirk. "Now *Myles* is the boy you should be focusing on. A thoroughbred who comes from old money." She winked and I rolled my eyes again. *Were we talking about boys or horses?* "Now if you want advice about how to catch that one, use your Irish boy toy to make him jealous. Have him catch you kissing Brogan. Force him to claim you before he even has a chance to think about it."

I raised my eyebrows. "Does that really work?"

"As long as he has even the remotest attraction to you, it works every time. Men. They're all such predictable creatures." She took a long swallow of red wine. "You just have to know how to wind them up and then watch them dance."

I turned away from her, considering the plan. The thing was, I had no need to make Myles jealous. Myles was mine for the taking. He was fun to flirt with, fun to have following me around, I supposed. But he wasn't the boy who set my heart on fire. I wondered if I had the nerve to go through with a plan like Ginny's. A powerful thrill shot down my spine. I wanted it to work. I wanted to make him jealous. I wanted to force his hand, to make him claim me. But the *him* I was referring to was not Myles. It was Brogan I wanted. Brogan Ramsay.

CHAPTER EIGHT

Brogan

Christ, I was so fucking upset I was still shaking. Upset at myself. I had meant to shock her, to unbalance her the way she'd been unbalancing me since the day she'd walked into my office. Instead, I'd merely succeeded in exposing myself and telling her things I hadn't meant to tell her.

"Goddammit," I swore under my breath as I got out of my car and slammed the door behind me, clicking the key fob. I'd left Lydia's room and Greenwich, heading for the Bronx. I needed to put space between us. I just needed to reclaim my emotions and I needed to do it in a place where I held all the power. Despite owning one of the prime pieces of real estate in Greenwich, the location still had this way of making me feel like the gardener's son. *Less.*

I pushed the door of The Black Dragon Tavern open, the pungent smells of stale beer, grease, and dirty mop water assaulting my senses. I didn't usually come here at night—preferring to sit on the open patio—but it was one in the morning and if I wanted to be around other people, which I did, inside at the bar was my only choice.

"Brogan Ramsay," I heard from a corner and turned to nod at a couple of the regulars. "What's three thousand ninety-nine divided by seven hundred thirty?" Aidan McGonegal called out, holding up his phone, his finger poised on what I knew to be the calculator.

"Four point two four five two zero five," I answered easily. The corner erupted in hoots and hollers, one guy pretending to fall out of his chair. I smiled, turning to the bartender and ordering a whisky.

"Bang on," Aidan yelled, his calculator just a couple seconds behind. More hoots and applause sounded from behind me and I chuckled.

"The lad is wicked good with numbers," I heard someone else say. Yeah, this was a good call, what I needed. I took a sip of the whisky and massaged the back of my neck.

"Brogan Ramsay," I heard to my right.

I looked up and saw an old man, a glass of amber liquid sitting on the bar in front of him. I nodded, frowning slightly. "Do I know ya?" I asked.

He smiled. "Father Donoghue. We haven't had the pleasure. I know ya by name, and I know your friend, Fionn." *A priest? I'd never known Fionn to keep company with holy men.*

"Ah. Well, nice to meet ya, Father. Any friend of Fionn is a friend of mine. What church do ya work at?"

He shook his head. "Oh, no, I don't reside in a parish any longer. There was a wee," he raised the pitch of his voice and held his thumb and index finger together, "bit of a scandal some years back. These days, I hold confession from this bar stool right here. The title and a few job duties kind of stuck, shur ya know like." He chuckled, looking none too upset about whatever scandal had occurred that had evidently resulted in his ex-communication. I shrugged. Who was I to judge? I was a fallen man, too.

"I don't usually see ya around these parts this late at night," he said, taking a sip of his drink. "Now Fionn, that's a different matter. That boy's always on the tear, and always with some new floozy on his arm. Ya know when I say floozy, I mean no disrespect. God loves all his children, even the ones who dabble in dubious ethical behavior."

I smiled what felt like a weary smile. "I don't usually have the need to imbibe at all, truth be told, Father."

"Ah, so what's chased ya here at such an ungodly hour, son? Money or a woman? Since I've heard ya have more money than the Almighty himself, me guess is a woman."

I sighed, leaning my chin on my hand. The truth was, it felt good to confide in someone about my own dubious ethical behavior. Maybe confession really did cleanse the soul. "Lydia De Havilland."

"A woman, aye. She doesn't want ya, I gather? Well, why not? You're a fine-lookin' sod."

I shook my head. "It's not about that." I turned to him. "Seven years ago she did somethin' that resulted in my family bein' thrown out on the street."

"Ah. I see. She betrayed ya."

I nodded. "Aye. And because of it, I promised I'd never beg again, never be brought to my knees."

He appeared to consider that for a moment before shaking his head. "Ya can't avoid it. Life brings us all to our knees at one point or another." He smiled suddenly. "I find when it does, ya are in a bloody convenient position to start prayin'." He chuckled and patted me on my back a couple times. I mustered a quick smile. "Also, son, if ya find yourself in love with a woman, on your knees is a rather beguilin' place to be."

I chuckled, suddenly having a pretty good idea about the topic of the *wee scandal.* But the statement simultaneously amused me and brought a strange ache. Never again would I touch Lydia in *that* way. *Even though her skin had felt like velvet beneath my hand earlier.* No. Never again would I touch Lydia.

"The thing is, Father, now the tables are turned, and *she's* the one who needs savin'." I stopped, looking around the bar, seeing only Lydia's beautiful face in my mind's eye. *Malevolent,* beautiful face I reminded myself. Blue-green eyes filled with evil. All right, perhaps I was being a *wee* dramatic. Filled with *deception*. That was more accurate.

"Sounds like that would be a good place to find yourself. Tables turned on the woman who brought ya low once upon a time and Bob's your uncle! Well done. Sláinte!" *Cheers.* He held up his drink.

I looked back to Father Donoghue's craggy face, staring momentarily into his sharp blue eyes that didn't appear inebriated at all, despite that he was sitting in a bar late at night with a drink in his hand. He turned in his seat and began to bring the glass to his lips.

I frowned. "Only—"

He turned back toward me, lowering the glass. "Aye, yeah, *only.*"

I couldn't help smiling. "Is there always an only, Father?"

He smiled back, a hundred tiny creases appearing at the corners of his squinting eyes. "Aye, when it comes to a woman, there's always an only, son." He smiled again as if this made him happy for some reason. "I will surmise that in your case, the *only* is that ya would not hate her so much *now* if ya didn't love her so much *then.* And there is such a thin veil between love and hate, me boy. As wispy as the mist on an Irish mornin'."

I let out a breath, raising my glass to my lips and taking a drink, letting the alcohol burn slowly down my throat. He was right, perhaps. I had loved her then with a fierce boyish infatuation. But I had loved a girl who hadn't really existed, and I needed to remind myself of that. I had loved an idea, an image, a beautiful face and a sexy body. And yet . . . if that was true, why did she *still* make me feel this out-of-control need, this confusion and hunger and lust?

There is such a thin veil between love and hate.

Okay, so the feelings I'd had for Lydia had been more than simple lust. It hadn't been *just* her beauty that intrigued me. She'd affected not only my body but my heart. And *that* was why I needed to exorcise her from the part she still claimed. I needed to break her like she'd broken me and finally be rid of her. The love I had felt for her was false, based on lies. And if the love was false, the hate was false, too. I would ruin her, humiliate her, and then there'd be nothing left except peace. She had never really known me.

That must have been very difficult for you.

I set my glass down on the bar just a tad too roughly, causing the remaining liquid to slosh out. I threw some cash on top of my tab and raised a hand to the bartender, standing and nodding to Father Donoghue. "Thank ya for the listenin' ear, Father. It helped."

He nodded, a small, knowing smile on his lips. "Ya be well, Brogan. Ya know where I am if ya need me."

"I do. Thank you. Slán, Father."

"Slán, me boy."

I left the bar, pausing outside the door, taking a deep breath of the night air, smelling gasoline, the garbage can halfway down the block, and the spices and fried food smells from a food truck parked a little way down the street. I felt better, more in control than I'd been when I'd entered the bar.

A boy walking alone with his hands in his pockets caught my eye, and I watched him for a minute. He eyed the food truck, and I recognized the look on his face: desperation, hunger.

I began walking toward him as he moved surreptitiously through the small crowd of people talking and laughing as they waited for their food. His hand snaked up and grabbed an order as it was set on the counter and a number called out. He made to duck through the people closest to the counter when a burly guy, probably having just left a bar after a night of drinking, clamped his hand down on the kid's arm. "What the fuck? That's my number, you little thief."

Walking up to both of them, I laughed. "Whoa, sorry, that's what I always order. My friend thought it was mine." I looked at the kid. "I haven't had a chance to order yet, pal." I clapped the big dude on his back, taking the food from the boy and handing it back, giving him a small shove. He looked confused but moved along. "What'll you have?" I asked.

The kid glowered at me, attempting to break loose of the grip I had on his arm. He smelled like unwashed hair and dirty laundry. I could smell him even over the stench of the grease and food code violations wafting off the truck. I ordered the largest burrito they sold, and we stood waiting with the rest of the crowd. I could tell he wanted to run, but the allure of food was too great.

When the order came up, I paid and handed the food to him. He unwrapped it greedily and began stuffing it in his mouth. He followed me as I made my way to the sidewalk and sat down on a bench a little way down the block. "Sit down," I commanded. He hesitated, shooting me a nervous glance but finally relented, sitting at the furthest end of the bench from where I was sitting.

"Stealing food from drunks at two in the morning is the best way to get yourself beaten to a pulp or taken down to juvy."

"I was just hungry," he grumbled around the food.

"Yeah. I can see that. How old are you?"

He paused before answering, his mouth still full. "Eighteen."

"Finish chewing and then tell me how old you really are."

He chewed the oversized bite in his mouth, his eyes moving away from me before he said, "Fourteen."

I leaned forward, resting my forearms on my thighs and lacing my fingers in front of me. "Who's supposed to be feeding you at home that's fallen down on the job?"

He regarded me for several moments, another bite of food in his mouth before he again swallowed and answered, "My ma." He glanced up the street and then said, "She got herself hooked on heroin again. Took off last week with a boyfriend, and I haven't seen her since. She'll come back at some point, but there's no food in the house and—"

"What's your name?"

He shook his head. "I'm not going to foster care. No way. Got put in there for a couple months when I was twelve, and I'll never go back. Never." He shook his head again to make his point.

"You're old enough to work. How'd you like a job?"

He stopped chewing as he balled up the burrito wrapper, setting it in the paper tray and putting it next to him on the bench. "Nah, mister, I don't do that kind of stuff."

Oh you would if you became desperate enough. I should know. I shook my head, pushing aside the sudden feeling of self-disgust as best as I could. "It's a clerical job mostly. You'd be running errands for my business after school. It's not the most exciting job, but it pays well enough, and you'd be able to feed yourself."

His eyes narrowed, and I could see the wheels turning in his head as he tried to figure out the rub. I took a business card out of my wallet and handed it to him. "My office is nearby. You go to that address on the card tomorrow and ask for Fionn Molloy. He'll set you up with the forms you need to fill out. You don't feel right about it, you can leave. You only stay employed if you don't bunk off school."

He nodded, a light of hope brightening his expression. A lump formed in my throat and I quickly swallowed it down.

"Are you from here?" I asked.

"Yup. Born and raised."

"I've never seen you around."

"My ma just moved us to a basement apartment up the street a couple months ago."

I nodded, standing. "Don't lose that card."

"I won't. Hey," he stood up, too, "thanks, mister."

I nodded over my shoulder as I headed for my car. Pulling out my phone, I texted Fionn.

Me: Sorry looking kid is going to come by tomorrow with one of my cards. Set him up with a job.

I got in my car and headed toward my apartment in the city. A minute later my phone beeped.

Fionn: Jaysus. You plannin on adoptin the whole of NYC?

I chuckled, throwing my phone down on the seat. It rang a second later. Figuring it was Fionn, I picked it up, but before answering I glanced at the screen. *Courtney.* I sighed and threw my phone back on the seat. I didn't have the energy for Courtney's neediness right now. And if she was calling in the middle of the night, she was especially needy. I felt a momentary twinge of guilt but squashed it down. "Not tonight, Courtney," I murmured into the silence of my car. I was needy myself, and I knew seeing her now would only end somewhere I'd regret. And for now, I had enough regret to last a bloody lifetime.

CHAPTER NINE

Lydia

By Thursday, I had read four books cover to cover. Brogan had a decent-sized library, and so I spent a lot of my time there. I should have considered this a mini vacation of sorts, but I was too antsy and keyed up to really relax. From being at the office from eight till five every day for the last few years, worried about the financials, attempting to turn the company around, to . . . doing nothing? A difficult adjustment to say the least.

I had rearranged and organized all of Brogan's dresser drawers—who put T-shirts in the top drawer anyway? Everyone knew top drawers were for underwear and socks. Only it seemed Brogan either only owned one pair of underwear or didn't wear any at all. I tried not to think too much about that.

I was still shaken and confused about what had happened between us in my bedroom and a lingering feeling of sad despair filled my heart. I hadn't even considered the possibility that Brogan and his family had suffered to the extent he described. I hadn't known where they went when they left our home, had often wondered if they'd gone back to Ireland to be with family, had hoped Brogan's father had found another job quickly, but never once had I pictured them destitute and starving. Anguish gripped me, and I wondered if I had just been too self-centered to consider the depth of hardship his family might have suffered back then. I had been young and sheltered, and though I thought myself worldly, I hadn't been. Not in the least. "You were," I muttered to myself, "just a stupid, selfish girl."

And at the moment I was lonely. Brogan and I had been friends once. Maybe I just needed to remind him of that to get on better footing with him. Suddenly it wasn't even all about my company. Suddenly I just wanted to let Brogan know how sorry I was, how I would do *anything* to change what I'd done to him back then. If only I could.

I pulled his business card out of my purse and grabbed my phone before I could overthink anything.

Me: Did you take all your underwear with you so I wouldn't rifle through it?

I immediately saw three dots indicating he'd read my message and was responding. But the dots remained there for a good ten minutes. Why was I picturing him standing somewhere, trying to figure out why I was being playful with him and waffling about what to write back? More likely he was just busy and had started a message and been interrupted. I wondered again at what exactly he did business wise.

Brogan: The fact that you're asking this question is proof I was right to do so.

I laughed and let out a relieved breath. Smiling, I typed him back.

Me: And btw, who puts jeans in the top drawer? Is that some kind of Irish thing?

Brogan: Aye. Now stay out of my drawers or I'll have to sic my nasty little leprechaun on you. Goodbye, Lydia.

I remembered how he'd always leave me when we were younger, the Gaelic word for goodbye.

Me: Slan, Brogan.

Again, I saw the three little dots indicating he was responding, but then they disappeared. He must have changed his mind and decided to leave it at that.

Grinning, I tossed my phone aside. Surely Brogan joking with me was a good sign. Feeling lighter, I went to his office to organize something there. When I saw business cards for an event floral arrangement and a catering company sitting right on the top of his desk, I paused only momentarily before calling each one, hoping they were the ones he'd hired for his party. When I'd confirmed they were, I posed as Brogan's secretary and had them go over what Brogan had ordered and made some small tweaks. He most likely wouldn't notice, and he'd done a decent job, but he was missing a woman's touch. And after all, he had asked me to work the party. I could hardly do a good job if I was unprepared for exactly what he'd ordered.

On Friday the gardeners arrived and started manicuring the lawn and grounds. I went outside and gave them some direction. *Why not?* I was the only one in charge, and Brogan *had* said I was part of the party staff, so I might as well start working. If I knew how to do anything from my upbringing, it was to throw a fancy party. That and shop, but Brogan didn't require my skill in that arena. He dressed immaculately. Classy and masculine and, oh, whatever. Shaking my head, I continued walking the grounds, noting things the gardeners had missed so I could make sure they touched them up before leaving.

As I walked between some trees, I caught movement in the window of the small house behind Brogan's. Biting my lip, I paused and then walked toward it. I took a deep breath before knocking. There was a long silence before I finally heard someone inside moving toward the door. It swung open to reveal a young woman with curly, dark brown hair and the same icy-blue eyes as Brogan's. I let out a breath. "Eileen?" I asked, although I knew immediately who she was. The last time I'd seen her, she'd been a frail pre-teen with leg braces. Now she was a beautiful young woman. She must be what? Nineteen now? Twenty?

She regarded me coldly before saying, "Lydia De Havilland. Imagine this. I never thought I'd see ya again. You're just as beautiful as ya ever were."

I smiled at the lilt of her accent. "You look wonderful, too. Your legs . . ." I gestured my arm downward, smiling with happiness for her. I hadn't ever really known her, never exchanged more than a handful of words over the three years her father had worked for us, but I remembered her being painfully shy and awkward.

"Yeah. No more braces. My brother found a brilliant surgeon and Bob's your uncle, here I am fixed up good as new."

"That's wonderful." There was an awkward silence in which she simply stared at me. I squirmed under her disdainful perusal. "I haven't had a chance to ask Brogan how your father's doing?"

"Our dad's dead."

My heart sunk. "Oh, I'm so sorry," I breathed. She merely shrugged. Another awkward silence ensued.

"Your brother didn't tell me you lived back here."

"Well, I do."

I nodded. This was not going well. It was time for me to go. "Okay, well. I'm just . . . staying at Brogan's house temporarily." I felt the blush rising in my face. Had Brogan told Eileen about taking over my company? About offering me a . . . sort of job or . . . something? "Working there, I mean."

She gave me a small smirk. "So I heard."

I licked my lips and let out a small breath. She hated me as much as her brother did. I turned to go. "Okay, well, it was nice to see you. I'm glad to know you're doing so well."

"Lydia, wait," she said, stepping onto her small porch. I turned just in time to catch the hard slap across my face. Stunned, I brought my hand up to my stinging cheek, my widened eyes finding hers. They were cold and full of contempt.

"That's for breakin' me brother's heart," she said before walking back inside and slamming her door in my face.

I stood there, blinking repeatedly. I now knew that a physical slap hurt almost as much as the bitchy, *behind my back but within earshot* catty comment from the women I'd once called friends. And yet, there was almost a certain *relief* in being slapped by Eileen. I wasn't sure I wanted to examine that too closely at the moment. And I wasn't sure I could ever face Eileen again without feeling every inch of heat on my skin. I wanted to hide, I wanted to leave, I wanted this to be over. But that wasn't an option. My hand on my cheek, humiliated and shaken—yet with that confusing relief running just beneath the surface—I didn't even recall the walk back to Brogan's house.

****

The caterer arrived bright and early Saturday morning. I spent the next several hours directing the setup of round tables and chairs on the expansive lawn, getting the band and the bartender situated, and showing the florist exactly where I wanted all the floral arrangements. I had her drape flowers on ribbons behind each chair and do several garlands along the porch railings. The effect was charming and lovely. I smiled up at the clear blue sky, dotted with a scattering of fluffy white clouds. It was going to be a beautiful day—lots of sunshine, but not overly hot. It was the perfect day for a garden party.

Satisfied with the results of the setup, it was time to shower and get dressed. I hadn't packed many dressy outfits, not knowing exactly what I'd be doing here, so my choices were limited. But I had a black, sleeveless dress with a floral, lace overlay that I thought would work well for a garden party. After blow-drying my hair, I put it up in a loose updo, pulling a few pieces down to frame my face. Happy with the result,

I did my makeup, dressed, put on a pair of strappy black heels, and went downstairs.

Therese, the head of the catering company, shot me a strange look but then smiled and said, "The appetizers should be ready in half an hour or so. Mr. Ramsay arrived a few minutes ago and is upstairs changing."

"Oh. Okay, thank you. Everything looks great." I started to head upstairs when Brogan appeared at the top landing. I sucked in a breath. He was gorgeous in a black suit that fit his strong physique to perfection, and his dark hair was still slightly wet from a shower. Our eyes held as he descended the staircase, and I clasped my hands in front of me, those old familiar feelings of girlish infatuation rushing through my blood.

"You look very handsome."

"Thank you." He looked me up and down, a small disapproving frown on his face.

I smoothed my hands down the skirt of my dress. "Is this not okay? I didn't bring a lot of clothes—"

"It would be fine if you were one of the guests. You're part of the staff, Lydia."

"Oh." I paused, confused and embarrassed. "I mean, I know. But I still have to mingle and make sure everything runs smoothly. What else should I wear?"

"You're not running this event. You're working it. You should wear a catering uniform. Therese brought an extra one for you."

Oh God. When he'd said I'd be working this event, he meant as a server. My face flushed. My stomach dropped. "Oh," I breathed. "Oh right. My . . . my misunderstanding." I shook my head, my hands fidgeting at the lace overlay of my dress.

Brogan's lips thinned, and he looked very uncomfortable. "Everything looks nice—the flowers especially. Thank you for organizing that."

I waved my hand. "It was nothing. My mother always said the flowers are what speak to a host's taste and artistry. Hydrangeas were her favorite," my voice trailed off as more blood rose in my face, making it feel hot. I was babbling. *Shut up, Lydia. Just shut up.*

"Hydrangeas are *your* favorite. At least they were," he said softly.

I blinked at him. What had he said? *Oh.* I felt dizzy like I was about to faint. I needed some water. "Oh, well, yes, mine, too. You remembered."

"I was a gardener, Lydia. Flowers were part of the job."

"Right." He had been a gardener, yes. Now he wanted me to be his server. And given his cold tone, I had been dismissed. I pulled my shoulders straight and let out a breath. "Well, I'd better go get changed."

Brogan nodded curtly, something in his eyes that I didn't have the awareness or time to try to read. I hurried away, turning the corner into the kitchen and standing against the wall for a moment to get my bearings. *God, I was an idiot.* I banged the back of my head lightly against the hard surface behind me. "Idiot, idiot, idiot," I chanted. I'd thought Brogan wanted me to *organize* his party, to help plan it. Instead, all he wanted was for me to work it as part of the serving staff. I felt like sinking into the floor at my stupid assumption. I took several deep breaths. I *wouldn't* sink into the floor. Okay, fine. He wanted me to carry trays around and serve his guests. Fine. And why not, really? I was sort of jobless as of now—or at the very least, my employment situation was in limbo. So I could use a job as a matter of fact. I wasn't too good to be a food server. Lots of wonderful, talented people worked serving food, sometimes temporarily, sometimes not. I'd spend a couple hours offering the delicious dumplings I'd put on the menu, and then I'd make Brogan sit down with me and spell out the terms of this ridiculous arrangement. This would settle the score from my long-ago wrong—*surely*—and we'd move forward from here. So what if we had joked a little bit via text? Obviously it'd meant nothing to him and it shouldn't mean anything to me either. We weren't friends, he hated me, his *whole family* hated me, and I needed to continue to remind myself of those important facts.

I found Therese and asked her for the uniform she'd brought, and she retrieved it for me. Talk about eating demeaning humble pie. Therese either thought me completely vapid and stupid, or pitied my embarrassing faux pas. My guess went toward the former.

Ten minutes later, I was outfitted in the same black pants and white button-down shirt as the rest of the catering team.

After wrapping a short black apron around my waist, I grabbed a tray of hors d'oeuvres and followed the other servers out to the party. The first guests were just arriving, and I spied Brogan near the gate, a blonde woman in a strapless yellow dress holding on to his arm as he greeted his guests. My heart sped up slightly. Ugh, he'd brought a date. Of course he had. *A different woman.* Not Anna and not the woman I'd seen him with at the garden party. Apparently he had at *least* three on call. Good for him. Variety was the spice of life and all that. I was going to ignore the ache in the pit of my stomach. I had a job to do.

A blond-haired man stood next to Brogan, leaning toward him and saying something that made Brogan laugh. My eyes caught on him momentarily. He was as tall as Brogan and almost as handsome, dressed all in black as well. They looked like two fallen angels—one dark, one fair. *Look out, ladies of Greenwich.* I straightened my spine for the tenth time since I'd donned this outfit and walked directly toward Brogan. If I was going to survive this with my pride intact, I needed to show him immediately that this was not going to humiliate me quite as much as he might hope. I was not going to shrink from this. I was going to do it, but I did still have some self-respect left.

Brogan's eyes widened when he saw me, and I noticed him fidget slightly. "Sir," I said, holding the tray toward him, "crostini with caramelized onions, melted cheese & sage?" I raised one eyebrow. "They're delicious. I sampled one myself before coming out here. You can dock it from my pay of course. I wouldn't expect anything less." I smiled sweetly. Brogan's mouth set in a grim line. Our eyes clashed while in my peripheral vision I saw his date narrowing her eyes. I heard someone clear his throat and glanced at the man standing next to Brogan.

"I gather you're Lydia," he said, his lips twitching in a held-back smile and a twinkle in his eye. His Irish accent was strong. I looked back to Brogan.

"I'm just part of the serving staff. Please enjoy the party." I turned and walked away, my head held high, and my tray thrust in front of me like a shield.

Behind me, I heard the blond man whistle and say, "I think I'm gona start gettin' meself good and hammered. I have a feelin' this party's gona go tits up *real* quick."

"Shut up, Fionn," I heard Brogan grumble before I moved too far away to hear more.

I went inside to grab another tray and when I came out, I sucked in a horrified breath. Lindsey Sanders and crew were just walking through the gate. I ducked back inside the house and took a moment to gather myself, breathing deeply. That bastard had invited them on purpose—he knew very well they had been my high school clique. He was not only going to make me serve his guests, he was going to make me serve the people I'd once led. *Associated with. Been.* If anyone had told me Brogan Ramsay was capable of this level of ugliness seven years ago, I wouldn't have believed it. I had spent time with the group he'd invited today, but I had never treated him with the blatant rudeness they had. *Chin up, Lydia.*

I moved around the perimeter of the party, trying to avoid Lindsey etcetera. Maybe they wouldn't even notice me. After all, they'd been trained to pretend the people who served them were invisible. I'd just hope to blend right into the background.

Turning, I offered the hors d'oeuvres I was carrying to the people standing behind me and froze when I saw it was the man named Fionn and Brogan's sister, Eileen. Eileen stared at me with a slightly shocked look on her face and Fionn smiled slightly. I lifted my chin. "Sweet potato rounds with herbed ricotta and walnuts?"

"Don't mind if I do," Fionn said, loading up a napkin with the small appetizers and popping one into his mouth as he winked at me. I almost smiled, but didn't. He was Brogan's and Eileen's friend. I had to assume he was enjoying my public disgrace at least to some extent.

"No, thank you," Eileen said, the tension in the air palpable. I swallowed, making a small curtsy before I turned and walked away. *A curtsy? Really, Lydia? What the hell was that? A curtsy! My God.*

"It can't be," a loud female voice said. "Lydia De Havilland? Seriously?" I halted and turned slowly back in the direction of Fionn and Eileen. Standing several yards away from them were Lindsey and company. "Oh my God," Lindsey breathed, bringing her hand to her chest and stifling a laugh.

I smiled a tight smile as they moved toward me. Holding the tray up, I tilted my head, and asked, "Appetizer?"

Lindsey burst out laughing even harder, looking gleefully happy with this turn of events. She put her hands on her hips and did a full circle around me, looking me up and down before she burst out laughing again. "My, *my,* how the mighty have *fallen,*" she said, barely disguised delight in her voice.

I smiled again as if this situation didn't faze me in the least, but I felt the hot blush in my cheeks that was surely giving me away. It felt like every guest in the yard had suddenly turned to look at me.

I simply smiled. "I hope you have a wonderful time," I said, turning and trying to hurry away. But my heel stuck in the grass and I tripped slightly, causing the girls behind me to giggle maniacally. Straightening myself, I took a deep breath and continued inside.

The vultures had descended, and now I was going to be consumed.

After that, I wasn't left alone for a moment. You would have thought I was the only one working the party, not that I was one of a dozen servers. Just when I'd delivered a requested glass of champagne to Lindsey, Daphne dropped her napkin and needed another. Then Bridget Baker wanted more of "those delicious little thingamabobs," and no sooner had I brought out a sample tray of every appetizer we'd passed through the crowd, Crystal Adler needed me to fetch a wet cloth so I could help her wipe an invisible stain off her Louis Vuitton clutch. I kept a smile plastered on my face, acting as if I were pleased as punch to meet their every need, not allowing them to see me sweat.

I caught sight of Brogan several times, standing to the side, his jaw clenched as he watched me being run around relentlessly. His date still hung on his arm, obviously trying to get his attention with her chatter, but he didn't seem to notice her at all. Apparently he was having too much fun watching me. I held my head higher, increasing the size of my smile. My cheek muscles wobbled with the effort of holding it in place.

On my way back into the house, I almost collided with the man named Fionn. "Oh, sorry," I said, scooting past him.

He leaned close to me as we passed and murmured softly, "Good on ya, Lydia," and winked. I wasn't sure what he meant, but in any case, I hardly had time to try to figure it out because someone else had me running to do her bidding.

I came back out with a tray of mini desserts and the seltzer water with a twist of lime Maya Richards had asked me to pick up for her at the bar, breezing past Fionn who was again standing with Eileen.

I delivered the seltzer water to Maya who proceeded to spill it on the lawn. "Oh phooey!" she exclaimed. "Clutzy me. Fetch me another one, would you, Lydia?" She smiled sweetly.

I resisted the urge to claw her eyes out and instead took a deep breath and said brightly, "No problem, ma'am. I'll get another one for you right away." Maya turned away and began speaking to the woman next to her as if I suddenly didn't exist.

I inclined the dessert tray toward Lindsey who looked annoyed. I supposed I wasn't giving her the show she was hoping for. Tears perhaps, or maybe a complete and total emotional breakdown, clawing at my face, dropping to my knees and declaring that as God as my witness, I'd never work in catering again. "Something sweet?" I asked, giving her my most innocent smile.

Glaring at me, she took a small dish of chocolate mousse off my tray, picking up the tiny spoon and dishing a bite into her mouth. "Mmm," she murmured, a glint of something evil coming into her eyes. *I'd seen that look before.* Right before she'd decimated someone socially in the cafeteria. But before I could figure out what she might have in mind, a huge spray of chocolate mousse hit me square in the face, splatters of it raining all over my hair and down the front of my shirt.

"Oh goodness!" Lindsey gasped. "This silly little spoon just *slipped.* I'm so embarrassed!"

I heard an intake of breath and everything seemed to grow quiet all around me. Had the band stopped playing? A glob of mousse that was stuck to my eyelashes fell onto my cheek and started sliding down my face slowly. Lindsey dropped her bowl back on my tray and snorted into a napkin. As I stood there, it seemed that the entire party had stopped and everyone was staring at me. Vomit rose in my throat as humiliation and loneliness engulfed me. *I didn't have a single friend here, not one.* I'd tried so hard to hold on to my composure, but standing there with food purposefully splattered on my face was the final straw. I couldn't do this. It hurt too much. Horrified, I glanced around at all the staring eyes, some mildly sympathetic, others amused.

Sucking in a huge breath, tears filled my eyes and I turned and ran toward the house as fast as my feet would carry me. Out of the corner of my eye I saw Brogan start after me, and so I kept moving, dropping the tray on the table in the foyer and running up the stairs to the bathroom. I slammed the door behind me and stood against it, breathing heavily, tears streaming down my face and mixing with the chocolate.

I heard voices outside the bathroom and hurried over to the sink, using a washcloth to wipe my face clean. For a moment I simply stared. The black eye makeup I'd applied so carefully earlier now streaked down my face, my white shirt splattered with chocolate, my hair droopy and wilted from all my running around. Dropping the washcloth, I put my hands over my face and allowed the tears to fall freely. I was an utter mess. The mirror image of my life.

"Lydia?" I heard a female voice say from the other side of the door. I took a deep breath, figuring it was Therese wanting to fire me. That was good because I was happy to be fired. But when I swung the door open, Eileen was standing there.

I sighed, turning away. "If you're wanting to slap me again, you're going to have to stand in line this time." I walked back to the sink and picked up the wet washcloth and started to dab at the chocolate stains on my white blouse. After three or four dabs, I threw the washcloth back in the sink. These stains would never come out.

Eileen came to stand next to me, and we stared at each other in the mirror for a few seconds, her gorgeous and perfect, me splattered, smeared, and defeated. Eileen tilted her head, giving me a small smile. "Ya need to get back out there," she finally said.

I gave one small laugh. "No way. I'm throwing in the towel. I call uncle. Maybe that Bob guy you mentioned. I call Uncle Bob."

She turned toward me, grabbing my upper arms so I was forced to face her as well. "No way are ya gona give those shite-flingin' primate bunch of bitches the satisfaction of gettin' the last word." She glanced at my stained shirt.

"It was mousse." I sighed.

She waved her hand as if one thing was basically the same as another. "Mousse-flingin' socialite bunch of bitches. Whatever. Both require the same basic brain maneuverings—those being slow and basic."

I almost laughed, but the shame I felt left it stifled in my clogged throat. "I used to be the leader of those bitches," I admitted softly.

She nodded. "Right. Which is why ya have insider information on exactly what would annoy the shite outta them the most. Now, what is it?"

I stared at her. "I . . . I don't know. They think I consider myself better than them."

She cocked her head. "I think ya might be, as much as that fact shocks me." She regarded me for a moment. "That's why ya have to get back out there and let them know they didn't get the best of ya, and they never will no matter how much shite they hurl your way." She looked me over. "Ya always were prettier than any of them, too. That's another reason they hate ya, I'd guess. Shallow as all hell, mostly because they have nothin' else except the superficial goin' for them."

I sighed. "I shouldn't care *what* they think," I said. "I shouldn't care what anyone thinks."

She looked at me thoughtfully. "Em, well," she said after a long moment, "we're made to care, aren't we, though? Find me the person who doesn't care a whit what anyone else thinks of them and I'll show ya someone very lonely. The trick, I believe, is to know whose opinion matters and whose doesn't." She paused and I thought how very wise she sounded for such a young girl. Then again, if anyone would know something about being shunned by others based on superficial things, it would be the girl who had worn braces on her legs for most of her life.

She gave me a small smile before continuing. "Ya gettin' back out there proves to them *and* to ya that those girls *don't* matter. They do not get the satisfaction of watchin' ya break over their petty antics." She worried her lip as if she were strategizing. Slowly, my cold despair was being replaced with warmth.

"Why are you helping me?" I asked. "Yesterday you hated me."

She looked me in the eye. "I believe in slappin' someone once and movin' on. I've moved on now. Have ya?"

"Um . . . sure."

She laughed, a sweet, musical sound. "Okay, wash your face. I'm gona re-do your makeup and then you're gona be forced to wear a different shirt. Unfortunately, the *only* choice is gona be one *quite* a bit smaller, like." She gave me an innocent shrug, and I laughed, a genuine one this time. "My brother is gona self implode."

"Your brother is the one enjoying himself. He arranged this."

"Oh no, Lydia. My brother might be actin' like a man baby, but I can promise ya he's not enjoyin' himself." She grinned. "Which is gona make it all the better."

"Wait, you slapped me for hurting him yesterday, and now you want to help me upset him?"

"He brought this one on himself. He's just gettin' what he deserves in this case. Now wash."

I turned to the sink and did as she said while she slipped out. I was drying my face and smoothing my hair when she knocked again, entering the bathroom with my makeup bag and a new white shirt. "I grabbed this from your bathroom," she said, holding up the makeup bag. "The red-haired girl on the caterin' staff had an extra shirt with her." She tossed it to me.

I looked at it. "The one who looks like she's twelve?"

Eileen grinned. "Yeah. I need ya to go get your laciest bra."

Fifteen minutes later, when my hair and makeup were done and my shirt was as buttoned up as a shirt three sizes too small would get, I looked at myself in the mirror. "I look like a prostitute."

Eileen came up behind me, tilting her head slightly, sizing me up before she gave me a pleased smile. "Aye. A high-class prostitute," she qualified. "One who dates married politicians."

My startled eyes met hers in the mirror, and I burst out laughing, thinking she was just what I had needed. I had needed a friend. And Eileen Ramsay had shown up. Life was full of surprises, and this was one I would never have expected.

CHAPTER TEN

Brogan

I rubbed my jaw as I surveyed my party. My stupid fucking party that had gone to hell in a hand basket. I'd set it up to go down just the way it had, so why did I feel like the devil himself? Watching Lydia run away from the group of bitches I'd invited purposefully to torment her hadn't offered the least bit of satisfaction. On the contrary, it had filled me with anger and made me want to protect her from the situation *I* had put her in. I'd thought about chasing after her, but I was probably the last person she wanted to see right now. I'd let her lick her wounds in her room and go to her after the party.

Despite all my internal justification, I knew I was acting unreasonably when it came to Lydia. I fucking knew it, I just couldn't figure out why. Or maybe I just didn't want to. "Fucking *feck,*" I muttered, clenching my jaw harder when I saw Fionn and Eileen heading toward me.

"Where's Tiffani with an i?" Eileen asked, taking a sip from the champagne glass in her hand. For a second I had absolutely no idea who she was referring to. Ah, my date. Right.

"Mingling I guess," I said. She might have left for all I knew.

Fionn turned to Eileen. "She got tired of him ignorin' her and not movin' his eyes from that poor servant girl. What was her name again?

Ah, Lydia. Poor, trampled Lydia. I hear she deserved it, though. So why then, I must ask," Fionn questioned, putting his finger on his chin as if in thought, "does my dear friend and your dear brother look so miserable about it?" He shot me a taunting smile.

"Fionn . . ." I said, a warning in my tone. Fionn simply laughed.

"It's true. Ya don't look like you're enjoyin' your victory, brother dearest," Eileen said, giving me an innocent smile. I scowled at her.

"I think Brogan has found himself in a *be careful what ya wish for* scenario," Fionn mock whispered, leaning close to Eileen as if I couldn't hear him. "Either that or he has a brutal case of indigestion. Sour stomach? What else is it referred to? Ah," he held up a finger, "*heartburn.*"

"I'd have to agree, my perceptive friend," Eileen said, letting out a dramatic sigh.

"What I want to know is why exactly this is so damned funny to you two?" I asked through my clenched jaw.

Eileen took another sip of champagne, glancing around as if looking for something specific. Technically, she shouldn't be drinking any alcohol at all since she wasn't twenty-one, but it was a private party, I'd let it slide. "Your misery is of your own makin' this time, Brogan. In exactin' your revenge against the De Havilland family, you've turned yourself into exactly what ya claim to despise. *These* are ya friends now?"

"All of a sudden you're on her side?" I asked, knowing I sounded like a petulant child and hating myself just a little bit more. *Of course the people here weren't my friends.*

"I'm on *your* side. *Always.* Which is why I'm against this. It's beneath ya. I disliked her for hurtin' ya. Slappin' her yesterday felt mighty good. But I didn't want to ruin her life for it, or watch her suffer the same treatment we once endured by that group of purposeless bitches." She nodded over to Lydia's old high school friends who were still laughing and twittering, most likely reliving every moment of bossing Lydia around like she was their own personal Cinderella.

I looked at Eileen, my guts twisting. "You slapped her yesterday?"

She nodded, and I clenched my eyes shut for a moment. "Well, yeah. She took it like a champ, just like she's doin' today. I have a feelin' she believes she deserves this. Which is part of why she's takin' it. But the girl has some pride, too. Damned if I don't respect her for it."

I didn't even bother to look at Eileen. I knew she was right. I opened my mouth to respond when the door to the house opened, and a girl with a tray walked outside. I almost choked when the tray was lowered. Lydia. *Oh shite.* She had obviously cleaned up her face and had redone her makeup. The sun was shining on her pale hair, and she looked bright and shiny and so beautiful I hardly wanted to look at her. But when my eyes lowered, a low snarl came out of my throat of its own free will, my muscles clenching tightly. The white button-down shirt was way too small, the buttons barely closing over her full breasts, the lace of her bra clearly visible through the stretched material, even from where I was standing. The top four buttons weren't even closed at all, giving an easy view of full, creamy cleavage. For a moment my vision dimmed the way it sometimes did when I was being overly stimulated in some myriad of ways.

"Did he just growl?" Eileen asked Fionn. My eyes remained on Lydia. This was ridiculous. Why in the hell was she back out here? Hadn't she had *enough?* And why the ever-loving *feck* was she dressed that way?

"I think he did," Fionn remarked from somewhere seemingly far away. "How very primitive, like. *Or* it's the heartburn again. Ya wanna hear me theory?"

"I *do* wanna hear your theory, as a matter of fact," Eileen said.

"I thought ya might. Me theory is that our friend here still loves the girl, and it's bloody *killin'* him right now to see her hurtin'."

"Insightful, my wise friend. Fair play. Ya might just be right."

"I think so," Fionn said.

"For fuck's sake, enough is enough," I said hoarsely, heading straight toward Lydia. She seemed to have seen me because she turned in the other direction and made a fast beeline for the exact group of girls who were having so much fun tormenting her. *Why?* What in the hell was she doing?

She marched right up to the group of coiffed vultures and beamed a smile at them, holding her tray forward. "Dumplings, anyone?" she asked, pushing her cleavage forward. "They're soft and delicious." They turned toward her and for a second I wished I had a camera. Their shocked, clueless expressions were so perfectly priceless. *Point to Lydia.* Obviously being completely unprepared for her return, the girls simply took a dumpling, their expressions remaining confused, and Lydia turned and marched away. I caught up to her.

"This is enough, Lydia. Go inside. You're excused from this party."

"Excused?" she asked, not stopping, forcing me to follow along behind her like a moronic puppy dog. "Oh no. I wouldn't dream of allowing you to excuse me now, Brogan, not when your revenge hasn't been properly satisfied. Don't deprive yourself of my complete and utter humiliation. I'm sure those girls have something more devious up their sleeves than flinging food. Then again, they're not the brightest bulbs in the bunch—take it from me—so they could be out of ideas. We'll have to wait and see. You must be on the edge of your seat to find out. I know I am."

I almost groaned. "Lydia, please, it's enough. *I've* had enough. Please go inside." Good fucking God, now I was saying please to my . . . archenemy? I suddenly wanted to laugh at the thought of the term Fionn had used once to describe her.

She shook her head, a beatific smile on her face as she headed toward another small group chatting and laughing. "Dumpling?" she asked, smiling around at the group. As the women took the dumplings, I watched as the men used the opportunity to examine Lydia's cleavage at length and in close proximity. Disgusting lechers. Why the *hell* did I have such disgusting lechers at my house? I hated disgusting lechers. But apparently I had invited a whole horde of them to my home to partake of my food and drink.

"Oh, hello, Brogan," one man finally said. I had no earthly idea who he might be, other than a disgusting lecher. "I haven't had a chance to say hello. Nice party." Then he babbled on about something inane and useless that I supposed I was meant to listen attentively to. Lydia took the opportunity to duck away and head to another group nearby to offer more of her soft, delicious dumplings.

"Are you okay, Mr. Ramsay?" the man in front of me asked, a concerned frown on his face. "Bit of heartburn, is it?"

"Em, yeah, excuse me," I muttered.

By the time I caught up with Lydia, she was filling a tray with champagne from the bar. "Lydia, put the tray down and go inside," I said. "I insist."

She turned away from the bar. "I can't just yet, Brogan. The crowd standing by the band is *parched*. If I don't get this champagne over to them immediately, there's likely to be any number of dry throats. Trust me when I say you don't want it to be known that you let your guests suffer dry throats at your first party. There could be negative gossip and as anyone who—"

"I couldn't care less about negative gossip," I growled.

"You should, Brogan. I'm just a lowly server *now*, but as you may or may not remember, I used to run in different circles and among the rich and shallow, negative gossip can ruin someone more quickly than carrying," she leaned toward me and whispered loudly, "a knock-off Hermès purse." She pretended to shudder and I stopped, feeling my lips tip up in the barest hint of a smile, mixed with a small measure of surprise.

Lydia. God, how did I forget how you once made me laugh?

She passed out the champagne and then rushed off. I stood staring after her, not knowing what to feel, the same way I'd felt after we'd joked a bit on text. I had felt a strange, confused happiness then, just as I felt now. Before I could even spend a moment more thinking about it, Lindsey and her group surrounded me. They'd been too busy running

Lydia all around to bother me before, but they had me cornered now. I sighed internally. Lindsey had attempted to hang off me at every event I'd seen her at since I'd been looking at real estate in Greenwich. Her obvious flirting and obnoxious conversation, mixed with the way she repeatedly touched me, was barely tolerable. In truth, I hated it. I hated her scent. I hated the feel of her talon-like fingernails, even through the material of my shirt.

"Brogan," she sing-songed, leaning in and kissing my cheek. Her heavy perfume, mixed with some sort of competing hair product, overwhelmed me, causing my head to swim for a moment. "I haven't had a chance to compliment you on a *wonderful* party! I was just telling my girls it's my favorite of the year so far." She batted her eyelashes, her eyes wandering down to my crotch.

A moment from a summer's day seven years ago filled my mind. Lydia and her girlfriends had been splashing and laughing at her pool. I'd walked by pushing a wheelbarrow filled with soil, and I'd heard Lindsey say, "God, if it wouldn't cause my father to have a conniption, I'd be all over that hot gardener boy. He makes slumming it look irresistible." I'd cringed, feeling hot shame move up my neck as the rest of the girls had started laughing. But when I'd looked at Lydia, she wasn't laughing. Instead, I watched as she stuck her foot out and tripped Lindsey who was too caught up in a giggling fit to notice. Lindsey had screamed as she went flying into the pool, flailing and belly flopping into the water on a loud smack. Lydia had winked at me and cocked one of her sexy hips as she'd feigned shocked concern for Lindsey. I'd turned my head to hide my laughter. Yes, Lindsey had always been a malicious bitch. Nothing had changed. So why didn't I harbor any ill feelings toward her? Why didn't her past mistreatment bother me? In fact, I barely remembered it.

There is such a thin veil between love and hate.

Lydia had *never* been malicious, not like them.

Not until that day. Maybe that's why it had hurt so bloody much. But standing here, watching her now, I remembered the way she'd appeared nervous, unsure. It had inspired tenderness in me then, and witnessing her discomfort today aroused the same instinctive protectiveness. And it *burned.* Heartburn, then, yes.

God, Lydia.

I cleared my throat just as Lydia came up to us, holding her tray out. "Cream puffs anyone? They're sweet and luscious." She smiled sweetly, her eyes challenging me not to look at her cream puffs, the ones threatening to spill out of her shirt at any second. I coughed into my hand, just barely managing not to choke, turning away slightly as Lindsey glared daggers at her. "No? Well, your loss. You'll never enjoy cream puffs like these ones. One hundred percent all natural ingredients. Nothing phony." She looked pointedly at Lindsey's *cream puffs*, obviously overinflated with phony ingredients. Lindsey gasped, placing her hand on her throat and widening her eyes as if she couldn't fathom the bold, impudent behavior of the girl serving her food.

With that, Lydia whirled away, to offer her cream puffs elsewhere. I pressed my lips together, not knowing whether to laugh uproariously or kill someone—possibly myself. Jaysus, help me.

Lindsey heaved out a disgusted breath. "God, Brogan, you've got to consider hiring classier help. Being from the working class yourself, surely you understand what's acceptable and what's not. You'd be completely within your rights to fire her on the spot. You're showing remarkable restraint." She clasped my arm, rubbing her phony ingredients against me. "It's very generous of you," she sighed, "but as you know, your staff reflects directly on you . . ."

I shook her off. "So do your friends." I looked around at Lindsey's followers, the women who were standing there idiotically waiting for their next instructions from the leader of their den of stupidity. "You'd all be wise to remember that." I enjoyed Lindsey's outraged intake of breath as I walked away.

The rest of the party went by far too slowly for me as my guests took their time drinking my liquor, eating my food, and making themselves at home on my property. I made the rounds once or twice but couldn't stomach more than that. Lindsey and her brainless bunch had apparently left early, but the mindless self-centered chatter of the other overinflated egos in attendance was more than I could handle today. Especially when I constantly had one eye focused on Lydia as she moved through the crowd as if she herself were the hostess of this mess of a party even though she wore the uniform and role of a servant.

I might have even been able to see the humor in it if my emotions weren't all twisted in a tangle of frustration, anger . . . and guilt. I felt like the biggest bastard who had ever lived.

Finally, finally, the guests started leaving, and I breathed a sigh of relief. Fionn and Eileen had evidently had a grand time witnessing my misery, standing off to the side and cheering each other and placing bets of some kind or another. Miserable Benedict Arnolds that they were. They finally came up and said their goodbyes, not seeming to mind in the least that I focused my most evil glare upon them and told them I was happy to see them go. They walked off laughing.

Those dwindling stayed another hour and then I made my way inside and tipped the staff that was packing up. Lydia was helping to clean the kitchen and when the catering staff began leaving, Therese gave Lydia a big hug and winked at her. Lydia had apparently won *her* over, too. Therese barely gave me a glance as she picked up the last of her things and headed for the door. And *I* was the one who had given her an overly generous tip.

Checking outside that everything was cleared away and all staff gone, I returned inside feeling relief that the party was over.

"Lydia?" We needed to talk. The kitchen was clean and empty, so I went upstairs, but both her bedroom and bathroom door were open. Frowning, I returned back downstairs. My heart picked up in speed. She wouldn't have left, would she? Why shouldn't she? I was a fecking arsehole to the nth degree. What reason did she have to stay? If it were me, I would leave after today, too. I *should* be happy to be rid of her. This had all gone arseways, just as Fionn had predicted.

So why did I feel a desperate misery descending over me?

I turned when I heard a small sound come from the living room, my heart hammering as I rushed in. Lydia was collapsed in a chair, her feet sitting on the coffee table, her high heels on the floor beside her. Relief swept through me. *She hadn't left.* But then my eyes moved to her feet. *Oh feck.* Her feet looked awful—swollen, with angry red welts in several places where her shoe straps must have been. I entered the room and sat down on the coffee table in front of her, taking her feet into my lap. Her tired eyes cracked open half-mast. *God, she was exhausted.* Another wave of guilt crashed over me. It must have taken everything she had in her to perform the way she did today. And yet she hadn't cracked, not once. And she hadn't let on about the state of her injured feet either. I felt . . . proud of her, yet also fearful and confused.

"Unhand me you spiteful villain," she slurred, but then she let out a deep moan of pleasure when my thumb pressed into her arch. I prayed she didn't feel what that sound did to the place right above where her foot was now resting.

"I have turned myself into a villain, haven't I?"

She cocked one eye open. "A conscienceless devil," she agreed. "Balor himself."

I let out a startled chuckle. "You remember that story?"

Her lips moved very slightly into what I thought might be the attempt at a smile. "Hmm-hmm. Balor can kill someone just by staring at them with his evil eye. I remember every story about Irish gods and devils and banshees and will-o-the-wisps you ever told me. I remember what you said about clovers, how they're lucky because the three leaves signify yesterday, today, and tomorrow. Each time I see one, I think of you. I remember it all, Brogan."

My heart squeezed tightly, and I felt slightly breathless. "Today was a mistake," I let out on an exhale.

"A mistake? You mean you mistakenly arranged for me to serve you and your guests? Your *friends?*"

I shook my head. "No, no, that's not what I meant."

She sighed. "I know what you meant." She attempted to rise, but I gently pushed her back into the chair. She watched my hands on her feet for a few minutes, letting out another small moan that raced straight to my cock. "Do all your employees get such personal treatment, or am I special somehow?"

Oh Lydia, I wish you weren't.

My lip quirked up into a small smile. "I figure I owe you this much. How in the hell did this happen anyway?" I held one foot up, turning it slightly so I could assess the full damage. At least there weren't any major blisters.

She nodded down to her shoes on the ground. "They were the only black shoes I had. I would have bought a more comfortable pair if I had known I'd walk the equivalent of seventeen miles today while hefting heavy food-laden trays over my shoulders. I have a newfound respect for those in the food serving industry. If you meant to teach me a lesson about—"

"Forget what I meant to teach you," I rasped. "I'm a stubborn jackass." She opened her eyes and stared at me for a moment. God, she was so beautiful, even exhausted and looking like she might pass out at any moment, her bruised and battered feet sitting in my lap. I wanted her. God, I'd never stopped wanting her. How could I? She had been the only person to ever really *see* me, I was ready to admit that now. I wanted to take her in my arms and kiss her until we were both panting with need. I wanted to feel her naked body against mine again, to dip my fingers into the place only I'd ever been, to feel the slippery wetness of her arousal, to know she wanted me, too. I wanted to bury myself inside her and forget where she ended and I began. I was hard and aching with the very thought of it. I clenched my eyes shut. I'd orchestrated my own demise. I was going to go down and go down hard. *Again.*

Lydia's eyes moved lazily up my chest until she met my eyes. I could see a vein beating steadily at the base of her throat. Did I affect her, too? I'd never been sure—not then and not now.

My thumb found the small hollow under her ankle bone and here, too, I could feel her pulse. I rubbed my thumb over it in light circles, feeling the gentle throb under her skin, a reminder that the heart beat everywhere, controlled every inch of the body. When I met her eyes again, they were filled with questions. Questions I wasn't sure I'd be able to answer, even for myself. "Better?" I finally managed, nodding to her feet.

Her lips parted as if she thought to say something, but then they closed and she only nodded. "What happened to your date anyway?" she asked.

"She left with Rodney Calloway, Sr."

She raised one delicate, blonde brow. "Rodney Calloway, Sr. is ninety and in a wheelchair."

I shrugged. "When she realized I was distracted by you, she looked into other options."

Her eyes widened slightly and she stared at me. I'd surprised her with my admission about being distracted by her. But I suddenly found I wanted her to know. *You turn me inside out, Lydia. You always have.* "You used her," she finally said. "I thought you hated game playing."

"We used each other," I answered, not missing the reference she was making to herself. She was right, though. I'd acted like a hypocrite in so many ways since this had begun that I could hardly keep track. I sighed, my shoulders heavy with self-disgust. *Arseways.* Totally arseways.

"I should go to bed," she said after a moment.

I nodded, releasing the foot in my hand. "There are some things we need to talk about. Can we do that over dinner tomorrow night? I'm working from my office here tomorrow."

"Sure." I helped her stand up. When she started to hobble toward the door, I couldn't bear it. I swept her up into my arms and though she made a small, startled squeak, she didn't tell me to put her down. Surprisingly, she wrapped her arms around my neck and allowed me to carry her. When I kicked the door to her bedroom fully open so I could enter with her, I nodded toward the bathroom. "Do you want me to run you a bath?" I asked. My voice was hoarse as I pictured her naked, wet limbs hanging over the edge of the tub as she soaked in the hot, steamy water. I cleared my throat and tried to clear the image. But she shook her head.

"No, I just need to go to bed. You can put me down. I'll be okay."

I let go of her legs and lowered her gently, her body sliding against mine. "Goodnight, Lydia."

I needed her to stop looking up at me with her kind, beautiful eyes, somehow seeming to see through my confusion and despair.

I needed her skin not to be so soft, so silken that I didn't want to let go.

I needed her to stop being so alluring, mesmerizing, irresistible.

"Goodnight, Brogan." *I* needed to be the one who broke away before I did something totally stupid that she didn't need any part of after the day she'd just endured, the day that I had *caused* her to endure. I turned away.

"Brogan," she called. I turned back. "To my mind, we're even now."

"Even?"

"Today. It settled the score between you and me. You can try to dish out more, but I'll fight you from here on out if you do. Just so you're aware." She lifted her chin, challenging me.

I almost smiled, but held it back. Fierce, exquisite girl, with swollen feet, her golden hair cascading around her stunning face, and her . . . cream puffs falling out of her too-small shirt. She had absolutely nothing to bargain with, and yet she stood there as if she held all the cards. Then again, perhaps she did. Perhaps she had all along. She watched me as I watched her, a small wary look on her face as if she was waiting for me to do something, but she wasn't exactly sure what. Finally, I simply nodded and left her room.

CHAPTER ELEVEN

Lydia

"Good morning," Brogan said, glancing back over his shoulder quickly as he flipped a pancake on his griddle. "How are your feet?"

My eyes ran down his jean-clad backside. God, I'd forgotten what an amazing ass Brogan had. He was wearing a brown T-shirt that showed off his back and arm muscles. I dragged my eyes away before he caught me staring.

"Better," I said, taking a seat at the bar and twisting my still-wet hair up into a messy bun and securing it with a rubber band from my wrist. In actuality, my feet were still sore, although I wasn't limping any longer. A good night's sleep and a long soak in the tub this morning had helped my feet *and* my muscles. My mood was buoyed by the fact that we were finally going to talk tonight and perhaps my life could resume again—at least in some manner. I would think about how I was going to attempt to solve what would be a new set of problems once Brogan laid out his terms. "You cook?"

"I can manage the basics," he said, smiling at me. I blinked. *Brogan Ramsay just smiled at me—a sincere one*. I had even caught a glimpse of teeth, the slightly overlapped front tooth causing my heart to speed up just as it had always done. He must really be feeling guilty to show me teeth. Well good, he should. Although he still hadn't actually apologized, I wasn't going to try to force him to. Like I'd told him last night, yesterday had evened the score between us. Now I was hopeful he'd return De Havilland Enterprises and come up with a reasonable payment plan. We could both go on our merry ways, no permanent harm done. So why did that thought bring a twinge of disappointment, no merriment at all? It wasn't as if I'd enjoyed more than a moment or two in Brogan's company this week. And yet . . . I believed in being honest with myself. There was still something between us—something I was having difficultly defining. Perhaps it was only a physical attraction, unrequited lust, the possibility we'd make sexual magic together if we really had the opportunity this time around. And whatever it was would never be fully known because our relationship—if you could call it that—was of a temporary nature and based on the exaction of revenge. I chewed at my lip, considering my mixed emotions.

Brogan brought a plate piled with fluffy pancakes to the breakfast nook and placed it on the already-set table. I saw there was already a plate of bacon, a plate piled high with potatoes mixed with what looked like onions and peppers, and two glasses of orange juice at each place setting.

"That's a lot of potatoes," I noted.

"I'm Irish. I like potatoes," he teased. "Coffee?" I nodded, and he poured two cups from a pot on the counter, bringing them with him to the table where he took a seat across from me.

"Thank you for this," I said, nodding at the food.

"My pleasure." We both dished up plates and the next few minutes were spent eating.

"God, this is good," I said, spearing another bite of fluffy pancake. "I didn't realize your domestic talents were on par with your gardening abil—" My eyes widened and met his, my stomach dropping at my own mindless, rude comment. "You know what I mean."

Brogan finished chewing. "Lydia," he said, an amused look on his face, "it's okay. The last time you knew me, I was a gardener. Actually, not even a gardener. A gardener's assistant. It's fine."

"Assistant or not, you were the hardest worker I've ever known," I said softly. "I'm not surprised you're so successful now. You did the work of two men on our property."

He paused with his coffee cup halfway to his lips. "You noticed that?"

"I noticed everything you did," I said, my cheeks warming. I lifted my chin. "I was a proper stalker. I took my job very seriously."

He tilted his head, his expression slightly bewildered. Had he really not known? I didn't think I'd been that subtle.

I took a sip of juice. "Anyway, you're a businessman now. Will you tell me about what you really do?"

He finished chewing. "We can get into all that later tonight."

"Okay. But I'm holding you to this conversation," I said, raising a brow.

He gave me another small smile. "As you should. What are you going to do today? I noticed my sock drawer hasn't been organized by color." His lip quirked. He was teasing me. *Huh.* I grinned. *He was a man, there were only two colors, black and white. Therefore, a two-minute job.*

"I can get to that this afternoon. But um . . . I have an errand I was going to run today while you're working."

"An errand?"

I nodded, picking up a piece of bacon, dipping it in my syrup, and biting off the end. "Actually, I'm going to go see my old house. My friend Daisy told me the family that bought it from Ginny moved." I took another bite of bacon and chewed and swallowed before continuing. "I won't be able to go inside, but I'd just like to walk around."

Brogan was studying me intently. "Why?"

I shrugged, trying to go for nonchalant. "My father died my first year of college. It was more sudden than anyone thought it would be. He'd been lingering . . ." My voice drifted away as I pictured receiving that terrible phone call, Stuart's voice choking back tears as he delivered the news, collapsing on my bed, and sobbing into my pillow. I'd been alone. Somehow I'd picked myself up and made flight arrangements. Somehow I'd picked myself back up a dozen times since then. I took a deep breath. "Anyway, I came home, of course, but everything happened so quickly. It was as if I were in a fog, you know?" I gave Brogan what felt like a sad smile. "I went back to school, but then we found out about the debt . . . Ginny put the estate up for sale and it sold quickly . . ."

"You never got to say goodbye," Brogan supplied. *I never got to say goodbye.*

I met his eyes. "No," I whispered. "I never did. Not to my father, and not to the home I'd grown up in. After graduation, I came home from college and it was just all . . . gone." I did a fluttering movement with my fingers, a gesture that came from sudden sadness, nervousness at sharing this part of myself with him. I stilled my hand, replacing it on the table. "I just thought I'd walk around a bit. Maybe it's stupid, but I feel like I need to. And I don't know if I'll ever get another opportunity."

"It's not stupid," he said, reaching his hand across the table and placing it on top of mine. His skin was warm and lightly calloused, and suddenly, the only part of my body I was aware of was the small portion of skin he was touching. His hands were beautiful. It was something I remembered first noticing about him as I watched him work in our gardens. His fingers were long and slender, his hands elegant but strong. When I glanced up, our eyes met and held for several beats. I cleared my throat, removing my hand from under his. It took me another moment and a sip of coffee to get my bearings.

"I'd like to go with you."

I frowned. "I don't know if that's—"

"I won't get in your way. I'll just accompany you. I guess maybe I never really got a chance to say goodbye either." I watched his face, a bleakness moving through his eyes and I swallowed, a sudden lump in my throat as I recalled that long-ago evening: watching Brogan stride across the lawn, his head down and his shoulders tense even as the sprinklers drenched him.

"Okay," I said softly. "It's big enough for the both of us to wander separately I suppose." He gave me a small smile.

We finished our breakfast, and I offered to clean up while he did what he needed to do in his office. Once that was accomplished, I went upstairs and blow-dried my hair and put it in a ponytail. I was wearing a pair of linen, army-green shorts and a black blousy, button-down shirt. My feet were not going to tolerate anything other than my flip-flops so I slipped those on, grabbed my wallet and sunglasses, and went downstairs to meet Brogan. He was just coming out of his office.

"Just give me a second, and I'll be ready." I nodded, not knowing why exactly I felt nervous. I guessed because it was the first time I was going somewhere *with* Brogan. Strange because I'd been living in his home for the past week. *Not that he'd been living here, too, though.* But either way, this felt different. Maybe it was because of *where* we were headed together.

Brogan came downstairs a minute later with his shoes on and held the door open for me as he grabbed his keys out of a basket on the table right next to the door. I followed him to his car, and we drove the twenty minutes to my old home in relative silence as I watched the scenery out the window. This was the place I'd grown up and still loved so much, from the miles of gorgeous shoreline to the sprawling back country. As we neared the Merritt, the landscape became more pastoral, with green, rolling hills, beautiful stone walls, and large pastures where horses grazed. It was an extremely affluent area, but what I'd always loved the most about this part of Greenwich was the charming country feel, even though it was so close to New York City. Everything around me whispered *home.*

Brogan pulled into the long curving driveway of what had been my home until I was eighteen. A swell of emotion hit me as I stepped out of the car, gazing upward at the beautiful stone Georgian mansion that had once belonged to my family. I looked around slowly. The landscaping was clearly untended, the home indeed unoccupied. Swallowing down a lump, I turned to Brogan. "If you'd have just waited a little bit, you could have had this house."

He studied me for a moment, a strange expression moving over his face. "I wanted a property with a guest house for Eileen," he said softly. "She's in college at Fairfield University."

"Oh," I said. Fairfield University was about a half hour from Greenwich. I hoped I'd get more of a chance to visit with Eileen and hear about her life, especially after she'd been so kind to me yesterday. "That's great." Our gazes held for a moment before one side of his lips tilted up. Almost a smile.

I turned and walked up the stairs, and using my hand as a visor to shade the sun, I looked into one of the windows to the side of the massive door. My eyes moved around the empty foyer, the sweeping staircase that I had bounded down so many times . . . I saw myself as a little girl running down it on Christmas morning, as a young woman in formal gowns, gliding down, trying to look as sophisticated as possible as some date or another waited at the bottom . . . Sighing, I stepped back. "Mind if I . . .?" I used my finger to gesture to the yard and the surrounding property.

"Of course," Brogan said, seeming to know exactly what I was asking and stepping back. I wondered what he was thinking, where he would wander, but I pushed it out of my mind. I needed to take this time for me.

"I'll meet you back at the car in a little while." He simply nodded.

I strolled around the property for a while, letting the many pleasant memories fill my mind: listening for the sound of my dad's car every evening and running to the driveway to greet him, throwing my arms around his neck as he laughed and swung me around. I remembered how my mother had loved the snow and how the first snowfall was always a magical day in our home. My mother's laugh would be filled with joy as we made snow angels and caught snowflakes on our tongues. I remembered my mother coming into my bedroom to kiss me goodnight, before she left for a night out with my father. I remembered her perfume, something light and feminine that I didn't know the name of. I remembered how she'd give me Eskimo kisses and tell me that someday I was going to fall in love with a man just like she'd fallen in love with my daddy. And someday I'd make a little girl as pretty as me. *Oh Mama.*

As I walked around the fence of the pool, I remembered laughing with my girlfriends so many summers as we slathered on sunscreen, read magazine articles aloud to each other, and gossiped about boys. Closing my eyes, I inhaled the familiar scent: grass, flowers, and the faint smell of horses nearby, a smell that lingered even though all the animals had been sold. I turned around and looked toward the stable. It would be my last stop.

As I strolled there, a feeling of peace came over me. There was no particular reason for it—I felt sad, lost, my life in upheaval and nothing was certain and yet . . . there it was. I wanted to believe that for just a moment, my beloved parents had used the breeze to caress me and tell me everything would be okay, and that somewhere deep inside I knew it was true. *I miss you both so very much, and wish you were here to stand by my side.* I'd felt adrift for so long, and recently—even before Brogan had taken over our company—the resilient façade had started to crack a little. I realized now that a large part of it was that losing both parents by nineteen had been so grueling—*harrowing*—and I'd never fully acknowledged that deep pain. That searing loss. Yet, being within the grounds where I'd been raised brought welcome comfort. Soothing smells. Calm . . .

Both my parents had died here, but it was the *living* I was remembering. And God, I'd needed this.

I tried the back door of the stable. Surprisingly it was open. The light inside was dimmer, dust motes twirling lazily in shafts of sunlight coming from the skylights above. The smell of old wood, hay, and the faint scent of the horses that had once lived here mingled together in the still air. I walked to the stalls and stood staring into the empty space. My eyes filled with tears. "Oh Maribel," I whispered. She had been my horse and part of this property I'd grieved the hardest for when Ginny told me she had to sell it. She'd reassured me she had found a good home for her, but I still missed her even though so much time had passed. "Are they good to you?" I whispered.

Bending my neck, I rested my forehead against the rough wood. I heard a small sound and whirled around. Brogan was standing by the open door, looking unsure, his hands in his pockets. For just a moment I simply stared at him. He looked so much like the boy I'd once known, the boy I'd wanted desperately to be mine, the boy I'd once . . . *loved.* Yes, I'd loved him. Some would say I hadn't known him well enough to love him, that I'd loved my own fantasy of him, that I'd simply been young and fickle, that perhaps I didn't even know what love *was*. But I didn't believe it—even now, all these years later and with the eyes of a woman. Something in him had called to me, something about him had spoken to my heart in a way no one had before or since. Even now, standing across from each other in the dim light of the stable where we'd first made love, there was so much bitterness between us, so much heartache and resentment, and yet my heart recognized something in him I could feel but didn't know how to name.

"Hi," I whispered. Brogan walked toward me, never taking his eyes from mine. The expression on his face was so intense, so filled with the same yearning I'd known in his eyes before. It shocked me—*touched me*—filled me with warmth for him, because I recognized what it was costing him to let me see it. When he'd stepped right up to me, I tipped my head back to look up at him, my breath catching. He brought his hand to my face and used his thumb to wipe the tear from my cheek.

"Lydia," he said, his voice low and hoarse. "Mo Chroí."

A princess? No, no longer. But it was what he'd always called me, and so it was special for that reason alone, especially when said that way. I shook my head back and forth. "I just . . ."

"I know," he said. "I know." I leaned in to his touch. Maybe it was because I was emotional. Maybe because it just felt so good to have someone touch me with tenderness in that moment. Or maybe it was because it was Brogan, and we were back together in the place where I'd once loved him, and he was showing me a glimpse of his own vulnerability. Maybe it was all those things.

I felt like I'd gone back in time for just a moment and I wanted to grasp onto it and do it better this time. I wanted another chance . . . another opportunity to make things different. And though I knew it couldn't be so, right then it felt possible anyway.

My breath rushed out and I put my hand over Brogan's heart and felt it beating steadily under my palm. "Lydia," he said again. *A question, an answer, a prayer.*

His eyes changed, and I sensed his intention before he even moved. He was going to kiss me. For the second time in my life Brogan Ramsay was going to kiss me. And I wanted him to—possibly even more than the first time. My heart beat out the plea and my lips parted a moment before his head came down and his mouth met mine. The contact immediately sent waves of pleasure radiating through me in an overwhelming rush of heat. I whimpered and wrapped my arms around his neck at the same moment he pulled me against him. His head tilted and his tongue swept into my mouth and my tongue met his, sliding against it in a delicious caress. It felt like a symphony rose in every cell of my body as I became reacquainted so easily with his taste, his touch, the way he reached his hands up the back of my shirt so he could run his fingertips over my skin. I gripped him, but kept my hands still so he could focus on exploring me. *I remembered.* I remembered the foggy, tortured look on his face when he was experiencing too much stimulation at once, the way he'd halt his movements based on mine. Not always able to give and receive at the same time. But there was a dance I'd begun to learn long ago and I heard the melody—felt the rhythm—as he pressed his body against mine. I heard it and my body responded as if it was sung only for me.

I know you, Brogan. I've never forgotten.

I moaned again, our tongues sliding and gently dueling. I loved the taste of him—mint and Brogan, that indescribable something that was only him and no one else.

Our kiss became urgent, Brogan's fingertips moving lightly over every part of my skin that he could reach as if he were trying to convince himself I was really there. I felt the hard press of his arousal against my stomach and pressed back toward him. He broke from my lips, panting. "I . . ." he said, looking down at me with glazed eyes. "I . . . God, Lydia." He brought his mouth back to mine again, and we kissed for long moments. I sagged against Brogan, my body limp with need. He took my weight, holding me up with one arm around my waist while he worked my mouth like he had been born to do just that, feathering his lips down my throat and sucking at the hollow spot at the base of my neck. I was throbbing between my legs, my underwear soaked. I wanted to beg him to lay me down on the ground, undress me, spread my legs wide and fill me with his hardness, and relieve the terrible empty ache within me. If I didn't stop now, I was going to do just that. I was going to beg and plead and demand.

Breaking from Brogan's mouth, I took in a big lungful of air. "We have to . . . we . . ." I panted, trying to organize what I was trying to say.

"I know." He pulled me toward him as we both caught our breath. I rested my head against his chest, trying once again to figure out what I was feeling. "I want you, Lydia," he said, laying his forehead against mine and letting out a shaky breath as if in this, he was admitting defeat.

I tipped my head back and looked up at him. Our gazes seemed to tangle before I looked away, off to the interior door behind him. There was still so much between us, so much unresolved, untold. I would not lie to myself; I wanted him, too. Desperately. But it wasn't enough. It hadn't been *then,* and it definitely wasn't now. Taking his hand I started toward it, pulling him behind me. He followed. When we stepped into what had once been a small, temporary bedroom, I let go of his hand and looked at him.

"What about this, Brogan? What about what happened here? Will you ever really forgive me? Is this," I swept my hand around, indicating all that had happened here that day, "really over and done with for you?"

His gaze broke from mine, and he looked around the now-empty room, his eyes lingering on the place the small cot had once been. The place where we'd both lost our virginity what seemed like so long ago.

I walked over and stood in the spot, a wave of melancholy coming over me as I thought back to my stupid teenage dreams. "I had envisioned it like this. You'd pull me close and kiss me." I brought my fingertips to my lips re-enacting the drama of my girlish imaginings. "Your lips would be so soft, so gentle. I'd imagined kissing you so many times. I'd lie in bed and think about it, my hands wandering over my skin, pretending they were *your* hands touching me, stroking me. I imagined how you might taste, how your skin might smell—like boy sweat and grass." I closed my eyes and inhaled and then smiled a small, dreamy smile, placing my hands over my heart. When I opened them, Brogan had a small baffled frown on his face. "Myles would burst in and demand to know why you were kissing his girl. '*Your* girl?' you'd say, before you could even think too much about it. 'She's *my* girl. I claim her, right here, right now. My princess. She's mine and no one else's.' And then we'd . . . I don't know, hop on one of the horses and ride off into the sunset." I dropped my arms, sighing and looking around. "I never was very good at tying up the loose ends of a plan after I'd orchestrated the exciting part." I looked at Brogan, beseeching him with my eyes. "I was sixteen and stupid. I was young and spoiled and selfish. And I should have just told you I loved you rather than setting you up. I'm sorry, Brogan. I never meant to hurt you." I shook my head. "I never meant for things to turn out the way they did. I'm so sorry. I'm so very, very sorry." My words faded away to nothing.

Brogan's expression was a study in confusion. He opened his mouth to say something and then closed it. Finally, he tilted his head and asked, "You wanted *me?* You pulled that stunt so that . . ." He ran his hand through his hair, looking down at the floor as if it might hold the answer he was apparently looking for. After a moment, he laced his hands behind his neck and just stood that way for several minutes, grappling with something. I waited, not understanding what he was so confused about. Finally, he dropped his arms loosely by his sides and met my eyes. "You did that for *me*? You did that so I'd fight for you?"

I nodded my head slowly, eyeing him. "Why did you think I did it?" I asked.

"I thought . . ." He shook his head. "I thought you used me to make Myles jealous. I suppose it doesn't matter." Only, it looked like it did matter. It looked like it mattered a great deal.

"No, I wanted *you.* I wanted you so much I couldn't think of anything else. So much I was willing to use every trick in the book to get you. Every stupid, manipulative trick." I sighed and walked a few paces and turned around, pressing my back against the wall and sliding down to the floor. He joined me where I sat, his shoulder touching mine as we stared straight ahead.

"We went to your house the next morning, you know, my father and I. I ran to him after Stuart . . . after Stuart fired your father. I ran to mine, and he was sleeping so I woke him. He told me we'd go see your family first thing in the morning. He promised he'd fix it. He liked you. He would have. He would have fixed it. But you were gone."

"We left that night," he said. "I couldn't bear to stay another minute." He leaned his head back and hit it twice against the wall.

"Brogan . . . I . . . I want to tell you something." I swallowed heavily. "We . . . looked for you. At least, Stuart was supposed to have put every effort into tracking you down. My father was ill, so he gave that task to Stuart. I wonder now . . ." I looked down at my hands. "But anyway, we looked for you because . . . because I was pregnant." I felt his body freeze next to me before he sat up abruptly, his eyes looking straight into mine.

"Lydia, my God." He took in a sharp breath. "You had—"

"I lost the baby. I was three months along and . . ." I shook my head, a sudden flood of grief taking me by surprise. I sucked in a shaky breath, almost shocked by the power of anguish overwhelming me. But I wouldn't cry now. Not in front of Brogan. "Everyone kept saying, 'Oh, it's for the best, Lydia.' They kept *saying* that and I *hated* them for it. I hated them because if it was for the best then why did it hurt so much? They were talking about my baby. They were saying it was for the best that my baby was gone." My voice sounded dull, emotionless despite the grief that pommeled my heart. "Even when I left for college, I was *still* so bitter. Then my father died and—" I sucked in a breath and Brogan pulled me into him, tucking my head beneath his chin. My breathing slowed as I felt his trembling increase. Brogan's hold on me was tight and after a few minutes, he seemed to calm, his muscles relaxing and the trembling abating. I tilted my head back to look at him. His face was waxen and he looked slightly shell shocked. "Lydia, God, I—"

I placed two fingers on his lips, stopping his words. "You don't have to say anything. I'm sorry I just sprung that on you. I didn't plan it." I wet my lips. "It's just this place and . . . maybe I shouldn't have said anything at all—" Brogan sat up taller and pulled me up, his hands around my upper arms, so I was looking straight into his eyes.

"Jaysus, Lydia, it was my baby, too. Of course you should have told me. I'm just so," he shook his head, looking for a moment as if he were a lost little boy, "so sorry you went through that alone. I didn't even consider . . ." He released me and ran a still trembling hand over his face. "I guess we both suffered . . . in different ways," he said blankly, staring at the wall behind my head.

"No, you had to scrounge for food to eat. You had to do things you hated doing. You—"

"Goddamn it! We're not going to compare our sufferings now," he yelled suddenly, moving me away from him and standing up. I came to my feet, too, my legs feeling shaky beneath me. He raked both hands through his thick hair, clutching fistfuls. "This is so fucked up." He released a large breath. Bringing his hands to his hips, he said, "Your brother did find me."

I shook my head in confusion. "What?"

"Stuart, he found me in the Bronx a couple months after I left."

"No, that can't be—"

"It is. Ask him. He dropped off a bag of things we'd left at the house in our haste to leave. Nothing of any value—one of Eileen's shirts, a plastic bowl . . ." He suddenly laughed, but it morphed into a grimace. "He looked around at the rat-hole we lived in and then he left."

I leaned back against the wall. "He must have had a reason," I whispered. "He must have . . ." Had my brother truly hated Brogan that much? Why had he done that to *me?* He *knew* how desperate I was to find him. He knew.

"Oh, he had a reason. But his reasons were all about him. Tell me, Lydia, will he apologize, do you think? Will he ask for your forgiveness?"

I let out a long breath, massaging my temples. I felt a headache coming on. "I don't know. Likely not. I know you hate him for what he did, for what he caused, Brogan, but we can't change it. We have to find a way to move forward. We have to find a way to find happiness *now.* You're a rich, powerful man who became successful against all odds and at such a young age. You must be *proud* of that." I moved closer to him and took his hands in mine. "And do you know the positive that came from what *I* experienced? I grew up, Brogan. I grew up real fast when I was dished up a big serving of painful reality. My scheming hurt you, and I'll regret the consequences that you suffered because of it for the rest of my life. But my scheming hurt me, too. And I learned that life isn't all about me. I learned that every choice has an outcome and I learned that holding on to bitterness is a poison that eats away at you from the inside."

Brogan looked at me as if I might be crazy, his features harsh and unflinching. But as his eyes moved over my face, something gentled in his expression. "Lydia, so forgiving. If only I could let go the way you've seemed to be able to."

"You have to, Brogan. You have to or it will ruin you *inside*."

"Maybe I'm already ruined, Mo Chroí."

I shook my head. "No, I don't believe that. You can make this right." I squeezed his hands. Looking into his handsome face, those almost otherworldly blue eyes, I thought that what I really saw there was an aching loneliness. "You can," I whispered. "I know you can." But his silence told me he didn't agree.

CHAPTER TWELVE

Brogan

I spent the rest of the day in my office, but I didn't work. I sat staring at the wall, a drink in my hand, contemplating everything that had happened in the De Havilland's former stable earlier that day. My gut clenched, and I closed my eyes again at the memory. *She'd been pregnant.* She'd been pregnant and alone. Yet, all these years, when I thought of Lydia, I had thought of nothing but my own misery, my own damaged pride. "Selfish fucker," I muttered, throwing back the remainder of my drink. I'd come inside her that day, and yet I had never even considered pregnancy because I'd been too caught up in my own suffering.

She'd tried to find me—or at least Stuart had been sent to find me. I was gripped by a wave of hatred so fierce I felt like it might knock me to the ground, as I remembered the disgusted look on his face when he'd come to our apartment and the way he'd left without saying a word about Lydia.

I might have eventually forgiven him for what happened in the stable after I'd made love to Lydia—*maybe.* But I could never forgive him for not telling me Lydia was carrying my baby when he'd had the opportunity. What if it was the stress of her situation that caused the miscarriage? I'd have a six-year-old . . . I could hardly wrap my head or my heart around it. *We'd created a life.*

And God, she'd asked me to meet her that day not to use me but because she'd *wanted* me. I was still reeling from her confession, was still hearing her voice in my head. *And I should have just told you I loved you.* My heart squeezed. I hadn't even considered it, had only seen it through the eyes of someone who felt so unworthy of her. And now, to some extent, because of my own devious acts, I still felt just as unworthy. *Arseways. What a fecking understatement.*

So what happened now? Where did this leave Lydia and me? I laid my head back against my chair and stared up at the ceiling. What a bloody mess I'd made of everything. I knew I wanted her, but what did that mean? We still had the same intense physical attraction between us. Hell, all she had to do was look at me and I was fucking hard. Kissing her today had been the most pleasurable thing I'd experienced in years, far better than any sex I'd had in the time we'd been apart. She seemed to understand me in a way no other woman ever had, and it made me feel . . . both safe and vastly *unsafe* in the same breath.

But the real question when it came to Lydia was, would it be a good idea to pursue more, whatever *more* was? Or had I created a situation where she'd never trust me and wonder at my motives, even if she understood the true nature of my desire for revenge? I wouldn't blame her if that was the case. God, I'd acted like a child and a fool. And even knowing that, there was still so much I couldn't let go of, not even for her. Namely, her fuck-up of a brother. Jaysus, the arsehole was making a bad situation worse. I hadn't even imagined that was possible. But clearly I had underestimated the complete and utter idiocy that was Stuart De Havilland. I let out a long sigh. I would have to figure all this out, but first, I needed to get dressed for dinner. I had to make some proposals to Lydia, and I had no idea how she was going to take them.

The doorbell rang with perfect timing, and I opened the door to the kid working for the restaurant delivery service holding two large cases in his hands. After tipping him, I placed the items in the oven and refrigerator as indicated on the instructions and went upstairs and showered, changing into a pair of slacks and a button-up shirt.

I could hear what sounded like a hair dryer being used in Lydia's room and my heart sped up in anticipation of being alone with her tonight. Despite all we had hanging over us, inside I was seventeen years old again. And that feeling both filled my blood with an excited anticipation unlike anything I'd experienced since I *was* seventeen and made me feel powerless and vulnerable at the same time.

And I should have just told you I loved you.

I stepped out into the hall at almost the same moment Lydia did, and we both stood staring at each other over the short distance, her words from earlier repeating in my head. *Lydia.*

"Hi," she said softly.

"Hi." She was wearing the same black dress she had been wearing before I had her change for the party yesterday, and this time, I took the time to appreciate her in it. My eyes moved from her slim legs, to her sweetly curved hips, to her luscious breasts, up to her beautiful face, and her shiny blonde hair. "You look beautiful. Your hair, it's different."

She smiled, running a hand down it. "Oh, I just straightened it."

"I like it." God, I *sounded* like a seventeen-year-old. But Lydia only smiled and walked toward me.

"Thank you. You look nice, too. Where are we going?"

"I ordered dinner in tonight. I thought it'd be easier to talk without worrying about a bunch of people all around us."

"Oh," she said, sounding a bit surprised. "Okay. Actually," she stopped once we'd reached the bottom of the stairs and took off her heels, sighing with what sounded like relief, "that sounds great. I'm also not sure if I'm ready to face Greenwich society again so soon."

I flinched slightly, feeling like the arse I was all over again. I took her by the hand and led her to the kitchen where I began taking the warmed food out of the oven. I handed a bottle of wine and an opener to Lydia. This all suddenly felt surreal to me, as if, unwittingly, and in only a week, Lydia had somehow become a fixture in my home. My mind was whirling with too many emotions to try to sort—I'd been at it all day and suddenly, I just wanted to sit across from her and have dinner and talk about mundane topics. I wanted her to make me laugh, and I wanted to ask her all about her life now. I wanted to know what she'd studied in college, and I wanted to hear about whether she liked her job. Or *had* liked her job before I came along. I closed my eyes for a second as another wave of shame hit me. So yes, I wanted this to be a real date, but it couldn't be. I had guaranteed that with my actions.

As we brought the last of the dishes into the dining room, I said, "What if I'd come up to you at a party a few weeks ago?"

She slid into her chair, a look of confusion passing over her face. She tilted her head to look up at me. "What do you mean?"

"I mean," I continued, taking my own seat, "what if I'd walked up to you at a party and asked you out?"

She furrowed her brow, obviously considering my question very seriously. "I . . . I mean, I would have been happy to see you, Brogan. Happy and surprised and . . . I would have said yes. I would have hoped we could mend our friendship, that I could apologize and that you'd accept it." The look on her face was wistful as if she were wishing things had happened just that way. *God, so did I.*

I nodded, a wave of regret passing through me. *Things could have been different.* But they weren't. And now they couldn't be, and I had to tell Lydia why. She raised her glass, a small smile on her lips. "To mending friendships." *Oh Lydia.* But I raised my glass, too, offering her a small smile.

We dug into our food, roast beef tenderloin with a Caesar crust and a side of roasted potatoes and mixed vegetables. Lydia let out a small moan. "God, this is good. You must be thrilled to be eating something I didn't cook."

I chuckled. "Actually, you're a good cook." I decided not to mention, in actuality, I had barely tasted her cooking. I'd been so busy watching her, thinking about her as she'd served Anna and me. *Anna*—another woman I'd used for my own selfish purposes—to make Lydia jealous. I blamed so many others for the wrongs done against me, and yet my own sins were piling up faster than poker chips during a winning streak.

Lydia and I ate in silence for another few minutes. After taking a sip of wine, she said, "So are you going to tell me what you do for work, or is it top secret?"

"I'll get to that. But first, we need to discuss us."

"Us?" she asked, her voice slightly breathy.

I cleared my throat. "Us, meaning you, me, and your brother."

She nodded. "Right, of course." I moved my food around on my plate for a moment, trying to come up with the right words for what I was about to say. She waited, a nervous expression on her face.

"Lydia, your brother has gone from bad to worse."

She frowned. "What do you mean? I just talked to Stuart a few days ago. He texts me almost every day."

"It's easy enough to lie in a text. You can't see the person." I paused, my eyes running over the beautiful lines of her face. "He's gambling again."

Lydia looked suddenly ill. "Gambling?" she whispered, shaking her head back and forth. "He doesn't have any money, though. He can't be gambling. What is he gambling with?"

"He's been gambling on credit. And he's been losing."

She closed her eyes briefly, placing her fork down on her plate with a soft clatter. "On credit. Are you sure?"

"Very."

She let out a slow, deep breath. "Okay. If you'll give us the company back, I know I can get it on solid ground again financially. Then I'll have the means to help Stuart and—"

"I'm not giving you the company back, Lydia."

Her eyes widened, and she sat back in her chair. "I know what he did to you was horrible, Brogan. I know, I do. But look where you are and look where he is. Surely you can let go of some of that hatred. After this morning, I thought maybe—"

"It's not a matter of me hating him anymore." I leaned forward, my elbows on the table. “Where do you think your brother is gambling? Whose credit do you think he's using?"

"I . . . I don't know."

"He's dealing with the mob. And the mob doesn't take kindly to people who can't pay back their debts. They're notoriously unforgiving on the matter."

"Unforgiving," she murmured. As the full impact of what I was saying hit her, tears filled her eyes. "Please, Brogan, there has to be another way. Could we not . . . could *I* not be given the responsibility to turn the company around? Surely I could raise the capital to pay Stuart’s debts. Despite all his faults, he's . . . he’s all I have. The only family I have left in the world." She paused, looking at me as if trying to read the thoughts in my mind. “If I have to, I'll sell it and pay Stuart's debts, and I'll pay you back, too. We can work out a payment schedule for the debt Stuart will still owe you—"

I shook my head back and forth slowly. "It'd be unlikely you'd get any decent offers once a buyer looked into the company finances. Frankly, it wasn't even worth the amount Stuart lost to me." *But it had been what* I *wanted. The only thing I'd wanted at the time. Or at least the only thing I'd been willing to be honest with myself about wanting.*

"Unlikely, but not impossible," she said faintly.

"And you don't have time for that anyway." I didn't mention the fact that even without Stuart's recent suicidal decisions, I wouldn't have given the company back just so they could end up exactly where they'd started. She simply didn't have the resources. My eyes met hers, and I flinched at the fear I saw in her blue-green gaze. *Feck.* If Stuart were here now, I'd tear him limb from limb.

She nodded. "Okay, well, this isn't your problem, obviously. I'll figure something out." She started to rise.

"Sit down, Lydia. Please." She paused, her gaze sweeping over my expression and then did as I asked.

"I have an offer for you, and I have some demands."

"An offer? Demands?" she repeated blankly.

"Years ago, I did some work for the men who hold Stuart's loans. I might be able to buy him some more time to pay them back."

"Why would you do that?" she asked. "You planned this. Isn't it what you want?"

I pressed my lips together. "Dammit, Lydia, you have no idea what these men will do to your brother if he doesn't pay them back, what they'll do to *you.* I'm not a bloody monster. I admit I wanted your brother ruined, but not tortured and dead." I closed my eyes briefly. Admitting aloud that I had orchestrated her brother's ruination didn't bring me the pleasure it once had. In fact, it brought a peculiar feeling of sadness and shame.

"I will not take responsibility for your brother's fuck-ups, but I will take responsibility for my own. *And* I will try to help him because of you, Lydia. Because I want to keep you safe." I shook my head, pausing before I said, "I want you to come live with me in my apartment in New York City."

Her eyes widened, and she stared at me for a moment. "Is that necessary—?"

"Yes. And it's what I insist upon if I'm going to try to help Stuart."

She licked her lips, sucking the bottom one between her teeth for a moment and the movement made my guts clench. "For how long?"

"I don't know. For as long as it takes to make sure you're not in danger."

She appeared to consider the situation I'd just explained to her. Perhaps to find a way out . . . an alternative. "What will happen with De Havilland Enterprises in the meantime?" she asked, obviously hoping that once this was over she'd have a chance to reclaim her company. *Would she? Would I eventually give it back? Sell it back on some payment schedule?* I had told Fionn I wouldn't, but now things had changed.

"I have a team in there now whose sole specialty is bringing back companies on the brink of financial ruin."

"I see." Her eyes wandered away again, the wheels in her mind obviously turning. "And then will you sell it? Once it's on solid ground, I mean?"

"I don't know. I haven't decided anything yet."

She nodded. "My father—"

"I know. Your father created that company from nothing. He worked hard every day, and he made it what it was before your brother got his hands on it. He loved it. He was extremely proud of it."

"Yes," she said quietly.

"I'm not out to ruin what was your father's dream. I'm trying to revive it."

She let out a breath. "I guess . . . I guess that's more than what my brother was doing."

I didn't say anything. She already knew how I felt about her brother. "I was trying, you know—"

"I know. I know that." I'd had the men looking into the company finances look into Lydia and Stuart's personal finances as well. Lydia had been putting practically every dime she earned back into the company in a number of ways—advertising, endorsement, even making up for the shortfall in payroll in the last several months. And though I was sure she hadn't fully realized it, Stuart had been spending ten times as much as he was earning, underhandedly raping the profits that should have been put back into the business. Lydia had been fighting an uphill battle, one destined for failure all along. And now she was broke. Not just broke, practically penniless. I didn't even know how she'd managed to buy the groceries I'd sent her out for. I'd felt sick to my stomach this morning when I'd received the details from my investigators.

"I suppose I'll need to find a job," she said eventually as if her mind had been following the same path as mine.

"I'd be happy to keep you on at De Havilland Enterprises. But I will not hire your brother back. And I can't have you going back to work until his issues have been resolved."

For the first time since we'd begun speaking, her eyes filled with hope. "You'll let me keep working there?"

"If you'd like to, yes. Did you enjoy it?"

Her eyes skittered away. "Mostly. It's kind of hard to say, I mean, I never really got to enjoy it per se. I was always sort of in desperation mode." She let out a small, brittle laugh.

I reached across the table and took her hand in mine. It felt cold and small, and I wanted nothing more than to take her in my arms and tell her everything was going to be okay, that she didn't have to be in desperation mode anymore. I couldn't though. I couldn't because I didn't know if that was the truth or not. I was still trying to catch up with the way things had changed course.

She stared down at our hands for a moment and when she slid hers out from under mine, she used it to pick up her wine, taking a long sip. "I should call my brother . . . warn him . . ."

"It's already been done."

Her eyes lingered on my face for a moment. "How did he take it?"

"Not well."

"Maybe I should try. Maybe he'll listen to me."

"Has he ever listened to you, Lydia? Even once?"

Watching her face pale was heartbreaking. It was as if she were scrolling through years worth of interaction and examining her brother's actions. I could hear him shouting at her to shut up. Repeatedly. By the look of pain on her face, and the way she couldn't meet my eyes, she had found her answer. Her next words, said so softly, made me cringe inside. "No. I suppose not." She looked lost, almost . . . guilty, as if she were somehow to blame for his failings.

I sighed. "Leave it for now. He knows what he's up against. He knows where he stands, and he knows he needs to lie low. There's nothing you can do for him."

Her eyes shifted away as she took another sip of wine. After a while, she seemed to relax a little bit, taking another bite of her dinner, though it was probably cold by this time. We both ate in silence for a few more minutes. I didn't say anything, allowing Lydia to come to terms with everything we'd discussed. She'd taken in a lot tonight and still maintained her dignity and strength, and I admired her for it.

"So, what is it you do to earn all this money that you use to *acquire* failing companies such as ours?" she asked finally. "I know you won ours in a poker game, but I assume you've acquired failing businesses before, since you had a team in place so quickly at De Havilland Enterprises?"

"Accurate assumption." I paused. "I do a little bit of everything." She raised an eyebrow, and I took a sip of my wine, relaxing now, too. She'd listened to what I had to say and though she hadn't said the words, I knew I had her agreement about coming to live with me in New York and letting me provide the protection she could very well need. Helping Stuart in any manner whatsoever made me furious and disgusted, but if it meant keeping Lydia safe, I'd do it anyway. And truth be told, even though Stuart had made his own choices, my actions had caused a new level of desperation, and I couldn't ignore that fact. *Arseways.* "You might remember I'm good with numbers."

She nodded. "Yes, of course."

"The short of it is that I earned enough money to use my talent to make some very profitable investments. I did that for a few years. I still dabble in investing, and I own a number of businesses that I have at least some involvement in, but mostly, I do what I want to do."

She stared at me for several moments. "You . . . do what you want to do. What does that mean exactly?"

I shrugged. I knew I was being evasive, but it was difficult to describe what I did—I had never attempted to put it into words before. "Whatever comes up. Nothing illegal, if that's what you're thinking."

She considered me for another moment before saying, "And the money you earned to begin making the investments?"

"That, Lydia, is another story and not something I feel like discussing right now."

She ran her pointer finger around the rim of her wine glass. "Some of it has to do with what you told me the other night—"

"Some, yes."

She licked her lips again and blood rushed to my groin. The relief of her agreement to my proposal, combined with the wine, was causing my thoughts to turn in a different direction—back to Lydia and how much I wanted her.

"The man at your party, Fionn. He works with you?"

"Yes. He's my business partner. I met him a couple months after I'd moved to the Bronx. He was in a similar position as me. Desperate. We became a team of sorts, I guess you'd say."

Sadness moved across her features. "He seems like a nice guy."

"He's the best man I've ever known."

She studied me as she nodded. "I'm glad you . . . had somebody watching out for you," she said softly.

"He did what he could."

We were both quiet for a moment before Lydia asked, "And once you have me safe and sound in New York City, what exactly am I supposed to do, contained in one apartment all day long?"

I swirled the last sip of wine and brought it to my lips, finishing off the glass. "I have a whole new set of drawers and cabinets there for you to re-arrange."

"Ha ha."

I laughed. "I suppose I could give you some work to do for my company. Let's see how it goes."

She nodded, and I stood up to begin clearing the dishes. When the table was cleared and the food was put away, I poured us each another glass of wine. Turning to her, I asked, "Tired? We could take our wine down to the water." Why did asking her that make my heart jump with nervous anticipation? Why did I feel like I was asking her out on a date and if she said no, I'd be crushed? We'd settled things between us for now. She had no real reason to spend any time with me at all.

"That sounds nice." I let out a relieved breath. "But I think I'll change into something a little more comfortable."

"Okay."

I finished up in the kitchen and then sat at the counter and answered a few emails on my phone. Twenty minutes later when Lydia still hadn't come down, I became restless. What was taking her so long? Grabbing the half bottle of wine and our glasses, I decided it was time to go get her so we could catch the last of the sunset. Glancing out the window I saw the wash of red and orange was already low on the horizon, the clouds tinged in gold.

"Lydia?" I called, knocking lightly on her door. When I didn't get an answer, I opened it slowly, calling her name again. The room was empty and my heart lurched unpleasantly. *Had she left?* But then I noticed movement beyond the French doors and saw her. My heart rate slowed, and I moved toward the doors. She had changed into a loose blue dress of some kind that was falling off one shoulder. She was standing at the rail of the widow's walk—her hands joined on the ledge—watching the last of the sun as it slipped beyond the horizon. The lingering light cast her hair in a pale yellow glow—a few strands lifting in the summer breeze—and I could see the outline of her profile, the mouthwatering shape of her body beneath the light material of the dress. *I was entranced.* I stood there for a moment just watching her, memorizing this moment, and knowing that for me, there would never be another woman as beautiful as Lydia De Havilland standing on my balcony watching the day slip into dusk.

CHAPTER THIRTEEN

Lydia

The door clicked behind me and I turned. *Brogan.* He held a wine bottle against his body with his bicep, the stems of two wine glasses between his fingers. He looked debonair and sexy, and I took a moment to admire him. "Sorry, I just needed a minute. The sun was setting." I inclined my head toward the water where the last vestiges of light were dwindling, causing the surface of the water to look as if a thousand diamonds were dancing upon it. "If I lived here, I'd never watch a sunset from anywhere else."

Brogan's shoulders seemed to tense for a brief moment and then he stepped fully onto the walk, pushing the door closed behind him. He moved toward me, handing me my glass.

I had come upstairs and changed, when all the events of the day had seemed to catch up with me all at once: the emotional trip to my childhood home, kissing Brogan, telling him of the pregnancy, Stuart, that our predicament had become worse. *Far worse.* And suddenly, I was so tired. Just weary to my soul. I'd spent the last seven years—or so it seemed—drifting from one heartache to another, one challenge to another, and I felt like I'd hit my limit. In that very moment, standing in the middle of Brogan's guest bedroom, a blue sundress gripped to my chest, I'd felt like every muscle was tensed with pent-up negative energy, and I just wanted to scream. I wanted to fall into someone, depend on another person, allow someone *else* to be strong for a while. And I didn't have anyone to do that—no one at all. I'd made some peace with my parents' deaths today, but returning to our old estate had also been a reminder that I was completely, utterly alone, and the reality of that felt like a sudden, gripping despair, the cracks in my heart splintering, widening.

I'd dressed and stumbled to the widow's walk, wondering at the women who had stood on a structure just like this and felt their *own* despair, their own desperate loneliness. I'd turned and there he was as if he were the answer to a question, as if he'd somehow known I needed . . . someone. And maybe it wasn't just someone I needed. Maybe I needed *him*. And maybe that was another reason I was so damned scared.

Because I had a feeling needing Brogan Ramsay again was going to ultimately break my heart.

I turned back to the water. "Do you know why this is called a widow's walk?"

He leaned a hip against the rail and took a sip of wine. "Because they offer an unimpeded view of the sea. Women would walk them as they looked out to the water waiting for a glimpse of their husband's ship. And often, their husband would never return."

I nodded, again picturing the nameless, faceless woman who might have walked one very similar to this long ago, her dress billowing in the wind, a handkerchief balled in her fist, tears streaming down her face as she waited for her beloved. "I studied history in college." I paused, taking a sip of wine. "It's always been the women who have had it the hardest, you know. We're always the ones who have to wait—for your ships to arrive, your wars to end, your pride to be soothed, for your bodies to be returned from some battlefield, some foreign land. We're always the ones stuck while you men fight for the things that are so important to you for reasons we can't understand. We wait, and we wonder, and we hurt."

He tilted his head, his eyes searching mine. "The men have been the ones to fight the battles, to be killed, wounded, scarred, captured."

I shook my head. "Waiting. The waiting, the uncertainty, the not knowing. It's the greater heartache, the greater torture. Can you imagine, coming here night after night, pacing . . . pacing, being so powerless to do anything except wait? Like a slow death . . ."

Brogan was looking at me in that intense way he had, as if he was trying to figure out the things I wasn't saying to him. And truthfully, I didn't know if there was anything I wasn't saying to him, or why I was suddenly so filled with pain for the women who had suffered the fate I was describing. Maybe I was just . . . emotionally distraught, overburdened.

"What did you want to do with a history degree?" he finally asked.

I shrugged, letting out a pent-up breath. "Teach most likely. I hadn't decided when it became clear I was needed at the company. I earned my degree, but I never really used it." I took a sip of my wine.

"It wasn't always your intention to work there."

"No. It was my intention to babysit Stuart." I sighed, the weight of that truth falling off my shoulders. "I've obviously done a piss-poor job."

"No, Lydia. You singlehandedly kept that company running in the black—even if it was always just barely. I've looked into the books."

I looked at him sharply. But of course he had. He was trying to fix things, trying to create a future for the company my brother had almost run into the ground. Of course he needed the details of exactly how that had happened, other than Stuart's penchant for gambling. Speaking of which, "Do you count cards, Brogan?" I asked the question that had crossed my mind several times since I found out Stuart had lost our company to him in a poker game.

He paused, a frown furrowing his brow, but then answered, "Yes."

Surprised, I turned my body toward him. "I didn't think—"

"You didn't think I'd admit to it after winning De Havilland Enterprises from Stuart in a card game? Why not? It's not as if I even work at it. It just comes naturally. I think it'd be more effort *not* to count cards."

"Is it really fair to gamble then? Isn't that—"

"Cheating? I don't believe so. But maybe we disagree."

Did I disagree? Not exactly, I guessed. He was only using his God-given talents. Still, if Brogan hadn't contributed to Stuart's downfall, would he, could he have eventually turned his life around? Or was *I* the fool for continuing to hope for that? By continuing to bust my own ass to keep our heads above water so he didn't have to? In truth, maybe Stuart had been headed for ruin with or without Brogan's involvement. *Take care of your brother, Lydie.*

"Will you show me?"

"Show you?"

"How you count cards."

He frowned, tilting his head, his tongue running over his teeth, just as the landscape lighting flickered on below, casting him in an aura of gold and drawing my attention to the blue of his eyes. Funny, in his office that day, I had described them to myself as icy, but I'd never thought them icy before then, and I didn't tonight. It was said eyes were windows to the soul, and if it was true, that soft, soft blue spoke of things I was almost frightened to acknowledge. And God, he was breathtakingly handsome—his masculine beauty was almost painful to look at because it made me want to possess him, and I didn't think that was wise. It hadn't been then, and it probably was less so now. "We'd have to play a game for me to show you."

"All right."

He nodded his head toward my room. "Let's go inside." I followed him off the widow's walk. The night was closing in, the sky turning a deep, twilight blue as the first stars appeared.

Brogan placed the wine bottle and his glass on the top of the dresser and I followed suit. "I'll go get a deck of cards." He left the room, and I sagged down onto the bed. What I should probably tell him was that I was going to sleep. But I didn't want to sleep. I wanted company. I wanted *his* company.

He returned a few minutes later, having changed into a pair of jeans that rode low on his lean hips and a black T-shirt that showcased his broad shoulders and muscular chest, *and* he was wearing his glasses. I sat up on my knees, and he joined me on the bed, sitting on the very edge. He'd grabbed our wine glasses and handed me mine. I took a sip and set it on the bedside table. He placed his on the wooden bench at the end of the bed.

Without a word, he took the cards out of the box and shuffled them effortlessly, his eyes remaining on my face as his hands fanned and folded the cards as if by magic. I couldn't help laughing softly. He raised a dark brow.

"What are we playing for?"

I gave him a wry smile. "You've already bankrupted my family. Plus, it would be a fool's bet on my part. You just admitted you count cards."

"I wasn't talking about betting money."

"What then?"

He shrugged. "Truth or dare."

"You'd end up getting all my truths and dishing up all the dares."

"How about if we play a game completely based on luck then? I'll still count cards, but it won't offer me any rewards. I'll just know what's coming. Winner gets to choose whether he or she wants a truth or a dare from the other."

"I thought in truth or dare the *loser* got to choose what they were willing to give up."

"I've never thought that was very fair. Why should the loser get to choose their fate?" His smile was lazy.

I thought about it, sucking on my lower lip. My heart was thumping at a quickened pace, and I wasn't sure I wanted to admit that what I felt was . . . excitement. I wasn't sure about the dare part, but I wanted Brogan's truths. This was my chance to get a few. "Okay."

He simply nodded, fanning the cards out once more and folding them back together. He placed them on the bed and nodded to them. "Cut?"

I did and then he picked them up and began dealing. "What are we playing?" I asked.

"War."

I raised a brow. "I thought we'd already played war."

He chuckled. "Oh no. Those were just the battles, Mo Chroí." But he tilted his head and looked up at me in that sweet, teasing way he'd done when we were teens that had always made my stomach do somersaults. *It still did.*

I watched him as he dealt the cards, noted the very slight scruff already on his jaw despite that he'd been clean-shaven that morning, the way his inky black lashes created shadows on his cheeks, even under the lenses of his glasses, the strong line of his jaw, the slight cleft in his chin, the way he held his mouth in that rigid way. And yet, I knew how soft it could be, the warmth of his lips, exactly how his tongue tasted—that exotic male spiciness that spoke to everything feminine inside of me. I wondered if he tasted the same everywhere, wondered at the flavor of his most intimate skin. I felt wetness pool in my underwear and achy pressure settled between my thighs at my own thoughts.

Brogan suddenly looked up at me, a knowing glint in his eyes as if he knew exactly where my thoughts had gone. He moved more fully onto the bed, grabbing a pillow and lying on his side, propped up on one elbow. *My God, the man was sexy.*

He turned over his first card—a six—and glanced up at me. I turned over my card—a queen—and gathered both. "My truth or dare?" I asked.

He shrugged. "We can play that way or we can wait for a war."

I bit at my lip. "Let's wait for a war. These truths or dares shouldn't be easily won."

"Nothing good ever is."

I grabbed a pillow as he'd done and stretched out next to him. Our positions felt very intimate, our bodies facing each other, our faces close. Of course, the fact that we were in bed—or rather *on* bed—together intensified the intimacy. We played for another few minutes before there was a war. I won. He gave me a small smile.

"I want a truth," I said immediately.

"Okay." I noticed his pulse beating steadily at the side of his neck and had the sudden desire to kiss him there. He watched me closely, seeming to still and I wondered what I'd revealed on my face that caused him to study me the way he was.

"How do you do it? The numbers, I mean."

He tilted his head, considering. "I honestly don't really know." He looked behind me, frowning slightly as if he was trying to figure out how to word his answer. "I've always seen the world in measurements. I constantly compute lines, relationships between objects." He looked at the wall to our right where two pictures hung. "Those pictures are a sixteenth of an inch off." I studied them. They looked perfectly aligned to me. "I notice all these things all the time. It doesn't bother me, and I don't think about it necessarily, it's just—"

"Part of you."

He nodded. "Yes. I see the world in numbers. Everything. And with actual numbers, it's like," he rubbed his fingertips together, "I can feel them. I feel their weight, their value." He furrowed his brow. "It's hard to explain. It's just . . . the way my mind works."

I nodded. I found it fascinating. I found *him* fascinating. Hadn't I always? But he looked slightly uncertain, picking up his cards and moving us away from the topic and back to the game.

We played for a few quiet moments, both of us sipping our wine here and there before there was another war. After I'd turned over a ten, I asked, "Who's going to win this round?"

Brogan's lip tipped up. "Me, most likely with a face card." Sure enough, he turned over a jack.

"Impressive," I murmured.

After another few rounds, we both turned over the same card. My eyes met his. "Another war," I said dramatically, breathing out the word. He laughed and my heart squeezed, suddenly realizing what a rare sound it was.

We turned over our three cards and then at the same time, revealed our final card. Me: three, Brogan: four. "Damn," I sighed. "All right. Do you want a truth or dare?"

He propped himself up a little higher. "Truth." He dragged his teeth over his bottom lip. "You said you haven't been with anyone, since me." He paused and my breath hitched slightly. "But have you dated? Is there anyone . . ." He seemed to still as he waited for my answer, but his expression didn't hold any hint of whether or not he cared overly much about my answer. I sat up and grabbed my glass of wine off the bedside table where I'd placed it and took a drink, returning to the position I'd previously been in on the bed.

"I didn't date much in college—not until the end anyway. I, well, the pregnancy . . . and then like I said, my dad passed away during my first year. After that, I kind of kept to myself. I dated a little bit during my senior year, but no one special. I've dated a little since I've been home, but mostly, the company and all our family problems have kept me occupied. I haven't felt like I had much to give to another person. Does that answer your question?"

He nodded slowly, and our eyes lingered for a few heartbeats, causing a warm flush to move through my body. Brogan picked up his cards and I did the same. My eyes ran down his muscular legs, my gaze resting on the way one foot rubbed unconsciously at the cuff of the opposite leg of his jeans. He was testing textures even with his feet. For some reason, that caused a shiver to run down my spine and my nipples to tighten.

After only two more cards, there was another war. When Brogan won again, I shot him a speculative look. "You sure you're not cheating somehow?"

He smirked. "I give you my word."

"Hmm." I gave him a suspicious glance and he chuckled. "Okay, shoot."

He reached over and grabbed his wine glass off the bench at the end of the bed and took a sip. Turning back to me, his expression was serious. His finger moved down the piece of silk at the edge of the pillowcase and I watched it, back . . . forth.

"The women," he finally said. "How did you know? How did you know that had been difficult for me?" A fleeting look of vulnerability passed over his face and I blinked. *Brogan.*

"I . . . I remembered you seem to . . ." I looked away, not sure how to phrase what I was trying to say. "You always seemed to have very heightened senses. I watched you." My eyes shifted away. I felt vulnerable myself, as if in answering this question, he'd understand just how *much* I'd watched him, noticed his every movement, every reaction, how much I'd thought about him. *He knew now.* "You always got this look on your face when you were dealing with two sensations at the same time—a sort of . . . pain almost, as if it were too much. It intrigued me."

"Yes," he breathed. "Yes, that's what it's like." Our gazes clashed, something powerful leaping between us.

"I know," I said. "I don't know exactly how I know. I just do. I did."

"My mother said I was a terrible baby, crying constantly." He laughed, a small sound containing little humor. His tongue found the imperfect tooth and ran slowly over it.

I tilted my head, watching him, taking my lip into my mouth again. His gaze moved to my mouth and lingered there the way mine had just lingered on his. "It must have been awful not to be able to explain what you were feeling, how everything was *too much*."

"I've never tried to explain it. And no one's ever noticed. I just—"

"Deal with it. Stand apart from people, hold your breath sometimes. I know."

His gaze leapt to mine, and he looked almost stricken for a brief moment. He cleared his throat but when he spoke, it was still slightly scratchy. "Yes." He picked up his cards and looked down at his hands holding them, looking as if he was grappling with his own thoughts. He didn't like that I knew that about him. I didn't blame him. I supposed he considered it very personal. Maybe even the most personal thing about him.

"Your eyes aren't bionic, though," I said, attempting to lighten the mood, to set him at ease.

He looked confused for a brief moment and then set his cards down and reached up and adjusted his glasses, his lip curving upward. "Bionic?"

I shrugged. "Yeah, you're sort of like a superhero with your bionic senses."

His eyes met mine, drooping lazily. He lay back fully on his pillow, folding his arms behind his head. "You know what else I can sense, Mo Chroí?" he asked. "You want me. I can smell it." His eyes wandered down to my crotch and then slowly back up to my eyes. He watched me, waiting to see how I'd react to that comment.

I felt color rush to my face. *Jesus.* "You're trying to shock me and make me uncomfortable because that's how I've just made you feel," I whispered. "But you asked me, Brogan. You asked me, and I gave you the truth. And now you're punishing me for it."

He kept staring at me, his expression seemingly a mixture of tension and shame and a small bit of confusion. He let out a harsh breath, closing his eyes. He removed his glasses and pinched the bridge of his nose. "You're right," he said. He sat up, tossing his glasses onto the bench behind him and then moving toward me until he was leaning over me. "But you want my truth, Lydia? I'll give you this one willingly. I want you, too." He paused, intensity vibrating between us as my pulse jumped and my breath hitched. "I want you so bloody much I feel like I'll die from it." As if in a dream, I leaned up slightly, and he gripped my upper arms and guided me until I was on my knees as he was, my body pressed against his, our breath mingling.

"We still have another round," I whispered hurriedly, glancing down at the cards. I needed to think. I needed to get my thoughts in order. This was . . . this was . . .

"It's a war," he said evenly. "And I win. You don't have any high cards left."

I licked my lips, believing him. *Wanting to believe him even if he wasn't telling the truth.* "And what will you ask of me? Truth or dare?"

"Dare," he said immediately.

"Brogan," I breathed, knowing where his thoughts were headed, knowing the nature of what he'd ask of me. And knowing I'd agree. My eyelids fluttered against my will. "We'll destroy each other. Again. You know we will." And yet, my hands came to his shoulders and I clutched him there, my actions contradicting my words of protest. I felt the current of our electricity running beneath my palms—the spark that had always existed between us. We'd indulged it once, and it had ruined us both. I feared now would be no different . . . and perhaps worse.

"Then let's at least destroy each other properly this time." His voice was low and slightly gravelly, and a shiver ran down my spine. He brought his lips to my neck and licked down my throat. I moaned a desperate sound of longing as if it had been lodged in my airway for seven long years. Sensation shot straight between my legs, my nipples hardening.

"Brogan . . ."

"Lie back," he instructed. I looked at him questioningly, but did as he said, scooting up the bed until my head was on the pillows where I slept. "I'm going to cash in on my dare."

CHAPTER FOURTEEN

Brogan

Her eyes held mine, waiting. Her breath seemed to be suspended as I moved closer to where she now lay. "I want ya to show me," I said, barely controlling my voice. I could hear my accent emerging and I didn't attempt to control it. I suddenly *wanted* to be myself with her, not the cleaned-up, polished version I'd extended so much effort to become. Not him. Not right now.

Tonight I was reminded again just how much she'd known me—the *real* me. More than anyone else. And she'd been right that my initial reaction had been to punish her for her knowledge and insight. Because it scared me and made me feel raw . . . but it was also a freedom. A freedom I hadn't felt in seven long years.

She blinked. "Show you what?"

"Show me how ya used to touch yourself when thinking of me. Show me what ya did, Lydia." *I'd lie in bed and think about it, my hands wandering over my skin, pretending they were your hands touching me, stroking me.* I'd moved those words aside earlier because we'd been discussing more important things, but I couldn't move them aside now, nor did I want to. I wanted to explore them thoroughly.

I'm cashing in on my dare.

The pulse in her neck jumped, color rushing to her cheeks. I had been halfway turned on the entire time we'd been playing cards, but now I was practically *buzzing* with need, my erection pressing painfully against the zipper of my jeans, suddenly so aroused, I could barely focus.

Her eyes lingered on mine for several moments, her pupils dilated, her lips parted, before her expression softened into acquiescence—and something I swore looked like relief. She was going to do as I asked. A hot rush of desire headed south and landed between my legs, my entire body tightening. *Holy feck.* I watched as she began unbuttoning the buttons down the front of her dress, her blue-green eyes trained on my face. Christ, but she was gorgeous. I tried to hold eye contact, but my gaze was wrenched to what she was doing with her hands, each new glimpse of skin making my heart rate increase and my breath catch. When the last button came undone, her dress fell open, revealing her silvery-blue bra and underwear. She shrugged the dress off her shoulders, slipping her arms free. My eyes roamed over her greedily, and I heard a small groan come up my throat, unbidden. It'd been so long since I'd seen her like this, and she was even lovelier than I remembered.

Lydia. Beautiful. My everlasting dream.

Her hand moved tentatively down her flat stomach until she came to the waistband of her underwear. She paused momentarily, as if she was rethinking what she was doing, and I swallowed, desperate to watch. Desperate to taste, to touch. Just . . . desperate. *Please don't stop.*

"One summer day," she said, her voice low and breathless, "I was lying by the pool and you were nearby shoveling mulch into our flowerbeds." Her fingers slipped beneath the waistband of her underwear and my eyes followed as if in a trance. "After an hour or so, you took off your shirt and used it to mop up the sweat on your face. God, Brogan," she let out a small sigh, "you were the most beautiful boy I'd ever seen. I watched your muscles tighten and flex, the way sweat gathered at the base of your back and gleamed on your chest, and it was all I could do not to move my hands just as I'm doing now."

Her lips parted on a small moan and she closed her eyes as her fingers dipped lower. My cock throbbed helplessly. *Jaysus.* I wondered if

I might embarrass myself by coming in my pants before I'd even touched her.

"That night I was lying in my bed, and I was still so turned on. I kept picturing those lines on the inside of your hips and the way I could see veins on your stomach that disappeared into your pants. I wanted to trace those veins with my tongue. I wanted to find out where they went. I closed my eyes and let my fantasy take over. You had stopped your work and joined me at the pool. I pretended you had asked if you could cool off and then hadn't been able to resist the sight of me in my skimpy swimsuit and had come over to my lawn chair and climbed on top of me." She let out a breathless little whimper as her fingers moved beneath the thin material of her underwear, pleasuring herself. I watched, fascinated, as her cheeks flushed with arousal and the pulse in her neck beat insistently under the delicate skin of her smooth throat. My eyes heavy, my head foggy with desire, I watched as she used her other hand to reach up and unhook the clasp at the front of her bra, her beautiful breasts popping free of the lace as she shrugged off the skimpy material. Oh, dear God in heaven. My dick pulsed again, and I felt pre-cum practically pouring out of my tip, my blood heating another three million degrees.

"I pretended my own hands were yours, Brogan. I've always loved your hands." Her fingers continued to move inside the underwear she was still wearing and she used her other hand to run one finger around a nipple. I watched, entranced, as it puckered. She moaned. "You'd know just how to touch me, just what I liked, what I needed. It was the first time I brought myself to orgasm."

"Lydia," I said, my voice shaky and sounding as if it were coming from somewhere far away. I moved closer, taking her hand from beneath the lacy material of her underwear and replacing it with my own. Her eyes popped open, hazy with lust. I watched her for a moment, waiting for some sign of approval. She closed her eyes again and arched into my hand. I let out a harsh exhale of relief, moving closer. She brought her hands to my arms, gripping my biceps. The room went dim. "Lydia," I choked out. I didn't know exactly how to tell her that if she touched me, I'd lose all control. *Please understand, Lydia. Please understand because I need you too . . . so much right now.*

She opened her eyes again, comprehension pouring through the lust, and I let out a relieved breath. *She. Understood. She . . . knows me.* Reaching over her head, she held eye contact as she gripped the bars of the bed frame. My heart pounded more fiercely in my ears, blood rushing through my veins like molten gold. She was the only woman who'd ever made me feel this way. *Mo Chroí.*

I pulled her underwear down her legs and tossed them on the floor. Then I moved over her as she let out another small gurgling sound in her throat. "Let me show ya what I would have done if I had really been there," I murmured. "First I would have tasted your sweet nipples." I leaned my head down and rubbed my lips on her breasts, feeling the texture of her skin there—like hot satin—and then I licked one hardened peak, swirling my tongue around it several times before moving to the other one. Lydia's breathing increased, and she let out another sweet whimper. "God, you taste good, Mo Chroí. Like milk and honey. Still. Sweet and creamy." No woman had ever tasted this good before, no woman had even come close. *I know your flavor, Lydia, and I can't forget it. No matter what I do, I can't forget.*

"Brogan," she sighed, pushing her breast toward my face. God, I loved my name on her lips.

I sucked and kissed her nipples for several minutes until she was panting with need. *Need me, Lydia. I want you to need me.* I kissed slowly down her smooth belly, my tongue dipping into her bellybutton, learning the flavors and textures of every part of her. I licked over one hipbone, feathering my lips over that smooth, taut skin, moving lower.

"I would have headed here next," I said. "I would have needed to taste ya. I would have been dying for it then just as I am now." I moved my nose just over the core of her and inhaled. She was all honey here, with just a touch of salt. Something about Lydia had always seemed *decadent.* Hadn't I always felt ravenous with hunger for her? I'd lick her and taste her and eat her in small bites until I'd had my fill. My mind went fuzzy for a brief moment with the intensity of the moment, my senses on overload.

When I leaned in and kissed Lydia's bare vaginal lips, she let out a small gasp, her hands coming off the bars of the bed momentarily before she seemed to catch herself and put them back where they'd been. I adjusted my position, lowering my head again, taking in more of her fragrance. "God, Lydia, you smell like heaven. *My* heaven."

"Brogan, please," she gasped. "Please . . . I need you."

Triumph surged through my blood at her words.

I used my fingers to spread her wetness, circling her swollen clit slowly, and she gasped and moaned. "God, you're soaked," I said, wanting to sink inside her so badly I was desperate with it. Desperate to join with her, to feel her heat surrounding me, to make her scream with pleasure. *Finally.*

"Yes, yes," she moaned.

Leaning forward, I took her clit between my lips and sucked gently, feeling the way her heart beat here, too. Lydia writhed under me, pressing herself against my face.

"Oh God, oh God," she moaned, opening her legs wider to give me more access, the movement making me shudder with satisfaction. I used my tongue to circle the swollen bud and then pushed one finger inside her wet opening, feeling the snug clench of her muscles around my finger. It was almost enough, but not quite. I moved my finger in and out and I sucked and licked her as she uttered indistinguishable sounds, syllables that started as words and left off in breathy gasps. I was mindless, too, the only thought in my head her satisfaction, my only goal to leave Lydia boneless with pleasure. This time I wanted to do it right. I wanted to fuck her in every way possible, and so thoroughly she'd never want anyone else to touch her except me. I growled against her wet flesh, and she bucked into me, screaming as she came against my face.

A fierce burst of pride moved through me as her body shuddered and clenched with pleasure. "Oh, oh Brogan," she moaned. "Oh God, yes."

Moving up her body, I brought my mouth to hers before she'd even opened her eyes. We kissed deeply for long moments before I brought my hand back down between her legs and used the heel of my hand to massage her pubic bone gently, right above her still throbbing clit. "Come for me again, Mo Chroí," I said, putting my mouth back on hers and probing her lips with my tongue. Her mouth stopped moving, and I opened my eyes to see that hers were opened, too.

"I . . . I don't think . . ." she whispered against my lips, but then her head fell back on a moan as I continued to work my hand. "Oh God, Brogan, I think I am, I—" She arched into my hand on a small scream as she came again, moving her head back and forth on the pillow. I circled my hand more and more slowly until I came to a stop.

Lydia opened her eyes, her expression baffled and drunk with pleasure. I smiled and she blinked.

"Shall we see how many times I can make your sweet body come tonight?" I whispered, leaning in and kissing her again. Her hands, which had still been gripping the bed, let go and fell limply above her head, her eyes falling closed.

For a moment, I simply watched her. God, I was stunned at how beautiful she was, limp with pleasure and waiting for more. My heart thrummed with excitement, my stomach muscles clenching. *All mine tonight.*

I sat up quickly and got off the bed, going into the bathroom. Several months ago, Fionn had brought a housewarming gift when I'd first purchased this property. It was filled with liquor, massage lotion, and other items he'd deemed home essentials. I'd just remembered there were condoms in it, too. Sometimes Fionn was bloody, fecking brilliant. I went quickly to the linen closet and grabbed the box from the still unopened basket and returned to the bedroom where Lydia hadn't moved a muscle.

Tossing the box on the bedside table and stripping quickly, I moved over Lydia again. "Are ya okay?" I asked.

Lydia's expression gentled as her eyes moved over my face. She placed her open palm on my cheek. "Yes." She removed her hand and brought her lips to mine and kissed me. I melted into her. Her hand moved between us, and she wrapped her fingers around my cock as I sucked in a breath. I closed my eyes as her hand moved up and down my length, causing delicious bliss.

"Is tú amháin a bhí ann i gcónaí," I breathed, not sure if I'd said it out loud or not.

It's always been you, and no one else.

She stroked me again and again, leaning up slightly to watch her hand on my hard, pulsing flesh. Another small bead of pre-cum leaked from my tip and I groaned. "I need to be inside ya. I can't wait anymore."

She leaned back as I grabbed the box of condoms and tore it open, unrolling one and sliding it over my erection, my shaking hands making the job take twice as long as I needed it to. Lydia watched, her gaze growing hazy again. As I came back over her, I moved her arms back over her head, this time to rest on the pillow.

"Will I ever be able to touch you?" she murmured.

"Yes, Mo Chroí. Just not this time. It's been so long. Please, just not this time." She nodded, and I used my hand to guide my cock to her entrance. Her cheeks were still beautifully flushed, her lips wet and swollen from my kisses, and I gazed at her as I pressed inside, my body breaking out in a light sheen of sweat at the tight clench of her warm inner muscles squeezing my shaft. It felt so bloody good, so good. So right. *Inevitable.* This was my victory, I realized with sudden clarity. Right now, this very moment. Not money, or a company, or any amount of power. *This.* But it still wasn't enough. *More, more, more*, I wanted more. I was buried inside Lydia and even now, I wanted more of her. I always had. I felt drunk and joyful and confused and vulnerable.

I began moving and a burst of pleasure made me gasp. "Ya feel so good," I murmured as I moved more quickly, the intense pleasure gripping me so I couldn't help but to speed up my thrusts, reaching for the climax I needed so desperately. I reached up and laced my fingers with Lydia's, holding her arms over her head on the pillow as I brought my mouth back to hers, thrusting my tongue in her mouth to the rhythm of our lovemaking. She wrapped her legs around my hips and moaned into my mouth. Goosebumps broke out on my skin as I held my orgasm at bay, waiting for the one I sensed might be approaching for Lydia.

After about a minute, I let go of her hands, balancing myself on one elbow next to her on the bed and bringing my other hand between us to find her small spot, still sweetly swollen. I used my thumb to rub it gently as I pounded into her, filling and retreating.

We were both moaning, Lydia meeting me thrust for thrust, when her body tensed, and she broke from my mouth, sobbing out another orgasm. The feel of her falling apart beneath me—the clenching of her inner muscles—sent me flying over the edge, and I thrust into her one final time, groaning out my own climax as the pleasure swirled through my abdomen, to my cock, and all the way down to my toes. I gasped. "Holy fuck, Lydia, God." I had never come so hard in my life. I circled my hips slowly, trying to draw out every last bit of pleasure.

Finally, I pulled out of her slowly, and Lydia let out a small whimper. I smiled against her neck, feeling amazed and . . . satisfied. The most satisfied I'd ever felt in my entire life. This . . . this was what I'd wanted all along. *Her.* Always her. I rolled off Lydia, pulling her with me, holding on. We were both breathing heavily, Lydia's face pressed to my chest. I suddenly realized there was wetness rolling down my skin and I startled, leaning up to look at her face. "Hey," I said, "what is it?" She tipped her head back and her gaze was watery, her lip trembling as tears rolled down her cheeks.

"I'm so sorry," she whispered, her eyes widening as if she was as perplexed as I was by her tears. "I, I don't know why I'm crying. I just, I . . ." Her words were lost in a small sob, and she buried her face back against my chest. I pulled her tighter, offering her words of comfort. A pressure formed in my heart. Was she already regretful about what we'd done? Had she not wanted this?

"I don't regret what we did," she said as if reading my mind. "I wanted it. *So much.* It was incredible."

I turned so we were facing each other and used my index finger to tip her chin up, looking into her impossibly lovely face, drenched in emotion. I thought I understood, though. "You've been carrying a lot, Lydia. For a long time. You've had so much on your shoulders, and no one to help, no one who really understood." And what we'd just done had broken the dam. "Making love to you was intense for me too." I kissed the tip of her nose. "I feel it too, Mo Chroí."

"You do?" she squeaked.

I nodded, pulling her close. "Let it out, Lydia. Let it go. Let me hold you." *Need me, Lydia.*

She curled up in my arms. And she cried. I continued to utter quiet words to her, mostly in Gaelic, the language I associated with comfort and felt safe to use without considering my words. And so I let them flow freely from my lips.

"Hush, mó ghrá."

Hush, my love.

"Mo aingeal."

My angel.

"Mó shaol."

My life.

Once her sniffles and sobs quieted and her tears seemed to dry, I pulled back, looking down at her. Her eyes were closed and her lips parted slightly, her breathing slow and normal. She was asleep. "Mo Chroí," I whispered, smoothing her hair back before I slipped out from beneath her. She mumbled softly in her sleep and turned over, bringing her knees up. I watched her sleep for a moment before going to the bathroom where I flushed the condom. I stood at the sink for a few moments, holding on to the countertop as I stared at my own reflection in the mirror. I was grappling with so many emotions I hardly knew where to start sorting them out. I was blissfully happy to have made love to Lydia, but I was scared, too, not only of my own powerful feelings, but because of all the things that threatened to steal her from me just when I might have her back.

I let out a deep sigh, turning from the mirror and crossing my arms over my bare chest. I had created an impossible situation, and I was going to try to make it right, but there were so many reasons I might not be able to now. There were so many reasons I might lose Lydia again. I had survived it the first time, but I didn't think I'd survive it again.

I returned to bed where I climbed in and gathered Lydia to me, spooning her from behind. "Brogan," she muttered sleepily, scooting her butt back into my groin. Despite having just made love, my cock twitched against her arse with renewed interest. She let out a small snore and I kissed her shoulder, smiling against her skin.

I'd figure this out. I'd keep her close, and I'd make it right . . . somehow.

CHAPTER FIFTEEN

Lydia

I hummed softly, stretching my body and then turning over, burrowing back into my pillow. With the light in the room already bright, even behind my closed lids, I cracked one eye open as memories of what had happened the night before streamed through my mind. "Oh my God," I breathed, sitting up slightly and then falling back down on my pillow, my eyes wide open now, staring up at the canopy above me.

Brogan was gone, but it must have only been recently that he'd vacated the bed because when I glanced at the pillow he'd slept on, the impression of his head was still there. I smiled at the memory of his arms around me, his feet tangled with mine, something I noticed each time I half woke throughout the night. *I had never had that, but I had loved it. Loved being held. Cocooned.*

When I thought about what had happened before that, I squeezed my legs together, feeling the slight ache where Brogan had been. Butterflies took flight in my belly. Did I feel embarrassed? Regretful? Maybe I should, but I didn't. I only felt deliciously sore and wonderfully satisfied, my limbs like jelly. And I felt . . . peaceful, despite no resolutions to life's problems. In fact, if anything, I'd learned that things were more complex and challenging than I thought they were.

I cringed slightly when I remembered bawling in Brogan's arms, but he'd been right. I'd just been so overwhelmed by the intensity of what we'd done, by all the mind-bending orgasms, all the pent-up emotions, all the long-held worries and problems that finally broke free in a flood of tears. I'd never cried about any of it, and the pressure had been building for years. The power of our lovemaking had finally broken the dam. And I *was* just a little embarrassed about that part, but I also thought it was the main reason I felt so good, *cleansed*. Even stronger somehow.

I swung my feet out of bed, glancing at the clock, my eyes widening when I saw it was almost noon. Walking naked to the bathroom, I brushed my teeth and tried to smooth my hair into some semblance of normalcy. Realizing it was impossible, I turned on the shower and got in, sighing as the hot, pelting water relaxed my muscles even further. After washing my hair and shaving everywhere, a small thrill went through me when I wondered if I'd sleep with Brogan again tonight. *I wanted to. God, I really did.*

But I was also a little nervous about where this left us, and I still had the worry for my brother hanging over my head. The only thing I could hope for was that Brogan was able to buy Stuart some time and that Stuart would see this as a sort of wake-up call to get his life together. I felt relieved that Brogan was willing to do anything to help Stuart at all. I knew he wasn't doing it for Stuart, I knew that. He was doing it for *me* and that filled me with warmth and gratitude. And I'd help Stuart in whatever way I could, too, but if truth be told, maybe Stuart wasn't cut out to be a businessman. I'd never thought he derived much pleasure from it. He'd never seemed to really enjoy the business aspect of De Havilland Enterprises. What he'd enjoyed were the financial benefits—the ones that, eventually, he'd all but made certain would completely dry up.

Perhaps there was something else that would make Stuart happier anyway. In some ways he'd never been given an alternative—it had always just been expected that he'd run the family business when our father passed. I had to wonder now if he'd been given more of a choice, would he have chosen to do something different.

Standing in my bra and panties after having just blow-dried my hair, I heard a knock on my bedroom door and called, "Come in." Brogan came into the bathroom a few seconds later and stopped in the doorway, his eyes roaming my body. My heart lurched and a tingle started between my legs. He was wearing another pair of worn-looking jeans, resting low on his hips, and a white T-shirt with some bar logo on it. He came up behind me and wrapped his arms around my body, leaning down to nuzzle my neck. I bent it to the side to give him more access, shooting him a small smile in the mirror. I let my eyes linger on the way we looked together: him so tall and dark, me blonde and—though I'd never been called short at five seven—so much smaller in comparison. In so many ways we were opposites, and yet, in so many ways, we seemed like the perfect fit. *We always had.*

"How are you this morning, or . . . *afternoon*?" he asked, kissing my ear again and inhaling against my hair. A thrill shot through me. *He didn't seem to be regretful. I needed that. His happiness, too. How many years had I gone without happiness? And when had I stopped noticing?*

I turned, wrapping my arms around his neck as he brought his arms lower on my waist. I tipped my head back to gaze into his face. "Very relaxed," I said. "I guess I needed the sleep . . . among other things. You sure do know how to treat your employees, Mr. Ramsay."

He chuckled. "I suppose you are still my employee, for now. Good thing there're no rules against fraternization at my company."

I raised a brow. "How convenient for you."

"Very," he murmured, bringing his lips to mine. He kissed me slowly once before pulling back. "It's killing me to cut this short, but unfortunately, I have a meeting in the city, and I have to get you all set up at my place there. Another game of war later?" He cocked a dark brow.

I laughed, letting go of his neck and scooting past him. "I thought we made a peace treaty last night."

"Is that what that was?" he asked. I heard something in his voice that caused me to turn, my shirt held to my chest. The look on his face was troubled.

I stared at him for a second. "Isn't that what you want, too?"

"Yes," he said. "More than anything. I just . . ." He ran a hand through his thick, black hair.

I dropped my shirt and walked back over to him. "Brogan, I know we have a lot to work out, and things are up in the air, but," I licked my lips and glanced away for a moment, gathering my thoughts, "I'm hopeful that if we work together, if we're honest with each other, we can figure it all out." *God, how I hoped that was what he wanted, too.*

Relief washed over his face and he let out a breath, kissing my forehead. "Get dressed. Your cream puffs are distracting me. And then meet me downstairs."

I laughed as he winked and left my room.

****

An hour later, I'd packed up, we'd eaten a quick meal, and I'd run over to say goodbye to Eileen. She'd given me a brief hug—she'd been leaving, too, for an afternoon class—and told me she was coming to dinner at Brogan's place in New York that week and we'd catch up then.

A few minutes after that we were in Brogan's car, heading for the city. He'd promised me he'd send employees for my car in the next few days so we didn't have to drive separately.

We chatted easily about mostly mundane things over the forty-five minute drive to the city. As for me, I was relaxed, but also somewhat drained emotionally from the night we'd had. I needed to take a break from the heavy topics of the day before and just sit back and listen to the radio, enjoy the scenery, and engage in easy conversation. Brogan seemed to feel the same way.

It was almost two when we pulled into the underground garage of Brogan's building in Manhattan. He grabbed my bag from the trunk and took my hand as we headed toward the nearby elevator. He keyed in a code and then pushed the button for the top floor, and we rode in silence for a minute.

"Do you split your time between here and Greenwich?" I asked.

"I spend more time here actually. But Eileen prefers Greenwich, and it's closer to school for her. I wanted her to live at the main house there, and I would have taken the guest cottage, but she insisted on having it the way it is."

I nodded, a small pang of envy making me realize how much I wished for the ease and obvious mutual respect in their sibling relationship. I'd never had that with my brother, and I wondered if I ever would. The soft ding of the elevator doors sliding open brought me out of my thoughts, and we stepped into a large, open vestibule. I followed Brogan as he walked to the only door on the floor. *Wow.* There was another keyless entry next to his door and after keying in the code we stepped into his apartment.

I was a girl who'd grown up in luxury. I was no stranger to high living, but this was jaw dropping even for me, *and* I knew, for New York City in general, where even a modest apartment could easily go for several million dollars. My apartment, which was decent enough, was a slum compared to this.

I walked into the large open area, marveling at the tinted floor-to-ceiling windows on three walls, showing off dramatic skyline views. The furniture was classy and urban, a perfect fit for the open concept space. I did note that this place was decorated with a more masculine hand than the house in Greenwich and had a feeling that although Eileen had helped with that house, this place was all Brogan.

I turned to him. "It's gorgeous."

He had been watching me as I walked about, and he seemed pleased with my approval. "Let me show you around."

I followed Brogan as he led me to the kitchen right off the main living space. It was modern and beautifully done in shades of white, black, and dark gray with a bar and three bar stools and the far wall done all in brick. "Nice," I murmured.

He pointed out three closed doors down a small hallway that led to his office, a workout room, and a bathroom and then led me up a set of open black stairs to the second floor.

He seemed to hesitate before he turned right and showed me to a guest room where he placed my bag on the bed. It was a simple space done in shades of pale blue and cream with nothing more than a bed, a dresser and a nightstand, but it featured the same stunning floor-to-ceiling windows and breathtaking city view.

Brogan walked to the window and showed me how to operate the shades that lowered from the ceiling at the touch of a button and then walked back to where I stood. "My bedroom's right across the hall," he said.

I studied him. He looked like he was struggling with something, but I wasn't sure what. Did he want me to ask him if I could stay in his room? Truthfully, I didn't know if I wanted that. And I thought for now, with him wielding all the power, it was best that I didn't. This situation was not going to last forever, but in the meantime, I thought it wise that I keep a certain distance from Brogan—even if that distance was just across the hall.

"Okay," I said.

He nodded curtly and pointed to a door next to the dresser. "Your bathroom's there. If you need anything, just let me know."

"I'll need more clothes. Can I run over to my apartment and grab some more stuff if I'm going to be here for another week or so?"

"I'll have someone run over for you. Go ahead and make a list."

"Is that really necessary? I hardly want some stranger choosing which bra of mine to pack with which outfit."

"Lydia, I don't yet know what's safe and what's not, and I'm not going to take any chances. I've just reached out to the people who hold Stuart's loans, but I haven't heard back. It's a slow process. These are not people you just call up on their personal cell phones. So until I do hear back, I insist you do as I ask—for your own safety and for your brother's as well."

I huffed out a breath. "Fine," I said, crossing my arms. "I'll make a list."

Brogan's lip tipped up in a small smile. "If you want me to go personally, I will. I'd enjoy rifling through your underwear. Plus, one good turn deserves another."

I raised a brow. "I didn't rifle through your underwear. You don't wear any."

He put his arms around my waist and pulled me close. "Are you sure? I think I might. It's difficult to remember. How about we explore the answer to that question later?" He kissed my neck and I laughed.

"Tease," I muttered. He brought his head up and gave me a crooked grin and my heart seemed to stop for a fraction of a second. *God, he had the power to slay me with his grin.*

Stepping away, he laughed softly. "Make yourself comfortable. Call me if you need anything. And text me that list. I'll be home in a couple hours."

Home. I nodded. "Okay. Oh hey," I said, and he turned at the door, "can I use your computer? I need to charge my laptop."

"Help yourself. There's no password."

He left my room and a few minutes later, I heard the front door click shut. I experienced a moment of loneliness as I stood in this strange, quiet apartment. Funny, because I was *used* to being alone, but suddenly, seemingly in less than a couple of days, I was used to Brogan's company. *I wanted Brogan's company.*

I took a few minutes to unpack my bag and set my toiletries in the bathroom, and then I headed downstairs and went into Brogan's office. It seemed pretty stark and unused and I wondered if he actually did any work here or if it was more for personal use. There was a photo on his desk of two kids and I picked it up, looking closely, able to tell immediately it was Brogan and Eileen. It must have been taken in Ireland because Brogan looked like he was about twelve and Eileen looked about eight, her legs in the braces I'd known her to wear when their father had worked for us. My heart clenched at the open, joyful smile on Brogan's face. He'd been happy and untroubled. I wondered if that had been the last time . . .

Replacing the picture where it'd been, I opened his computer, deciding to do a little work since I had the opportunity and now knew for sure I still had a job. I spent the next few hours answering and sending emails, checking in on projects, and doing what work I could remotely. A call to my secretary updated me on everything going on in the office.

"Lydia," Trudi said, lowering her voice in the way I knew she did when she didn't want her phone conversation to be overheard, "we all think the team you brought in is wonderful and, well, Stuart being replaced was probably the best thing that could have happened for the company and hopefully for him as well. We know he was Edward's son and your brother, and I do hate to say it, but he just wasn't cut out to run a business." She sighed. "And it's good you're taking some time away while the team is here."

I'd been taken aback. The word circulating was that all the recent happenings were *my* doing? Perhaps it was only rumor . . . After all, I was the only one left and the other employees didn't know Stuart was, or had been, the sole owner of the company, though he acted as president. *Interesting.* As we spoke, I noted the hopeful excitement in Trudi's voice, and it made me glad to know the company was being taken care of in my absence. Or perhaps more to the point . . . because of my absence.

Brogan's phone rang repeatedly, annoying and distracting me, but I let it go to voicemail. *Who still had a landline anyway?* I had my cell phone sitting on the desk beside me, and if anyone needed to get a hold of me, they would have called that number.

Once I'd finished working, I closed Brogan's computer and went into his kitchen and dug through the refrigerator. It held a small amount of food, but I found a yogurt that hadn't expired and an apple that still looked decent and ate it in his living room in front of a late afternoon talk show.

By the time I'd finished the food I was already bored. Sighing, I cleaned up and went up to my room. Despite doing a whole lot of nothing for the past week, I still wasn't used to being idle, and I definitely wasn't used to feeling like a caged animal.

Picking up my phone, I dialed Stuart's number. Just as it'd done for the past couple of days, it went straight to voicemail. I left him a brief message, telling him I was worried about him and to call me. Just as I was putting my phone down, it chimed with an incoming text.

Brogan: Fionn is bringing dinner by. He has the door codes. I'll be home asap.

Me: Okay. Everything all right?

Brogan: Just held up.

I sighed. *Well, okay.*

An hour later, I heard the beeping of the keypad outside Brogan's door and a second later, Fionn's voice called, "Lydia? It's Fionn."

"Hey," I said as I descended the stairs. Fionn stood in the entranceway. He grinned, holding up several brown paper bags. "Howya? I hope ya like Chinese."

"I do. Thanks." When I got to the bottom, I said, "By the way, it's nice to officially meet you." I shifted awkwardly. "The other day was . . ." I drifted off, not knowing exactly how to finish that thought.

Fionn laughed. "The other day was gas. It's not often I see Brogan snookered. I knew then we'd be mates." He winked and I let out a confused laugh. I followed him into the kitchen where he set the bags on the counter.

"What does snookered mean exactly?" I asked. Fionn paused in unloading the food from the bags.

"Em, it's a heavy defeat." He grinned and I laughed.

"Ah. And you're happy your friend was defeated?"

"Lydia, there's not a thing in this world I wouldn't do for Brogan, but I told him he was gona make a bags of this whole situation if he insisted on doin' things the way he thought he needed to, and so some defeats are victories in disguise. I like to think that party was one of them. Maybe even for the both of ya, shur ya know like." He winked again.

"Okay, um, make a bags . . ."

Fionn leaned against the counter. "Ya want a lesson in Irish slang, Lydia?" he asked, laughing again. I loved the way he said my name, the same way Brogan said it when his accent emerged: faster than those with American accents, and with an emphasis on the *a*.

"Yes," I said. "Can you stay for dinner? I'd love it if you would."

"Well, that's the best offer I've had in donkey's years." He glanced at me as he started unpacking a bag. "That means a long time."

Grinning, I grabbed dishes, napkins, and silverware and took them to the small table next to the kitchen. Fionn carried over the numerous cartons of food and retrieved a bottle of wine from the wine fridge at the end of the island.

He opened it and brought that over with two wine glasses. Pouring, he said, "Okay, the first thing ya gotta know is how to greet someone. Ya ask, what's the craic? It means, what's up, what's the news?"

I remembered Rory had asked me that at Brogan's office what seemed like a hundred years ago. "What's the craic?" I nodded. "Okay. What about the shur ya know like phrase?"

"Em." He nodded to the cartons, indicating I should start, and I grabbed one with some kind of noodles in it and started dishing it onto my plate. "That's just a sayin' like ya might put 'ya know' on the end of a sentence."

"Got it."

We ate dinner, talking and laughing, Fionn teaching me enough slang to get me started and educating me on some sayings.

Saying, "Relax the cacks," meant "Calm down." "I'm as sick as a small hospital today," meant "I'm feeling rather ill," and was usually used after a heavy night of drinking. The question, "Do you fancy a few scoops?" meant, "Would you be interested in an alcoholic beverage?" scoops pertaining to *pints* in particular. "Her face looks like the back of a bus," referred to a very unfortunate-looking person, as did a woman with "a body from Baywatch, and a face from Crimewatch."

I had to believe Fionn made up some of the phrases himself as they were too outrageous. But by the time we were done eating, we'd finished off the bottle of wine, and I was laughing me cacks off, which meant laughing my pants off. I didn't remember ever laughing so hard, and my cheek muscles hurt.

The keypad beeped and Brogan came through the door. "What's the craic?" I called out, raising my empty glass of wine.

Brogan closed the door, an amused look on his face as he walked toward us. "I see there's a party going on without me."

I smiled at Fionn, but when I looked more closely at Brogan, he looked worn and tired. "You okay?" I asked. "Are you hungry?"

"Yeah." He sat down and grabbed a container, taking my fork and eating straight from the takeout box.

"Should I open another bottle of wine?" Fionn asked.

"Definitely," I said. Fionn stood up to grab a bottle.

"Did everything go all right today?" I asked Brogan. "Any news on my brother?"

"I'm negotiating with them. I don't have a definite answer yet." His gaze skittered away from mine, and I wondered if there was something he wasn't telling me.

"Oh," I chewed at my lip, "okay. Do you think—?" I was interrupted by the ringing of the doorbell.

Brogan's brow furrowed, and he set the container of food down. Whoever it was downstairs rang again. "Jaysus," Brogan muttered as he stood up and walked to the monitor near his door. He opened the cover and looked at the camera, seeming to still. I heard him utter another curse, his shoulders moving up as if taking a fortifying breath. He pressed the button, and a woman's hysterical voice came over the speaker.

"Brogan, let me up!" It sounded as if she was crying.

"Be the Lord Jaysus," I heard Fionn mutter. I looked over at him in confusion, and his face was tense. He glanced at me and there was none of the amused laughter that had been there only moments ago.

"Courtney, this isn't a good time," Brogan spoke into the monitor. "I'll call you."

"He's getting *out*," she screeched. "Oh my God, Brogan, I've been calling you for *days,* and you haven't answered. Let me *up*!" Brogan leaned his head against the monitor. I watched him, nervous dread moving through my stomach. Who was she?

He turned toward me, our eyes meeting across the expanse of the room. "I'm sorry, Lydia," he said softly before he pressed the button, allowing access to the screaming woman on the street below.

I felt my face blanch, but I blinked, trying to gather myself. I'd just been happily sipping wine and laughing, and now something I didn’t understand was about to happen and apparently it wasn't good.

Brogan looked at Fionn. "Will you—?"

"You don't have to do this, Brogan," Fionn said quietly. They traded a few quick, tense lines in Gaelic, the language flying by me so quickly I couldn't even attempt to grasp a word. But then Fionn sighed and nodded. "Yeah."

Brogan turned as the pounding on his door began and opened it. A brunette woman—I *thought* it was the woman from the first garden party I'd seen him at in Greenwich—rushed into his apartment and threw herself at him.

"What's happened, Courtney?" he asked.

She sucked in a huge sob, gathering herself and standing straight. "He got parole."

"Parole?" Brogan sounded confused. "They said—"

"I know what they said!" she yelled. "They changed their minds. I don't know! All I know is he's getting out next month. Oh Brogan, I need you. Hold me. I just . . ." she sobbed again. "I need you to hold me." She threw herself into his arms again and he let her, wrapping his arms around her. My stomach dropped. Not knowing what to do, I stood on shaky legs, my buzz suddenly gone, and took my dish to the counter.

My movement must have registered with her—*Courtney*—because she straightened up, pulling away from Brogan and looking around him to me. "Who's she?" she demanded. I blinked, flushing under her disdainful scrutiny.

Brogan turned and his face was ashen, full of regret and . . . fear? "Courtney, Lydia." He extended his head toward me, not offering either of us more of an explanation about the roles we played in his life. What *should* he say? "Courtney, this is Lydia, the woman whose life I set out to ruin and ultimately gave three mind-bending orgasms to last evening." A hysterical laugh rose in my throat, and I coughed to disguise the small sound that managed to escape. Maybe I was still more buzzed than I thought.

Courtney narrowed her eyes, and I saw that though she was beautiful, she was perhaps a few years older than Brogan and me. Her gaze moved to Fionn, and back to me, presumably coming to the false conclusion that I was with Fionn. "Fionn," she said, her voice cold.

Fionn's laughing demeanor was gone as he nodded back at Courtney.

Courtney turned back to Brogan, her face crumpling. "Take me upstairs, Brogan, please, darling." *Darling?* Brogan put his hand on the small of her back and led her toward the stairs, not glancing back once. What the *hell?* Jealousy and disbelief assaulted me. He was taking her upstairs to his bedroom to *hold her*? After what we'd done last night? I looked at Fionn and his lips were thinned, his eyes sympathetic. He let out what sounded like an annoyed breath and shook his head, placing his hands on his hips.

"Who is she?" I asked in a loud whisper. Upstairs, I heard the door to Brogan's bedroom close and felt vomit move up my throat. Had that just really happened? *Should* I be as hurt as I felt? He hadn't made any promises to me and yet . . .

"He'll have to tell ya that. I'm bloody sorry." He shook his head. "I do think it's time ya and I got bolloxed and moved on to the epitaph portion of our Irish slang lesson."

I blinked at him, feeling sick and confused and angry. I needed to get out of here. "I'm leaving."

Fionn nodded. "I can't let ya do that, Lydia. It's not safe for ya to be goin' anywhere, especially not before Brogan's had a chance to fix the mess with your brother."

I glanced up the stairs. Surely after Brogan calmed that hysterical woman down, he'd be back to explain things to me? Or was this another part of his revenge? My stomach twisted. Had he *planned* this like his other dates had been planned, at least in part, to upset me? No, no, we were past that. *Right?* Plus, the look on his face had been one of discomfort and remorse. Or maybe that was all an act. Had last night been an act, too? Oh God, these thoughts were causing my head to ache.

I held my glass toward Fionn. "Fill me up, Fionn. All the way to the bloody top."

CHAPTER SIXTEEN

Lydia

I felt myself being lifted and let out a garbled resistance. "Quiet, Lydia, you're drunk. I'm putting you to bed," came Brogan's voice.

"I'm plastered," I amended, cracking one eye opened. "And you're a tool. A *quare* tool. And a wanker."

"I know I am," he agreed as the room spun. I groaned. "Goddamn Fionn," he muttered.

"I love Fionn," I said. I thought I felt Brogan's body tense, but I was too drunk to care. I did love Fionn. Fionn and his wine. I loved Fionn's wine. "And Fionn loves me," I asserted.

"Fionn loves everyone." *Not Courtney. And seriously, if Fionn didn't like someone, they must be a bitch. A scanger.*

"And you're a tool," I said, trying to organize what I was saying out loud and what I was saying in my own head. "And a wanker. Fionn helped write me off the map." I hiccupped. "You know what that means, wanker?"

"Yes, Lydia, I do."

He paused at the top of the stairs as if trying to decide which room to turn toward. "Don't you dare take me in your room, you tool," I slurred. "You still smell like her." He did, and it was making me sick. It was a strong, spicy perfume that made my head spin more than it already was. I could only imagine what it was doing to Brogan. And yet, he'd been the one letting her rub all over him. That same smell was probably all over his sheets, too. And who cared? Who cared about Brogan? He was a tool. And a wanker. A feckin' manky prick.

"I know I do," he said, letting out a tired sigh, as he turned toward my room. He placed me gently on the bed, and I opened my eyes, staring up at him. His face was in shadow and set in a grimace as if *he* was currently feeling tortured. But that's what he had done to me earlier. And it'd hurt so much I'd drunk two bottles of wine. And yet it still hurt, only in a fuzzy, bleary way that was better than the sharp pain that had sliced through me watching him walk up the stairs to his bedroom with *that* woman.

"You hate me," I said. "You want to hurt me and hurt me and hurt me."

He shook his head. "No, God, Lydia, no. But I have, and I'm sorry. I'm so sorry." Finally the apology I'd been waiting for, and it only brought more hazy hurt. I turned away from him, onto my side and let my eyes fall closed. My head was spinning and I was so tired. I just needed to sleep.

A minute later I heard the quiet click of my door being shut, and a second after that I drifted back into a dreamless sleep.

****

I woke up feeling like hell. Groaning, I opened my heavy lids and looked around, trying to get my bearings. Memories of the night before came flooding back, and I groaned again, louder this time. I sat up, massaging my temples and squinting against the small amount of muted sunlight showing through the closed blinds.

Stumbling to the bathroom I brushed my teeth thoroughly and dared a glance in the mirror. I looked scary: mascara smeared on my cheeks, my eyes red, and my face puffy. My hair was sticking out in every direction.

That's when I noticed the note on the counter along with a bottle of water and two Tylenol. I picked up the note.

Lydia,

These will make you feel better. I'll be home early so we can talk. Please give me a chance to explain.

Brogan (the tool . . . wanker, etc.)

How dare he joke with me? I crumpled it up and hurled it toward the small garbage can next to the sink but missed and stood staring at it bleakly where it landed on the floor. Why that depressed me so much, I wasn't sure. Maybe I just couldn't handle one more failure right now, even a very small, insignificant one. I left the stupid note on the floor and threw back both Tylenol tablets and drank the water.

After a long, hot shower, blowing my hair dry, and putting on some makeup, I felt and looked a little better. I threw on a pair of jean shorts and a loose, blue and white striped V-neck T-shirt and went downstairs. The apartment was empty. I stood at the island and drank a glass of tomato juice—not my favorite but all Brogan had as far as juice in his refrigerator—and forced myself to eat a piece of dry toast.

Fresh anger gripped me when I noticed the unwashed wine glasses next to the sink. I was not staying in Brogan's apartment today waiting for him like some faithful, mistreated puppy dog. Perhaps he hadn't made any promises to me, but I deserved more care than what had happened last night. He didn't even have enough respect to stay home this morning and offer me an explanation as soon as I'd woken up. Instead, I was supposed to spend the day bored out of my mind, waiting for him to grace me with his presence and his sorry explanation? *No way.*

We're even now, I'd said. Only perhaps in his mind, we weren't. Not yet. Perhaps I was a fool for thinking so.

You can try to dish out more, but I'll fight you from here on out if you do. Just so you're aware. A fool, maybe, but that's what I'd told him and that's what I'd meant.

I threw my clothes back in my bag, grabbed my purse, and let myself out the door of his apartment into the small, private lobby.

I pushed the down button for the elevator and waited impatiently for it to arrive. Once it did, I jumped in and stood in the corner against the wall as it made its way down. Lost in my own head as I stepped out, I nearly missed the burly looking man in a black suit standing by the outside doorway. *Surely not.* Through the glass, I could see that he was smoking and chatting with a woman who had been walking past with her dog. They were laughing as the dog yapped and the woman tossed her hair, flirting. Stepping back inside the elevator and pushing the close door button, I bit at my thumbnail. I didn't know if the man was someone hired by Brogan or not, but I wasn't going to risk it. Not like he could detain me—I wasn't a prisoner. But I didn't want to deal with being held up. Since Brogan lived in a building without a doorman, I hadn't considered that I wouldn't be able to simply walk out the front door without being noticed. I rode to the garage level and stepped off cautiously, hoping that if Brogan *had* put security on the building, it had been for those arriving, not those leaving. I remembered that you needed a security code to get in this elevator.

I weaved through the cars instead of walking along the ramp and exited out a side door. Looking both ways, I hurried across the street and only then let out a breath, feeling both a sense of accomplishment and still that unpleasant pit in my stomach.

I hailed a cab a couple blocks from Brogan's building and gave the driver my brother's address. Ten minutes later we pulled up in front of Stuart's building.

While I had apartment hunted in questionable neighborhoods to save on rent, Stuart was living in the Meatpacking District, one of the most expensive neighborhoods in the city. As I exited the cab, tipping the driver and thanking him, I gazed up at the sleek, glass luxury building, feeling a wave of resentment wash over me. Men, wankers and tools, all of them! The anger fortified me and I stiffened my spine as I breezed past Stuart's doorman.

The concierge dialed Stuart's number and after several tense seconds where I thought Stuart wouldn't answer, I heard his voice come through the line and the concierge announced me and then nodded toward the elevator bank. When I arrived at Stuart's floor, he was standing in the doorway of his apartment waiting for me, shirtless, his jeans unbuttoned.

"Christ, Lydia, you should have called and told me you were coming over." His voice was slightly slurred and rough. Had he still been sleeping? Or perhaps drinking before noon? *Excellent.*

"Nice to see you, too, Stuart. I'm fine, thanks," I said, brushing past him into his apartment, putting my bag down near his couch. His apartment smelled like dirty dishes and funk and looked as if he hadn't cleaned it in weeks. Or as if he'd just had a massive rager here. There were liquor bottles and half-full food cartons littering his coffee table, and two lamps were overturned.

I turned toward him as he shut the door. "Do you have a shirt you could put on?"

He sighed, but grabbed what looked like a dirty garment off the couch, sniffing it before pulling it over his head. "How are you?" he asked.

"I'm fine I guess. I've been calling you."

He looked at me blearily for a moment, his eyes red and bloodshot, before he ran a hand through his hair and headed for the small kitchen to the right of his living room. I followed. "I know. I was told not to have any contact with you." He held up a bottle of water.

"Sure," I muttered, taking it and drinking a big sip before replacing the cap. I needed to hydrate. I still didn't feel one hundred percent. "Told by whom?" I asked.

"Brogan Ramsay." His facial muscles ticked as if in response to uttering the name of Lucifer himself.

I paused, frowning slightly. "I didn't think that pertained to the phone."

He shrugged and took a drink from his own water bottle. "How did he treat you in Connecticut?"

I frowned. Apparently Stuart wasn't overly concerned about me in any capacity. He was at home, not calling me, having a drunken pity party instead of concerning himself with my welfare. "Fine. He's trying to protect me, Stuart. Protect me from the men you owe money to now." I couldn't keep the tremor of anger from my voice.

He exhaled a big breath, leaning on the counter, fidgeting slightly before crossing his arms as if to force his body to still. "This is all his doing, you know."

I shook my head. "You can't blame him for your own foolish choices, Stuart—"

"You think me losing was an accident?" he gritted out. "*Either* time? They set that up, too, Brogan and that other Irish fucker. The blond one."

I shook my head. *Fionn?* Fionn wasn't any part of this. *Was he?* "They didn't hold a gun to your head and force you to gamble!"

"Not the first time, but they *did* guarantee I'd lose. You remember how good Brogan was with numbers. I bet anything he was counting cards, the motherfucker. And what was I supposed to do after that? I'm ruined. And so yeah, I gambled again. What other possible way did I have of earning any money? Was I not supposed to try anything I could? Was I not supposed to take every chance I had available to try to win our father's company back?"

I rubbed my temples. Hadn't that been the reason I'd given myself? Work for Brogan and beg him for our company back? That I wouldn't allow the regret of not trying anything and everything I could, even if it meant risking my pride?

And yet, after hearing the hope and excitement in Trudi's voice yesterday about the results the team Brogan had brought in were achieving, I was questioning what I had once fought so hard for. Despite my current feelings for Brogan Ramsay, what if . . . what if what was best for De Havilland Enterprises—what would *actually* keep my father's dream alive—was for Brogan to run it? *God, I couldn't think clearly.* The wine from the night before was still muddling my thoughts.

Stuart rattled on. "They're orchestrating my entire downfall, and now they're trying to make it look like they're going to help me. But they're not. Mark my words. This is just another part of the overall scheme," Stuart spat out, twitching again. "They won't be happy until I'm dead in the ground."

God, he was paranoid. How had he deteriorated so quickly? "They don't want you dead, Stuart. You're lucky they're trying to help you out of the mess you yourself created."

"Oh really, Lydia? I'm supposed to be *thankful? I* created this mess? Brogan Ramsay created this mess. We'd be at our desks right now at our family company if not for Brogan Ramsay."

I sighed. Brogan Ramsay *had* created this mess. *Originally.* Not that things were fine and dandy even before he'd come along. My feelings for him, and this situation, were all warped and confused. But regardless, Stuart had made things worse. Stuart had created a situation that not only ended in his financial ruin, but perhaps his very life. *And mine.* Regardless of what Stuart thought, Brogan was not behind *that. Right?*

"You shouldn't be here," Stuart said flatly.

I pulled out a bar stool and sat down. "I know. But I had to talk to you, to check on you. You're my brother. I worry about you." *Take care of your brother, Lydie.*

His face seemed to soften, a look of sadness passing over his expression. "I worry about you, too, Lydia. God, I'm such a failure. I'm so sorry." His voice was hoarse as if tears were lodged in his throat.

I remembered a time when I'd heard that same tone in his voice. Stuart had been about twelve, and he'd come home with an art project he'd done that received an honorable mention in a school art fair. His eyes had shone with happiness. I'd gushed over it. It had been *good.* It was a portrait of our house, the sprawling lawn, horses grazing in the pastures beyond. He'd looked so proud as he showed it to my father. My father had taken a brief glance at it, grunted noncommittally, and then said, "You need to focus on things that matter, son. Scribbling on paper isn't going to earn you any money in the future."

My brother had agreed, but he'd looked crushed and to my knowledge he'd never drawn again. My heart gave a lurch of sympathy. Sometimes I felt like Stuart had never grown up. He was still that twelve-year-old boy who would always be a failure in his father's eyes. But I couldn't be his babysitter *forever*. It was killing me. Even before all of this—even before Stuart had lost our company in a poker game—it had been killing me. I could admit that now.

I took a deep breath. "This is going to be okay. *Somehow*. What's done is done, and we both need to take responsibility for our parts in this mess. And maybe something good can come from it. But in the meantime, you have to clean yourself up. Debt or not, mob or not, you're going to have to come up with a plan for your life once this is all figured out."

He nodded, pressing his lips together. I didn't miss the expression of hatred that quickly passed over his face—hatred aimed at Brogan I could only assume. I paused before saying, "Hey, Stu, can I ask you a question? Brogan told me you found him in the Bronx all those years ago. That when I asked you to find him, you did. Only, you never told me. *Why?*" I couldn't help the hurt in my voice.

Stuart looked confused for a moment, but then his expression cleared, understanding coming into his eyes. "Yeah, I did. So what?"

I frowned and tilted my head. "You *knew* how important it was to *me* to find him. I was *pregnant*, Stu, was carrying his baby. Why? Why did you keep his whereabouts from me? And why didn't you tell him I was trying to find him?"

He let out an impatient breath. "You were better off without him, Lydia. I took one step into that hellhole they were living in and I couldn't . . . I couldn't allow him to be a part of your life. *Our* life. You would have never been free of him."

I grimaced at the coldness in his tone. "That wasn't for you to decide," I said, the injustice of what he'd done to me crashing down on my shoulders.

"I was protecting you! And him as a matter of fact. Though I'm sure that selfish bastard wouldn't see it that way. He could barely afford to feed his little sister. There were bugs and . . . mold growing on the walls, Lydia. *Mold!*" He screwed up his face in disgust. "How was he going to take care of a *baby* when he could barely take care of himself?"

Anguish gripped me as I pictured Brogan and Eileen in a place like that. I shook my head. "Our father would have given him a job. Our father would have helped them. You *know* he would have. You know it now and you knew it then." And that was the real reason he had remained quiet about Brogan's whereabouts. *Oh God. Stuart, how could you?*

"It's in the past anyway," he muttered, having the grace to look partially ashamed. "If I could change it I would, Lydia, I swear to you, but I can't."

I stared at him, trying to hate him for what he'd done to me, to Brogan, but only able to muster up a numb sense of pity. And it *wasn't* in the past. Surely even Stuart could see that it was anything but in the past. His current situation should be proof enough of that. *Our current situation.*

"You should get home," he said. "It's better that you're not here. I think they're watching my building. I've seen strange cars pass by out the window." He glanced to the large expanse of glass, and back to me, a twitch in his shoulder making it jump slightly. Was he paranoid or was he really being watched? "Your place is safer."

"Maybe. I'm not sure. I was staying at Brogan's apartment here in the city until this morning."

He looked shocked. "What the *fuck*?" he practically yelled. "I thought that was over. Lydia, he better not—"

"It's not like that," I lied. "He just thought it was safer there."

"That's a load of shit. It's part of his plan. He wants to turn the last person on earth who's in my corner against me. And then he'll ruin you, too. You have to see that! You have to see that he's not done with us."

"I—"

"Stuart?" a female voice called. I looked back to see a woman with bleached blonde hair wearing what looked like one of Stuart's button-up shirts and nothing else walking toward us from his bedroom. I turned toward Stuart and raised a brow. *Seriously?*

"I have to *eat*," he defended. "I can't even leave my apartment. How am I supposed to get food?" He must have forgotten about all the options for grocery and food delivery in New York City. Although apparently *his* "food delivery service" also included plenty of liquor, possibly drugs—though I had no idea how Stuart was paying for them—*and* sexual favors. I might throw up.

The woman nestled into Stuart, and he wrapped an arm around her. "Who's she, Stu?" she asked, shooting me a flirty smile. *Really?*

"I'm Lydia," I said, "Stuart's *sister*. Nice to meet you."

"Oh hi, I'm Jewel." She looked up at Stuart. "You coming back to bed, baby?" *Well, that was my cue.*

I stood up from the bar seat. "I've gotta go."

Stuart detached Jewel from his side and met me as I headed toward the front door, picking up my bag. "You sure you're okay?"

"Yeah, I will be."

"Stay away from Brogan Ramsay, Lydia. I swear you're safer away from him. There's something not right about this whole situation, and he's behind every bit of it."

"All right, Stuart," I said, because frankly, I *intended* to stay away from Brogan Ramsay. "Things are going to be okay," I murmured, though I was beginning to sincerely doubt that was the case. He nodded at me and let me out.

As I rode the elevator downstairs, I leaned against the wall, considering the current situation. Yesterday, I had thought I knew Brogan, understood him, and today . . . I realized I didn't know him at all. I knew nothing about his life. He'd been evasive about his business, there were women who just popped out of the woodwork—that made three I'd seen him with now—and apparently at least one had some sort of hold on him. And as for his feelings for me . . . would I ever know for sure *how* he felt? A wave of despair washed over me. I had hoped . . . what had I hoped? I chewed at my lip, considering that question. I had hoped Brogan and I were moving back toward where we'd been so long ago. Yes, I could admit that now. But that was impossible. We'd been innocent teens then. And now, we had so much baggage, so many obstacles between us. And what hurt the most of all was that for a brief moment, I had believed it possible anyway. Despite *everything,* I had believed.

My heart heavy, my mind troubled, my travel bag suddenly seeming to weigh twice as much as it did before, I stepped out onto the street and debated which way to turn. The truth was, I wasn't sure where to go. I'd been warned away from living at my own apartment, but other than that or Brogan's place—which I refused to return to right now—I didn't really have anywhere else to go.

Trying to move that depressing thought aside, I stood for several minutes debating before taking my phone out of my purse. I had several missed calls from Brogan, but decided not to answer him right away. Instead, I dialed Daisy's number.

"Lydia Loo," she answered in a sing-song voice. I smiled despite my pitiful current circumstances.

"Hey Dais." I stepped around an older couple walking hand in hand along the sidewalk. "What are you doing?"

"Shopping for an outfit. Will you be at the Christenson's Fourth of July party?"

"Um, no. I don't think so. Daisy, I need to catch you up on," I moved to the far side of the sidewalk as a large man with white-blond hair came walking straight toward me, not looking like he was going to change course before we collided, "some stuff that's been going on." I continued to veer right and the man did the same, clipping me slightly as we passed each other. I gasped as I felt something sharp poke my side, letting go of my bag. The asshole had been holding something sharp.

Had it dug into my side as he passed?

"Lydia?" I heard Daisy say. "Hello? Are you still there?"

I turned to glare at the man and he leaned in to me, hissing in my ear, "Remind your brother what happens when we don't get our debts repaid."

My blood ran cold as I fell toward him. He held on to my upper arms for mere moments before he let go and disappeared into a group of people walking by in the opposite direction. I lurched forward, my hand going to the spot on my side that had been struck with whatever he'd been carrying.

"Damn crap connection," I heard Daisy saying from the phone still clutched in my hand. "If you can hear me, I'll call you later," Daisy said loudly. I dropped the phone on the ground, the screen shattering.

As I tripped and fell to my knees, someone off to my left gasped. I brought my hand from my side to my face. It was bright red with blood.

I'd been stabbed? Oh my God, I'd been stabbed!

CHAPTER SEVENTEEN

Brogan

My heart lurched in my chest as I pulled over across the street from Stuart De Havilland's apartment. It was the only place I could imagine she would go. I'd arrived home, and she'd been gone. I couldn't exactly blame her, but I'd still felt my stomach drop with sudden, icy fear.

I'd rushed downstairs and jumped in my car, driving the ten minutes to Stuart's apartment, my heart racing as I banged on the steering wheel and blared my horn at people going too bloody *fecking* slow.

I pulled my car into a no parking zone, and jumped out, starting across the busy street. She had to be here. Where else would she go? *Feck me.* I needed to fix this, but first, I needed to find her and make sure she was safe.

Relief pounded through my blood when I spotted Lydia exiting Stuart's building. *Thank God. Thank God.* I increased my pace, pounding my fist on the hood of a BMW that blared its horn at me.

As I started across the flow of traffic on the other side of the center median, I saw a man walk quickly past Lydia, grab her upper arms and move on. Something about the movement seemed strange, but before I could think too much about it, Lydia turned in the direction the man had continued walking. *Oh shite. No.* Clutching her side, she stumbled forward, falling to her knees.

"Lydia!" I yelled, breaking into a sprint. The sharp sound of squealing brakes barely penetrated the fog of panic I felt. "Lydia!"

I made it to her at the same moment an older gentleman was stooping to help her up. "Miss, are you okay—"

"Lydia," I rasped, pushing the man aside.

"I was just trying to help," he muttered from somewhere seemingly far away and then obviously moving on.

"Brogan?" Lydia said, confused and pale.

I pulled her to her feet. "Can you stand?" I asked, my voice shaking.

Had the man knocked her over on purpose? She weaved toward me, her hand again going to her side, a look of startled confusion on her face. I looked down to her waist and saw the bright red stain coming through the fabric of her striped shirt. *Oh Lydia, Lydia.* Oh *feck.*

My breath came out in wild pants as I walked her across the sidewalk to stand under the awning of a closed service entrance to Stuart's building.

I looked quickly back in the direction the blond man had gone, but didn't see a trace of him. *Fedor Ivanenko.* The unusual height . . . the white-blond hair . . . it had to be. I wanted to roar with rage and helplessness. I wanted to sprint after him and pound his face into the concrete. But if I was right about who that'd been, he would be long gone by now. The mob didn't hire hit men who didn't know how to make a quick getaway.

I moved Lydia until she was leaning against the inside wall of the entryway and inched the fabric of her shirt up, my hands shaking. I used the hem of her shirt to clean away the blood in order to assess the wound, my heart beating out of my chest. When I'd cleared some of it away, I saw it was mostly a flesh wound, deep enough to need stitches, but not deep enough to cause real injury. "Thank God," I breathed. "Thank God. Are ya okay?"

"I, I think so," she said. "I was just walking down the street and . . ."

"I know. Did the man who did this say anythin' to ya?"

She bit her lip as I continued to apply pressure to the wound with the bunched up material of her shirt. "He said . . . he said, something about reminding my brother about what happens to people who don't repay their debts." Her eyes met mine, wide and full of fear. "Oh God, Brogan, he was one of the men Stuart owes money to. I thought you said you were working with them and that—"

"Motherfuckers!" I swore, dropping my hands and leaning back against the opposite wall. "We need to get out of here. Can you walk?" I guided her hand to where I had been using mine to apply pressure to her wound.

"Yes. But wait, what about Stuart? He might be—"

"Fuck Stuart!" I started to pull her.

"No!"

I attempted a calming breath. Was she really going to dig her heels in now? "Lydia, you're bleeding. I need to get you safe and get you bandaged. Stuart is fine. This was a warning for him already set in motion. I talked to the men holding his loans this morning and we're almost done negotiating a deal." What I didn't say was that after this, it was done. I'd agree to anything. The warning meant to convince me had worked in just the way they'd planned. I glanced down to the blood-soaked material where Lydia held her hand as I worked to control my breathing. "Now please," I said, more gently, "come with me."

"You really almost have a deal worked out?"

"Yes."

She hesitated briefly before allowing me to lead her from the doorway. "Wait, my bag, my phone . . ." she uttered, pointing to where they both still lay near the curb. The fact that she'd brought all her belongings gutted me. *She'd meant to leave. Permanently.*

I led her there quickly and picked both up, noticing that the screen of her phone was shattered. Once we were across the street in the safety of my car, I reached behind me into a gym bag on the floor of the backseat and retrieved a small towel. "Here," I said, handing it to her, "this is thicker than your shirt. Apply it to your wound." My hands trembled as I wiped them on my pants so they wouldn't be slippery with blood and then started my car, pulling out into traffic. *Needed to get her back to my apartment. Needed to make sure she was safe.*

I glanced over at Lydia who was leaning back in the seat, her face pale, her hand pressed to her side. *This was my fault.* Christ Almighty, *enough.* I wanted to scream and break things. I bloody hated myself for this. And Lydia would too, if she didn't already. Clenching my jaw, I forced myself to focus on just getting us home.

As I drove, I made a quick call to Fionn, explaining the situation and telling him to send Margaret to my apartment. He didn't ask questions, just took directions, said he'd handle it and hung up. My shoulders relaxed slightly.

Ten minutes later I pulled into the underground garage, and five minutes after that, I was leading Lydia through my apartment door. I guided her immediately to the bathroom in her bedroom and had her sit on the edge of the tub. Digging in the cabinet under the sink, I found the first aid kit and returned to Lydia. "I need you to take off your shirt," I said. She hesitated, but lifted it over her head. The cut on her side was bright red and stood out in stark contrast to her creamy skin. And it sent the message loud and clear: *you are not safe, not anywhere, even on a crowded street. We own Stuart De Havilland, and now, we own you and those you care about.* I knew how these men operated. I'd worked for them. "Does it hurt?" I asked, my voice hoarse with the rage I was barely holding back.

"Not much," she said softly, but she took in a sharp breath when I dabbed rubbing alcohol on it.

"I'm going to kill those bastards," I muttered under my breath, rubbing antibiotic ointment on her skin. She let out a tired-sounding sigh.

"Are you really helping Stuart? Do you promise you are?"

I glanced up at her as I laid a piece of bandage on the cut and lifted her hand to apply pressure to it the way I had before. "I gave you my word I was, Lydia. I talked to them this morning. It's why I left before you woke up." I thinned my lips, not wanting to think about the bargain I'd been hesitating to make.

Her eyes moved over my face as if she was trying to determine whether I was telling her the truth or not. "I shouldn't have left. I just . . ."

"I understand," I said. We needed to talk. As I was opening my mouth to say so, the buzzer sounded from the street. "That's a nurse to stitch you up."

She frowned. "Do you really think that's necessary? It's so small and it doesn't seem too deep . . ."

"Aye." I didn't want her to have a scar, a reminder of the way in which I'd failed her. "Just a few. When it heals, you won't even know it was there."

"Oh, well, okay. If you think so."

"I do." I turned at the doorway. "I can bring you some lunch when it's done."

She nodded. "That sounds good." My eyes lingered on her face for a moment. She looked tired—likely from getting wasted the night before—but she also looked weary as if the events of last night and today were weighing heavily on her mind. *Feck.* Just when I'd erased that look from her eyes, it was back again. Because of her fuckwit brother, but also because of *me.*

I hurried down the stairs and rang Margaret in and then waited by the open door. She stepped out of the elevator with a small bag in her hand. "What did ya do now, Brogan Ramsay?"

I couldn't help smiling at the sight of Margaret's warm, open smile. She had provided nursing care for Fionn or me more times than I could count, whether it was back in the days when we ourselves got in fights we couldn't avoid on the streets, or whether she answered our call to help someone else who didn't want to make a trip to the hospital for one reason or another. She was good and kind and didn't force answers we didn't want to give.

"My friend got attacked in the street—a knife. She needs a few stitches."

"Aye, so Fionn said. Do ya know who attacked her?"

"Aye."

She studied me for a moment. "All right, well, where is the girl then?"

"She's upstairs in the guest room on the right." I walked her to the stairs and as she ascended, I said, "Thanks, Margaret." She nodded, not looking back.

When she'd disappeared around the corner, I took my phone from my pocket and texted the men I'd met with that morning.

You have a deal. I want your word that no harm will come to Lydia De Havilland ever again.

I paced in a small circle at the base of my stairs until my phone dinged a few minutes later with one simple word.

Deal.

A knock sounded on the door, interrupting me from my murderous thoughts. Fionn. "You could have let yourself in," I said.

He shook his head. "I didn't want to disturb anythin'—like maybe Lydia in the act of cuttin' off your ballsack."

"Funny," I muttered, knowing I probably deserved it.

"How is she?" he asked, his smile disappearing.

"She's fine. Just shaken, I think. Fuck me straight to hell, Fionn, they knifed her right in the bloody street. They could have killed her if they'd wanted to, and no one would have been able to stop it." Fionn winced slightly, taking a seat on my couch. I sat down across from him, leaning my head back for a moment, letting out a long exhale, trying to relax. I'd been tense for two days it seemed. "I let them know they have a deal."

Fionn leaned forward, resting his forearms on his knees. "It was a warnin', Brogan. But they'll call 'em off now that you've made a deal.

She's safe."

"Yeah." I sat up straight. Fionn was regarding me. "I fucked up," I admitted.

"Yeah, ya did. Ya made a bloody balls out of everythin'. Now ya gona make it right."

"I'm trying. God, I'm trying."

"That's the shot." Fionn smiled. "Who's got ya back?"

I smiled despite myself. He always had. "Thanks, mo chara."

"It's gona be all right. You've done this kind of work before. I know ya don't want to, but, it's not a bad thing to stay on the right side of the mob." He shrugged.

"Yeah," I said, not wanting to get into the reasons I'd been hoping they'd take a cash deal instead of bargaining with my talent for numbers. I'd even offered to pay double what Stuart owed them, and they'd turned me down.

"Now what are ya gona do about Courtney?" Fionn asked, probably as much to turn my mind from the deal I'd made with the mob.

I sighed again. "Manage her as usual."

Fionn shook his head. "Ya need to tell her to feck off. She's manipulatin' ya."

I wasn't stupid. I knew she was. I just wasn't sure what to do about it. Because she was also legitimately scared. Due in large part to what I'd done all those years ago—or more to the point, what I *hadn't* done.

"And now," Fionn continued, "she's gona come between ya and Lydia. Ya should have seen Lydia's face when ya went upstairs with Courtney last night. I almost kicked your arse meself, ya wanker. But I can see you've been kickin' your own arse so I'm gona be satisfied with that. *For now*. Ya don't want to tumble with me, mo chara. Ya know that doesn't end well." He winked. We'd only gotten in one physical fight, when we were younger, over something trivial that I could barely recall now. It'd been a straight draw, and we'd both shook hands and let go of whatever the issue had been.

I let out a small sound that might have been a laugh if it contained any humor at all.

We talked business for a few minutes, Fionn telling me about the kid I'd caught stealing food from the food truck and how he'd set him up with a courier job. So far he was a hard worker and was doing well, which was good news.

Talking mundane business helped calm me and get my mind back on track. After a bit, Margaret came downstairs and said Lydia was all taken care of, no problem at all, and she'd given instructions on how to care for the stitches over the next few days, which she gave to me as well. I thanked her profusely, kissing her cheek as she left.

Once Fionn left, I made Lydia a sandwich and carried it up to her room, knocking softly. The room was dim, the bathroom fan was whirring, and she was curled up on the bed, fast asleep. I watched her for a few minutes, despair making me feel sick. I could have lost her today. And I'd only just gotten her back.

CHAPTER EIGHTEEN

Lydia

I came awake slowly, my eyes adjusting to the dim light, my memory temporarily held at bay, though I had the feeling something wasn't quite right. I enjoyed the brief moment I knew I had before recollection would tumble in, making me aware of exactly what the *something* was. As I turned over, the minor ache in my side brought the happenings of earlier that day rushing back. I let out a small sigh, sitting up slowly so as not to pull my stitches.

"How do ya feel?" I startled slightly, noticing the outline of Brogan sitting in the chair by the window.

"This is the second time I've woken up to you sitting in the dark in my room, uninvited," I said. "It's kind of creepy. Are you trying to give me a heart attack?"

He stood and came over to me, sitting on the edge of the bed. "No, Lydia. I don't want to do a thing to hurt ya. Not ever again." He sighed, tossing something on my bedside table.

I looked over, seeing what was a dark yellow folder, dirty and tattered, notes written all over it in what appeared to be Gaelic. I looked back at him. "What's that?"

"It's nothin' now. What it was, though, was the thing that kept me goin' when I had nothin' else."

I sat up higher, propping myself on the pillows behind my back, bringing my legs up so I was sitting Indian style, and reached over and clicked on the small reading lamp on my bedside table. It illuminated the room with a soft glow, allowing me to see Brogan gazing at me with those soft blue eyes, his expression grim.

"What do you mean?"

He ran a hand through his short, dark hair. "When we left your estate that day . . ." he paused as if just the very mention of *that day* still brought a deep ache with it, "we traveled to the Bronx. We had actually started out there before my dad applied for the job with your family. We'd heard there was a big Irish population, knew a few folks who knew folks. Anyway, that's where we returned. We found a small fleabag apartment to rent, and my dad, he," he inhaled and let it out slowly, "he pawned my mam's wedding ring just to come up with the security deposit and first month's rent."

"Brogan," I whispered.

He shook his head as if I shouldn't stop him now. "In the beginnin' I did anythin' I could to earn some money—just to feed us. I got in with some other guys—Russian lads—in similar positions who knew how to make some quick cash. We, ya know, scalped tickets, acted as lookouts, delivered messages, stuff like that. I knew I was workin' for mobsters, but I didn't care. It was feedin' my family when I had no other way to." His expression was defensive for a hint of a moment, but it slipped quickly into shame before he averted his gaze.

"Of course," I said. "I admire you for doing whatever you had to do to survive. It was very brave."

He paused for a brief moment as his eyes met mine. He shook his head, almost imperceptibly before he looked away again, continuing. "My dad, he looked for work and claimed he couldn't find any, but it's hard to find work when you're drunk nine hours a day."

Even in profile, I could see that another look of despair crossed his face and a lump formed in my throat. *Oh Brogan, if I had known . . . I would have done anything to help you.* Guilt surged through me once again at my own teenage naïveté. I hadn't even considered Brogan's family was experiencing that type of poverty, had no real knowledge of struggle, desperation. And I was so ashamed of my own ignorance.

"I met Fionn who was in a desperate situation, too, and we became friends." He gave me the first glimmer of a smile. "Of course, it doesn't take long for Fionn to grow on ya. But it was more than that. I trusted him when it was hard to trust anyone. And it made it so it wasn't so lonely, ya know? The scrapin' and scroungin', with Fionn it almost became . . . fun—he made a game of it. His own survival tactic, I suppose, but it helped me, too. Helped . . . balance me, I guess. And he's never let me down. Not once. Even when I deserved it. Even when I asked him to do things that went against his own morals. Which makes me a shite friend."

I leaned forward and placed my hand on top of his where they sat in his lap. I was still uncertain about *us*, but I cared about him and couldn't ignore his pain. "You'd do anything for him, too. I can see that and I know he does as well."

He took a deep breath. "Yeah. I would. Anythin'." He paused before continuing. "Anyway, we did any job we were asked to do. Through different jobs, they found I was good with numbers and started givin' me tasks that were more administrative in nature. Eventually, I was helpin' to do their books, accountin', stuff like that. Some of the guys I worked with were real arseholes. I saw them do things to others that turned my stomach, and I did nothin'. Not a feckin' thing, though it went against everythin' in me." He paused, the expression on his face so bleak my breath caught.

"If you had, they might have fired you, or worse. You needed that money. It was smart to keep quiet. Look where it got you in the end." I lifted my chin, asserting my point, defending him . . . to himself.

"Lydia . . ." he said quietly but didn't look at me. Again the small head shake as if he couldn't accept my statement. "I started keepin' some records, names, took things with me I shouldn't have, told myself I'd get them back for the way they preyed on others who were helpless for no other reason than because they could. *Someday* when I had the power, I told myself."

"And it helped," I said.

"Yeah," he said. "It helped knowin' that though I couldn't do anythin' *then*, I could and would do somethin' *later*. I put the files in that folder, and I took it out and looked at it whenever I didn't think I could do it anymore. But . . . the job, it paid better than any of the more menial jobs, and I was also grateful because Eileen was gettin' some of the treatments she needed. I'd been savin' up for her surgery—the plates she needed in her legs to straighten them permanently. I got us out of the slum we were livin' in, moved us to a nicer place in the Bronx—the building I work from now. His lips tipped up slightly, and he took a deep breath. "And it meant I could quit the thing I hated the most."

I tilted my head questioningly, a cold shiver moving through my body. Brogan ran his tongue over his front tooth, once and then again, his expression vulnerable and pained. I waited, completely still. "Earlier on when I was still doin' low-level jobs, one of the other guys let me in on a service a few of them were performin'. It was a sort of side business and a lot of the guys seemed perfectly happy to be picked for the job. I knew the mob dabbled in prostitution, but I didn't consider that they hired out male prostitutes as well." He grimaced as he said the word, and my heart squeezed, my stomach knotting. "One of the women—mostly married women whose husbands were much older—would place an order, and we'd be sent out."

"Brogan . . ."

He shook his head. "I know. I didn't want to do it. Just the idea of it was . . . distasteful to me on so many levels. Fionn tried to talk me out of it. But Fionn was only takin' care of himself, he didn't have others dependin' on him. And I thought if I could just earn enough money to get Eileen her surgery, and if I could just earn enough money to start makin' some investments, I would stop, no real harm done."

"Only . . ." I whispered.

His eyes met mine, and he gave me the smallest hint of a smile, though it didn't reach his eyes. Talking about this was hurting him, and part of me wanted to tell him he didn't have to continue, but the other half wanted desperately to understand his past, to understand *him*.

"Yes, only." The smile slipped from his face. "I pretended they were you," he said, his voice gravelly all of a sudden. "Only sometimes—mostly maybe—that made it worse instead of better."

My breath caught. "Brogan," I breathed.

He shook his head. "And they weren't you. You were right, I hated the way they smelled, the way they'd grab at me, the way they'd rake their fingernails over my skin. They liked all sorts of . . ." he trailed off. "Anyway, I hated it. I hated them, and I hated you more, too, because being with those women made me long for you twice as hard and you'd betrayed me—or so I thought at the time. Still wantin' you like I did didn't make sense. My mind couldn't justify it, though I still felt it desperately, and I hated you even more for it."

My eyes filled with tears, but I didn't reach for him this time. I could see he was struggling, and it seemed he needed space to get through the telling of this part of his story.

"I started keepin' records on them, too. In my folder." He let out a small, brittle laugh. "My *feckin'*, ridiculous folder. But some days, I'd look through it, and I'd imagine what I'd do to them when I was the one with the power, and it was the only thing holdin' me up. The idea of revenge took hold and became the thing that strengthened me when there was nothin' else." He paused for a moment. "You were in there, too, you and Stuart."

Yes, of course. Of course we were. And in some small, possibly twisted way, I was glad because it meant we had helped him survive when he had little else.

"But then I got the job doin' some of the mob's accountin' and I was able to quit. Eventually, I moved up to launderin' money. That's when I did make enough money to make some investments and I doubled some of it by gamblin'. I paid for Eileen's surgery. My dad, he . . . drank himself to death." Pain for him made my stomach clench and he paused for a moment as if he was experiencing the same thing. He looked back down at his hands. "But he watched her walk without her braces right before he died." My heart squeezed, but Brogan's expression didn't change.

"My own wealth started growin' in leaps and bounds. And once I started amassin' wealth, power, I used it to run the women and their husbands out of New York in one way or another—bribes, job transfers, things of that nature. I *couldn't* run into any of them, didn't *ever* want to be reminded of how low I'd once been, didn't even want those women in the same *zip code*, and I finally had the power to make that happen." He shrugged and glanced at the folder. "I keep it now to remind me where I once was and how far I've come."

Oh Brogan. He carried so much pain, so much bitterness, but I had to wonder if the person he was having the hardest time forgiving was himself. I had to wonder if the real reason he kept that folder was to remind *himself* why he shouldn't be let off the hook for his own choices. We were both quiet for a minute.

"Courtney was one of those women," I finally said softly.

"Yes. I'd seen her a few times. It was a little better with her than with some of the others. Her husband was twenty-five years older than her and not a nice man from what I knew, although I think she genuinely loved him. I think, mostly, she was lookin' for someone who was gentle with her, someone to pay her attention."

My fingers twisted in my lap, and I was ashamed of the jealousy that overcame me in a moment when Brogan was revealing his pain to me. This was not about me. This was about him. This was about the ways in which he'd survived.

"One night, her husband came home unexpectedly from a business trip and walked in on us." *Oh God.* "It was ugly. Courtney begged and pleaded with her husband to let me leave, to just let me go. And he did." He paused, looking down at his hands. "I could have refused to leave. I could have begged for him not to hurt her, too. I could have. But I had vowed never to beg anyone again. I had vowed never to give anyone that kind of power over me, and so I didn't beg. I didn't even stay. I walked away. I just . . . left her there. And he beat her to within an inch of her life. She was in the hospital for months. I had no idea she was in that kind of danger when I left, but I should have, I . . ."

I sucked in a breath and leaned toward him, putting my fingers under his chin and turning his face toward me. Our eyes met, his filled with pain and self-disgust. "Brogan, you can't believe you're responsible for that. Even if you did beg, even if you tried to stay, he would have thrown you out. He would have hurt her anyway. Then, or maybe later. You were not responsible for him being a sick, violent man or for him hurting her the way he did."

His smile was sad. "Maybe. I'll never know and it's another thing I have to live with." He looked down again and I studied him for several moments, recalling what Courtney had said when she burst into his house.

"He went to prison for what he did to her and now he's getting out?"

"Yes."

"And what does she expect you to do? You made your choices, but, Brogan, she made hers, too. She bears responsibility for what happened to her as well. Probably most of all."

He shook his head. "She wants me to protect her, keep her safe."

"You feel responsible for her? That's madness. You can't spend your entire life paying for something that wasn't your fault."

He shrugged. "It didn't seem like such a terrible price to pay before—"

"Before what?"

"Before you came back into my life. Before it became obvious she'd put a wedge between us. And I don't want that. I just want you, and I wish I had gone about this differently. I have so many regrets."

I swallowed, his words music to my ears. I *wanted* him to want me over her, but . . . "Does *she* think you want her?"

He shook his head adamantly. "No, no. It's not like that. I've been honest with her. She uses situations like last night to get to me."

"And you let her."

"I have in the past, yes. I admit to givin' in to the guilt I feel when it comes to Courtney. And things were completely different before two weeks ago. I didn't think it would hurt anyone that I provide comfort to her if she needed it, if I spent time with her at social events, things like that. But last night when Courtney showed up, I just needed to spell out the situation for her in private. Because in the past I've been there for her, but I can't and I won't be anymore. I'm sorry, Lydia. I'm sorry for what you thought, what I put you through. But I couldn't talk to her in front of you. It wouldn't have been right to do that—not to her, but mostly, not to you."

I blinked at him. "You . . . told her about me?"

"A bit, not much. She doesn't need all the details of my personal life, whether she thinks so or not."

I worried my lip, considering all he'd said. "I'm not sure what to say." It was true, I didn't. I just needed to digest what Brogan had told me.

"You don't have to say anythin' right now. I'm sorry I've further complicated things. I was unprepared for this. You have to know that. Fionn said this whole thing would go arseways, and he was right."

I gave him a small smile. "Arseways," I muttered. "A complete mess."

He gave me a slight smile and then nodded to where my stitches were under the T-shirt I'd changed into. "How are ya?" *Ha-ware-ya?* His brogue had been pronounced during the telling of his past.

"I'm fine. It's just a scratch. And you were right—I shouldn't have gone out, especially not to Stuart's. I was so hurt and . . . stubborn." *Stupid really. I took responsibility for this.*

Brogan stood up. "I was negotiating this morning with the men who hold Stuart's loans, but I hadn't agreed to their terms yet. I have now. It's done."

I blinked. "So you did buy more time for Stuart?" I asked,

hopefully. "Thank you, Brogan."

"The debts are mine now."

Confusion rushed through me. My mouth opened to speak, but when I realized I had no idea what to say, I shut it again. Finally I managed, "Yours? I don't . . . I don't understand."

"I took on Stuart's debt. He's free and clear, and I have their word they will not extend him more credit."

"But . . . but, why?"

"Because I set this all in motion, and because I will not risk ya, that's why."

My heart sped up. *I just want you.* I stared at him, not knowing exactly what to say, feeling overwhelmed with all the information he'd just given me and experiencing what felt like a hundred different emotions at once. I put my hand on my stomach as if I could hold myself together from the outside.

"You must be starving," he said and though he had misinterpreted my movement, I was grateful he'd changed the subject. I needed time to process. I was completely overwhelmed in every way.

"I am actually," I said slowly.

He smiled, the first real one I'd seen since he'd arrived home the night before—what now seemed like a million years ago. "Then let me feed you."

CHAPTER NINETEEN

Brogan

I leaned back on my pillows, halfheartedly watching ESPN, considering everything that had happened since yesterday afternoon. *Jaysus.* Courtney showing up had been the cherry on top of a shit pie. I'd wanted to claw my eyes out at the situation. But what could I do except take Courtney to a place where she'd calm down, and I could explain to her why she was *not* allowed to come barreling into my apartment anytime she wished, demanding I cater to her emotional needs?

Of course, once I'd gotten her upstairs, she'd made it clear her needs were of the physical nature, too, as they usually were, and I'd practically had to fight her off me.

I'd always deemed her touch tolerable. But I'd been comparing her to the other women I'd been with and in that regard, she *was*. But *now*, I was comparing her to Lydia and the difference was drastic enough to make me cringe when Courtney put her hands on me.

I'd made a mistake when months ago, at the time I was planning on taking over De Havilland Enterprises, I'd first seen Lydia as she exited the building after work one evening. I'd stood across the street watching her, my heart lodged in my throat, my emotions all over the place. She'd laughed as she'd called out a couple words over her shoulder to a man in a suit who obviously worked there, too, and the man had laughed back, waving, continuing to look over his shoulder at her even as she walked farther down the block.

I'd been shaking with what I had called anger at the time, but now knew was the longing she'd always elicited in me. It was still there, after all these years, and that knowledge *burned* clear to my bones. I'd felt confused, hopeless, and I'd gone to Courtney's. I'd told her a few surface details about my plans to ruin someone who had done me wrong long ago, and she'd offered words of comfort that had eventually turned physical.

It was the first time I'd slept with her in years, and the first time ever without money exchanging hands, but it still left me feeling dirty all the same. I'd hated myself for what I'd done. Not only did it leave me feeling dissatisfied and empty, but it had encouraged her. It had been wrong. And the truth was, it wasn't even sex I had wanted that night. I just hadn't wanted to be alone.

I sighed. Of course, I hadn't mentioned that to Lydia, but what good would it do and did it really matter? If she had been sleeping with someone months ago, I wouldn't want to know the details.

Courtney hadn't been happy about Lydia, not that I'd told her much, but at least she hadn't thrown the fit I'd imagined she would, and I'd walked her out an hour after she'd arrived. Of course, by that point, Lydia and Fionn were passed out drunk on my couch.

And now . . . not only was I taking responsibility for Stuart's debts, I was paying them off by doing something I vowed I'd never do again. I was going to help the mob cook their books and launder several large sums of money.

I'd been negotiating simply to pay off Stuart's debts with cash, but it hadn't been what they wanted, and what choice did I have? I'd made a deal years ago to buy my way out by making them several large investment deals that had paid off in spades. And I'd set up accounting systems that other men could run. I'd gotten out, but I'd still stayed in their good graces, and they'd allowed me to gamble in their underground clubs even though they must have suspected I counted cards.

I'd promised myself I'd never again *have* to do anything that wasn't of my own choosing, that I'd never again find myself beholden to anyone, and here I was, right back where I'd started.

I raked my hand through my hair. I'd made a bloody mess out of everything. I was going to participate in illegal activity again to rescue the man I'd set out to ruin. I would laugh my arse off if I could summon the humor.

Thinking of what they'd done to Lydia, though, had me grimacing rather than laughing. If I hadn't been stubborn, if I'd made a deal with them thirty minutes before she was attacked . . .

And now it was my arse on the line instead of Stuart's, mine and Lydia's, and perhaps Fionn's and Eileen's too. *Jaysus fecking Christ.* Of course, the difference was, I had the means to repay what was now *my* debt.

Bile rose in my throat as I thought back to watching Lydia fall to her knees from across the street and knowing that if they had wanted, she'd be dead. She'd be dead and it would have been my fault for hesitating in agreeing to their terms. Again, *my* hesitation, my unwillingness to take action, would have cost someone else physical harm—only this time it would have been Lydia, and it would have killed me, too.

I heard a scuffling in the hallway and got out of bed, muting the TV.

Lydia was standing on the other side of the door, and she startled when I pulled it open. "Hey," I said, "you okay? Is it your side? I could change your bandage if you need me to."

She shook her head. Her blonde hair was loose and falling around her shoulders, and she was wearing a pair of small cotton shorts and a tank top. My blood heated instantly. "No, my side is fine. Honestly, it really only needs a Band-Aid. I guess I'm having trouble sleeping because I slept so much this afternoon." She moved from one foot to the other, biting her lip uncertainly.

My breath caught and hope soared. "Do you . . . do you want to join me?" I asked, opening the door wider. "Or we could go downstairs. I'm just watching TV in here. But I could turn on a movie or something."

She smiled, nodding her head and looking past me at the TV in my room. "That sounds good."

She joined me on my bed, and I flipped through the movie channels, both of us agreeing on a comedy that had recently come out. "I could make some popcorn," I said, smiling over at her.

Her eyes went to my mouth and seemed to soften. "I love to see you smile like that," she said. "It seems so rare."

"I've been doing it more since you've been around," I said honestly.

She moved closer, fluffing the pillows behind us. "No popcorn. This is perfect." She settled back, stretching her legs out next to mine.

I wasn't sure how I was going to manage being on my bed with Lydia and focus on a movie, but once she started laughing at the funny parts, I couldn't help but to laugh with her. The movie wasn't even that funny to me—a sort of stupid, slapstick film, but Lydia was laughing so hard it was contagious, and I found myself laughing, too.

It didn't seem like the laughter was hurting her side so I decided not to bring it up. I didn't want to put a damper on this lighthearted night by mentioning what had happened earlier today. I had to trust she'd know her own physical limits. And watching her now was making me happy.

Lydia was always laughing when she was a teenager. I remembered her flitting from one place to another like a brightly colored hummingbird, full of life and laughter, flirting with everyone who crossed her path. But looking back at it now, not through the eyes of a besotted seventeen-year-old boy who thought he could never have her, I saw it was harmless flirting, the kind that let everyone around her know she *enjoyed* them. I also understood it better now because Fionn was the same way. He charmed everyone he came into contact with, because he truly *enjoyed* people and he couldn't help letting them know.

I smiled over at Lydia, overjoyed to see that carefree part of her personality on display—even if only for a couple hours. After the day we'd had—after all my doubts and fears over telling her the details of my past—relaxing and watching a movie with Lydia felt like a small miracle. It felt like she might be giving me a second chance, but I didn't even dare ask her. *Nor expect it.*

I watched as she grinned at the screen, that wide smile that I hadn't seen on her face since she was sixteen, the one she'd always seemed to quickly amend when it slipped through, as if she didn't like something about it. She wasn't hiding it now though, and I let my eyes linger on her, soaking it in. *Beautiful.*

When the movie was over, I flicked it off, still chuckling. I lay back on the pillows and Lydia turned toward me, smiling. "That was terrible," she said.

I laughed. "You seemed to be enjoying it."

"I did, but it was still terrible." She laughed, but then went quickly serious, the wheels in her head obviously turning. We stared at each other for a minute. I wanted her, but I was afraid to make a move after she'd suffered an attack today, not to mention what happened the night before. Plus, I'd revealed so much to her earlier. I still felt insecure and unsure about what she thought of me, about where we stood. But would she be in my bedroom if she wasn't interested in me physically anymore? Was she thinking the same thing I was? That she wanted to make love more than she wanted to breathe?

"Lydia—"

"Let's talk," she said.

"Talk?" I blinked.

"Yeah, like, let's have a sleepover and stay up talking."

"A sleepover? Stay up talking?"

She nodded. The sleepover part sounded promising, the talking, not so much. "Yeah. Didn't you ever have sleepovers when you were a kid?"

I shook my head. "My mam was sick for a long time."

Her eyes widened and she frowned. "You were robbed of so many things," she said sadly. She took a deep breath. "Okay, well, it's never too late. We can make up for the sleepovers you never had."

I wanted to tell her that the only sleepover I was interested in with her was the one where we were both naked and her legs were spread open, but I was pretty sure the sleepover she was talking about was of a different nature.

"What do you want to talk about?" I asked.

"First," she said, "you need to get in your PJs and we need to get under the covers."

"My PJs?" I asked, confused.

"Yeah, your PJs. Your pajamas."

"Do men wear pajamas?"

"You don't?" She frowned.

I raised a brow. "I'd think you'd know that better than anyone considering you took inventory of my clothes."

She laughed softly. "Hmm. Now that I think about it, you're right. How about sweat pants?"

"Workout shorts?"

"There you go. Perfect. Go get changed and come back."

"Sleepovers seem to have a lot of rules," I grumbled, mostly due to sexual frustration. Not only did this sleepover involve lots of talking, but it also involved clothes. But I did as Lydia told me to and changed into a pair of workout shorts and returned to bed. Lydia frowned. "What?" I asked.

"No shirt?" She shook her head and licked her lips.

"I think it's a better idea if we both wear shirts." That buoyed my spirits. She was still affected by me, too. Maybe this sleepover would turn into something more than . . . talking. I grabbed a T-shirt and put it on. Although, if I was really going to make an issue of it, I'd mention that her tank top really didn't leave much to the imagination and I was having a particularly difficult time not letting my eyes wander down to her cream puffs.

Lydia turned the covers back and slipped under them. I joined her, turning toward her on the pillow. She reached over her shoulder and flicked off the lamp, casting the room in near darkness.

"I've never spent the night with another woman," I said.

She tilted her head on the pillow, blinking at me for a moment. "You haven't? Never?" She paused. "Brogan, haven't you been with anyone other than . . . those women." *Those women.* Funny, that's how I thought about them, too.

"No."

"No," she whispered, sounding disbelieving. "Haven't you dated at all?"

"No. I mean, not unless it was for your benefit." I shot her a small smirk, and she let out a breathy-sounding laugh, her forehead wrinkling in confusion.

"Well, but . . . *why?*"

"I guess I've been so focused on accumulating wealth." *Safety.* "I haven't really had time." I was quiet for a moment and Lydia waited, watching me. "And I guess my past . . . maybe I just . . . wanted to distance myself from it for a while . . ." That felt right although I wasn't sure I wanted to delve into it too much—not right now at least.

We were quiet for a moment before she said, "You have to find a way to release it, Brogan. The women, your choices, the shame, you have to find a way to let it go. Learn from your mistakes, but don't let them define you now. Find forgiveness, for them and for yourself."

I let out a breath. "I've tried. I just . . . I can't hold on to the emotion."

She shook her head. "Forgiveness isn't an emotion. Forgiveness is a choice. And sometimes it's one you have to choose again and again." She licked her lips. "For instance, take my stepmother, *ex*-stepmother that is. I wanted her to be a mother figure to me so badly, or at the very least an older sister figure, an aunt, something, anything." She paused. "I realize now she just wasn't capable. I've forgiven her for the things she wasn't able to give me, but if I see her at a party, I throw back a lot of alcohol and avoid her like the plague. And I have to choose again, in that moment, to forgive her for the ridiculousness that comes out of her mouth." I chuckled and she smiled. "I'm just saying, you don't have to be best friends just because you forgive a person. It's really about setting yourself free of the hold they have on you."

"And what about your brother? Isn't constantly forgiving him really just sending the message that you'll tolerate anything? His choices affect you. They have for a long time."

She looked at me thoughtfully, if not a little uncomfortably. "Yes, you're right. It's easier to forgive a person when their bad choices don't wreak havoc on your own life, when you can distance yourself." She sighed. "I guess, sometimes, you have to be the one to cut ties if you're truly going to forgive. And it's more complicated than it seems. I wasn't trying to make it seem overly simplistic."

She looked troubled and perhaps slightly lost, and so I reached over and took her hand, lacing my fingers through hers. "This sleepover has suddenly taken on a somber tone."

She laughed softly. "You're right. We'll save somber for when we have a bottle of wine open."

"I'd lay off the wine for a while, Mo Chroí. You're a dirty talking drunk." I raised a brow.

She laughed softly and then was quiet for a moment before she asked, "The other night in ah, bed . . . what did you say to me in Gaelic?"

I paused. "I believe it was something very complimentary about your cream puffs."

She laughed again and the mood lightened. We talked about less serious topics after that. She told me about going away to college, her roommate Beatrice who had snored like a trucker, listened to techno music constantly and lived, seemingly, on a diet of candy corn and Red Bull, about coming back home, about her life now. I listened to her talk, smiling and absorbing every word, and I had to admit, I liked my first sleepover, despite all the talking. Or maybe because of it. Or maybe I just really liked the girl I was having a sleepover with.

I told her about my childhood in Ireland, my mam, the cancer, and even a little bit about my dad before he'd been ruled by the bottle, and I found that it felt good to talk about them, even if only a little. Apart from Fionn, and Eileen of course, I hadn't come across anyone who had lost both parents so young.

"I wanted this with you," she murmured. "When we were teenagers. I dreamed of this." I smiled softly at her. Funny, we'd both been dreaming of the same thing, yet we'd both been dreaming alone. I didn't want to dream alone anymore. I hoped to God she didn't either.

We'd slept together in the guest room in Greenwich, but having her in *my* bed brought an even deeper joy and satisfaction. I loved whispering with her in the near dark of my room, loved the look of her freshly scrubbed face right next to mine on the pillow, loved the soft sound of her voice, the way her words faded away as she started drifting off to sleep in the middle of a sentence.

I don't remember falling asleep, but at some point in the deep of the night, I came half awake, realizing Lydia and I were tangled together, her smooth thigh thrown over my leg and her breasts pressed against my chest, her breath warm on my throat. I pulled her closer, burrowing my nose into her sweetly fragrant hair, feeling a calm sense of happiness flow through me.

When I woke up next, it was morning and Lydia was gone, but when I got up and opened the door to my bedroom, I heard the water running across the hall in her bathroom and smiled. I brought my arm to my nose and inhaled. *Lydia.* Her scent lingered on my skin.

I brushed my teeth, shaved, and took a shower, and then dressed quickly in dress pants and a button-down shirt.

When I got downstairs and turned the corner into the kitchen, Lydia was sitting at the table dressed . . . as a man. "Em," I said, squinting my eyes at her.

She grinned. "Hi," she said, "I mean, hi," she said again, lowering her voice a few octaves.

"What exactly is . . .?" I used my finger to indicate her state of dress—a button-down shirt stolen from my closet it seemed, rolled up to her elbows, a pair of loose jeans—and her hair bundled into a baseball cap, and the small . . . I squinted again . . . drawn-in mustache?

"I'm coming to work with you today," she said. "I thought you'd feel safer about me accompanying you if I was in disguise."

"Disguise?" I walked closer, leaning my hands on a chair back. "Lydia, that's the worst disguise I've ever seen."

"Oh!" She held up her finger, grabbed a pair of sunglasses sitting next to the toast she was eating and put them on, smiling.

"Just as bad."

Her smile vanished. "Well, of course it's not meant to trick you." She removed the sunglasses. "But it should work just fine in general. Plus, you said you'd come to an agreement with the men holding my brother's loan. Surely the risk is decreased now, right?" I pressed my lips together and then sighed.

"Please, Brogan," she rushed on, standing and walking over to me. "It's so boring being locked in an apartment all day alone. And you told me you might have some work for me to do for your company. Wouldn't it be better if I was actually *at* your company so I could ask you questions if I need to?" She put her arms around my waist and gazed up at me, and my eyes wandered to the mustache.

"This is disturbing," I said. "Really disturbing."

"Please?" She blinked up at me, flirting in that shameless way I remembered. Only now . . . it made me smile. Even though I had no bloody idea how to flirt back. Fionn would know. But I had a feeling that sort of thing either came naturally or it didn't. And for me, well, it didn't.

I sighed again. "Fine. But you stay inside with me. I'm serious, Lydia. Let that small ache I'm sure you still feel on your side be a reminder of why what I say is very important." I didn't think she was in danger today, but I wasn't going to take any risks. And either way, she'd be with me. I'd make *sure* she was safe.

I ate a piece of toast and finished getting ready and then we went down to my car, pulling through a coffee drive-thru en route. Fifteen minutes later, I parked across the street from what was my former home, and now my offices in the Bronx.

We got out of my car and I grabbed Lydia's hand as we crossed. She grinned. "I'm glad to see you're confident enough in your masculinity to hold another man's hand in public."

"You're not a man."

"Yes, but other people don't know that."

We stepped onto the porch and I pulled her to me, wrapping one arm around her waist, and holding my coffee in the other hand.

I grinned. "I'm confident enough to do this, too." I pulled her closer and kissed her lips, running my tongue across the seam so she opened on a surprised inhale of breath. I heard the door open in front of us and cracked one eye open. Rory was standing there, a baffled look on his face as he watched me kiss the young . . . man in my arms.

I pulled back, clearing my throat. "Rory," I greeted as I took Lydia's hand, pulling her behind me and past Rory who was still standing in the doorway looking completely blindsided. I almost asked him why he wasn't at school, but remembered he'd told me it was a teacher in-service day.

I brought Lydia into my office and pulled a chair up next to mine. She stood there watching me, looking around. "Things were so different the last time I was here," she said softly.

A wave of guilt washed over me when I thought about how I'd treated her that day, the offer I'd made and my dark intentions toward her. "Yeah," I said. "You were a woman then." She laughed and I smiled, letting out a breath. I didn't want the easy rapport we'd developed last night to go away. And though things were far from perfect, and I still had several unpleasant tasks staring me down, in that moment, watching as she settled herself at my desk, the only thing I felt was happiness.

CHAPTER TWENTY

Lydia

Brogan had set me up with a list of tasks, and I had gone to work right away. I went back and forth between Brogan's office and the file cabinets in a small room off the waiting area. Each time I did, Rory looked at me skeptically, but I just nodded, wanting to laugh at his confusion.

I also noticed the way he followed Brogan around, watching him closely and imitating his mannerisms. I didn't think Brogan noticed. I didn't even think Rory was aware, but he obviously hero-worshipped Brogan. This situation with Brogan's new man-friend must really be throwing him for a loop. Though I figured part of his confusion stemmed from the fact that he was unsure whether I was actually a man or not. I wanted to giggle, but I held it in and resolutely went about my tasks.

Going through a few of the files Brogan had me working on, confused me. *What sort of business was this?* "I do what I want now," he'd said. Only it seemed what he did was . . . help people. I bit my lip. *What did he get out of this?* How did you make a business out of helping people who were in bad situations? Did he charge them an exorbitant interest like one of those check cashing places that loaned you money before payday? I leafed through several more files, but if that were the case, there was no record of it here.

A little before noon, Fionn came striding in. Brogan and I were in his office and he paused in the doorway, one eyebrow cocked as he stared at me. "Em . . ."

I laughed. "Hi, Fionn. What's the craic?" I winked and Fionn let out a breath, walking into Brogan's office.

"I thought that was ya, Lydia. But I didn't want to be wrong and offend Brogan's new, wee lad secretary." He sprawled in the chair in front of Brogan's desk. "We gona go deal with that mug, Rudy Dudley?"

Brogan sighed and rubbed at his eye. "Yeah. Just give me a minute to take my anti-nausea medication." Fionn chuckled.

"Rudy Dudley?" I asked.

"Aye," Fionn said. "A real chancer, tight as a duck's arse. He owns some slums in South Bronx and our client has hired us to," he paused as if considering his words carefully, "use our powers of persuasion to convince him to make some repairs."

Hmm. "A chancer. A . . . dodgy character." I grinned, proud to have remembered a word from my Irish slang lesson. I turned to Brogan. "And your client is . . ."

"Sally Hodges. She has a three-year-old and a six-month-old living in a shithole where the rats are bigger than the cats."

I cringed. But if Sally Hodges lived in this rat-infested shithole, she must not have the money to move elsewhere. And if she didn't have the money to move elsewhere, how did she have the money to hire Brogan and Fionn? "I'm coming with you," I said.

Brogan shook his head. "You wouldn't want to be anywhere near this place, trust me."

"I'll stay in the car. But I'm coming." Brogan considered me for a second, but then nodded his okay.

Ten minutes later, we were pulling up in front of a crumbling, three-story brick building. I leaned toward the backseat window, looking up at the structure as Brogan and Fionn got out, telling me they'd be back in twenty minutes, Brogan locking the doors with his key fob.

Although the street was nice, with lots of old, large trees, the building in front of me was a definite eyesore.

I sat in the car for several minutes, watching two boys kicking a ball on a patch of brown grass. I glanced up at the building one more time.

Overcome with curiosity, I got out, walking quickly to the door I'd watched Brogan and Fionn enter, wrinkling my nose when I stepped into the lobby. It reeked of trash and something dead. I hoped whatever had died was of the animal variety.

Stepping through the debris, I climbed the stairs, following the raised voices. I stayed hidden around a corner for a minute listening to the conversation.

I heard Brogan say, "Mr. Dudley, we've catalogued a hundred and fifty housing code violations in this building. Frankly, I hardly want to waste the finances or the energy bringing a lawsuit against you, but there are seven women and thirteen children living here who deserve better than the fucking, dirty shithole you're providing for them. And unlike your tenants, I have the means to do something about it."

"Now listen here, *boy*," an older voice spat out. I peeked out from behind the corner and caught the old man's eye, and pulled myself back against the wall, my heart pounding. *Damn!* "Who's that?" I heard him demand.

Biting my lip, I pulled my ball cap off, quickly scrubbed at the mustache I'd drawn on with eyeliner that morning and unbuttoned the top two buttons of my shirt, un-tucking it and tying it at the side of my waist. I took a deep breath, fluffed my hair and stepped out from around the corner, smiling brightly. Brogan was walking toward me and when I shot him a smile, his forehead creased right before his eyes widened.

"Oh, hi, sorry I'm late," I sing-songed. Brogan frowned, and I stepped around him, reaching my hand out to Mr. Dudley. "Mr. Dudley?"

"Uh . . ." said the tubby old man with the greasy, white hair sticking in every direction from his head and every other orifice I could see. He looked at me, to Fionn and then back to me. I glanced around him into the dirty garbage pit he referred to as his apartment and tried not to grimace at the smell wafting out. My eyes caught on a bookshelf near the door—a bookshelf featuring a folded American flag in a small glass holder and several medals and plaques. I squinted my eyes, reading the inscriptions quickly. When I looked back to Mr. Dudley, he was trying to look down my shirt.

"Mr. Rudy Dudley, former US Marine, recipient of the Silver Star?"

He puffed up, standing taller, looking at me more closely. "That's right. How'd you know that?"

I pointed behind him to his bookshelf, smiling and cocking one hip out. "The Silver Star," I said, putting one finger up to my lips and puckering up as I tapped them. "That's for gallantry in action, right? Why, Mr. Molloy, Mr. Ramsay, we're dealing with a bona fide hero right here. You boys hardly need to *threaten* him with doing the right thing. Doing the right thing is in his blood." I sighed. "Mr. Dudley, you have no idea what an honor it is to meet you. There are so few real *men* nowadays, don't you agree?"

Mr. Dudley straightened even further, smoothing his wrinkled wife beater down his paunchy stomach and flicking something dried and crusty at the hem. "Uh . . . yeah. Yeah! You're right, young lady. In my day, heroes were *respected*." He shook his head. "Not anymore." He shot a glare to Brogan and Fionn who were watching our exchange with blank looks on their faces.

"Well, I respect your service to our country, your bravery, and I admire the fact that you want to provide safe and secure living conditions for the women residing here—the women who are counting on you to be the hero they need. But, Mr. Dudley, I understand it's an overwhelming job and perhaps you've hesitated while trying to come up with the most strategic plan for making the fixes and repairs necessary. Am I right?"

"Uh . . . strategy . . . yeah. That's right. If you're not strategic, it'll all go to hell. Every last bit of it!" he yelled, looking off behind me as if expecting someone else to appear.

I nodded sympathetically as his eyes moved back to me. "You're so right. Again, Mr. Dudley, the sound thinking I'd only expect from a war hero such as yourself. Here's what I propose: if I can get your guarantee that you'll fund the cleanup project and hire the professionals necessary, I'll send a crew made up of Mr. Ramsay's employees, free of charge of course, to get rid of the garbage and debris littering the uh . . . grounds and main foyer of this property."

Mr. Dudley nodded. "Main foyer, right." He narrowed his eyes, and tilted his head, considering me.

"You've got a deal, Miss . . ."

"De Havilland. Lydia De Havilland." I grinned. "Mr. Dudley, you're a gentleman and a patriot."

Mr. Dudley, shockingly, grinned back, showing me a mouthful of crooked, nicotine-stained teeth. "Miss De Havilland, will you be by to check on the progress?"

I hesitated. "Uh, absolutely. Of course."

"I will see you then." Again, he smoothed his shirt, licked his palm, and reached up, attempting to tame his wild hair. Well, that was gross. And anyway, it was a useless effort—his hair remained looking like one of those freaky troll dolls. And how I wished he had not just raised his arm higher than his shoulder.

He turned to Brogan who was standing there with a look that was simultaneously baffled and disgusted. "Mr. Ramsay, I'll go inside right now and start setting up the appointments to make the fixes you outlined in your letter. Good day." He nodded to both men, smiled at me again, and closed his door. I heard him whistling from the other side.

I rubbed my hands together, turning from the door and walking back to the stairs. "Are you coming, boys?" I called to Brogan and Fionn. "Or are you both going to stand there looking gammy?" I heard Fionn's deep laughter as I headed down the stairs and grinned to myself.

****

Happy hour at the bar named The Black Dragon Tavern was already shaping up to be quite the party. Brogan, Fionn, and I snagged one of the last booths, Fionn raising his voice to place our order with the waitress over the hubbub. "I took the liberty of orderin' for ya, Lydia. Ya gotta drink like the true Irishwoman ya are if we're celebratin' ya joinin' our company today."

Brogan nodded. "As an office assistant. Temporary."

"I much prefer working in the field," I insisted.

"Not when the "field" is a rat-filled, asbestos-poisoned slum," Brogan grumbled.

"I don't know, mo chara, I think Lydia proved the field is exactly where her specific talents are needed, shur ya know like."

"We would have achieved the same result eventually," Brogan said.

"Aye, in donkey's years. We were shapin' up to make a balls of it first," Fionn said.

"Would you have *preferred* to spend money and time on a court case?" I asked. "Sure, you could have crushed him eventually. But Mr. Dudley just needed his ego stroked a bit by a female. You men seem to find that very convincing."

"The lady is right," Fionn said. "Us lads do like to be stroked. I can't deny it." He winked and I rolled my eyes. "Now," he went on, "like Lydia said, we can apply the funds we were plannin' on usin' to convince Mr. Dudley to do the right thing elsewhere, like."

The waitress delivered tall glasses of thick-looking black liquid I assumed was Guinness.

Fionn raised his glass. "To Lydia, and to a bleedin' deadly day in the field. Fair play to ya. Sláinte." He grinned and took a long drink. I followed suit, taking a mouthful of the strong beer, blinking and giving my head a small shake once I'd swallowed it down.

"Well, that'll put hair on your chest," I said, my eyes watering.

"Let's hope not," Brogan muttered. "I like your chest just the way it is." I laughed, nudging him.

Brogan seemed to spot someone at the bar and started to stand. "Hey, I need to go say hi to someone. I'll be right back."

"Oh okay," I said. He got up and I watched as he wove through the crowd, women looking back over their shoulders at him as he moved by. Though I bristled slightly with jealousy, I didn't blame them. And on top of the jealousy, I felt a strong surge of pride. *I* was going home with him tonight.

I looked at Fionn who was watching me with a small, knowing smile on his face.

"How are ya feelin'?" He glanced at my side where my stitches were. I hadn't even thought of it all day.

"I'm fine." I frowned slightly. "Brogan seems to have taken it harder than he needed to. It's just a scratch, and he solved a situation my brother put me in."

"He blames himself for turnin' your brother down the path of destruction in the first place. Tryin' to convince him otherwise is brutal, like."

"I suppose it was his initial intent." I bit at my lip. "A moral dilemma . . ." I murmured, still not completely sure how to organize it in my mind, especially because I was so close to the subject.

"I daren't say that Brogan knew completely what his initial intent really was, Lydia." Fionn took a long sip of his beer, appearing to use the time to consider his next words. "And aye, a moral dilemma. Brogan ain't that grand with moral dilemmas." He paused. "Brogan is savage with numbers, but when it comes to emotions," he frowned, "he can be fairly feckin' . . . black and white, either, or. It's like with numbers, his brain is nimble and complex, but with emotions, he can be a spanner." *A spanner. A person lacking wisdom.* He smiled, looking slightly guilty for his wording perhaps. "I don't mean it unkindly, like. He just has a bloody hell of a time seein' shades of gray when it comes to matters of the heart. Eileen says when he was six, he was doin' high school maths, but he'd wallop someone over the head if they mistreated the class pet. He's a man now, but sometimes with emotional subjects, well, he gets there, but it's not always a pretty process."

I smiled softly, nodding. "I do know what you mean. But it's part of what I always loved best about him." I realized the truth in my statement as it came from my lips. "The intensity . . . how fierce he is in his convictions," I murmured. "The degree to which he feels things."

"Aye, Brogan, he . . . doesn't give his heart easily, whether it's as a buddy or more, but when he does, it's yours forever. He doesn't know any other way to be. Do ya hear what I'm sayin'?"

I swallowed, feeling overwhelmed by the statement. Had Brogan given me his heart? Truly? I nodded yes, my eyes moving away, distracted by the questions in my head. We were both quiet for a minute before Fionn spoke again.

"I'm glad to see ya worked through the Courtney issue."

I took another drink of beer. It was definitely growing on me. I took a moment to savor the rich texture and the roasted flavors. "Yeah, he told me about her," I said once I'd swallowed. I pressed my lips together and frowned slightly. "You really dislike her, don't you?"

Fionn reclined back in the booth, seeming to take up the entirety of the side he was sitting on. "Aye. And the feelin' is mutual."

"I can't imagine anyone not liking you, Fionn."

He grinned. "I know, right? Clearly, she's not the full shillin'." He winked. But his expression was serious as he said, "Speakin' of moral dilemmas and Brogan seein' them differently than ya or I might."

I breathed out a small laugh. "Yeah, that intensity is a double-edged sword, isn't it?"

He nodded. "Aye. Like ya said, when he feels somethin', he feels it strongly, more strongly than most I think. Whether that's love or anger or guilt. And it makes him easy to be taken advantage of if the subject of his emotion is a manipulator. Courtney is a manipulatin' cow."

I sighed. "Well, I think he cleared things up with her."

"Jaysus, I hope so. If I never have to hear her whiny voice again it'll be too soon."

I took another sip of beer. "Fionn, can I ask you another question?"

"Anythin'."

"Your business . . . it seems like, well, it seems like you help people for a living."

"Not for a livin', no. There's no livin' to be made in helpin' people."

I tilted my head. "Then . . ."

He shrugged. "Brogan has a number of businesses that make a profit, too. But with or without those, he has more money than he can spend in this lifetime. Helpin' others is what he chooses to do with it. He gives jobs to folks who need them, he helps families find safe, clean housing, and sometimes he helps people with the money to pay this month's heating bill. Sometimes he brings lawsuits against slumlords because no one else can afford to. He helps those who are helpless."

Oh my God. He helps the helpless, and punishes those who prey on the helpless. "Like he was once." I felt a tightening in my chest.

"Aye."

I blinked at Fionn for a moment. *The man is a walking miracle. Proof that hope lost can be turned into hope restored. In Brogan's case, not only for himself, but for the others he assists. Could the man be more complex?* "Doesn't Brogan realize that he got back at everyone who ever wronged him simply with the way he lives his life?"

"No, he hasn't quite made it there," he said, a worried frown on his face that made a chill go down my spine for some reason I didn't quite understand in that moment.

Brogan came back to the table right then, interrupting my thoughts and causing me to startle slightly. There was an older man standing next to him.

"Lydia, I wanted you to meet a friend, Father Donoghue." *Father? A priest?*

"Hello, Father," I smiled, "nice to meet you."

"Well, it's a true pleasure," he said in a thick brogue, smiling broadly. He looked to Fionn. "Fionn, me boy, what's the craic?"

"Aye, dead on, yerself, Father?"

"Dead on. I don't usually see ya without a bird on ya arm."

Fionn looked around. "I'm about to remedy that, Father. Care to join me?"

Father Donoghue laughed. "Ah, no, no, only one woman for me. That was me Mary Catherine. God rest her soul." He looked to Brogan. "She was my *only*. And ack, what an *only* she was." Brogan smiled conspiratorially at him as I frowned in confusion. Weren't priests supposed to be celibate? Fionn stood up and clapped Father Donoghue on his back.

"I'll see ya later," Fionn said, shooting us a grin.

"Fionn," I called and he turned. "Thank you." He returned my smile, nodding before slipping into the crowd.

"Father, will ya join us?" Brogan asked Father Donoghue.

"Can't tonight, me boy. I have an appointment, but I'll take ya up on that kind offer another time, like."

We said our goodbyes to him, and Brogan slid back into the booth. I scooted close to him, hooking my arm through his.

He leaned in and whispered in my ear, "I want to take you home."

"Another sleepover?" I asked, tilting my head innocently.

"In a manner of speaking," he said darkly.

I felt a buzz begin between my legs, my nipples hardening against the thin material of my shirt. It had been a near torture to sleep in a bed with him the night before and not touch him. But I'd thought we needed a night like that—a night that was about something other than sex.

The ground I was on with Brogan felt anything but solid, my emotions careening between extremes from one moment to the next. And now that I understood what part of his business was really about, I was even more confused. I admired him so much for helping those in similar situations to the one he'd once been in, but I also understood his need to punish those who had made victims of others, and I still felt like I might be in that category. His feelings for me must be so convoluted. Would we ever be able to truly trust one another? Would he ever truly be able to let go of the past we shared? Especially because Stuart would always be in my life. There was no getting past that. Brogan might forgive *me*—and

I was hopeful he did—but I was doubtful he could ever really forgive Stuart. And where did that put me?

Pushing complicated thoughts aside, I looked to the far corner of the bar where a band was setting up.

I nodded over to them. "Are you familiar with that band?"

Brogan nodded. "I've heard them play once or twice. They're an Irish band that only plays locally."

"Can we stay for a little bit and listen to them?"

Brogan looked like he was going to protest for a minute, but I put my hands in the prayer position and smiled sweetly. He rolled his eyes, laughing softly, and relented. We finished our beers as the band played and I ordered another, although Brogan didn't.

The lead singer's voice was smoky and sensual. I was buzzed from the beer and Brogan's closeness *and* the way his thumb rubbed lazy circles on the top of my hand under the table. Brogan was telling me stories about some of the characters in the bar, and I was laughing and I felt young and happy, sitting next to a gorgeous, complicated man who fascinated me.

There were reasons I shouldn't feel so carefree, perhaps, but for just that moment it felt too good to deny. The liquor emptied my mind and the music filled it and I laughed and let everything else float away. It'd be back soon enough. This moment, though, this moment was mine. Brogan's and mine.

But I could also tell he was overwhelmed by the noise and the smells of this loud, crowded public place. He had tolerated it for me, which made me feel warm, but I didn't want him to overextend himself. "I want you," I whispered. "Can we go?"

He met my eyes and his were bright and filled with the same need I felt. He grabbed my hand, lifted his other one to Fionn across the bar who was sitting on a barstool with a redhead in his lap. Fionn lifted his hand in response and Brogan wove us through the crowd, my hand gripped in his until we stepped out of the loud bar into the fresh, warm summer air, the music muted behind the walls now. We walked quickly to the back lot where Brogan had parked earlier.

"How will Fionn get home?"

"Fionn will find a way," he said, letting me in the car. I had a feeling the redhead sitting on his lap would be happy to give him a ride. Pun intended. I giggled to myself and Brogan glanced over at me, raising a dark brow.

It felt like a million years before we were pulling into Brogan's garage, Brogan grabbing my hand again and almost running toward the elevator. I laughed and he shot me a heart-stopping smile over his shoulder. Once in the elevator, I leaned against one wall, Brogan against the opposite. "You know what's going to happen when we get upstairs, right?"

My heart rate spiked, lust careening wildly through my veins. "Yes," I whispered. Yes, and I wanted it. I wanted it more than I'd ever wanted anything in my life. *Did everyone feel this way about sex? I'd only had it a few times, but I felt addicted. Addicted to Brogan. To how he made me feel. Was it just him? Something told me it was.*

We stared at each other across the short distance between us in the elevator, and I swore I could hear both our hearts beating, the anticipation of feeling Brogan moving inside me again so sharp, I almost moaned. I clenched my thighs together, feeling a burst of pleasure in the small movement and Brogan's eyes went lazy. "Jaysus, Lydia," he said right before the elevator doors opened.

We barreled through the front door of his apartment, and as soon as the latch clicked behind us, Brogan had me pressed against the wall in the foyer. My chest heaved as I gazed up at him, his expression hungry, light eyes intense. His lips crashed down on mine, and he pushed his tongue into my mouth as I groaned, eagerly accepting it. As we kissed, Brogan's hand moved up my waist to my breast, his thumb lazily circling my hardened nipple. I gasped, pushing my breast toward his hand. "Oh God, that feels nice," I breathed.

His lips moved to my neck and he used his teeth to nip lightly at my skin. I sucked in a sharp breath and jumped slightly, letting out a small shivery laugh. He smiled against my skin, nipping lightly again and then dragging his tongue up my throat, finally bringing his lips back to mine. "You can always trust me," he whispered against my mouth. Our eyes were open and we stared at each other—the feeling of intimacy all the greater for the short distance between our gazes.

"Spoken like a true villain," I said, my voice breathy. I felt his lips curve again, his eyes squinting slightly with his smile.

"Am I still the villain?" he asked, bringing his hand to my hair and weaving his fingers into it. "I keep losing track." Without waiting for an answer, his eyes slid closed, and he slipped his tongue into my mouth. I moaned, accepting him, meeting his tongue and using my own to tangle and entwine. Our kisses grew more feverish, my blood boiling, Brogan's body hard and solid against my own.

"I can't be slow tonight, Lydia," he finally growled, breaking away. "I don't even know if I can make it upstairs. But . . ." He brought both hands to the buttons of my shirt, his mouth trailing down my throat as I tipped my head back, leaning on the wall behind me.

Our mouths came back together and as he undid my buttons, he began walking backward, pulling me with him. He finished with my shirt and pushed it off my shoulders. As it fell to the ground, he unbuttoned his own shirt. We were a tangle of open mouths, probing tongues, and grasping hands. Our clothes were being removed piece by piece and left strewn across the floor as we made our way toward the stairs.

My breath came out in heavy pants as I struggled with Brogan's belt buckle. "But?" I asked. Glancing up at him, I saw that his expression was filled with both lust and the slightly pained look he got when he was overly stimulated. I paused, thinking I understood. He was desperate and full of need, but he didn't know how to rush things without experiencing a certain amount of discomfort. "We can slow down," I murmured.

"I don't want to slow down," he said, taking over at undoing his belt. He had it off in about two seconds flat and was unbuttoning his pants when we got to the stairs. He climbed up three steps backward pulling me with him, and I pushed at his chest so that he was forced to sit down. He let out a startled laugh as his ass hit the stair and I grinned down at him, moving onto his lap so that my legs were on either side of his hips, our pelvis's meeting.

"You're in good hands," I whispered against his lips right before I kissed him, rotating my hips in his lap.

"Spoken like a true villain," he murmured when our mouths parted.

I smirked at him and then licked down his throat slowly. There it was, that salt I'd always associated with him *before*. I let it settle on my tongue as if it were a fine delicacy, rotating my hips again, the throbbing ache in my core intensifying to a steady drumbeat. Brogan gasped and I felt his erection jump against my belly. I reached between us, into his open pants and caressed his hard flesh, eliciting a moan from him. "The mystery is solved," I whispered against his mouth, not having met with the barrier of an underwear waistband. He smiled back, obviously understanding my meaning.

We kissed and kissed right there on his stairs, my hand wrapped around his erection but unmoving so as not to cause him too much stimulation just yet. Just the feel of the hard, thick, hot flesh in my grip made me wild with desire. Brogan's fingers dug into my hips, until he finally broke away.

"Lydia, God, I'm so—"

"I know. Me too."

Somehow we made it to his bedroom, though I didn't think our lips ever parted and by the time we got there, we were both completely naked.

He reached into what looked like his unpacked overnight bag sitting on a chair near the door and grabbed a box of condoms, tossing them on the bedside table. I raised a brow. "Expecting to get lucky?"

His eyes moved down my naked body before he met my gaze, smiling charmingly, if not a little dazedly, and I couldn't help laughing. "Just hoping," he said, wrapping his arms around my waist as I ran my hand through his thick, glossy hair and kissed him again, smiling against his lips.

He fell backward onto the mattress, and I went down on top of him, the feel of his hot, bare male skin against mine so wonderfully erotic, I found myself wanting to simply writhe against him. He scooted up toward the headboard and I followed, kissing slowly down his chest. He groaned.

"Tonight, it's my turn to touch you," I murmured, feathering my lips over his pectorals, flicking my tongue out to taste one flat nipple. I listened to his breathing, his reactions to determine if what I was doing was pleasurable for him. In this way, he was very easy to read.

I was born knowing your body's language, Brogan. Trust me.

I feathered my lips over the hard muscles of his upper abdomen and he sucked in a breath, his hips coming up off the mattress slightly. A thrill went through my belly.

When I glanced down, he was so hard his penis was lying against his stomach, the tip almost purple it was so engorged with blood, the veins prominent. I clenched my thighs together and continued lower until I reached his cock, wondering if he'd be salty there, too. I flicked my tongue out to taste it, and Brogan let out a guttural hiss. *Yes, just the bare hint of salt on clean skin.*

"Okay?" I murmured against his swollen flesh.

"Yes, God, yes," he groaned, sitting up slightly, the muscles of his stomach tensing and bunching as he used his hands to gather my hair at the top of my head. He gripped it, pulling slightly and causing a delicious tingling in my scalp. I thought he had done it because the feeling of my hair tickling his skin while my mouth was on his cock was too much, but something about him gripping my hair and controlling my movements turned me on so much, I moaned, bringing my lips back to his cock. I licked him from base to tip and then took the head into my mouth, sucking gently.

"Ah, God, Lydia." He said something in Gaelic that sounded like neeus mo.

Licking at him again, I said, "You have the control. Show me what you like."

He didn't answer, but I heard him suck in another breath. I had never done this before and wasn't sure how good I'd be at it, but I also didn't want to overwhelm him or do something he wouldn't like. He already sounded like he was on the brink of torture. I just hoped it was the good sort of torture.

Using one hand to fist the base of him, I brought my mouth over his cock and used my tongue to swirl around it. His grip became tighter in my hair, and he pulled gently until my mouth came all the way to the tip, and then he pushed, filling my mouth again. He repeated this movement several times as I increased the suction until he was panting so loudly, the end of each breath was punctuated by a small, deep groan.

"You're going to be the death of me," he rasped and then muttered something else in Gaelic as he let go of my hair and pulled me up by my arms until I was straddling him. I felt flushed and overheated, throbbing with arousal.

"Put your tits in my mouth, Lydia," Brogan said, and I moaned again, my skin prickling as I scooted up his waist and leaned until my breasts were right at his face and he sucked one sensitive nipple into his mouth, giving it a hard pull. I cried out loudly, pleasure arcing from my breast to my clit as I squirmed on top of him. He gripped my ass with one hand as he licked and sucked at my nipples, using the other hand to run one finger up and down the crack of my ass, spreading the slick wetness from my core. It felt like my eyes were going to roll into the back of my head as I rocked on top of him, his mouth and his hands working magic on my body. After a few minutes, an orgasm slammed into me so intensely I arched my back and screamed with pleasure, collapsing on top of him and whimpering softly, overcome and shocked by the intensity of my climax. He hadn't even touched me between my legs. *Holy hell. How had that happened?*

"Put me in, Mo Chroí," Brogan said, sounding like he was barely able to form the words. He reached over to the bedside table, grabbing a condom. He ripped it open with his teeth and then reached behind me. I looked over my shoulder fascinated and turned on by the sight of him sliding the condom quickly over his erection.

I scooted back a little and lifted myself up slightly and wrapped my hand around his cock, fitting it into the wet opening of my body. *Oh God, yes.* I moaned at the feel of him entering me, my vaginal muscles leaping in a small aftershock.

"Oh Brogan. God, God," I murmured, pausing and riding out the small, unexpected burst of bliss that the contact of our most intimate parts had brought on.

"Mo Chroí, I'm gona die a brutal death if I don't get in ya," he groaned out. I let go of his shaft and sunk all the way onto him, impaled completely as I leaned back and began to move slowly, letting out a satisfied sigh.

He gripped my hips and exerted pressure until he was moving me the way he wanted—slow at first and then faster as his head went back on the pillow. His skin flushed, his lips falling open, the muscles of his arms and chest taut with strain and glistening with perspiration, the rippled muscles of his abdomen flexing as he made masculine sounds of pleasure. *So incredibly sexy.* His erotic male beauty was utterly mesmerizing, and I sucked in a breath, wanting to memorize the way he looked in that moment. *I was doing that to him.*

As I moved, he muttered words in Gaelic, words I didn't understand but thought I knew all the same. *Yes, yes, don't stop, please, oh God,* I imagined was what he was whispering in that beautiful, mysterious language.

Brogan moved me faster and faster, his cock sliding into my drenched core over and over, his hips pumping from beneath until he slammed into me one final time, yelling out and arching his head back deeper into the pillow beneath his head.

I collapsed on top of him again, and he brought his arms around me, holding me as we both trembled, drifting back to earth, our breathing slowing, our thundering hearts finally returning to normal.

In a haze, I used my fingertip to trace a vein under the skin of his bicep and made a deep, satisfied hum in my throat, finally raising my head to look at him.

He looked drowsy and half drunk with pleasure. "That was . . ." He trailed off, not seeming to know how to continue.

"I know," I said sleepily, smiling against his skin.

After a few minutes, I attempted to sit up, our slick bodies peeling apart. I felt boneless and heavy limbed. Brogan scooted out from under me, moving me gently onto the pillow as he got up and went to the bathroom to get rid of the condom, I assumed. A minute later I heard the bath running and a few minutes after that, Brogan came back into the room, picking me up and carrying me to the bathroom where he deposited me in a tub of warm, bubbly water. I sighed out, leaning my head back.

The nurse, Margaret, had said to keep my stitches dry for twenty-four hours, but it'd been longer than that. I smoothed the waterproof Band-Aid down anyway, to make sure it was secure. It was obviously healing well—I hadn't thought of it once in all our . . . maneuverings.

"Are you going to join me?" I asked, my lids heavy.

Brogan dropped the towel he'd wrapped around his waist and stepped in, leaning back against the opposite side. For a minute we simply watched each other, something intense and erotic leaping between us. This was the most intimate moment I'd ever experienced. Brogan ran a wet hand through his hair, leaving it tousled and standing straight up.

I smiled. "You are so handsome," I said. He gave me a crooked, shy smile and I felt butterfly wings stir in my stomach. I tilted my head. "You must know."

He cupped a handful of water and brought it to his face, sputtering slightly and smiling at me, teasing. "The only woman I'm interested in appealing to is you," he said, his expression suddenly serious.

I gazed at him for a moment wondering how it was that this beautiful, complex man wanted me, wondering what it was about me that made him desire me the way he seemed to. "What does neeus mo mean?" I asked.

Brogan grinned. "It's spelled n-í-o-s m-o," he answered. It means *more*." He raised an eyebrow. I used my hand to swirl the bubbles in front of me, and he glanced down at one of my nipples poking through the water, his gaze darkening.

"What about ledehull?"

"It's three words, l-e d-o t-h-o-i-l. It means *please*." I licked my lips and his eyes moved to my mouth. So I'd been right about what he was saying. "I'm going to have to be careful what I utter around you," he said, a teasing gleam in his eye. "I'm far less safe than I thought."

"Far less," I agreed, smiling back. I sat up, moving toward him until I was lying over him, my face in front of his. His hands went to my ass and he rubbed it gently, bringing the water up and over my skin. "Teach me how to say something in Gaelic."

He considered me for a moment, moving a damp piece of hair behind my ear before saying something that sounded like, "Iss le Brogan may." I repeated it and his eyes moved over my face, his gaze somehow soft and intense at the same time, his lips tipping up as if very pleased. He leaned forward and kissed me softly, uttering something that sounded like, "Iss latsa mo chree."

"What did you have me say?" I asked, nuzzling my nose along his and letting out a small moan as his fingers massaged up my back.

He leaned toward my ear. "I had you say, I love Brogan's large, extremely competent penis." I let out a surprised laugh and shook my head, pinching his nipple lightly.

"Ow."

I laughed again, raising a brow. "And what did you say back?"

"I wholeheartedly agreed with your assessment of my penis."

I continued to laugh, even though I suspected he was lying because the name he called me—the word that sounded like mo chree—*princess,* had been on the end of his statement. I brought my lips to his, kissing him as he smiled against my mouth. "Someday I'll learn Gaelic, and then I'll know all your secrets," I whispered before licking along the seam of his mouth. He moaned and opened to me.

We played in the water for a little while longer until I was squirming again and Brogan was hard. He got out and toweled himself off, his erection jutting out in front of him. He helped me out, drying me thoroughly and applying a new Band-Aid before lifting me and carrying me back to the bed as I laughed.

"I can walk, you know."

He placed me on the bed, following me down, rubbing his hard cock on my thigh. "Not after tonight," he said darkly, nipping at my neck as I laughed and squealed for mercy. He kissed me thoroughly then and the mood changed. He made love to me slowly and sweetly this time and I fell asleep in his arms, not waking until the sun was lighting the room in a soft, golden glow, welcoming us to a brand new day.

CHAPTER TWENTY-ONE

Brogan

The next few weeks went by simultaneously in a haze of bliss and a blur of regret.

Lydia came to work with me every day, exerting her feminine charm in situations I would have handled completely differently, and astounding me with the ease in which she achieved the positive results that likely would have taken Fionn or me weeks or months. She was that bright hummingbird I remembered—flitting everywhere, coloring my days with spirit and vibrancy, completely in her element.

And the nights . . . the nights were filled with bliss beyond my wildest imagination. Lydia learned what I liked as if my body was the subject and she was the most committed student who ever lived. I began to trust her in a way I didn't think was possible to trust a woman, which in turn allowed me to relax and enjoy the sensations she aroused in me. She always seemed to know when something was bordering on too much or when there was room to push me to greater heights, and I in turn, learned my own limits through my surrender to her. She had never been with anyone else, but in some ways, neither had I. In bed, I had *never* known true surrender, I had never known joy.

I felt hunger in the way I'd known hunger before, only this time I was even more insatiable. I knew I'd never be satisfied, never have enough, never be filled no matter how much I partook. She was a buffet of the finest delicacies life had to offer me, and I wanted to binge and devour every luscious morsel. I wanted to be sure that what I needed and wanted so desperately would always be available to me—I didn't want to feel this faint panic after every time we made love, the way I'd felt *before* when I'd had to scrounge for every small meal.

But that was the way of hunger, wasn't it? Even as it was being satisfied, there laid the knowledge it would need to be satisfied again . . . and again.

So I studied her body, too, worshipping every inch of her skin night after glorious night, learning the scents and textures of every part of her, not satisfied until she had an orgasm so intense she screamed my name. And then we'd sleep wrapped in each other's arms through the night.

And I knew I loved her. Deeply. Intensely. I had *always* loved her, even when I hadn't wanted to. But now it was different. I had wanted to give her the world when I was seventeen, and now I could. I had wanted to give her my heart, and now I could. *I would.* Every part of my heart.

And yet . . . I was still in the midst of cleaning up the mess I myself had created. I had Fionn take Lydia to dinner under the guise I had more work to do while I repaid her brother's debt to the mob in the form of illegal number crunching.

I hated it—it made me feel owned and powerless, and yet it was the price I had to pay to make up for the situation we were in. I just didn't want Lydia to know. I didn't want her to be burdened with the information, I didn't want the knowledge of illegal activity to put her in any more potential danger, and truthfully, I didn't want her to feel less about me. I was not the stand-up businessman she thought. And when we worked together at my office, solving a problem for a family who had no one else to turn to, she looked at me as if I were some sort of hero. I didn't want to tell her I wasn't. I was just a man who was still scrabbling and cheating and trying to justify the means to an end I was dreaming about so hard it felt like an obsession.

I wanted Lydia. I wanted her forever. And I ached for her to want me back. I wanted her to admire me, to respect me. I wanted her to love me. *Me. She* had *loved me. Would she now?* And sometimes, as I gazed at her in the moonlight of my bedroom, our limbs tangled together, our bodies intimately connected, I dared to hope she might.

I knew that once I finished this final job, Lydia wouldn't be in danger, and realistically, she could safely move back to her own apartment. Yet, I *wanted* her with me. She didn't seem in any hurry to leave, which gave me further hope she didn't want our time living together to end either.

We had both been distracted by everything going on and hadn't remembered to send someone to get more clothes for her, and so after work one day, I accompanied her to her place so she could pack a few more things.

I'd seen her apartment from the outside, a modest brick building in Brooklyn, but the inside was even more modest than the outside. When I saw the difference between where Stuart and Lydia lived, I wanted to beat Stuart De Havilland's arse even more than I had before.

What kind of arsehole let his sister live in a small, run-down studio when he lived in luxurious high style? I thought about Eileen and how I'd kick my *own* arse before I'd watch her struggle if I could do anything about it, if adjusting my lifestyle meant making things better for her. Then again, I'd done things I'd regret forever to make things better for Eileen. Maybe there was some sort of happy medium. Fionn enjoyed telling me I didn't always need to be so *extreme*. And yet I wasn't sure how to be anything else. *Extreme* had gotten me where I was today.

"Do you think we could spend the weekend in Greenwich?" she asked as she packed.

"Sure," I said distractedly, tracing a large crack in her wall with my finger and frowning. "Why?"

"I just thought it'd be nice to get out of the city, enjoy some sunshine," she said. She came up behind me, wrapping her arms around my waist and laying her head on my back. I dropped my hand from the wall and looked at her over my shoulder.

"Anythin' you want, Lydia," I said, my voice cracking before I cleared my throat. She smiled and pulled away.

I walked to her refrigerator and pulled the freezer open, noting two piles of Budget Gourmets and two ice trays, nothing more. I stared glumly at the small boxes of frozen food. *Budget* frozen food.

The first time I'd seen Stuart after I'd decided to take over his company, he'd been dining at one of the most expensive restaurants on Madison Avenue. I'd wanted to get a fix on him, find out what kind of life he was leading, how much he might be tempted to lose to me in a poker game. I'd found out he was already addicted to the lust of the game. I just hadn't delved any deeper into Lydia's life. *If I had* . . . would it have changed my mind? Would it have caused me to change course? I wanted to believe it would, but I wasn't so sure . . .

This though, right here, this was the life I'd interrupted. This was the life I'd set out to *ruin*.

I love you and you were living here and I hate myself for it. How can you not hate me, too?

If only I'd walked up to her at that party, like I'd mentioned to her in Greenwich. If only I'd found a way to let go of the past and returned to her and begged her . . . but no, I'd never beg. I'd promised myself I'd never beg again. And yet for Lydia . . .

"Are you hungry?" she asked, interrupting my thoughts.

I slammed the freezer door closed. "No," I said. "Ready?"

The expression on her face was mildly confused, but she smiled and we left her apartment and returned to mine. That night I made love to her three times, unable to get enough, unable to quench the longing, knowing somehow I was at risk of losing her, of being left hungry *forever*, and not being able to figure out why I was so gripped by fear.

****

When the concierge at Stuart's apartment building called his line to announce me, the pause was so long I thought I was going to have to grab the phone and threaten Stuart to let me up. But just as I was about to do so, the concierge looked at me and nodded toward the elevators.

A few minutes later I knocked on Stuart's door and he answered as if he'd been standing right behind it waiting for me. "Stuart," I greeted, working not to grimace at the foul odor that permeated his apartment. God, had something died in here?

"What do you want?" he asked sulkily. I narrowed my eyes at him as he closed the door. He looked awful, far worse than he had the last time I'd seen him. Either this situation was severely stressing him out or he was consuming more drugs and alcohol than I'd imagined. Maybe all of the above. "I'm busy."

"No, you're not. Your only job these days, *evidently*, is drinking and doing a fuck ton of nothing."

A muted sort of anger took hold of his expression, as if it was the best he could muster at the moment and under the influence of whatever he might currently be on. "You're the one who told me to lie low," he growled.

"Lying low doesn't mean sinking into a state of utter uselessness," I shot back. "If it hasn't occurred to you, you have some decisions to make with your life."

"Fuck off."

"I plan to." I wouldn't stay a moment longer than necessary in this cesspool-smelling hellhole. Then it hit me: Stuart De Havilland had probably thought the same thing when he'd come to *visit* me in my own personal hellhole all those years ago. The circumstances were different and Stuart's hellhole was one of his own making, and still featured one of the best addresses in the city. And yet . . . it was a hellhole all the same. A pit of despair. I hesitated. "But first, I came to let you know your debt's been paid off. You're off the hook. And the men with whom you took out credit will kill you before they extend more, is that clear?"

He regarded me suspiciously. "You paid off my debt? I thought you were going to buy me more time."

"What good would that have done?" I asked. He kept staring at me, the wheels in his head turning as fast as they were able. "You'd never be able to pay them. Especially not at the rate you're going."

"You did this for some reason," he grated. "What is it?"

I stared at him, tamping down the anger his reaction evoked. I was fucking whoring myself again for this bastard, in a manner of speaking anyway, and the best he could give me was suspicion. I hadn't expected a thank you, but even so . . . "I did it for your sister," I said honestly. "I did it because I care about her. And for some reason, she cares about you. And if you have any decency at all, you'll take this second chance and get your life together, for her, if not for yourself."

"You've got something up your sleeve, you Irish fucker."

I let out a weary sigh, glancing around at his trashed apartment, noting there were napkins and magazines and receipts littering the table surfaces and even some floor space, all of them featuring drawings and doodles. I looked more closely at the swirls and small pictures. I envisioned him sitting alone in his apartment, in a drug-and-alcohol-induced state, obsessively creating art anywhere and everywhere. It was odd and unsettling. And yet, it wasn't only amateur doodling, it was . . . good. It was really good. "You could go back to school and study art," I murmured, almost to myself. "It seems like—"

A look of rage so sudden and intense came over Stuart's face that it startled me. He barreled toward me, his fists flying. I easily sidestepped him, but he seemed to be possessed by something stronger than himself as he came at me again. I ducked and then struck out with my fist, connecting with his jaw as he let out a loud grunt and whirled backward, falling onto his couch, the anger seeming to drain from him as he gripped his jaw. "You *asshole*," he choked. "I will fucking kill you someday." He kept rubbing at his jaw, looking strangely lost now.

Despite the threat, the only thing I felt was pity.

Stepping over a lamp lying on the floor, I moved toward his apartment door, shaking my hand. It'd been a long damn time since I'd had to punch someone.

"I'm broke," Stuart said flatly. "I don't even have enough money to eat, much less figure out a plan for my life."

I paused, the doorknob in my hand. He couldn't know it, but it was my Achilles heel, the thing I couldn't walk away from without helping—*hunger*. I blew out a breath, reaching into my pocket for my wallet. The vision of him throwing the hundred-dollar bill on the floor and me having to bend to retrieve it floated through my mind. I supposed I should feel vindication in this moment—the tables had turned in such a literal way. So why instead did a sad ache fill my chest?

I had a little under a thousand dollars in cash on me. I took it all from my wallet and laid it down on the table next to the door. "Be well, Stuart." And I left.

CHAPTER TWENTY-TWO

Lydia

I walked out of Brogan's home gym, rubbing a towel over the back of my neck as my breathing slowed. I'd used his treadmill for a slow, five-mile run, and though I felt invigorated, it had been harder than it should have been. I was out of shape. I needed to get back on the regular exercise wagon.

As I stood under the hot spray of the shower, I hummed the tune of the song the Irish band had played the night we went to The Black Dragon. This morning I felt free, light, unencumbered.

Although I checked in with Trudi almost every day, I had taken a small step back in recent weeks, knowing De Havilland Enterprises was doing just fine. And honestly, it was a relief to let go of the constant worry, to let the capable team Brogan had put in place take on the responsibility of what I had been carrying mostly alone for so long.

In the weeks since, I'd gone to work with Brogan every day and it almost scared me how much I loved working with him—or not even with him precisely, although that was wonderful, too. I just loved doing what he did. Problem solving for others who didn't have the means to be creative in the ways we did was fun and challenging and more gratifying than anything I'd ever been involved in to date.

My father had always given charitably, and I would, too, as soon as I was financially able, but this was different than that. This was offering my *talents* and my *heart* in a way that was useful to others. And the reason my love for it scared me was because I knew it was temporary. I had my own job to go back to at some point soon. Which was a good thing, but . . . I'd miss the lilting accents, the kids running in and out, the cheeky boys who I could make blush with just a look, the colorful characters we worked with in one capacity or another, the bursts of Gaelic that rang out like sweet bird chatter throughout the day. And the way I felt *valuable*—not because I had money, but because of *me*. It was really the first time I'd felt that way. *Ever.*

Rinsing the last of the conditioner from my hair, I let out a sigh. Yes, I'd miss it terribly. Maybe I could convince Brogan to let me volunteer a couple of days a week after work.

Brogan—intense, complex Brogan. A shiver ran down my spine just thinking about what we'd done the night before. *Foreplay that had lasted for hours . . . we'd both come mere seconds after he'd slipped inside me.* I couldn't get enough of him. But it wasn't just sex—I loved talking to him, too. Loved being curled up in his arms, listening to his deep voice, noticing the places where his accent broke through and knowing it was always telling, informing me what to listen closely to, what topics affected him the most. He had a few small "tells" and I knew only the people closest to him knew what they were.

As I toweled off, I heard my cell—the one Brogan had replaced for me after mine had been shattered on the street—ringing from the kitchen counter downstairs, but ignored it. I pulled on my clothes—a pair of black, silky shorts and a thin pale gray sweater that fell off one shoulder. I heard my phone ring again and ran down the stairs to grab it, wrapping my wet hair in a messy bun and securing it as I went. I grabbed my phone on the final ring. "Hello?" I said breathlessly, noticing Daisy's name right before I picked up.

"Lydia?" she asked, tears in her voice.

"Dais? What's wrong?"

"He's cheating on me," she said, hiccupping. "I suspected it. I have for a long time. I guess I," she let out a small sob, "I just didn't want to believe it."

I sat down on Brogan's couch. "Oh honey . . ." I breathed. "Are you sure? I mean—"

"Yes. I followed him last night. He said he had a business meeting, but I just got a weird feeling. I've been getting a lot of them lately so I followed him to a hotel. He met a woman in the lobby and they went up to a room together. I followed and waited fifteen minutes before I knocked and he answered the door and," she let out another sob, "he was shirtless and she was in bed, Lydia."

My stomach dropped. There was no way to put a positive spin on that—no way to read it any differently than she had. "Oh God," I whispered. "Oh Daisy, I'm so sorry. I don't even know what to say. What did *you* say?"

"I couldn't say anything!" She sniffled. "I hightailed it out of there and sobbed in my car. I don't even remember driving home."

"Did *he* come home?"

"Yeah. He got home fifteen minutes after I did and tried to apologize . . . tried to explain . . . but, there's just no explaining that. And Lydia, it was his secretary. I recognized her as soon as I saw her in the lobby. I was just stupidly hoping they were there on some business together. Even as I followed them upstairs, I kept hoping. I mean, how cliché can you get, right? He even mocked a coworker that got caught cheating with his secretary last year—said how predictable it was. We *laughed* about it, you know, like if you're going to cheat, at least be original about it. And then . . . and then . . . that. The fucking hypocrite. Oh my *God,*" she wailed. "Do you want to go shopping? I'm headed to the city now."

I blinked. "Shopping? No, Daisy. Shopping, sadly, is not going to fix this, honey. I don't even know if shopping will put a Band-Aid on this. Listen, I'm in the city at Brogan's. He's working, and I'm here alone. Do you want to come here? We can talk."

"Brogan's?" she asked.

"Oh Daisy," I sighed. "I have so much to catch you up on. But that can wait. We're going to talk about you first, okay?"

"I *don't* want to be alone right now," she squeaked. "Is that okay?"

"Yes. Just drive carefully, and I'll be waiting. I'm going to text you his address. There's a garage under his building, okay?"

"Okay. Thank you, Lydia."

"Of course, Dais." We said goodbye and I hung up and texted her Brogan's address, pursing my lips with anger. That jackass! How *could* he? I kicked the chair next to the couch, which only resulted in a dull ache in my foot. "Fucker," I muttered aloud.

As I blow-dried my hair and put on a little makeup, I felt so angry. Gregory was such a bastard. No woman deserved to be cheated on. *Ever.* I wasn't sure how Dais would rebound from this. Just as I was sliding some gloss onto my lips, I heard the doorbell ring. It was Saturday, and Brogan had told me he had some work to do, but had acted a little dodgy about exactly what it was, just as he'd been doing a lot of lately. He promised he'd be back early and take me out to dinner. This was good as it meant he was less concerned about the potential safety issues involved in going out in public.

I pressed the button on the camera to the street and saw my brother. Frowning, I pressed the intercom. "Stuart?"

He looked around as if expecting someone to suddenly attack him and then leaned in to the intercom. "Lydia. Let me up. Hurry."

Hesitating and biting at my lip, I said, "I don't think that's a good idea, Stu. Let me come down."

"No! Someone's following me. Let me up, Lydia." He sounded so panicked, my skin prickled. Hesitating again, but only briefly, I pressed the button allowing him entrance. I waited by the door until I saw him outside on the other camera screen. I opened it and he rushed in, practically barreling me over.

"Whoa. What the hell, Stuart?"

"Why are you still here?" he demanded. I shut the door, turning toward him. "I saw him leave a while ago. I waited for you, but you never came down. Now's your chance to leave."

"Brogan's not keeping me here against my will," I said. "He just wanted to be sure the men who held your loans didn't pose a threat any longer," I explained, walking past him into the kitchen and behind the island. I had never even told him about the stabbing. What was the point? It was over, and there was nothing he could do about it now.

He followed me into the kitchen, standing across the island from me. "He supposedly paid off those loans," he said. "But he lied. He lied. There are men following me. And if they don't get me first, he will." He glanced to the window as if, even now, they could see him. "There are men trying to kill me. And he knows they'll kill you, too. That's why he's keeping you here," he growled, twitching in what turned into a sort of grotesque shudder.

I frowned. "Stuart, what's wrong with you?"

He threw up his arms. "I don't sleep!" he yelled. "You wouldn't either if you had a hit out on your life!"

I shook my head. "You're wrong. Brogan paid off your debts. You're free and clear, Stu. No one is trying to kill you."

He shook his head almost violently. "No, no, no. You're wrong. He lied. He won't be satisfied until I'm dead and then he'll ruin you, too. He'll make you fall in love with him and then he'll be the one with all the power. Whatever you do, Lydia, don't get feelings for him. He's a liar and a cunning devil."

"Stuart, *God*, do you hear yourself?" He sounded insane.

"I have proof," he said, taking something out of his back pocket. He unfolded a piece of paper and threw it on the counter.

"What's that?" I asked, looking down at it suspiciously.

"He owns our old house in Greenwich," he said. "He bought it two months ago. I looked it up on the Internet. He bought it through a corporation, but he owns it. It all came back to him."

I frowned, picking up the paper, a printout from the Fairfield County auditor's website. It took me a minute to read through it, but it looked like Stuart was right. I knew for a fact Brogan owned the company that now owned our old property in Greenwich because of the work I'd done for Brogan. I tilted my head in confusion, trying to understand why Brogan would have bought our house and not told me the day we went there.

"It's all part of his master plan," Stuart said, twitching again and rubbing at his neck. "Me, dead, you under his thumb, and him," he gestured his hands around as if he was trying to communicate what he was thinking but was having a hard time getting there, "master of the domain where he once worked as a servant," he finally blurted out.

"He was our gardener, not a servant," I mumbled, casting my gaze to the side, confusion overwhelming me. "And that sounds pretty dramatic, Stu."

"This whole fucking situation is dramatic, Lydie," he said, using a nickname he hadn't used since we were kids. "Machiavellian revenge plots, mobsters, *hit men*? I didn't make any of *that* up."

A cold lump of dread was sitting in my belly. "I just need to talk to him," I muttered. "I just need to ask him . . . I'm sure . . ."

Stuart stared at me, a horror-stricken look on his face as he began to back up. "Oh my God," he breathed out in a sudden rasp. "It's already done. You're in love with the devil."

I met his red-rimmed gaze. "He's not a devil, Stu. He's—"

He spun away, his hands on his head as he let out what sounded like a growl of defeat. "I have to get out of here."

I came from around the island, holding my hand out to him. "No, Stu, please, you look so tired. Let me make you some tea, and we can sit down. We can talk about this. And Brogan will be home soon—"

"No, no, no." He shook his head. "They're following me. I need to leave."

"No one's following you."

He scrubbed at his face. "I need some money, Lydie. Just whatever you have. Please. I can't go back to my apartment."

"I . . . I only have about fifty dollars on me." And that was only because Brogan had given me cash to pay for the dinner delivery we'd ordered the night before, but then gotten out of the shower before it arrived. He'd paid and the cash had remained in my wallet.

"Whatever you have, I need it. Now. Right now."

I took a long look at him. He truly looked awful, as if he hadn't showered in days, or slept, or eaten. But there was also a fear in his eyes I'd never seen before. Were people really after him? No, surely not. Surely he was sleep deprived, possibly still drinking . . . "My purse is upstairs," I muttered. "I can make you some food here, though."

"No. I need to go before he comes back. Give me the money." He held out his hand, moving his fingers back and forth. *Jesus.*

I stared at him a moment longer, not knowing what was best in this situation. "I'll be right back," I finally said, going toward the stairs.

He followed me. "You can come with me."

I shook my head and looked back at him. When we got to the landing, I said, "Where, Stu?"

He scratched at the inside of his elbow, his eyes jumping around the empty hall. "No, you're right. You can't come with me. You'd just be in more danger. But you need to get out of here. Promise me you'll find a way to get out of here and . . ." His words faded away.

I stared at him for a moment, waiting for him to finish, but it didn't seem he was going to, and he obviously wasn't waiting for an answer from me, so I simply turned and went into the guest room where my purse was on the dresser. I dug in my wallet and pulled out the money, two twenties and a ten. I opened my change purse, too, to see if I had a few dollars in quarters. I did and collected those as well. I turned and handed the money to Stuart. "Stuart—"

"Thanks, Lydia, I gotta go," he said, moving past me and out into the hall.

"Wait, Stuart!" He bounded down the steps and was already opening the door by the time I got to the bottom. "Wait, I—"

He turned, pausing, his eyes seeming to clear for just a moment. "I love you, Lydie. Mom and Dad would have been so proud of you." And then he walked out the door, closing it behind him. I stood in the foyer, staring after him for long minutes, rattled and confused.

****

I went back inside Brogan's apartment and stood staring out the window at the city beyond for a good long while as I considered Stuart's demeanor and everything he had said.

I felt worried and sickened, scared and confused. There was something wrong with Stuart—either it was paranoia or perhaps drugs, maybe both—but was the paranoia based on something real? Had Brogan told me he paid Stuart's debts and not really done so for some nefarious reason? I shook my head at the very thought. No . . . *no.* I didn't believe that. I wouldn't. I *trusted* Brogan. It had been weeks since I'd been knifed, and the threat had been about Stuart. So, if no harm had come to him . . . although . . . why had Brogan lied about buying my family's old estate? He had bought it *months* ago and that day when we'd gone there together, I'd said something to him about how it had gone up for sale, and he could have bought it himself, and he'd . . . what had he done? He'd said he needed a guesthouse for Eileen. He'd redirected the conversation. But *why?*

I wanted to trust him so badly, but doubts were assaulting me left and right. Speaking of doubts, what was he *really* working on today? And why had he pawned me off on Fionn so many nights recently while he apparently worked late? I hadn't wanted to pry too much before today, suspected maybe Brogan did jobs he didn't want me involved in for safety's sake, and I was okay with that, but now I needed answers. I needed reassurance. To know the truth, I would have to look in his eyes and watch as he answered all my questions. *That meant waiting until later.*

The buzzer sounded from the street and I walked quickly to the door, giving the screen a precursory glance, seeing Daisy's face and buzzing her up.

I opened Brogan's apartment door and waited for the elevator in the vestibule, pacing as I did so, going over my worries again. I needed to put them aside though as soon as the elevator opened because Daisy needed me. *What was taking so long?*

Finally, the elevator dinged softly. Even before the doors slid completely open, I heard Daisy laughing with someone and frowned slightly. Was Brogan home already? Daisy stepped out of the elevator smiling, although her eyes were red and puffy. I smiled back and started toward her, when Courtney stepped out from behind. I halted, my smile slipping. *Oh God. What now?*

"Lydia," Daisy said, "this is Court—"

"Yes, I know who she is." I sighed. "Hello, Courtney. Brogan isn't here."

Courtney gave me a smile, somewhat cat-like, but it moved quickly into a small frown. "Oh dear. Well, I'd tell you to leave him a message, but it's somewhat personal in nature." She tapped one long red nail on her front tooth for a moment as if in thought as my heart began beating faster. *What was she up to?*

She looked at Daisy. "Oh Daisy darling, you've confided in *me* about your philandering husband, the *prick.*" She put her hand on Daisy's shoulder. "And so I feel comfortable confiding in you. I had a pregnancy scare!" Her eyes widened as she turned her face to me. "I just wanted to let Brogan know there was no longer reason for concern. Until next time, I suppose." She laughed softly, her eyes narrowing ever so slightly. *Pregnancy scare? Next time?*

"You're lying," I said flatly. There was no way Brogan was sleeping with this woman. Or was that where he'd been going some nights . . .

Daisy looked confused as her head moved from Courtney to me. Courtney walked toward me slowly, sizing me up as if she was about to devour me and wanted to make sure I'd satisfy her appetite.

"No," she said. "I'm not. Ask him yourself."

"I will," I said, lifting my chin and crossing my arms, biting down on my lip that insisted on shaking.

One side of her mouth tipped up in some strange version of a smile, and there was pity in her eyes. My guts twisted painfully, and it took everything in me not to run inside and slam the door on her, make this stop, start this whole day over. I'd woken in Brogan's arms; his hand had been cupping my breast possessively.

"He told me about you as he fucked me. Did he tell you *that?* He told me how he was going to ruin you. He told me he was going to enjoy it."

My stomach dropped and a small sound came from my throat. *Oh God.* I put my hand over my mouth, to stop the noise, or perhaps the vomit that threatened. *Please make this stop.* Blood was rushing in my ears and my skin felt hot and prickly.

Daisy moved quickly to my side, glaring at Courtney. "Wait, who the fuck are you?"

Courtney's eyes moved slowly away from me, halting on Daisy. She tilted her head. "I'm the woman Brogan is going to marry once he's done demolishing her completely," she said.

And that's when I did turn and run into Brogan's apartment, straight for the downstairs powder room where I vomited up my breakfast.

I distantly heard Daisy speaking harshly and then the slam of Brogan's door and Daisy's heels clicking on the floor as she called my name. I groaned and a second later Daisy was behind me, holding my hair away from my face as I spat into the bowl. I stood slowly and she helped me to the sink, meeting my eyes in the mirror, hers red and puffy, mine wide and shocked.

"Pack your stuff, honey," she said as she turned on the water. "I don't know what's going on, and you're going to tell me. But either way, I don't think it's a good idea for you to stay here. We're going to get in my car, and I'm going to take you back to Greenwich. Fucking men," she muttered.

I blinked at her, my head and my heart aching. "Okay," I finally squeaked. I just needed *space.* I needed to get out of here and think. I couldn't do that in Brogan's apartment.

"He told me about you as he fucked me. Did he tell you that? He told me how he was going to ruin you. He told me he was going to enjoy it." Oh God, Brogan. *Why?*

I walked numbly upstairs and started putting my things into my travel bag, allowing the tears to fall as I packed.

CHAPTER TWENTY-THREE

Brogan

"Lydia?" I called, moving the large bouquet of endless summer hydrangeas to my other hand and closing the door behind me.

I went into the kitchen and put the flowers on the counter as I called her name again. *Where was she?* I wanted to celebrate. It was done. Stuart's debt was paid for. Finished. *Thank God.* A huge weight had been lifted from my shoulders. And now . . . I finally felt *hope* that the mess I'd created was going to be over, and Lydia and I could really move forward. I even wondered if maybe she'd agree to move in with me. I planned to bring it up at dinner. It felt soon, but then again, it felt like seven years too late.

I went upstairs calling her name for the third time, a tiny fissure of worry opening inside me when again, she didn't respond and I didn't hear the water running. *I didn't hear anything.*

Her room, cleared of all her personal items, hit me like a fist to the gut. I looked around helplessly. She was gone? *Why?* My heart slammed against my ribs as fear slid down my spine. Was she in danger? I saw a piece of paper sitting on her dresser and rushed to it, grabbing it.

Brogan,

I'm leaving to stay with my friend Daisy. Please don't call

me tonight. I'll contact you when I'm ready.
Lydia

I swallowed, reading the note a second time, trying to understand. *Why?* A sick hurt assaulted me. When I'd left this morning, everything had been fine. We'd made sleepy love before either of us were fully awake, and she'd kissed me and smiled as I'd left, telling me she'd see me later that evening. And now she was suddenly gone with no explanation? And her letter, it was so . . . terse.

I turned and stared blankly at the bed, remembering the night I'd revealed all my secrets to her. My eyes moved to the bedside table, blinking at it repeatedly as more sick hurt gripped my heart. The folder—my stupid, ridiculous folder—the thing that had once kept me going, it was gone. *Lydia had taken it with her?* I stumbled to the bed, my legs collapsing as I sat down on the edge, putting my head in my hands. Why, Lydia? I didn't understand. *Why?*

****

I sat at my desk staring blankly at the stack of papers in front of me. After finding Lydia gone, I'd come to my office in the Bronx. I couldn't be at the apartment. God, would I ever be able to be at my own apartment without her? She'd told me not to call her, but I'd done so anyway, getting only her voicemail. I'd give her a couple of days. And then I'd go to Daisy's and demand she talk to me. She owed me an explanation about why she'd left and why she'd taken my folder. My stomach felt sour and my head hurt. I'd been going over every moment of our exchanges over the past few days for hours and still hadn't come up with an answer.

Why? Why now? Where are you, Lydia?

My thoughts were interrupted by the muted sound of glass breaking. I stilled, listening intently and not hearing anything again for several minutes. Something on the street maybe. Although, since moving here, I'd worked in a business where instincts could save your life, and right now, something felt off.

I started to stand when I heard another faint noise, this time closer and from within the building. I sat back down and reached under my desk for the gun I kept there. And I waited.

I didn't have to wait long. A minute later, the door to my office clicked open and Stuart De Havilland entered, looking like death warmed over, shaking, and pointing a gun at me. *What the feck?* I kept my hands on my lap, not moving a muscle. "Stuart," I said evenly.

He lurched toward me and my hand reached toward my gun, but retreated when he fell into the chair in front of my desk, smirking at me as he took something he'd been holding between his upper arm and body and set it on his knees. *My folder.* My gaze moved from it to his face. I forced my expression to remain unaffected.

"You were a *whore*," he said excitedly, letting out a strange, high-pitched laugh.

"Where'd you get that?" I asked.

"My sister gave it to me," he said, watching me closely. Cold sickness moved down my spine but I worked not to react. Was he lying? But if he was, why was Lydia gone, and why hadn't she called me? Had she really betrayed me . . . *again?* Or . . . for real this time? Confusion and horror made me dizzy. *Surely she hadn't been lying to me.* Had she been working with Stuart all along to try and turn the tables? No. Impossible. *No, no, no.*

Visions flicked quickly and painfully through my mind—watching Lydia seemingly alive with happiness as she'd worked in my office, how others had softened with her presence, how the young people we worked with had almost found a mother/sister figure in their life. Someone they could trust. No, that *couldn't* have been a lie. I felt gutted by anguish. I wanted to fall to my knees and weep; the very thought brought a hopeless rage barreling through my chest.

Stuart twitched and the gun in his hand jerked, causing my blood pressure to spike.

"How about you put that down while we talk?" I suggested.

"No fucking way."

I let out a breath. "Okay then, have it your way. Let's get this over with. What do you want?"

"I want everything you have, you piece of fucking gutter trash."

"You want your company back? Fine, it's yours. I'll sign it over to you in the morning."

He waved his gun around and my hand inched toward my gun. "I don't want my fucking company back! Fuck my company! I want your money. All of it, every cent."

"Why would I give you my money, Stuart?"

"Because of this," he yelled, picking up my folder and waving it around.

"There's nothing in that folder that would persuade me to give you a dime," I lied. The truth was, there wasn't anything in that folder that would do the job of ruining me, at least not in the way Stuart was counting on. But for it to get out that I'd been a prostitute . . . that I'd kept the information in that folder at all, filled me with sick shame.

"You're lying, you piece of shit whore. These people in here—did you know the husband of one of the women who hired you to be her boy toy is running for state senate now?" *Yes,* I had known that. It hadn't mattered because they were in a different state now because of me. I'd done that and it was enough.

"The only one you'll affect by exposing what's in that folder is them," I said.

His eyes narrowed, and he twitched so violently he almost dropped the gun. *Jaysus Christ.* "You don't care that the world knows what you did?"

"Not really," I lied. But I'd always been a better poker player than him. And he was too far gone to remember that.

Rage contorted his features. "There's information on the mob in here!" he yelled.

"Only on low-level players who have long since moved on," I said. This was the truth. I shrugged, a slow movement using only one shoulder. I didn't want to startle him. "There's nothing in there, Stuart. Nothing I care about. You can go print every piece of information in the New York Times tomorrow, and it won't matter to me."

"You're lying," he choked out, but I heard the doubt in his voice. His arm was shaking, and I saw his finger tightening on the trigger. *Please don't make me do this, Stuart. God, please don't make me do this.* "You're fucking lying, you motherfucking liar."

"I'm not lying," I said as calmly as I could. "I can help you, though. I won't let you blackmail me. But I'll help you. Put down the gun, and I'll get you the help you need."

"Fuckyoufuckyoufuckyou!" he screamed, waving the gun at me, and panting as if he was having trouble catching his breath.

He suddenly seemed to calm, chilling me even more and causing my heart to gallop. "I hate you," he said, and that's when he stilled completely, pointing the gun at my head.

They say in moments of high stress your life passes before you in slow motion. But it's also the events of that moment. I saw his gaze shift to his gun and the brief glance back up at me. I felt my arm raise. I felt something graze the top of my shoulder. I felt the jolting kickback as I fired. I saw blood. Stuart's eyes widening in shock. I heard a gun drop to the ground. Maybe his. Maybe mine. I saw Stuart slump in the chair and fall to the floor of my office. I saw death.

****

I was at the police station for hours, telling the same story over and over. Finally at three a.m., they released me, a clear case of self-defense.

The evidence that Stuart had broken and entered into my place of business was clear in the broken glass on the floor of the front room, the same glass stuck in the bottom of his shoes, and embedded in the skin of his fist. He'd punched through the glass with his bare hand. It would take time for the autopsy results to come back, but I suspected they'd find high amounts of drugs and alcohol in his system. Add to that the fact he'd fired at me first with a stolen gun and there would be no charges against me.

I'd told the police I'd recently taken over De Havilland Enterprises in a deal Stuart was still bitter about. It was enough of a motive. Of course, I'd picked up the bloodstained folder and put it in my safe in the back room before I'd called the police. I'd burn it once I had the chance. It now represented not my salvation, but my utter self-destruction.

I felt numb as I walked out of the room I'd been in since I'd called the police last night. Fionn stood up from across the station, causing the first pulse of emotion to move through my chest since I'd dialed 911. Mo chara. *My friend.* He moved toward me just as Lydia walked out of another room. She froze when she saw me, her eyes large and shocked, bloodshot. She'd been crying. My heart plummeted. *Oh God, Lydia.* I immediately went to move toward her, to take her in my arms, to offer what comfort I could.

She watched me approach, her mouth open slightly, her head shaking back and forth as if to say what? No, don't let this be true? "No," she choked out. "No, don't come near me."

Her words felt like a physical blow and I stumbled, wincing. "Lydia," I breathed. "Please. I didn't want to. Please listen to me. I never would have—"

She hit me, pounding her fists into my chest. Her expression seemed to collapse in horror. "No!" she screamed, striking me harder. "No, no, no!" Her head shook from side to side as if in denial. "How could you? How could you?"

"Lydia!" I choked, trying to contain her, trying to wrap my arms around her. "Le do thoil. Is breá liom tú."

"You did this on purpose," she sobbed, her eyes pools of stark pain and bright blue, not even a hint of green. "He said you would. Oh God, oh God, oh my *God.*" Her legs buckled. The police officer, who had been leading her out of the room, caught her from the side as she punched at me again. "I'll never forgive you!" she cried, her beautiful face a picture of misery, her loud sobs echoing through the mostly empty room. "Never!" She collapsed against the officer and Fionn gripped my arm.

"Not here, mo chara," he said. "Let her be for now."

"No, Fionn!" I said, panicked, sick, reaching for Lydia.

The police officer supporting her led her away, throwing one scathing look over his shoulder as the last piece of my world seemed to drop out from beneath me. *Mo Chroí.*

CHAPTER TWENTY-FOUR

Lydia

Stuart's gone. I'm alone. Completely alone.

It's done.

He's done what he set out to do.

Desolated me.

****

"Hey, honey," Daisy said softly, handing me a cup of coffee. I glanced up at her, breaking away from my thoughts.

"Morning." My smile felt small and weak. Outside the window, the sun was already shining brightly, the trees rustling with bird play. It was supposed to be in the eighties—a gorgeous late August day. God, where had the summer gone? Seemingly swallowed up in a haze of misery and grief.

"What do you want to do today?" Daisy asked, placing her coffee on a side table and sitting down on the overstuffed chair across from me.

She adjusted her silk robe and brought her feet up under her.

I sighed. "I suppose I should do some job hunting."

I'd gone to De Havilland Enterprises the week after Stuart had been killed and resigned. Trudi had been stunned and saddened, but the company would do just fine without me. It had been operating without me for over a month and was all the better for it from what I knew. And I couldn't be there anymore. My heart wasn't in it, and working for Brogan was out of the question.

I'd received several paychecks directly deposited into my bank account since I'd first moved in with Brogan, and with those, I paid my last month's rent in New York City and moved out, putting my belongings in storage and going back to Daisy's where we now lived together in her luxurious mansion—the new home of the broken-hearted.

Because Daisy's husband, Gregory, had been so clearly in the wrong, starting the divorce had been an easy process, one he hadn't argued about. Not enough, as far as I was concerned. *Fucker.* Daisy was worth so much more than that scum. So we were both in mourning, although Daisy seemed to be doing better than I was, which didn't exactly make sense since she had lost a husband. Then again, I'd lost *two* people, a brother and a . . . what? What had Brogan been to me? Even now, I wasn't sure. My heart squeezed and I winced slightly, bringing my hand to my chest as if I could massage the agonizing ache away.

He'd destroyed my life in every way possible. No job. No money. No home. No family. My heart in tatters. He had achieved the *ultimate* revenge. I was utterly and completely obliterated. And the very worst of it was . . . I *missed* him, longed for him with an intensity that felt shameful. He'd betrayed me and killed my brother.

"Why work?" Daisy asked, bringing me back to the present. Right, I'd mentioned getting a job. "I'll support you in high style here. And if I get the divorce settlement I think I'll get, we'll be rolling in riches. We'll burn money on the lawn and dance around it naked. We'll melt gold and drink it like it's champagne."

I laughed softly. "As fun as that sounds, I can't have you support me, Dais. I need to figure out what to do with the rest of my life."

A wave of grief washed over me when I thought about how much I'd loved working for Brogan—and how, even now, I missed it. I shook my head. I wouldn't cry. I'd already cried an entire river of tears.

Daisy's expression softened. "I know." She reached over and picked up her coffee and took a sip. "What about going back to school? You mentioned before you might look into getting your master's so you could teach."

I nodded. "Maybe," I said. Of course, if I did that, I'd still need to get a night job. Not only did I need to pay my bills, but Ginny had *shockingly* been mostly supportive when Stuart died, and she'd helped pay for his funeral. I had promised to pay her back. I didn't think she expected it, but I was determined to anyway.

"And you'll stay here with me?" Daisy asked. "Please? It makes it so much better, you being here."

I studied her momentarily, wondering if she was saying that for my benefit, or if being here really helped her with her own grief. It seemed to me that she was actually the one doing most of the supporting and I suspected the former. I was so very grateful for her. I smiled. "Only if you let me pay you rent."

She rolled her eyes. "You can pay for our monthly alcohol."

"I can't afford that."

She laughed. "True. That's the biggest bill we have. Utilities?"

"Done."

She grinned. "Okay. Go get showered and dressed. Today we go out and conquer the world." She raised her arm, making a fist.

I breathed out a smile, raising my own arm, but lacking the enthusiasm behind the gesture. I could barely conquer my heart, let alone the world. I sighed. *Fake it until you make it.* That'd be my life motto, for now at least.

****

"You look hot," Daisy said. I turned, smoothing the skirt of my deep red cocktail dress, and adjusting one of the spaghetti straps. "It's the perfect fall color." *Fall. A new season. The same ache in my heart.*

"You sure? It isn't too short?" I'd bought the dress from the small boutique I had gotten a job at recently in the nearby town of New Canaan. It was close enough to be an easy commute, but far enough away that I didn't worry about running into anyone I knew from Greenwich. It wasn't so much that I was embarrassed about working retail, it was more that I was just too . . . raw to deal with being mocked. By Lindsey, for instance. I wouldn't be able to conjure up the moxy needed to successfully deal with her and I'd more than likely crumble. Best avoided. So yes, since Stuart had died, I'd been hiding to a certain extent, but sometimes hiding was necessary for self-preservation. But at least I had the semblance of a life now—a job, a goal. I worked weekends and a few nights a week, which was the perfect schedule to work around my online classes and still allow me plenty of study time. It'd only taken me three months to get here, and it was still only a start. *Three months since my brother had died, since my heart had been decimated.*

"Is that dress too short? With your legs? God, no." She leaned toward the mirror, checking her makeup, which was perfect. "Ready?"

I took a deep breath. This was the first social function I'd been to since the summer garden party I'd gone to what seemed like eons ago. The one where I'd first spotted Brogan. I pushed the thought from my mind. No, I *wasn't* ready. In fact, I wanted to rip this dress off, put my sweats on, and park myself in front of Netflix for the rest of the night. But I just nodded. Daisy had begged me to go to this event with her and I'd said yes. I wouldn't back out now. I owed her so much—I could muster the strength for this.

We went into the kitchen where Daisy opened a bottle of

champagne, laughing as it bubbled over into the glass she held. She topped off two flutes and handed one to me. "To us," she said. "To moving on."

I raised my glass. "To moving on," I repeated. God, I only hoped I could. I still felt like an empty shell, breakable, and too delicate to step out into the world. When would that feeling start diminishing? When would I start feeling whole again?

"Oh, hey, something came in the mail for you," Daisy said, nodding to a large envelope that sat at the end of her marble counter. I frowned slightly. Who knew where I was staying? Who knew me at all for that matter? I was completely unconnected to anyone except Daisy. And distantly . . . Ginny.

I set my champagne down and picked up the envelope. *No return address.* Tearing it open, I pulled out the stack of papers. I sucked in a breath and sagged against the counter as I read.

"What is it?" Daisy asked, her heels clicking on the stone floor as she walked quickly to me.

I brought two fingertips to my lips as my eyes scanned the pages, flipping through them. "Brogan, he signed De Havilland Enterprises over to me," I said, shaking my head in disbelief, my hands beginning to tremble. *What did this mean?*

"Let me see that," Daisy said, taking the stack of papers from me and looking through them as I stared ahead, unseeing.

"Lydia, he also signed your old house over to you, and," she flipped through the stack of papers, "it looks like he's set up an account to pay for property taxes," she paused, reading, "upkeep, lawn and grounds maintenance, etcetera." She set the papers down on the countertop, looking at me. "Do you think he's trying to make up for what he did?"

I shook my head, a pit opening up in my stomach, a fresh wave of anguish making me feel as if I couldn't breathe. "I don't know," I whispered. "Maybe he does feel some guilt for what he did. But," I shook my head back and forth again, "either way, it's him officially writing me off. There's not even a note in here," I said, tears threatening. I took a deep breath, determined not to cry. "Nothing, but these documents from," I picked up the stack of papers, reading the names at the top, "Shaw and O'Malley, Attorneys at Law."

Daisy's brow furrowed. "Lydia, maybe he doesn't know *what* to say. Maybe this is his way of reaching out to you in the hopes you'll reach back."

I turned that over in my mind, confusion and hurt warring with a small flicker of hope. In that moment, holding Brogan's fifteen-million-dollar gesture—whatever the gesture meant—I was suddenly certain of one thing. I didn't want the business back. I didn't even really want the house anymore. I wanted my brother back. I wanted . . . Brogan back. Neither one was possible. And none of it meant anything with my heart shattered in a million pieces. With the acknowledgment came more grief because it could never be. Everything was ruined and there was no way to fix it.

"He shot my brother, Daisy." My voice sounded small.

She was quiet for a moment. "I know, Lydia, but you read the police report. You know Stuart all but forced Brogan to shoot him," she said, her expression nervous as if she was afraid to broach this subject with me. "Do you really think he planned that?"

I didn't know. I had seen Stuart earlier that day. I'd known he was paranoid and half crazy. And the toxicology report that had come back from the medical examiner confirmed my suspicions that he'd been using heroin as well.

I'd gone over it and over it in my mind, wondering if my reaction that day had been born of grief and confusion, the pile-up of all that had hit me at once: Stuart's suspicions, finding out Brogan was hiding things from me, at least one being the purchase of my old family estate, Courtney's visit, her vile words, and then Stuart's death. I had *only* looked at it from the vantage point of shock and mistrust. God, I was so tired of trying to figure this out, of going over and over it in my mind and thinking I might come to some conclusion, some answer.

"Maybe—" Daisy started.

"No," I said, rejecting it all. "I can't think about this tonight. I can't wonder. If he wanted to talk to me, he would have made that happen. If he wanted to provide me some answers, he would. But he hasn't because either this was his intended ending or he knows that even if it wasn't, this is not something we could ever move past. There is no way for us to recover from this." *Was there?* I picked up my glass of champagne and downed it, closing my eyes for a moment, attempting to regain my composure.

Daisy chewed at her lip for another moment, as if she wanted to say more, but then raised her glass, apparently rejecting the idea. "Well okay, then. Let's get out of this house, have some fun, and we'll revisit this when you're ready." She downed the last of her champagne. "Let's do this." And with that we headed for the front door, stopping to grab our wraps and small evening bags.

Daisy's driver was waiting for us out front. We had another glass of champagne in the car on the drive to the city, and when we got to the art gallery where the exclusive charity event was being held, I was feeling better. We got out of the car, laughing and clutching our wraps against the cool October air.

Inside, people drifted from one display to another. I did my best to turn off my mind. I wouldn't think about what Brogan's unexpected gesture had meant. He hadn't had the decency to tell me, had made the choice to leave me guessing, and so I wouldn't spend a moment of my time obsessing. It was too painful.

And yet . . . despite my own assertions, my mind kept returning there. Had it been a peace offering? A way to reach out? Or was it really what I'd called it at Daisy's house, a way to completely cut all ties with me? But if that were the case, was it really necessary? He didn't need to give me ownership of my family company or my home in order to cut ties. *He'd already done that.* Perhaps then, it was his way of saying, "I win, but now I have no need for these spoils of war. Take them, they're nothing to me now." No, that made *no sense.* And . . . my heart rejected it. It felt wrong.

But then there was Courtney. He'd said he'd been clear with her about her place in his life—*out*. But where had he been those nights?

I thought back to the way he'd made love to me—tenderly, reverently. The way he'd looked at me, the way he'd touched me, I just couldn't accept that he was doing it vengefully or dishonestly.

I thought we made a peace treaty last night.

Is that what that was?

I massaged my temples. I was going to give myself a headache—again.

I left Daisy flirting with one of the event hosts by a large, bronze and silver sculpture of what looked like a pile of crumpled candy wrappers. I stopped and gazed at some of the paintings for a few minutes here and there, but mostly meandered. It felt good to be out, good to get dressed up, to remember I was still young, still attractive when I exerted some effort. Several men smiled at me as I passed, their eyes lingering a moment too long and that boosted my spirits, too. I was far from ready to date, but maybe someday . . .

"This is boring as hell," Daisy said, coming up next to me and taking my arm. "I made my contribution by buying a print near the front of the gallery. We can get out of here now."

I laughed. "We've only been here for half an hour."

"Yup. Twenty minutes too long. All the men here are rich businessmen. We've both sampled that variety. Let's go somewhere where the pickings are better." She pulled me and I followed.

"I don't want to sample any variety of men," I said. "But I'll follow you somewhere where there's a variety of alcohol."

We retrieved our wraps from the coat check and walked outside. "There's a restaurant across the street, a new hibachi place. Very young and trendy. Let's check out the bar." Daisy linked her arm with mine and we crossed at the crosswalk, moving as quickly as possible so as not to get chilled in the unseasonably cold weather.

The hibachi restaurant was dim and warm and smelled

wonderfully of savory, grilled meat.

"We're just going to have a drink," Daisy said to the hostess when she greeted us.

"Of course." She smiled, waving her arm toward the bar to our left.

We turned toward it as a small group who had obviously just eaten moved toward the restaurant door. My heart stuttered violently when my eyes met Brogan's. For the breath of a moment, something inside that was wholly uncaring of the rules and reasons of my head lurched toward him in joyous delight. Shock registered in his light-blue eyes, but then they immediately shuttered, moving away from me as if I was of no consequence at all. I stopped in my tracks, frozen, my gaze moving to the people he was with: Fionn, two older men I didn't know, and . . . Courtney. She saw me, her cat-like eyes registering surprise as well right before she hooked her arm through Brogan's and smiled at me, showing the bare hint of teeth. The message was clear in her expression: *I win.*

And I had lost. Oh yes, and it had been a slaughter.

"Lydia," Fionn said, stopping in front of me as the rest of them moved on. I blinked at him. Next to me, Daisy put her hand gently on my arm. Fionn didn't seem to notice her.

"I . . . I—" *Oh God.* I was going to faint right here in the lobby of this restaurant.

"How are ya?" he asked gently.

"I . . ." Fionn's eyes moved over my face, his expression worried.

"Lydia," Daisy said. Fionn's eyes jumped briefly to her and back to me.

"Listen, Lydia—"

"Fionn," Brogan said from behind me. Fionn glanced to where Brogan must have been standing and then off to the left.

"For feck's sake," he murmured. His gaze met mine again. "Lydia—"

"I have to go," I choked, turning, stumbling slightly, not knowing *where* to go. Brogan was at the exit.

"We have to use the restroom," Daisy said, her grip on my arm tightening. Fionn hung his head, his hand moving to the back of his neck, but he didn't stop us. Daisy pulled me and I followed, stumbling again. My legs didn't seem to want to work.

I held myself together until we got to the ladies' room and then I collapsed onto the small, velvet couch in the bathroom lobby, sobs moving up my throat so forcefully I couldn't choke them down.

I knew now.

I had wondered, and now I had my answer—Brogan had given me the business and my family home to assuage any guilt he might hold. *That* had been *his* way of saying anything we'd had between us was over. *Finished. Just like me.* And if the gesture itself didn't say so, Courtney's presence certainly did.

I realized then that, despite my grief over Stuart's death, despite my horror and confusion and deep despair, I'd held a kernel of hope in my heart that Brogan would come to me—*come for me*—and attempt to make things right. I'd hoped that I hadn't imagined he'd cared for me, that he might even love me as I'd loved him. I'd begun to admit to it earlier tonight when I'd opened that envelope, but I knew without a shadow of a doubt when I'd come face to face with him.

But now, now I knew. There *was* no hope, not even hope I wasn't ready to fully explore. There was nothing but a vast empty hole of grief and loneliness. And I knew in my heart I'd never recover from this, not fully. I'd known more loss than most would know in a lifetime, but nothing had carved such an irreparable hole as this.

As the bathroom attendant brought me tissues, Daisy sat beside me and held my hand as I cried on her shoulder for what must have been the hundredth time.

CHAPTER TWENTY-FIVE

Lydia

I resisted groaning when I heard the bell ring on the door of the boutique. There'd been a sale today, and I was dead on my feet. I was the only one closing, and I'd been cleaning up and hoping to be done with customers for the day.

Laying a white cashmere sweater that I'd just folded down on the pile in front of me, I turned, freezing when I saw Eileen standing in the doorway. "Hi," I said, blinking at her, not knowing the appropriate reaction.

Her smile was small and quick. "Hi, Lydia," she said. We stared at each other for a moment.

"How are you? Are you here . . . are you shopping?" I asked.

She walked toward me, shaking her head. "No, I'm actually here to see ya."

I tilted my head. "Oh? How did you know I work here?"

"Em, your friend Daisy told me."

"Daisy?" When had Eileen seen Daisy? And why would Daisy divulge my place of employment to anyone associated with Brogan? "I, uh . . ." I pursed my lips. "I'm sorry, Eileen, this is just . . . unexpected and I—"

She came just a bit closer, her pale blue eyes the precise color of her brother's. Looking into them made my heart hurt. "I'm sorry to just show up like this, Lydia. I was just hopin' we could talk. Maybe get coffee? I won't take up much of your time, I promise."

Oh God, this was not going to be good for me. I'd been doing okay in the weeks since I'd run into Brogan. Most days, I didn't even cry anymore. *And now . . .*

"Please?" Eileen pleaded.

I let out a breath. "Okay, sure. Let me, um, just finish up here and I'll meet you in the coffee shop next door. They're open for another hour or so."

Eileen let out a breath and smiled. "Okay, great." She started to turn. "Should I order for ya?"

"Oh, sure, uh . . . a raspberry Chai would be great."

She smiled again. "Okay." Turning, she walked out the door, the bell chiming again behind her.

I walked to it and turned the lock even though it was five minutes before the official closing time. It took me a few more minutes to close out the register and put the money in the safe in the back. Gathering my things and putting my jacket on, I then set the shop alarm and locked the door behind me.

Next door, Eileen was sitting at a table by the window. I sat down in the chair across from her, cupping my hands around the still-hot mug in front of me. "Thanks," I said, nodding down to the tea.

She gave me a small smile, taking a sip from her own cup. "How are ya, Lydia?" she asked. "Really?"

Surprised by the tenderness in her expression, I answered honestly, "I'm okay, mostly."

She nodded, pressing her lips together. "I'm sorry about your brother," she said. I nodded, not taking my eyes from her. "It must have been a terrible shock."

"Yes," I said, surprised by the tears that pricked my eyes. I missed Stuart, but I was also very aware of his issues and the ways in which he'd contributed to his own death. I'd been thinking about him a lot lately, now that the pain of losing him was diminishing, and I was ready to remember him as he'd really been—not some perfected version, but realistically, a very flawed man. And somehow acknowledging who he'd really been felt like a weight lifted from my shoulders. "He . . . wasn't perfect, not by a long shot. But . . . he was my brother. I miss him." *He was my only family left.* I looked to the side. "I miss . . . the possibility that he could have changed his life . . . grown up . . . I don't know. I'm not in denial about who he really was. I just wish he'd had a chance to change."

"I understand," she said before pausing again. "Me brother tortures himself for what happened." I blinked at her, before looking down into my tea, squeezing the warm mug in my hands. "He can't forgive himself, Lydia."

I swallowed down the lump in my throat. "Eileen . . ." Her name broke off in a whisper, my heart squeezing.

"Lydia, he needs your forgiveness. He doesn't think he deserves it, and he'll try to keep ya from givin' it, but God, he needs it so badly."

"I . . . I . . . I just . . . he betrayed me in other ways, ways you don't know about. He lied to me about buying my house and—"

"He didn't tell ya about that because he bought it originally as part of his bloody stupid revenge plan." She frowned, shaking her head. "And then, well, then when he realized the error of his judgment in that regard, he couldn't just hand it over. Ya still had no way to pay for the taxes alone. You'd only have had to sell it again, the way your family had to the first time. He'd made sure of that. He needed to fix the situation before he gave it back to ya. He thought he was doin' right by ya, Lydia. I know it's all twisted, but I swear to ya on me life, on the very legs I walk on, that me brother has a heart of gold unlike anyone I've ever known."

I swallowed. I wanted to put my hands over my ears and beg her to stop. She was causing me to doubt the carefully constructed walls I'd built since I'd left Brogan's apartment that day, the walls that were keeping me safe, secure. I needed those walls. I'd struggled to lift each brick into place. "Did he send you here?"

"Jaysus, no. He'd kill me if he knew I was here. But I had to try, because he's been spendin' time with that scanger, Courtney. She wants him to marry her, and I'm scared to bloody death he might eventually do it just to punish himself."

My stomach knotted. "Courtney told me he was already planning to marry her. That day I left his apartment, she came by and told me they were still involved, and he was going to marry her when he was done ruining me." I swallowed. The memory of that moment still brought bile to my throat. Eileen let out a small, high-pitched laugh, lacking any humor.

"The only one who had plans at that point regardin' marriage was Courtney herself. She lied to ya, Lydia. I don't know the particulars of Brogan and Courtney's relationship, but I do know he doesn't love her, and he never has. Her ex-husband's been released from prison and she's playin' the safety card as a way of stayin' close to Brogan. She has some strange hold on him, aye, but *if* he marries her, he will spend the rest of his days miserable, which is about what he's aimin' for, I do believe."

I wasn't sure if that was any of my business. I wasn't even sure I shouldn't hope for just that. And yet, the thought of it made me feel sick and desperate all the same. "But Eileen, he doesn't love me either. I'm nothing but a princess in his eyes," I said. "A mo chree, that's what he calls me. And maybe he's only ever wanted to knock me off my imagined throne." I stared unseeing behind Eileen, then moved my eyes back to her worried expression. "I saw him a couple weeks ago at a restaurant. Did Fionn tell you? That night, he looked at me as if I was nothing to him, as if he'd never known me at all."

"Aye, he's scared of ya. He's scared he's gona beg ya to forgive him, and that ya might. And he's scared that ya might not. He's all knotted up, and he bloody hates himself. I've seen it before, Lydia. He was only seventeen then, but I remember it well." She eyed me with meaning, reaching across the table and laying her small hand on top of mine, giving it a squeeze. "I'm havin' Brogan to dinner at my place on

Saturday. Please come, Lydia. Please. Just think on it. I won't lie to ya. He won't make it easy for ya. But I'm askin' ya, no I'm beggin' ya to try. Even if ya decide ya don't want to be with him again, if ya can only find it in your heart to forgive him and to help him forgive himself. Please."

I shook my head. "Dinner? Oh no, no, I can't, Eileen."

She gave my hand another squeeze before she pulled away. "*Please*," she repeated as she stood up. "Seven o'clock. And Lydia, mo chroí doesn't mean princess. It means *my heart*. When he's callin' ya mo chroí, he's callin' ya his beloved, the very thing that keeps him alive."

I sucked in a sudden, sharp breath as she smiled gently at me and walked toward the door. "Eileen," I called out and she paused. "What does, iss bra lum too mean?" I'd spoken the sounds slowly, hoping she'd understand.

Eileen tilted her head, pausing for a moment. "It means I love you," she said. She gave me one small, fleeting smile before she left, closing the door of the coffee shop behind her.

Please. I love you. Please. I love you. That's what he'd said that night in the police station, the day I'd screamed at him and told him I'd never forgive him. *Please*, he'd begged me. *I love you.* And I'd turned away. Again.

Mo chroí. *My heart.*

I sat there for a long time, not drinking my tea, a lump clogging my throat as I simply stared at the wall.

****

"What are you going to do?" Daisy asked, her eyes wide.

"I don't know, Daisy," I said, pacing across the plush carpet of her bedroom. She'd been getting ready for bed when I'd gotten home and I'd come straight to her room, needing to talk. "And anyway, why did you give Eileen the name of the shop I work at?"

She poured lotion from a small bottle on her bedside table and began rubbing it into one elbow. The soothing scent of lavender met my nose. "She seemed so distraught, Lydia."

I stopped pacing momentarily. "And I'm not distraught? I haven't been distraught for three months now?"

She changed elbows. "I thought maybe . . . well, perhaps you could help each other with your . . . distraughtedness."

"That's not a word," I snapped.

"Distraughtegy?"

I thinned my lips, noting her teasing expression.

"Distress. And this isn't funny. Not in the least." I folded my arms and continued pacing.

Daisy capped the lotion bottle, stood, and came over to me, halting my pacing by putting her hands on my upper arms. "Lydia," she said, "in these last three months, you've become like a sister to me. I like to think we've helped each other through our *distress.* But . . . I'm getting better, and you're . . . not. And I think it's because in my case, there are no loose ends, nothing to work through, but with Brogan, well, I think there might be. And I think you know that, too. I think it's eating you alive. And until you at least figure out how you feel about him and *talk to him,* it's going to *continue* to eat you alive."

I stared at her, wanting to reject her words, but knowing I couldn't. And now tonight, after talking to Eileen, I had so many doubts, so many unanswered questions I'd thought needed no explanation, could *have* no explanation. But what if . . . what if they could? I'd seen him in that restaurant and despite everything, my heart had still called out to him. My instinct had been to run into his arms and heal the terrible, heart-wrenching ache inside me—not grief over my brother's death, for that was healing on its own. The ache I still felt inside was the loss of . . . *him.* Either I was a complete and utter idiot, an explanation that wasn't completely off the table, or . . . or I still loved him, because my heart knew he was a *good* man who had made some bad choices, even if those bad choices had led at least partially to this terrible situation we were in now.

And yet, I didn't absolve myself of my *own* misguided actions. Perhaps I could have done more to help Stuart. He'd come to me first that day, and I'd known how messed up he'd been. I'd seen his desperation and his paranoia, and yet I'd let him walk right out the door, even giving him money, a measly fifty bucks, but still.

And before that, I'd made excuses for Stuart, worked double time to cover up his mistakes, which only allowed him to keep making them, leading eventually to him threatening Brogan with a gun. I wrapped my arms around myself, a shiver moving down my spine. I was *far* from blameless myself. "You're right," I whispered. "God, you're right."

Daisy let go of my arms and looked at me sympathetically. "Talk to him," she repeated.

I bit at my lip. "Eileen says he won't make it easy on me. She says he'll try not to let me forgive him, that he wants the punishment."

"Well," Daisy said, stepping back, "I guess you have to decide if you still believe he deserves it, and if not . . . what you're going to do about that."

"Yes." I hugged her tightly, holding on for a moment, wishing I could verbalize my love for her, too, but I was spent. *Emotionally exhausted.* I dragged myself to my room and quickly changed and brushed my teeth, falling into bed. I didn't think I'd be able to sleep, but surprisingly, once my head hit the pillow, I was out like a light almost immediately.

****

I *was in a large room, open at the top. I craned my neck back, gazing at the bright blue sky, billowy white clouds floating lazily by. When I looked back down, I realized the walls around me were filled with artwork, swirls and splashes of color decorating every square inch.*

Walking closer, I saw there were pictures woven into the splashes of color. One in particular caught my eye: it was a picture of our family home, the lush grounds beyond, horses in the distance. It was the one Stuart had drawn when he was young. I marveled at the beauty, the talent of which it spoke.

I felt a presence behind me and turned. Stuart was standing beside one of the walls, a brush in his hand. I took a disbelieving step toward him. "Stu?" I whispered? He smiled broadly.

"Simply wonderful, isn't it?" a voice asked from the other direction. I let out a small whimper, turning. It was my dad's voice. He was looking around at the walls, a proud smile on his face. And my mom stood next to him, as beautiful as I remembered her.

"Dad? Mom?" I breathed, holding out my hand as my heart leapt with joy. "Stuart?" They all smiled and I ran to them, Stuart joining us, as they wrapped their arms around me, forming a sort of huddle.

Tears ran down my cheeks as I caught Stuart's eye. He smiled softly and said, "Forgive me."

"Yes," I whispered. "Yes."

We held each other this way for a long time until I finally pulled back slightly, wanting to soak them in with my eyes, overwhelmed and filled with happiness. My dad smiled, taking my hand in his and placing something in my palm and closing it. I looked down, opening my hand slowly to reveal . . . a clover. I raised my eyes to my dad's and he nodded, his eyes warm with love, glancing at my mom who wore a soft smile on her lips.

****

I woke up sobbing. I clutched my pillow to my chest, as the last of my tears dried. I'd been crying—*I missed them so much*—and yet I felt . . . a deep peace settle over me.

A clover . . . they'd given me a clover. *Brogan.*

Yesterday, today and . . . *tomorrow*. I closed my eyes tightly for a moment.

Am I the villain? Brogan had asked. *I keep losing track.*

And I had lost track, too. Again and again. Even now, I wasn't exactly sure. Or maybe we were all villains sometimes, each one of us. Maybe the thing that determined how quickly we became heroes was the grace we were extended, not only by others, but by *ourselves.*

I had spoken to Brogan of forgiveness once, and yet *I'd* been unwilling to forgive, unwilling to extend him the very grace I'd suggested he needed in order to find peace. Forgiveness is a *choice,* I'd said. And yet I hadn't even given him the chance to explain, hadn't trusted him enough to even allow him that.

"I'll never forgive you," I'd screamed at him that night. I'd done the same thing to him that he had done to me, both of us caught in a vicious cycle of hurt and mistrust and revenge. I'd had good reasons, I could argue, but so had he. And frankly, I was done arguing, done justifying, done putting my pride and my hurt ahead of everything else, done speaking anything except the truth in my heart. *Mo chroí.*

My heart knew.

Brogan hadn't wanted to kill Stuart. Stuart had blamed Brogan for driving him to the edge, but in fact, Brogan had tried his damnedest to help him, paying off his debt and *saving* his life. Ironically, Brogan, who set out to ruin our lives had been the only one in a position to make them better. And that's just what he had attempted to do in the end.

If he had simply left us alone—if he had never set out to exact revenge—chances were that eventually, Stuart would've gotten himself killed by the mob, and perhaps me as well.

It was *Stuart* who had been so filled with resentment and self-pity and envy that he couldn't help himself, much less allow Brogan to. If he had, things could have been so different. I'd tried so hard to honor my mother's wish that I take care of Stuart. And yet, what I'd really done was enable his behavior by excusing him again and again. Brogan had been right about that. And so it had become a *burden*, not the act of love my mother had intended. I'd carried the guilt of that knowledge for so long, and it had kept me trapped, right along with Stuart.

My father had bestowed on Brogan the approval and affirmation that Stuart believed should have been his, and he'd always hated Brogan for it. It was the reason he'd kicked Brogan in the face all those years ago, it was the reason he'd left Brogan in the mold-infested slum later, and it was the reason he'd eventually shown up at Brogan's office with a gun.

Forgive me. *Yes.*

Sometimes forgiveness meant letting go.

The dream. Whether my parents and Stuart had really come to me or whether I'd known these truths in my heart all along and conjured my family up in my head to deliver the message, I didn't know. But it was clear to me now—I forgave Brogan, and he *deserved* my forgiveness.

Sometimes forgiveness meant holding on.

I loved him. Oh God, I did, I loved him. I *always* had. But love was not separate from trust—it couldn't be. And yet, I'd denied him just that. Guilt stabbed at me more harshly than the knife I'd felt in my side all those months ago.

Brogan was good and generous and moral, and he'd acted against *himself* as much as anyone else when he'd set out to exact revenge. But then he'd tried so hard to make it right.

I had thought all hope was lost, that there was no fixing the situation we'd found ourselves in. But maybe I'd been wrong. Maybe with love . . . with truth . . . with forgiveness, anything was possible. *Please help me make it possible, Brogan.*

I was going to go to him and offer my forgiveness and hope to *God* he'd forgive me, too. He might fight me, but I was going to fight back. I might fail, but this time, the cause finally felt entirely worthy.

****

I took a deep breath, gathering every ounce of courage I possessed as I knocked on Eileen's door. I heard footsteps coming toward me and resisted the urge to flee. The door flew open, and Eileen stood there. Her face broke into a huge grin. "Oh, thank ya, Jaysus," she said, hugging me tightly. I let out a small, surprised laugh. "Come in, come in." She ushered me inside, out of the cold.

My head moved around, hardly seeing the décor of her home, my eyes only set on finding one person.

"He's not here yet," she said. "He's drivin' in from the city." Footsteps sounded from the room beyond where we were standing in the living room and a second later, Fionn appeared in the doorway.

"Lydia," he said, happiness and surprise mixed together in his tone.

I smiled. "Hi, Fionn." He practically ran over to me, sweeping me up into a hug. I laughed again.

"We've missed the hell outta ya, Lydia," he said.

"I've missed you, too," I said honestly. "I'm sorry I didn't tell you when I saw you in New York—"

"Nah, I never would have expected to run into ya. Brogan not sayin' a thing was a load of rubbish. I told him so afterward."

"I suspect he didn't know what to say," I mumbled. "I didn't either."

"Courtney bein' there was my own bloody fault," Fionn said. "I told Brogan bringin' a woman would balance the mood in a way that would work to our benefit for that particular meetin'. I was tryin' to give him an excuse to contact ya and wanted to throw up on me shoes when Courtney the scanger showed up."

I gave him a wan smile. "It wasn't your fault, Fionn. Brogan makes his own choices." I wasn't sure whether Fionn's explanation should give me some hope or not. There was still so much I didn't know. *Deep breath. Forgiveness. Faith.*

"Well, let's hope he makes some good ones tonight." He winked.

Eileen took my coat and purse, and I walked farther into her living room, admiring the beautifully decorated yet comfortable space, noticing the same touches here that were in Brogan's house as well. "Something smells good, " I said. "Can I help?"

"Oh, no, no," Eileen said, walking toward the kitchen. "It just needs a bit longer in the oven. Do you want some wine?"

"Yes, that'd be great." I rubbed my palms on my dark jeans. God, the longer I had to prepare for this, the more nervous I was going to become. I just wanted him to get here already.

"I'm hopin' for the best," Fionn said. "But I fear he's not gona make this easy on ya. Are ya prepared?"

I looked at him, his expression worried, which in turn made my own nervousness notch up a few levels. "That's what Eileen said. And I . . . I think so. I'm going to try my best anyway."

"I'm just bloody thankful you're willin' to." I nodded, suddenly unsure about this plan. What were my reasons again? I couldn't remember why this had seemed a good idea two nights ago. "He's convinced himself he doesn't want ya to forgive him, and that he's doin' right by ya to stay away." He paused. "Bloody caveman," he muttered just as a loud knock sounded at the door. I jumped, my pulse skyrocketing. Fionn squeezed my shoulder gently and gave me a wink. I stood frozen.

Fionn opened the door and Brogan came in, wiping snowflakes off his hair. It had started snowing? In October? Snow always made me think of my mother and for the whisper of a moment, strength—*hope*—surged through me. "Mo chara," Fionn said. That's when I saw Courtney behind Brogan. My stomach dropped into my feet and the hope I'd felt a second ago fled. *Oh God.* I couldn't do this, not with her here. I wanted to sink into the floor, to run, to disappear. Instead, I continued to stand frozen, staring at them as they started to remove their coats.

Fionn appeared to have stilled, too, when Courtney had appeared. It was obvious he hadn't known she'd be with Brogan. "Jaysus fecking Christ," I thought I heard Fionn mutter under his breath.

That's when Brogan noticed me, his body going rigid as his face drained of color. He stared at me for the space of two heartbeats and then looked to Fionn, his lips thinning. "Don't do this, Fionn," he said stiffly. I felt my face warm, feeling embarrassed and lost.

Fionn smiled innocently, ignoring his words. "Of course, ya know Lydia," he said. Brogan's eyes met mine and then he looked away, down to the floor for a moment as his jaw ticked.

Courtney stepped forward. "Are you kidding me?" she looked at Brogan. "Did you know she'd be here?"

"She's me guest." Eileen said, coming from the kitchen, handing me a glass of white wine. I gripped it gratefully. "I didn't realize *you'd* be here tonight, Courtney," Eileen said.

Courtney smiled placidly, shrugging one shoulder. "Hopefully not for long." She put her arm through Brogan's. "I prefer to be home in bed in front of a warm fire on nights like this." She smiled meaningfully up at Brogan who was as still as a statue except for that same tick in his jaw.

Eileen's eyes darted to me and then to Fionn. "Well then, time to get good and plastered. What can I get ya to drink?" he asked Brogan and Courtney. Courtney asked for wine and Brogan said he didn't want anything. Fionn headed for the kitchen, shaking his head.

As he passed by me, he leaned toward my ear and whispered, "You're stronger. Ya can do this. Unbalance him."

My heart was pounding as Eileen led us to sit down in the living room. I sat down next to her on the couch and Brogan and Courtney sat down across from us on a loveseat, Courtney scooting as close to Brogan as she possibly could.

Brogan looked to be made of stone, his expression tense and completely unreadable. There was a moment of strained silence, and I noted that Brogan was leaned slightly away from Courtney. *One of his tells.* It gave me the courage to stay seated, not to run for the door.

I took a long drink of wine, setting it down on the coffee table in front of me and rubbing my shaky hands on my thighs. "I received the package you sent," I said to Brogan, hating myself for the way my voice trembled. His eyes met mine, and I swore for a moment, grief passed over his expression. But then it was gone, and I wondered if I was seeing my own emotions reflected in him, because despite this terrible, awkward situation, I wanted nothing more than to fall into his arms and ask him to comfort me. His cold demeanor—not to mention that awful woman—was the cause of the intense pain resting heavily on my chest. And yet, seeing him made me realize the *depth* to which I'd missed him.

"What package?" Courtney asked.

Brogan ignored her. "Good," he said.

I waited for more but when he didn't say anything else, just kept looking at me with that distant expression, I nodded. "Thank you."

His jaw muscles tensed, and he closed his eyes briefly, letting out a harsh exhale. "Jaysus Lydia, there's nothin' to thank me for." Fionn had just come out of the kitchen with two drinks in his hands, and at the sound of Brogan's harsh voice, a pleased look came over his face.

He handed a glass of wine to Courtney and held up his glass. "May ya never lie, steal, cheat, or drink. But if ya must lie, lie in each other's arms. If ya must steal, steal kisses. If ya must cheat, cheat death. And if ya must drink, drink with us, your friends. To me friends!" He started to bring his glass to his lips and added, "And ya, too, Courtney."

I almost laughed. I felt wound so tight and a burst of hysterical laughter seemed like it might release some tension. Courtney glared at him and Brogan uttered, "Fionn," in a warning tone, and so I simply took a small sip of my wine and replaced it on the table.

I couldn't do this. I put my hands on my thighs, ready to stand up. This had been a hideous idea. Or it might not have been if Brogan had shown up alone. *Why was she here?* But he hadn't, and I might have been able to plow ahead despite the chill of Brogan's silence, but I couldn't do this in front of Courtney. I felt shaky and sick. Eileen put her hand on top of mine before I could move.

"So, Lydia, what have ya been up to recently?" she asked, looking at me pointedly. I glanced at Brogan who was looking off behind me somewhere, that same muscle working in his jaw.

"Um, well, I . . . I re-enrolled in school. I'm getting my teaching degree. I hope to work at a college, teaching history when I graduate. And I'm working at a small clothing boutique."

Brogan's eyes snapped to mine. "Your teaching degree? A boutique? You own a company. Why wouldn't you work there?" He closed his mouth and grimaced as if asking me a question resulted in physical pain.

Courtney picked imaginary lint off Brogan's shoulder. "A teacher. I think it's sweet," she said, syrup lacing her tone.

I ignored her. "I actually don't want the company, Brogan. I contacted your lawyers and told them as much. You have the ability to run it far better than I can. From what I can tell, it's doing wonderfully." I paused. "Thank you for that. My father would have been very happy. I think . . . well, I think my father would have wanted it that way," I finished softly.

His hands clenched in his lap, and he ran his tongue over that front tooth as he stared off behind me again, the wheels in his head obviously working overtime—on what, I couldn't be sure. My pulse raced. *Unbalance him.*

When he looked back to me, his expression was raw, tortured. "This isn't a game, Lydia." I shook my head. "I gave ya the company because it's rightfully yours. Always should have been."

"No, Brogan, I'm not playing games. I don't want to play games with you. Not ever again." I took a deep, trembling breath. "I only want—"

"What about the house then?" He looked slightly desperate for some reason I didn't quite understand.

I shrugged. "I can't accept it outright, but I would like to work out terms we can agree upon. I won't be able to pay a lot on a teacher's salary, but maybe I could do some volunteer work for your company or—"

"No." My eyes widened at the emotion in his tone, the way his jaw clenched again, the despair that crossed his features.

Courtney's eyes looked slightly wild as her gaze moved between Brogan and me. "No, Brogan is correct. You really should focus on your little teaching job if that's your goal. He doesn't have time to pander to volunteers who—" She let out a loud squeal as Fionn made a strange tripping movement from behind her, spilling his drink all over her left shoulder. She stood suddenly as it dripped down her shirt.

"Oops," Fionn said, shrugging innocently.

Courtney's face turned red with rage. "You did that on purpose, you . . . you *clown!*"

Eileen sprang up, taking Courtney by the arm. "Let's not get upset over a wee spill," she said. "We'll get that right out. No problem at all. I have the best stain remover in me bathroom. Come with me." She practically dragged Courtney with her, Fionn disappearing into the kitchen. It was suddenly only Brogan and me sitting across from each other.

"Ya shouldn't have come tonight, Lydia."

Hurt speared through me. "I wanted to see you," I said. "I thought—"

"Ya need to get on with your life. I have no place in it anymore."

Grief clogged my throat. I stared at Brogan. The look on his face was hard, unyielding and yet . . . his tongue moved continuously over that front tooth, his fists clenched so hard his knuckles were white.

Brogan. Why are you doing this?

"I forgive you," I breathed. His face broke, raw emotion contorting his features. "God, Brogan, I'm sorry it took me so long to get here. I'm so sorry I didn't give you the chance to explain."

"No," he hissed, visibly swallowing.

I nodded. "Yes. It wasn't your fault. My brother caused his own death. You had no other choice but to defend yourself. And I'm sorry you had to, but I'm glad you did."

"No," he gritted again, letting out a small, strange choking sound. He uttered something in Gaelic, clearly a curse. "I won't allow it."

I stared at him. He didn't *allow* it? My forgiveness? Sadness moved through me in painful waves. "But that's the thing," I gripped my hands in my lap, "it doesn't matter if you allow it or not. I still forgive you all the same. I still . . . I still love you all the same. And God, I don't want to waste another seven years not letting you know it."

"Lydia," he said, the word filled with torment, breaking on the last syllable. He sat up straight, seeming to gather himself, his expression going hard again. Blank. He took a deep, shaky breath. "I'm not sure what ya thought comin' here tonight would accomplish, but I think ya should leave."

My heart squeezed so tightly I felt as if I couldn't breathe. He couldn't accept my forgiveness, or perhaps he didn't want it. Or maybe he wasn't ready to extend me his. All right then. He wasn't ready for any of this. It had taken me a while to get here, too. But I had said my piece. That would have to be enough. I had done all I could do. Now it was up to Brogan.

I stood on shaky legs just as Courtney's loud voice and clicking heels came toward the living room. She burst in, still rubbing at her shirt with a towel, Eileen behind her, Fionn coming out of the kitchen. I offered them what felt like a wobbly smile.

"Eileen, thank you for your kind invitation to dinner. I think, however, it's best that I decline."

Eileen moved toward me, her hand outstretched, glancing at Brogan. "Lydia, please stay, I—"

"No," I said, gathering my coat and purse. "Thank you, really, but I," I took a deep breath, "it's for the best that I go." Everything inside me hurt, as if I was a walking bruise.

"Well, I'd have to agree," Courtney interjected. Eileen shot her a look so nasty, she withered just a bit beneath it.

I looked once more at Brogan who was sitting as still as a statue, staring at the floor and then my eyes moved to Fionn who was glaring daggers at Brogan. I turned to the door and opened it, looking back over my shoulder once more at Eileen.

"Thank you," I said before I slipped out. Fat snowflakes were drifting from the sky as I walked quickly to my car, not allowing the tears to fall until I had pulled out of the driveway and was halfway down the street.

CHAPTER TWENTY-SIX

Brogan

"That's it," I heard behind me right before I was dragged up by my collar. Fionn's fist connected with my jaw in a sucker punch to end all sucker punches. I heard Courtney scream as I reeled backward, falling into Eileen's coffee table.

"What the *feck?*" I yelled, pulling myself to my feet.

"Yeah, that's right, get up, I'm about to hand your arse to ya on a plate, ya feckin' twat." Fionn danced around me, his fists raised, his head down.

I took a deep breath, putting my hands on my hips and glaring at him, ignoring his theatrics. "I'm not gona fight ya, Fionn." His hand shot out, connecting to my jaw again as I tripped backward over the coffee table, landing on my arse.

Shock and anger exploded through me. "Ya feckin' prick!" I yelled. "I'm gona feckin' beat the shite outta ya, ya mother feckin' dickhead!" I jumped to my feet.

"That's it," Fionn said. "Come on, ya wanker. What a silly cunt ya are. I'm done watchin' ya act like a bloody muppet."

That was it. I was going to kick his arse straight into next week. "I'm bloody sick of ya interferin' in me life," I said as I lunged for him, tackling him onto the couch. I raised my hand to slam it into his manky pretty-boy face when Eileen screamed.

"Wait!" I paused, my fist in the air. Fionn looked over at her, too. "Not in here. Beat his arse outside," she said to Fionn.

"Beat *my* arse," I said in disbelief. "I'm your *brother*."

Eileen crossed her arms. "Aye, and you're a bleedin' eejit."

Anger engulfed me. I had lived in utter misery for the past three months, limping through life as if every part of me was broken beyond repair. Worse, I felt sick and wrecked with grief over seeing Lydia tonight. Watching her walk out the door because I'd told her to . . . gutted me. And now I needed my arse beaten? By the people who were supposed to care for me? Suddenly a fight seemed like the best bloody idea I'd ever heard. "Fine," I growled, heading for the door, "let's do this."

Courtney was talking shrilly about something, but I didn't give a feck what it was. I ignored her, flinging the door open and stepping outside into a world of softly whirling white, fat snowflakes falling from the sky. *More snow?* I thought the few flakes from earlier would have stopped by now. It wouldn't stick I'd guess, but something about it felt magical for just a moment and gave me pause. But then I heard Fionn stomping behind me, and my anger bubbled up again.

I stopped in the open area in front of Eileen's house and turned. Fionn was already advancing on me and when he got within a few feet, he stopped. We stared each other down for a moment. "I gave ya a few months, but ya came to the wrong conclusions, ya stubborn gobshite. I didn't want to have to beat some sense into ya, but enough is a feckin' nough," he said. "I'm a bloody monkey's uncle if I'm gona watch ya self-destruct."

"This isn't your business, Fionn," I gritted, stepping closer.

"You're me business, Brogan Ramsay, whether ya wanna be or not. And I'm your business. I'm your *family*." He *was* my family. I loved him like a brother. His fist slammed into my stomach, and I doubled over. I grunted as I caught my breath, surprise and red rage spreading like wildfire through my veins. I was going to bloody kill my *brother* now. My fist connected to his jaw, and he stumbled backward.

"She forgives ya," he sputtered, spitting out a mouthful of blood, the red a bright splotch on the pristine white carpet of snow.

"I don't bloody *want* her forgiveness," I growled. *Goddamn it!* I'd *suffered* every day since she'd been gone, every *hour* an effort to get through. And I would be damned if I was going to go backward now. *Not that I'd moved forward very far.*

Seeing Lydia tonight had highlighted that fact and tormented me. I had already forgiven her. Her betrayal hurt, but I *had* put her in an impossible position. I could hardly blame her for trying to help her brother. But when she'd said those three words, *I forgive you*, I'd wanted to grab her and hold her so tightly we'd meld together and no one could ever separate us again. But I *wouldn't.* I wouldn't give in to my own selfish wants and take anything from her ever again. Even if she wanted to give me a second chance, I wouldn't let her. I didn't deserve any more chances, and she should have far better than me. Someday she'd fall in love with a man who deserved her, with a man who hadn't killed her brother, who hadn't set out to ruin her life and succeeded by every definition. I would do one thing right by Lydia—the *only* thing I'd ever done right by Lydia—I would let her go.

It doesn't matter if you allow it or not. I still forgive you all the same. I still . . . I still love you all the same.

Lydia. Mo Chroí.

Fionn came charging for me and I braced as his head connected to my shoulder and we went down hard, my back connecting to the ground in a jarring smack, the air releasing from my lungs in a loud whoosh.

I groaned as Fionn scrambled up until he was kneeling over me, his arm rising to hit me again. "She doesn't really forgive me, Fionn," I wheezed out. His arm halted in midair. I took a few deep breaths, my lungs expanding. "She thinks she does because she . . . she's generous and kind. But . . . she'll always remember what I did, who I am, and eventually . . . she'll leave me again, or betray me again," I gasped. "It'll just be a matter of time. I can't . . . I can't . . ." Fionn's fist slammed into my jaw.

"*Feck!*" I yelled. "What the *feck?*" My face felt like it was on fire.

"Jaysus. Still wrong, ya dopey dick," Fionn muttered, raising his arm again. I dodged his fist, rolling to the side.

We wrestled for a few minutes, a stick poking into my back so violently, I thought it might have broken through my skin. I yelled out and Fionn paused. I took the opportunity to nail him in the gut. He let out a loud whoosh of air, falling over. He groaned, clutching his stomach and I paused, which gave him just enough time to roll toward me again and attack. I went slamming to my back again and groaned.

"Okay, okay. Jaysus, what do ya want, Fionn?"

He fell to his back beside me with a small moan. For a few seconds, we lay looking up into the gently falling snow. The fat flakes melted as they hit my skin, feeling good against my hot, injured face.

"She forgives ya, mo chara. She loves ya. She's not gona withdraw it to hurt ya later. If ya want the games to be over, you're gona have to trust her. If ya want her love, you're gona have to give her your love in return and for the love of Jaysus, you're gona have to try to see the good in yourself. End your own torment, mo chara, forgive her and forgive yourself."

"I do forgive her," I muttered. And I really did. She hadn't meant any harm to me seven years ago, and in fact, had suffered painfully because of what happened that day. It was because of *me* she'd been put in a position to have to choose between her brother and me. It was because of *me* she'd taken my folder—the folder I'd ultimately burned. And for all of that, it was *myself* I couldn't figure out how to let off the hook. There was no question. *I* was the villain.

As if reading my thoughts, Fionn said, "If ya can't figure a way to forgive yourself, you're never gona trust *her* forgiveness." I sighed. I felt drained completely. "Ya made mistakes, Brogan, but you're a good man. Stop punishin' yourself and the rest of us along with ya. This is no atonement."

"I just need to think," I said. Fionn leaned up, his fist connecting to my face once again in a punch that made it feel like my eye had exploded.

I brought my hands to my face, rolling away and sitting up, facing him. "What the *feck?*" I yelled again for what felt like the tenth time.

"For the love of Jaysus, please stop your bloody *thinkin'*," he said, sounding as drained as I was.

I stared at him, his face as bruised and battered as mine felt, our shirts wet and ripped and bloody. And I started laughing. He stared at me for a heartbeat and then he started laughing, too, until we were both howling and clutching our bruised ribs in pain. I stood, groaning, my laughter fading as every muscle in my body screamed. I reached for his hand and he gripped mine, as I helped him to his feet. I pulled him into a hug, clapping him as gently as possible on the back.

"Ya got two women waitin' on ya, mo chara," he said when we'd pulled apart. "Make the right choice."

I exhaled, my breath coming out in a white puff. I looked toward the house where Courtney waited. She had shown up at my apartment tonight, crying in fear about her ex-husband, and so I'd brought her with me even though I'd known neither Eileen nor Fionn would be happy about it. Hell, I wasn't happy about it. So what the *feck* was I doing?

Fionn seemed to follow my thoughts. "Yeah, ya really are an eejit."

I let out a surprised burst of laughter. "I'm the eejit who employs you."

Fionn put his hand on my shoulder. "Listen, mo chara, next time ya get to thinkin' on some subject or another, a good rule of thumb is to ask yourself, what would Fionn do?" He attempted to smirk, or so I thought anyway, but it was all twisted and grotesque, his bottom lip swollen to twice its size, and the movement only made me laugh harder. *What would Fionn do?* Okay, then.

"Maybe I'll have a T-shirt made." I laughed, but it died quickly. I put my hand on Fionn's shoulder, filled with gratitude. Fionn would be the best damned friend a man ever had. *I ever had. That's* what Fionn would do. “Thank you, mo chara. Thank you," I rasped.

"You're feckin' welcome, ya wanker," Fionn said, smiling another hideous smile. I smiled back, only feeling a small measure of guilt for the state of him. I figured my face looked pretty bad too. I chuckled as we started for Eileen's door.

****

"**O**h for Christ's sake," Eileen said when she took in the sight of Fionn and me. I looked at Courtney who was sitting on the couch, still, her hands on her knees, looking straight ahead.

"Courtney, can I talk to you?" I asked softly. Her eyes met mine and she nodded. I saw Fionn and Eileen exchange a look before they both left the room, Eileen scolding Fionn for dripping blood on her carpet. I picked up a cocktail napkin off the table next to the couch and pressed it against my lip. I thought it was the only place I was actually bleeding from although I didn't take the time to glance in a mirror.

"I—"

Courtney held up a hand. "It would be the same."

I tilted my head, not understanding. "The same?"

"Bennett. Being with you would be the same as being with Bennett, wouldn't it? If I ever did succeed in actually getting you to make some kind of commitment to me." She rubbed her temples. "Which, God, I've put a whole lot of effort into." She sighed. "But it wouldn't work anyway. Oh, you wouldn't be unkind to me, not outright, anyway, and you'd certainly never hit me, but you'd never love me. You'd end up ignoring me, and I'd go looking for someone else to make you jealous, to fulfill what you weren't capable of providing." She laughed, but it had no humor in it. "I'd be right back where I started."

I couldn't help the sympathy I felt. I had never truly wanted her in *any* way, especially not in marriage. I realized now that it wasn't only the guilt that had inspired me not to tell her to feck off these last few months, but also the idea that it was exactly what I deserved: being tied to a woman I didn't love, and ensuring Lydia could *never* forgive me, even if she tried. But that hadn't been fair to anyone. God, Fionn was right. Sometimes my conclusions were . . . flawed.

I sighed. "Yes. I'm sorry."

She pressed her lips together and nodded. "These last couple months, you've never touched me, not once. And the two times I kissed you, the look on your face . . . it was as if I was . . ."

"Not her," I supplied, grimacing slightly. It felt cruel and yet, I owed her the truth. I owed myself the truth.

She flinched, but nodded again. "She's branded on your heart."

"Yes," I said softly. *She is my heart. Mo Chroí. And like my heart, to rid myself of her would kill me in the process. The truth of that thought hit me in the gut. All these months, that's how I'd felt . . . half alive, as if I were very slowly dying.*

Courtney stared at me for a moment, exhaling a deep breath. "I lied to her," she finally said. "The day you shot her brother. I went to your apartment and she was there. I . . ." she let out another breath, "I told her I'd had a pregnancy scare. I made it sound as if we'd slept together recently and—"

"Jaysus, Courtney," I gritted out, shock and horror sliding down my spine.

"Some other terrible things, too." She paused. "She looked like I'd just killed her best friend. I was happy at the time," she said, looking off behind me. "I thought I'd won."

I exhaled a large breath, running my fingers through my hair. It's why she had left. That's. Why. She. Left. *Feck!* She'd thought I'd been lying to her about Courtney. *Cheating on her.*

I spun away from Courtney, my mind reeling with the truths slowly dawning on me, what Lydia must have gone through that day . . . the doubt, the pain.

I'd found the printed proof that I owned her old family estate sitting on my counter, too. I'd known it had come from Stuart by the doodles at the bottom of the page.

So that day, so many doubts had been planted in her mind . . . she'd left, needing space and who could blame her? And then she'd gotten the call that I'd killed her brother. And suddenly, I knew beyond any doubt, that Lydia hadn't taken my folder. Stuart had. *How had he known? Because I had written all over the front in Gaelic.* He'd seen it and he'd taken it. *Oh my God.* I'd already forgiven Lydia for giving the folder to Stuart, had understood the position she'd been in, and yet realizing that she *hadn't* taken it, that she *hadn't* betrayed me, still made me want to weep with relief. And somehow . . . somehow it helped me forgive myself. Lydia hadn't believed I deserved to be betrayed. *I* had been the one who thought that. Not her, *me.* And it was the reason I had been so unwilling to allow her to forgive me.

It doesn't matter if you allow it or not. I still forgive you all the same. I still . . . I still love you all the same.

Oh Lydia. Mo Chroí.

Despite all she'd dealt with that day, despite everything that had happened, she had still found it in her heart to forgive me. She'd still found the courage to come here tonight. She'd sat across from me and the woman she thought I was involved with, in at least some capacity, and she'd told me she forgave me, that she loved me. Oh *God.* The *bravery* that had taken, the *goodness* that had taken. And the faith—the faith in *me.* The realizations spun through me so powerfully, I almost felt dizzy. I turned back to Courtney.

"Go," she said, resignation in her voice, sorrow clouding her expression. "I'm thinking Fionn will be very pleased to drive me home."

I paused. "Security detail—"

"Bennett's no threat, Brogan." She waved her hand and shook her head. "Yes, it's true he's paroled, but I lied about everything else. He wrote to me many times from prison asking for my forgiveness. Apparently he's found God. He's a changed man. And he's married to a woman he became pen pals with while he was locked up. It's very romantic. A book should be written."

Jaysus! I stared at her, releasing a pent-up breath, but suddenly feeling only pity for all her lies, suddenly seeing her not through the cloud of my own guilt, but as the lonely, troubled woman she was. I was more than angry with her. What a bitch. "Courtney—"

"Go," she said, harsher this time, waving her hand in the air again. "I need to hate you for a little while."

I nodded. "Aye," I said. *I really wanted to hate her for more than a little while.* I had yet to fully process all the implications of her revelations, but . . . *she* had been a large part of the reason Lydia left me that day. The reason why I'd been at the office that night. *Fecking hell.* I flung the door open and ran outside, headed for my car. The snow was already dwindling, the wind in the trees seeming to sing one word over and over again: *Lydia, Lydia, Lydia.*

God, I hoped she was still waiting for me.

Please be waiting for me.

CHAPTER TWENTY-SEVEN

Lydia

Why had I come here? I wasn't exactly sure. It even seemed somewhat illogical and self-torturous to return to this specific place after being rejected by Brogan.

I sighed, leaning back against the wall of the small room in my stable, where I was sitting, blowing into my gloved hands for added warmth. *This room.* I kept returning, somehow hoping for a different outcome than the one that had first occurred. Somehow hoping to make it right. Only we couldn't *get* it right. I'd tried. I'd bared my heart, offered my soul, and Brogan had told me I should leave. I'd driven around aimlessly for a while and somehow ended up here without really planning to. So here I was—alone—and I certainly couldn't make it right all by myself. So again, why had I come here of all places while Brogan was across town with . . .? Pain made my stomach tighten as if bracing for a blow. I closed my eyes, wrapping my arms around myself.

I stayed that way for several more minutes. Then the squeaking of door hinges replaced the silence of the snow-filled night. Creasing my brow, I stood quickly.

I saw a shadow cross the wall in the main room where a single bulb lit the large space. The room where I now stood, my heart beating quickly, was only dimly lit by what little light spilled in through the open door. I flattened my back against the wall, too afraid to call out.

When a shape appeared in the backlit doorway, I exhaled a breath I'd been holding. I'd know his shape anywhere—his height, the broad outline of his shoulders. *Brogan.* As always, my heart leaped toward him, joyous at his presence. I put my hand over the place where it lay under my skin, as if I could contain it in such a way. But it insisted in soaring with hope.

"He arrives in shadow," I said softly.

I heard him release a breath. "Just like a villain?"

My smile felt brittle, my heart rate picking up in speed. "No, sometimes heroes arrive in shadow, too. I . . . I suppose we keep trading the titles back and forth, don't we?" I'd been the villain once, too, here in this very room. I brought my hands in front of my body, gripping them together in anxiousness.

He took a step into the room, out of the direct light, allowing me to see him, allowing me to take in his bruised face.

I blinked. "God, what happened to you?"

He reached a hand up and rubbed his bruised jaw. The skin around one eye was tinged red, and he had a red cut along his cheekbone.

"Fionn and I had a talk," he said, one side of his mouth lifting in a small smile.

Ah. *Fionn.* I thought I understood. But then his smile faded and the pain in his expression broke my heart a little.

I shifted on my feet. "How'd you know where I was?" I asked.

"I didn't. I went to Daisy's first and didn't see your car. I came here next . . . Somehow I thought it might be where you'd go. Or maybe I just hoped."

"Oh." My breath hitched causing the word to break.

He paused, his eyes beseeching me, asking me . . . something. I waited, my pulse quickening. "Lydia, I . . ." He shook his head, a few snowflakes still sticking to his hair—the white crystals a striking contrast to the black strands. His expression was suddenly very raw. "I'm not very good at unrehearsed speeches. I . . ." He furrowed his brow, obviously struggling. I worked not to hold my breath as I waited, somehow knowing it was important to give him the time he needed to get his words right. "Well, Fionn says I have a way of complicating things that don't need to be complicated . . ." His eyes met mine. "Maybe he's right, and I think that if any place should inspire us to speak the simple truth, it's this place." I blinked back tears. "And so I'm just going to tell you what I should have told you at some party or another last year before I put my ridiculous revenge plan into action."

He walked closer, his pale eyes filled with what I thought was . . . fear. He was scared, but he was here. *He was here. Oh Brogan.*

He reached his hand out. My eyes wandered down to it. It was trembling and the sight filled me with tenderness. I took his hand in mine, the contact making me want to weep. He felt warm and solid and he gripped me as if he was never going to let me go. *Oh please don't let me go. Not again. Please be here to stay.*

"Lydia, it's so nice to see you after all these years. You look . . . God, you look even more beautiful than in my dreams. And I've dreamt about you so often. It scares me because each time I do, I wake up feeling hungry in that way I promised myself I'd never feel hungry again. Only this hunger can only be satisfied by you, and I'm . . . I'm not sure what to do about that." He ran his tongue over his front teeth, his eyes clear, blue pools of vulnerability, and I sucked in a shaky breath. "So I'm hoping you might have some ideas better than my own." I sniffled, tears pricking my eyes. He gazed at me so seriously, his expression so deeply pained. And I wanted to take him in my arms, but I didn't. "Before you say anything, you should know that, since I saw you last, I've done some things I'm not proud of, survived in ways that still bring me shame. But . . . but I'm hoping, God I'm hoping so hard that you can find it in your heart to understand and maybe help me forgive myself, because I've never been very good at that. But above anything, what I'm hoping is that we can get to know each other again and forgive *each other* for the things we did, both intentionally and unintentionally. Because I'd really like to take you somewhere warm where I can buy you a meal and then bring you back to my house and make love to you the way I wish I'd known how to do the first time."

I let out a small, sniffle-laden laugh and took a step closer to him, my heart swelling with love. "That would have been a lot to take in," I said, my smile soggy as a tear rolled down my cheek. He wiped it away with his thumb.

I pressed my lips together so they wouldn't begin trembling. "What about Courtney?" I finally whispered, my heart squeezing as I swallowed, bracing myself. Whatever he told me, I was going to try my best to understand.

"Courtney's gone back to New York City to her own life. I only . . . God, Fionn's right, I'm an eejit." He released a loud whoosh of air. "She was lying to me. She was manipulating me, and I let her. Partly because of my own guilt. But partly because as long as Courtney was around, it meant denying myself the option of begging you for forgiveness. I thought it'd make it easier on you *and* on me. I didn't *want* you to forgive me, and I was so scared I was going to beg you to do it anyway, because I wanted you back so damned badly. I haven't touched her, Lydia. She kissed me twice, and I let her, and I'm sorry about that, not only to you, but to myself because," he shook his head, wincing slightly, "she was all wrong. She wasn't you."

Another tear rolled down my cheek. He had kissed her while we were apart. Twice. But in all fairness, I had told him I'd never forgive him. *But he had kissed her twice.* "That was a really terrible plan," I said.

He nodded. "I seem to come up with a lot of really terrible plans when it comes to you." He shook his head.

"Well, it didn't work anyway because I do forgive you."

He brought his hands to my face, cradling it gently. "She told me what she said to you that day you left my apartment. It was a twisted version of the truth, Lydia. Since the day you walked into my office, I haven't been intimate with anyone except you. I haven't *desired* anyone except you. And that's sort of an understatement." He leaned his head down and put his forehead against mine, letting go of my face, our fingers lacing as our arms lowered.

I closed my eyes briefly, overcome with the memory of the rollercoaster of emotions of that day. I told him about Daisy calling with the news her husband was cheating, about Stuart coming over, and then Courtney showing up.

"Jaysus. No wonder," he said. And he told me about Stuart bringing his folder to his office that day, about how he'd told Brogan I had given it to him, a revelation that made me gasp with horror.

"No," I breathed. "I would never have done that. He must have taken it," I said, looking to the side, envisioning that day. "He followed me to my room, and he must have seen it and—"

"I know, Lydia. I already figured that out."

My eyes searched his, seeing the truth of his forgiveness there—forgiveness I hadn't even realized he was struggling with, forgiveness he'd bestowed before even knowing the truth. *Brogan.* I clenched my eyes shut with the pain of it all, with my own shame for making him wait for mine. We still had things to talk about, but . . . I knew in my heart everything was going to be okay. Still, regret gripped me.

"I should have talked to you. I should have trusted you."

He shook his head. "I should have charged to where you were and demanded you talk to me and answer my own questions that very day. If I had, I wouldn't have been in my office that night. And before that, I should—" I let go of one of his hands and brought two fingers to his lips.

"Let's not do this anymore. No more *I should haves*, no more keeping track of wrongs. Love doesn't keep a tally. Love doesn't seek to punish. I forgive you with my whole heart. And if you forgive me, then let's move forward from here. Let's trust each other. Let's be honest with each other, even when it's hard. Especially then."

"I didn't know how I was going to live without you, Lydia. I didn't know," he said, his voice hoarse. "I love you. *That's* my truth. It's always been my truth."

I smiled, my lips trembling, my heart soaring. "I love you, too."

He let out a breath, pressing his lips to mine, but not moving, as if the contact itself was all he could handle in that moment.

I brought my hands to his hair. "More," I whispered.

"More truth?" I smiled and though I'd meant more kissing, I didn't correct him. He kissed me briefly and pulled back, smoothing my hair.

"I want to have sleepovers with you every night for the rest of my life." He smiled gently. "I want to fall asleep in your arms and wake up to your face each morning. Someday, I—" he broke off, clearing his throat as he brought his arms around me, "I want to make another baby. I want a family. With you—only you. I want to love you and care for you and make you happy. I want to be your hero."

"Brogan," I said shakily, swallowing heavily. Tears spilled as relief and happiness flowed through every cell of my body.

"Tell me you want the same," he said, his voice an ache-filled whisper. "I'd get down on my knees and beg ya if ya wanted me to."

I shook my head back and forth, my gaze holding his. "I'd never ask it of you, Brogan. Never." The look that passed over his face was one of such raw tenderness, it caused my heart to clench.

"I know, Mo Chroí. Yes, I know."

At the sound of the name he'd called me all these years on his lips, I let out a small gasp of joy. I'd heard it before, but now I knew what it really meant and it made me dizzy with love. *My heart.*

"I want all the things you want, too. And God, I want to hear you call me Mo Chroí for the rest of my life. Every day." Brogan's mouth claimed mine then, his tongue entering me, as we both sunk to our knees, our hands moving over each other almost desperately. He released what felt like a small chuckle into my mouth and I pulled back in question.

"What?" I asked. He gazed at me lovingly. "I was just thinking that it's really cold in here, and I'd like to get you to a warm bed." His smile grew. "*And* that being down on my knees isn't really such a bad place to be when you're down here with me."

I laughed, pulling him close and resting my head against his chest as he nuzzled my hair.

After a minute we stood up and I looked around. *This room.* Warm joy filled my chest, the feeling that tonight, we'd come full circle.

The first time we'd left here, our hearts had both been broken and shredded. Tonight, those hearts had been put back together, restored. Complete.

Yesterday, today . . . and finally, *finally*, the miracle of tomorrow. I grasped Brogan's hand in mine and we walked out *together*.

EPILOGUE

Almost Two Years Later

Brogan

We were married beneath the sycamore tree next to the stable. This time, I was the one who waited for her. My bride arrived on Fionn's arm, wearing a white lace gown and a glowing smile, holding a simple bouquet of hydrangeas. Her beauty stole my breath. But then, it always had.

"Ná bí ach ag análú," Fionn whispered on a smile as he put Lydia's hand in mine and stepped aside.

Just breathe.

"Thanks for meeting me," Lydia said softly, a little shyly, her face radiant with love. I swallowed back a grin, turning to face her fully.

We said our vows as the sun set behind us, and when we were pronounced husband and wife, I took her face in my hands and kissed her with the overwhelming amount of love and passion I felt in my heart.

The small group of family and friends in attendance clapped and tossed flower petals at us as we walked back up the short aisle hand in hand, laughing with the pure joy of the moment.

Later, we danced under the stars, hundreds of candles in mason jars hanging from the trees and set on a few tables, casting the outside party area in a romantic glow. In the distance, the horses roamed the pasture, including Maribel who I'd bought back for Lydia when we'd moved into the house.

A few couples away on the outside dance floor, Eileen laughed as Fionn dipped her. Lydia smiled as she watched them for a moment and then looked at me, her expression soft. "She dances because of you," she whispered. My breath caught. Suddenly, right there, all the sacrifices, all the pain, it all seemed to make sense, and I felt filled with peace.

She dances because of you.

I smiled down at my beautiful bride, the woman I loved to utter distraction. "Did I ever tell you I received my first kiss right over there?" I asked, nodding to the stable. "A different summer, long ago."

She pulled back and laughed softly, smoothing a lock of hair that had fallen forward on my forehead. "What a coincidence. So did I."

I chuckled. "That same girl is going to be my last kiss," I whispered, kissing her lips. "And every kiss in between."

She smiled against my mouth. "She better be."

I spun her around and she laughed. Pulling her close again, I planted a small kiss on the side of her neck, inhaling her scent. "I haven't toasted you yet," I said, glancing at our guests laughing and conversing as some drank champagne and others, tall pints of Guinness.

Lydia hesitated before drawing back slightly and taking my face in her hands. "I won't be partaking in champagne for a while," she said, pulling her bottom lip between her teeth.

My eyes moved over her half-nervous, half-hopeful expression, understanding dawning. "You're—"

She nodded, smiling tremulously. "I think it happened at that bed and breakfast in Trim."

We'd recently spent three months traveling all over Ireland on an early honeymoon, touring old castles and monasteries, awe-inspiring natural attractions like the Cliffs of Moher, drinking in pubs, and falling in love more deeply than I'd even known possible.

As for me, I'd not only fallen in love more deeply with Lydia, but with my homeland, with the wild and ruggedly beautiful scenery. I'd felt filled with pride to show the woman I loved the splendor and history of the Emerald Isle and to call myself Irish born.

Our last week there, we'd visited the town where I'd been raised and stayed at a small bed and breakfast. It'd rained constantly and we'd spent lots of time holed up at the cozy inn, whispering words of love in the intimacy of our bed, making love over and over as it bucketed down outside the windows.

I swallowed heavily, my heart squeezing with happiness. "You're having a baby," I breathed, a smile breaking over my face.

"Is it too soon?" she asked.

"God, no," I said, pulling her close. It felt like I'd waited a lifetime for this moment. My mind whirled with the ways our lives would change, and the ways they wouldn't. "Do you still want to teach?" I asked. Her position at a local community college started in the fall, the reason we hadn't planned our trip to Ireland after our wedding.

Lydia smiled. "It's just two days a week. I still want to work at your office, too." She looked away for a moment. "And you can teach him or her Gaelic." She smiled, looking as if this thought pleased her very much.

I raised a brow. "We might keep secrets from you."

She laughed. "Then I better speed up my own lessons."

That night, after the cake had been cut, after the celebration had ended, and when the last guests had left, I kneeled down in front of my wife, kissing her flat belly over the white silk of her nightgown, already loving the tiny life inside her. The life we'd created in love, in hope, in forgiveness.

As Lydia pulled down the shoulder straps of her gown, the thin piece of material slid to the floor, allowing me to kiss other parts. And here, on my knees before the woman I loved, I realized Father Donoghue had been right—it was a very beguiling place to be. I smiled against her skin. For I now knew that being on your knees didn't have to mean groveling, it could also mean worship.

"With my body, I thee worship," I murmured, a line from our vows. I kissed her inner thigh and she moaned and sunk to her knees, bringing her mouth to mine.

"I'm going to spend my life worshipping you," I promised her again, sliding my lips down her neck.

She brought her hands to my shoulders, leaning back and allowing me more access. "And I'm going to spend my life worshipping you," she whispered. "Now take off your clothes so I can do it properly."

I laughed, doing as she asked.

Eight months later, our daughter, Catriona Grace, named after our mothers, came screaming into the world, displaying a fierce Irish temper, my black hair, and her mother's beauty. Fionn patted me on the back, a gleam in his eye, and told me my comeuppance for all the trouble I'd put him through had just arrived in a perfect eight-pound package. I had a feeling he was right, but I was too happy to care.

That night, as Lydia slept, I cradled my baby girl in my arms and told her an Irish fairy tale my father used to tell me. I remembered him not only as the man whose weakness had destroyed him and hurt me so much, but as the man capable of love and kindness. He had loved my mam so very much, and I understood that desperate love now. *Would I fall apart as he did if I had to move to a foreign country after losing the love of my life, and having to raise two children on my own?* Looking down at my daughter, I knew the answer was no. But my father hadn't been that strong. I didn't remember him falsely, but I forgave him, and it had brought peace to that corner of my heart.

There is such a thin veil between love and hate. I had chosen love.

When Catriona's eyes finally fluttered shut, her lashes two dark crescents on her petal-soft skin, I stared at her for a long time, marveling at everything we'd gone through to make it to this one, perfect moment.

I had set out on a mission to achieve what I had once deemed life's greatest treasures, and all along, what was most precious and powerful was *already* inside of me.

Love.

Trust.

Forgiveness.

And with these things, anything was possible. Anything at all. And there was no more beautiful proof of that than the small, beloved girl sleeping peacefully in my arms.

Acknowledgments

As always, my team is the wind beneath my wings!

Special thanks to my storyline editor: Angela Smith, for reading Ramsay in airports, on airplanes, and with your whole heart, wherever you were. We got to talk about this one over cocktails and it filled my soul!

Marion Archer, your insight and wisdom on all things grammatical is appreciated, but even more so, your insight and wisdom on all things human nature is valued even more. You make my stories better. You make my *characters* better. Thank you for doing it yet again with Ramsay.

Gratitude to my beta readers whose care, enthusiasm, and willingness to spend their valuable time reading my first ramblings is so very, very appreciated; Cat Bracht, Natasha Gentile, Heather Anderson, and Michelle Finkle.

Thank you to Elena Eckmeyer who not only beta'd Ramsay but read it a second and third time for grammar and consistency. I can't tell you how much this helps give me confidence in the final product. Thank you for having Brogan's back (those glasses were for you!).

Thank you to Sharon Broom for beta'ing and for proofing as well. I am so grateful for your friendship and for your support. Someday I *will* make it across the pond!

Thank you to Amy Kehl who not only beta'd Ramsay, but is the world's most dedicated pimp goddess. My appreciation knows no bounds.

Thank you to Karen Lawson whose attention to detail makes me look so good. I have unending faith in Karen's-Book-of-Knowledge and I adore you!

Gratitude and thumbs up to Nelle Obrien—you know why.

Special love and many thanks to my Irish language beta, Melissa Molloy. Thank you for reading Ramsay first and making sure I didn't have to use Google Translate in order to have my characters speak Gaelic. Without you, I'm sure I would have made a complete fool of myself and of them. Thank you for instructing me on how to swear like a proper Irish woman (even though I know *you* don't say those words), for teaching me how to speak a few important phrases of Gaelic, and most of all for making me fall so deeply in love with the Irish culture. I WILL come visit you someday—be warned. And have a pint of Guinness waiting for me. Readers, if you loved Fionn, you can thank Melissa.

Huge love to A.L. Jackson and Katy Regnery who—once again—provided hours and hours of laughs, support, advice, craziness, and friendship, while writing and promoting this book. You two are the best co-workers a girl could have. #SideEyesForever #TheGreatKind #MAK

Tina Kleuker, you make the world a better place. Not just the book world, the world in general. Thank you for all you do for me. If I listed it here, this book would cost ten dollars more to ship.

Thank you to Kimberly Brower, the best agent a writer could have. I value you so much. Thank you for being in my corner. Thank you for working tirelessly for me. And thank you for not blocking my husband's number.

To you, the reader, thank you for spending your time with my words and my characters. All of this, it is all because of you.

Thank you to Mia's Mafia. Your enthusiastic support is never taken for granted.

To all the book bloggers who love reading with a passion. Thank you for putting so much time and effort into what you do. Each review and recommendation is appreciated beyond measure.

To my husband whose love and support is beside me during the creation and release of every book, this one being no exception. Thank you for celebrating my successes, and comforting me in my defeats. Thank you for forgiving me when I need to be forgiven and for never failing to offer a sincere apology when you load the dishwasher incorrectly. Most of all, thank you for making me feel so very loved. Just like the Aries you are, your heart is pure gold and I am so very, very lucky to call you mine.

About the Author

Mia Sheridan is a *New York Times*, *USA Today*, and *Wall Street Journal* Bestselling author. Her passion is weaving true love stories about people destined to be together. Mia lives in Cincinnati, Ohio with her husband. They have four children here on earth and one in heaven. In addition to Ramsay, Leo, Leo's Chance, Stinger, Archer's Voice, Becoming Calder, Finding Eden, Kyland, Grayson's Vow, and Midnight Lily are also part of the Sign of Love collection.

Mia can be found online at www.MiaSheridan.com or www.facebook.com/miasheridanauthor.

CPSIA information can be obtained
at www.ICGtesting.com
Printed in the USA
FSHW010502251119
64468FS